KARL WEBSTER

THE AMSTERDAM GOOD MURDER GUIDE

a confession

a Bag of Elbows publication

Amsterdam

The Amsterdam Good Murder Guide is a work of fiction. Like any work of fiction, it is comprised not merely of things that never happened, but also of things that definitely did. The people too… I'd be lying if I said that any resemblance was entirely coincidental. Most of it is quite deliberate. Most of the locations are real too and hopefully they still exist. The weather is also real, albeit out of time. What's still entirely fictional, however, at least for now, is the vast majority of the morally questionable behaviour.

~breathe~

For the sociopaths.

We see you.

Time's up.

"Evil exists in the world not to create despair but activity. We are not patiently to submit to it, but to exert ourselves to avoid it. It is not only the interest but the duty of every individual to use his utmost efforts to remove evil from himself and from as large a circle as he can influence...."

— The Reverend Thomas Robert Malthus
An Essay on the Principle of Population (1798)

Prologue

This is the story of how I, Wesley Bell, became a serial killer. And I know that sounds bad — you hear "serial killer" and immediately you think: "bad egg". But bear with me. I'm the exception that proves the rule. I'm a good guy, and the nicest multiple murderer in history. You'll see.

It was my therapist's idea to write it all down. Not the killing of course. My therapist knows nothing of the killing. Heaven forfend. Rather, she hoped a written account of recent events might help put the kibosh on the weeping jags in Lidl. I figure it's worth a shot, and it seems only fair to give an honest account of what I did and why I did it. Fair to me, that is.

This then is my warts and all confessional — how I went from committed pacifist to defensible, some would say *righteous* serial murderer within the space of five months. What my therapist cannot hear, for legal reasons, you will hear, for judicial ones. And I know I don't have to hold back with you because, well... you don't exist. Not yet at least. And if ever you do exist, I can only assume I'm being held accountable in law and you, dear reader, are my jury. My future, therefore, is very likely in your hands. Let's hope you're up to the job.

Either way, this is my truth. It's also *the* truth. Having said that, I may have played fast and loose with language and time here and there — just to keep things fizzing along, you understand. I'm tempted to say you can always count on a begrudging serial killer for a fancy prose style, but in actual fact, I'm still just a hack.

So, shall we begin with all that David Copperfield kind of crap? Or shall we crack on with the chaos and death? I know, right? As if there's ever any choice...

I

August 2019

1

"I want you to *die*," said the old woman in the seventeenth century church courtyard. I laughed because I thought she was joking. Not that women hadn't wished death upon me in the past; they had, once or twice, but those women knew me well. All this woman knew about me — gleaned from the purple name-badge round my neck — was that I was a tour guide, and quite clearly, she did not care for tour guides.

"I want you to drop down dead right here and now."

I gasped.

"You should be *ashamed* of yourself."

"Well, yeah, that goes without s—"

"You're dis*gusting*."

I recoiled from her watery blue eyes and the venom they so adeptly conveyed. Most of my group were now standing awkwardly around, staring at the old lady as if she herself were a tourist attraction. One young Israeli was filming.

"You are destroying this city!" she cried, visibly upset.

I felt bad for her, but at the same time, I had to disagree. Partially. *Disgusting* I could accept. I am after all a human male. *Ashamed* too. Certainly. Shame is pretty much my go-to emotion, my comfort zone. But destroying Amsterdam? Nope. Not possible. I absolutely *adore* Amsterdam.

"How would you like it," demanded the old woman, "if I came to your home town with gangs of foreigners and did what you're doing to Amsterdam?"

"I would like that very much," I replied, instinctively visualising this sour-mouthed harridan trailing a handful of dismayed American tourists through the streets of Sunderland,

4

waxing lyrical about the city's *nineteen* branches of the world-famous Greggs bakery chain.

She scowled.

"Look, I'm not sure what you want from me," I said.

"I want you to *die.*"

"Oh yeah. You did say."

At this point, unable to hold his tongue any longer, a tall, well-dressed Sikh to my left said, "That's very rude, madam."

In response, the old woman actually hissed at the Sikh before turning abruptly and shuffling off in the direction of the church, muttering, most probably something about foreigners.

"Well, *that* was weird," said an Australian woman from somewhere within my flock. Some of the others, evidently gobsmacked, exchanged bemused sniggers and whispers.

"Yet another example," I said, "of that world-famous Amsterdam tolerance."

But of course, the Australian was right. It *was* weird. And, though I didn't know it yet, this was just the beginning of what would turn out to be — hands down — the third weirdest day of the weirdest year of my life.

1.2

Ordinarily, my working day consisted of two tours: history in the afternoon; Red Light District in the evening. Today, however, having received a panicky dawn text from Monica, I'd swapped my Red Light for her 11am.

The previous day had been Monica's 28th birthday and she claimed her visiting sister had been hit by a bicycle and needed her attention. I say 'claimed' because she'd been clubbing the night before. Therefore it seemed much more likely she'd been up till 6am drinking and dancing with lanky, proud-chinned Dutchmen. Snogging one or two too, I imagined. Much as it pained me to imagine such a thing — on account of me being in love with Monica — I imagined it anyway. So, in truth, I agreed to take her morning tour not just because I'm a thoroughly good egg, which I swear I almost am, but also because somewhere in the back of my mind, there lurked the distant fantasy that if I continued to cover her shifts and just be generally wonderful, then one day — just maybe — one day she'd kiss me too. But I always knew it was just a fantasy. I always knew that in reality, pale chinless gingers like me *never* get to kiss women like Monica Gandolfo. *Ever.*

One of my closest friends, Monica was also, indisputably, a goddess, plagued with supernatural beauty but blessed with the wit and confidence to survive it. That being said, nothing could escape the fact that this morning's death wish should really have been hers. What happened in the afternoon, however, was all mine.

It was a hot afternoon on the first of August, and as per usual, I turned up at Dam Square at 1.15. In the shadow of the National Monument, a 22-metre travertine memorial for the fallen of World War Two, I hugged hello with Henk, the 24-year-old Dutch-

Mexican Meeting Point Manager (henceforth MPM). Two more guides then arrived and with varying degrees of efficaciousness, we all helped organise and fraternise with the tourists as they began to amass. At 1:30, we escorted all 57 of them off the square and across the street, where we split them into three groups of 19.

With such a relatively small group, I always took a few moments at the start to find out where everyone was from. So I hopped onto a concrete bench by two giant immovable heads, gathered my tourists and began.

To my immediate right was a trio of people with rather singular physical characteristics. They *appeared* to be two middle-aged identical twin males and one slightly younger woman, either a sister, a cousin, or potentially an unrelated lover and sex dungeon captive, but one with eerily similar features. They all had large, unusually bovine faces, with heavy brows and prominent chins. They reminded me of something specific, but I couldn't quite put my finger on it. No matter. I focused on the first of these large-faced, frowning creatures and said, "And where are you from, Sir?"

"Nowhere," mumbled the man.

"*Nowhere?!*" I repeated, both amused and genuinely confused.

I glanced at the rest of the group, a few of whom were also laughing, but not for the same reason. "Norway!" a couple of them cried, correcting my genuine and to my mind genuinely hilarious misunderstanding.

"Oh, *Norway!*" I must admit, I found this deeply, *deeply* amusing. The Norwegians, however, did not. The female forced a brief half-smile that was really more of a grimace, but the males gave me nothing. They just stared, emotionless, like something in the wild. "I really thought you said *nowhere!*" I continued, trying to tease them out. "No?" No.

7

I moved on. I returned to the Norwegians frequently, however, throughout the tour. Partly I was trying to crack them, to squeeze something from them — a laugh, a smile, a genial roll of the eye — anything; but partly it was pure fascination. I'd never seen such otherworldly humans before and I wanted to study them, to learn from them.

Appearance aside, the most unusual thing about the Norwegians was their overwhelming apathy. They never laughed, they never spoke, they never nodded their huge heads in appreciation or affirmation. They gave me nothing, despite my desperate, brazen hankering for a connection. "Can I just check," I asked, between the first couple of stops, "do you speak English? Do you understand what I'm saying?" They nodded. "*Really?*" They nodded again. "Oh."

I tried not to show how defeated I felt, but the fact was, I needed their laughter. Making people happy, at least superficially, was the thing I loved most about being a tour guide, about being alive, maybe. Other people's laughter gave meaning to my life, and when it failed to materialise, I felt like I'd failed. Of course in reality I know, you can't please all the people, ever. Some people are an entirely different species.

In the break, I remembered — they reminded me of trolls. I'd seen a Swedish film about real live trolls and these Norwegians had the same abundant foreheads and dour, brutish expressions. This made me feel slightly better about the lack of connection. It wasn't me; it was them.

Sadly, they weren't the only inhuman participants on the tour. Neither, as it transpired, were they the only trolls.

1.3

"And you, Sir, where are you from?"

"Yorkshire, England," came the proud reply. My suspicions thus confirmed, a tiny smile flashed across my lips.

The Yorkshireman was large, blotchy and massively white. He looked mid-50s, but there was a deep-rooted bitterness in his steadfast scowl that could easily have added a decade. He wore an England football shirt — the white home strip — but I doubted he'd kicked a ball himself in decades. A giant belly stretched out the shirt, exposing the lower curve and giving him the profile of a heavily pregnant woman. On his legs were shorts with too many pockets. On his feet were sandals and knee-length white socks. On his head an elaborate combover. A large red drinker's nose sat atop the permanent scowl like a distended testicle. He looked like a cartoon caricature of an English Northerner.

"Where in Yorkshire?" I asked.

"You won't have heard of it."

"Try me."

"What's the point? You won't have heard of it."

Appearances are not always deceptive. This guy was precisely as contemptible as he appeared. "Humour me."

He relented with an angry sigh. "Osmotherley."

"Never heard of it." A couple of people tittered.

"What'd I tell you?"

"You were right. I should have listened."

I offered my most winning smile. He scowled and shook his head.

The first interruption came very early on, halfway through the preliminary overview. Generally, I welcome questions. A curious group is always preferable to a mute, apathetic one, but tourists who ask questions fall into three distinct categories, and not all are as welcome as others.

Some raise their hands like well-behaved schoolchildren. Not wishing to butt in or spoil the flow of the tour, they wait to be invited to speak. They consider the feelings of others before barging in with their own concerns. I adore these people. For me, if human beings are ever to survive as a species, it will be thanks primarily to people like these. Seriously, whenever anyone raises their hand and waits, it's all I can do not to wrap my arms around them and never let go.

Others wait for a suitable pause in the tour before speaking. This is the most common method and again, I'm always grateful for the thoughtfulness.

Then there are those who just interrupt whenever anything occurs to them, regardless of what the guide is talking about. Could be the weather, could be the war.

"During their occupation of Amsterdam, the Nazis killed at least 80% of the Jewish people living here — something like 65,000 of the city's 80,000-strong Jewish population, including of course, modern history's most famous teenage girl, A—"

"It was actually more than a hundred thousand."

For a couple of seconds I just stared, like an abandoned ventriloquist's dummy. Then I said, "That was in the Netherlands as a whole. I'm talking about just Amsterdam."

"Hmm," said Osmotherley Man. "Maybe."

"No, no," I insisted. "*Definitely.*"

He lifted his chins in a peremptory micro-nod, begrudgingly permitting me to continue. I swallowed hard and sighed. We had another two-and-a-half hours to get through.

When we moved on to the Dutch penal system — how they favour rehabilitation over incarceration; how this frees up the prisons, some of which have been populated by criminals from Norway and Belgium — Osmotherley Man said, "That can't be right."

"That *is* right," I said, refusing to stop. I looked instinctively to the Norwegians for support but then, remembering, gave up.

I should point out at this juncture that generally speaking, I am an enormous fan of people who participate in walking tours. For me, they exhibit a curiosity and a willingness to discover new things about the world that is absolutely something to be admired in a human. There are those, of course, though very, very few, who join such a tour primarily because it's potentially free and they have no intention of tipping at the end. Then there are those with no particular interest in the tour — they're just killing time. Then, of course, there are the sociopaths…

1.4

Aaaaaah, the sociopaths.

I always fancied myself a canny judge of character, even before my fifteen years as a journalist had honed my people skills to a pinhole. After journalism, however — five years in local news, five in national and five in glossy lifestyle magazines — I think it's fair to say that my razor-sharp powers of deduction and prognosis, alongside my knowledge of Shoreditch pop-ups and refreshing summer cocktails, were world class. I was particularly proud of my ability to weed out a sociopath.

I honestly believe — to this day — I can pinpoint sociopathic tendencies within the space of a ten-minute conversation. I can sniff them out, like a spaniel homing in on a tumour. (I also recognise that this could be nonsense. I know I'm not the sanest brick in the sanatorium wall, but I'm not so mad that I don't doubt myself constantly.)

Sometimes I feel like I'm catnip for sociopaths, like I attract them, but I know that's silly. I'm just very conscious of them, and undeniably fascinated. Meeting Rupert Murdoch when I worked for Sky News added to this fascination, and I've since read an awful lot about how they function. As a result, it could be argued that I'm just a touch obsessed.

Consequently, I do have a tendency to tar perfectly ordinary scoundrels with the sociopath brush, without necessarily knowing all the facts. But then, when it comes to sociopaths — who are after all, driving our species towards extinction — it is better to be on the safe side.

All of which is to say that, within fifteen minutes of meeting Osmotherley Man, I was pretty sure he was the latest socio to cross my path. There was a silent but palpable glee in his interruptions.

Even later in the tour, when the other tourists began to turn on him, I could still see him enjoying the turmoil, thriving on it. Nothing made him happier than the unhappiness of others.

At the second stop, I talked about how, back in the day, before getting back on their ships, sailors in the Red Light District would cross the street, from prostitute to priest, to confess their sins. "Now — and this will surprise many of you, but I swear to God it's true — in *those* days, the Catholic Church was actually quite corrupt. *I know, I know.*"

This always did well, but today it killed. Lots of hearty laughter and fake amazement. It also prompted Osmotherley Man to say: "You're being sarcastic. You're implying that the Catholic Church are corrupt today, am I right?"

I stared, unable, indeed, no longer even willing, to hide my frustration. "I am implying that, yes."

"How so?"

"How so *what*?"

"How are the Catholic Church corrupt? You can't just make these accusations and not expect to have to back them up."

Some groans from the rest of the group.

I rolled my eyes. "You mean *apart* from the child abuse?"

"You can't blame the whole church for that. That's just a few bad apples."

"Alright, what about stockpiling wealth while many of their congregation are languishing in poverty?" I was very pleased with *languishing*. "Or what about charging for services for dead people?"

"Doesn't happen," said Osmotherley Man. "You're misinformed."

"OK." I forced a smile. "Then let's agree to disagree, shall we?"

"I don't think so. I don't have to agree with anything you say."

"No, no. You can *dis*agree. We can *both* disagree. Do you see?"

"I do disagree," he said, with wilful belligerence. "Because you're talking rubbish."

I sighed. I knew that for the sake of the other tourists, I had to stop rising to his bait. I also knew from bitter experience, that arguing with a sociopath was an exercise in futility.

"You're right," I said. "I *am* talking rubbish, and I apologise. So..." I glanced back at the Norwegian trolls and raised my eyebrows. Unmoved, they stared like termite mounds. "...if you wanted to stay out of hell, you basically had to pay the Catholic Church for the privilege. So the sailors would go to the priest, and the priest would take a note of their sins, basically to see how much they were worth to God."

Osmotherley Man sputtered. I ignored him and moved on to the confession money, which the church would use to pay for everything from stained glass windows to jewellery for the Pope. "I have also heard," I continued, "that on occasion, the priests in the Old Church might use some of that confession money themselves, and go back across the street, to visit the ladies of the night."

Another derisive sputter, expertly ignored.

"Now obviously, in reality, I can't say for sure whether that happened or not, but it definitely, *definitely* happened." Usually this did very well, but today, thanks to the constant interruptions, my flow was off and there wasn't much reaction. This peeved me enormously.

Ten minutes later, I'd reached the Dutch East India Company, the second wave of Amsterdam expansion in the 1600s, and the so-called Golden Age. "You have to remember, the Dutch were going pretty much all over the world and pretty much anything that was being manufactured or grown anywhere in the world, they

14

snapped it up and brought it back, in bulk, to this tiny little country, where it had to be stored before it was sold. Much of it they stored in the upper fl—"

"Actually, they weren't going all over the world."

"*Lord* have mercy." I lost my patience. "They went to Asia, Africa, Australia. They went to North America, South America, the Caribbean. They went to India. They did go *pretty much* everywhere."

"They didn't go to Europe," he said. "They didn't go to the Arctic."

"Jesus Christ." This was another tourist, an English guy who'd also had enough. "Can you maybe give it a rest? We're not here to listen to you, mate."

"It is an interactive tour," replied the Yorkshireman deliberately, as if speaking to a known imbecile. "He said so himself at start. So I'm interacting."

"But they are not *helpful* interactions." This was a woman from Germany. "You are spoiling the tour."

This was an exciting first for me — the rest of the group turning on the disruptor. Maybe they'd lynch him.

"He said they went all over the world," insisted the Yorkshireman. "I'm just pointing out that they didn't."

"I said they went *pretty much* all over the world," I pointed out. "And I stand by it."

"Oh don't be such a petty bugger," snapped Osmotherley Man. "Come on. Get on with it, for God's sake."

I gasped, shook my head at the rest of the group and continued.

When the next interruption came, I said: "You are welcome to leave, you know. I mean, you're clearly not enjoying the tour. Maybe you'd have a better time elsewhere, doing something else."

"No, I'll stay, thanks. Someone's got to keep an eye on your lies."

A couple of the others laughed at the man's audacity, and we soldiered on to the break, when two couples left. One gave me a tenner and said they had an appointment at the Van Gogh Museum. The other couple gave me twenty and said they simply couldn't stomach any more bullshit from that *jackass*. They'd also bought tickets for the next day's Red Light tour, so they said they'd see me then. "I don't know where you get the patience," said the man before they left. "If I were you, I swear, I'd wanna kill the guy."

The next day, when I told him what had happened in the second half of the tour, he would remember his words, and he would cross himself.

1.5

In the second half of the tour, the Yorkshireman became a touch less belligerent. He'd had a pint of lager in the break and it seemed to make him drowsy. So instead of verbal interruptions, he focused all his spite on messing around with his phone (beeps on) and yawning.

Indeed, every time we stopped in the second half, Osmotherley Man would yawn, loudly and rowdily, at least once. No nervous novice nun yawns, stifled in a sleeve, these were loud, voiced yawns with an almost burlesque quality. They were also, if not entirely fake, wildly exaggerated, deliberately fabricated to irritate me and ruin the tour.

But I stopped biting. Yawns and beeps were much easier to ignore than idiotic interruptions and I knew it would all be over soon enough.

At the penultimate stop, on the intersection of Hartenstraat and the Keizersgracht, I hopped up and perched on the railing, as I always did when a railing was available. The fifteen tourists that remained gathered around me in a fairly loose conglomeration. Osmotherley Man was to my immediate right, leaning sleepily on a green electrical box, just close enough to be heard, yawning and beeping.

It didn't matter. He no longer mattered. Everyone was ignoring him and I'd actually started to enjoy the tour again. I was talking about the canals, and the thousands of bicycles beneath the surface of the water, when a wasp joined the group. It was wasp season. They were everywhere, annoying everyone. Wasps were the trolls of the insect kingdom. Every glass of wine or beer on every table outside every cafe in the city was awash with them. They were a nuisance at the best of times and they could easily derail a tour if

17

you happened to have a spheksophobe in the group. And in my experience, almost every group had at least one spheksophobe.

Unfortunately, the instinct of the spheksophobe was always to panic. In a worst case scenario, they would scream and run around in aimless circles, pointlessly flapping their hands. In this group, the spheksophobe was a Frenchwoman standing directly in front of me, maybe a metre away. As soon as the wasp descended and began to loiter between me and the Frenchwoman, I could see that a situation may be about to develop. The wasp was doing its thing. As they seem really quite brilliantly able to do, it had already identified and focused its attentions on the spheksophobe, and was now flying back and forth repeatedly above and around her face and head. Back and forth it flew, over and over, maybe thirty centimetres in each direction, with only a soupçon of variation in its trajectory. Then it would suddenly dive or dart in a surprising direction, and repeat the whole routine.

I could see quite clearly in the eyes of the Frenchwoman that she was on the verge of panic. I assumed she had history, some wasp trauma from her childhood maybe, so I decided to step in and counsel her before her anxiety got the better of her.

"OK, I'm just gonna stop for a second," I told the group, "because it appears we may have a wasp situation developing here. Now the key is not to panic. Ideally, ignore the wasp. It will get bored eventually, and fly away." I overcame an urge to fire an accusatory glance at the Yorkshireman and instead made eye contact with the Frenchwoman.

"You OK?" She nodded. "What's your name?"

"Isabelle."

"OK Isabelle. It's gonna be fine, I promise."

I resumed the tour, still monitoring the situation.

Eventually, the wasp settled on the sleeve of Isabelle's yellow coat.

"It's OK," I said. "Honestly, ignore it. I have much experience with wasps. Seriously. I'm a wasp whisperer." She did not look convinced.

I'd already chatted with Isabelle earlier in the tour. She was from Lyons, but she lived in Berlin. She was in her thirties, travelling alone and transfixed, in that moment, by the hateful creature making its way up her arm. "Don't even look at it," I said. She laughed and lifted her head. I gave her another reassuring smile. Then I continued with the tour.

As I talked, I watched the wasp crawl slowly up Isabelle's sleeve. I had just reached the point in the tour where I apologise for the behaviour of English football fans throughout the world. "And if there's anything any of you would like to apologise for," I said, "now would be the perfect moment."

Osmotherley Man was immersed in his phone and appeared not to be listening. One guy from LA at the back of the group raised his hand and apologised for Trump. A few people laughed. I nodded. "Apology accepted."

Meanwhile, with the wasp having made its way past her elbow, Isabelle was visibly trembling with the effort not to react.

"One more thing that ends up in the canals of Amsterdam," I said. "Between ten and twenty of this particular thing are brought out of the water every year. Something quite important. What are we talking about here? Any ideas?"

"Dead bodies!"

Isabelle screamed. It was a short scream, but surprisingly powerful. As she screamed, she threw up her arms and stepped backwards, treading on the foot of an Indian lady, who also cried out.

Isabelle's scream had been an involuntary reaction to the confluence of two distinct, relatively complex events taking place simultaneously. Either one of these events, had they occurred individually, might have caused her to scream, but the fact that they happened in concert goes some way to explaining the intensity of her reaction.

Firstly, one of the Norwegians had broken their silence. Standing right next to Isabelle and as quiet as a grave thus far in the tour, the female had yelled her response to my question in a high-pitched voice with a peculiar accent: "*Dead bodies!*"

Secondly, the wasp situation had progressed. Having previously crawled a little way past Isabelle's elbow, the wasp had taken flight, darted about a bit and landed once more on her upper arm. Isabelle was terrified but trying hard not to react. I got the feeling she felt sorry for me, having witnessed how much I'd already had to put up with on the tour. The last thing she wanted to do was exactly what she wanted to do, which was to start running around in small circles, flapping her arms and screaming. So she stayed still and suffered in silence. It was all going to be over soon. If she could just… hang on…. And then, in the exact same moment that the Norwegian cried out, the wasp left Isabelle's arm and attacked her.

As far as I could see, her instincts had been absolutely right. The wasp had indeed been heading directly for her face when her hands shot up to defend herself. Making contact with the wasp, one of the fingers of her right hand then batted it with considerable force towards my face.

At which point, my instincts also kicked in. I raised my right hand and in a wholly defensive move, volleyed the wasp with the closed fan of my fingers, making perfect full contact with its malevolent little body. Immediately the wasp changed direction and was sent hurtling eastwards, where, as it so happened, giving free rein to another unfettered, sociopathic, fake-looking yawn, stood the Yorkshireman, his mouth fully agape.

1.6

The moment the wasp hit the back of his throat, a gasp went up from the group and Osmotherley Man immediately, instinctively, clamped his mouth shut. I leapt down from the railing and, equally instinctively, stepped towards him to help.

He began making choking noises and clawing at his throat, not quite coughing, not quite retching. I took out my phone and dialled 112 as a man from Canada began to slap Osmotherley Man on the back. I honestly couldn't tell if he was trying to help him or was just using the moment to vent some accumulated frustration. If it was the former, he failed. Indeed, for a short while, with face red and eyes bulging wide and watering, no breath seemed to emerge from Osmotherley Man's body.

Through to the emergency services, I cried out in English, "A man is choking on a wasp!"

"Try to clear the airways," they told me. "Keep him breathing."

They'd send an ambulance from Spuistraat, just around the corner. It would be no more than a few minutes.

Osmotherley Man went down on one knee, one hand on the ground to balance himself, one still wrapped around his throat.

His breath came in strained, wheezing bursts, like his throat was only partially opened.

"How do I keep him breathing?" I cried, scanning the group for the medic that must surely be lurking inside one of them. No help was forthcoming. Nobody had even the first idea how to deal with the situation. Instead they all just watched in horror, almost all of them cradling their own throats empathetically.

Osmotherley Man continued to claw at his neck.

The wasp had not emerged.

"We need to get the wasp out!"

I tried to open Osmotherley Man's mouth with my fingers but he still found the strength to push me away quite forcefully.

His fading breath was now a staggered, half-hearted inhalation and I was convinced that if I didn't act, he was going to die. Which was when I remembered a trick I'd seen in a film. If I had a pen, I could use it to burrow into Osmotherley Man's trachea and let him breathe through that. I did have a pen. I located it in the side pocket of my rucksack and pulled out the ink chamber and the plastic stopper.

Osmotherley Man slumped forward onto all fours. Then he slumped further forward onto one side and rolled gracelessly over onto his back.

"What are you doing?" someone asked.

"I'm giving him an emergency tracheotomy," I replied, stepping forward with the plastic pen-tube like a knife in my fist. Although I couldn't quite believe the sentence I'd just spoken, this was definitely happening. If I didn't push my pen through his neck, Osmotherley Man was going to die. Then, for a second, it occurred to me. *Would that be a bad thing?* I paused, maybe even less than a second. *Of course it would be a bad thing. He's a human being, for God's sake.*

So I took Osmotherley Man's neck in my left hand and started pushing the dirty plastic barrel into his windpipe. *Salvador*! That was the film with the emergency tracheotomy, performed by James Woods, of all people. Woods may also have had a knife, however, because my pen wasn't going anywhere. Also, Osmotherley Man was *still* putting up a fight. At my request, the Canadian and the guy from LA took hold of his arms.

"I need to really... *pop* it in there," I explained, "through the walls of the windpipe. It's like gristle."

I tried to wipe away the red marks I'd left on his fat neck. His breathing was getting thinner all the time, with longer pauses between intakes as his throat swelled up and choked him. The ambulance was nowhere in sight, or sound, and it was up to me to save him.

"I hope this works."

Supporting his neck from one side, I stabbed the pen into his windpipe from a distance of ten centimetres. It didn't work. I was going to have to just push it in using brute force with the palm of my hand. I took a deep breath, put the pen back in position and started pushing.

Then, like a last-second reprieve at a public execution, came the mangled squeal of an approaching ambulance.

"Oh thank fuck for that."

I stopped pushing.

Seconds later, the ambulance screeched to a halt and the medics leapt out and took charge. Quickly and incredibly efficiently, while re-establishing with me exactly what had happened — a wasp, *completely unaided*, flew directly into this poor man's mouth — two paramedics injected him with adrenaline, attached an oxygen mask to his face, strapped him to a gurney and took him away in their ambulance, leaving me alone with fourteen tourists, all of whom, in a stupefied silence, now turned to face me.

1.7

"Dead bodies is right," I eventually said, followed by a few nervous titters. "Between ten and twenty people die in the canals of Amsterdam every year and the vast majority of them have a number of things in common."

I paused.

"I guess I should ask: are you guys happy to finish the tour? I don't really know what else to do."

Those that responded said that they were, that they might as well.

So we continued. As if nothing had happened. But obviously, something — something quite horrible — had happened.

At the end of the tour, a Scottish guy gave me a tenner and said, "That's got to be the weirdest fuckin' tour of your life, right?"

I nodded enthusiastically. "Without question."

For such a small group, they tipped very well. I assume they pitied me, or maybe admired how I'd handled the situation. Even the Norwegians gave me forty between them, although no more words were spoken.

Isabelle was the last person to approach me with her tip. She said, "You know, you may have saved that man's life."

"I guess," I replied. "But I may also have killed him. I mean, it was me who, you know… if I hadn't hit the wasp, it wouldn't have…."

"Mais moi aussi, if I hadn't panicked…."

I shrugged and puffed up my cheeks. "Do you fancy a drink?"

Although it wasn't the first time I'd considered it — Isabelle was an attractive single woman and I was a desperate single man, thirsting for the validation and gratification of romantic union — still the offer surprised me as much as it probably did her.

She laughed and looked at her watch. "But I have only twenty minutes before my Red Light District tour."

"Ah OK. But if you like — this is just an idea, off the top of my head — why don't *I* give you a Red Light District tour, just the two of us? Then we don't have to hurry. We can stop and have a drink along the way, and talk about death. What do you think?"

When, after a moment's hesitation, Isabelle agreed, we made our way back into *de Wallen* — as the Dutch call the Red Light District — and improvised a tour. A couple of hours later, we found ourselves in Café 't Mandje, one of the oldest gay-friendly bars on planet Earth and when Isabelle went to the bathroom at one point, I phoned the hospital on Spuistraat. When I enquired about the Englishman with the wasp in his throat, I was asked if I was a relative. I explained that I was the guide who'd phoned the incident in. I just wanted to know if he was OK. There was a pause.

"I'm sorry, Sir," came the reply. "I really can't tell you anything."

But it was there in her voice. Regret. Sorrow. Compassion. Whatever it was, it was obvious.

"He died, didn't he?"

"I...." she said. "I'm sorry."

When Isabelle returned, I told her what had happened.

Her mouth fell open. "*Merde.*"

"Maybe you were right to be afraid of wasps after all," I said. When she smiled, I leant forward and kissed her. Happily, she reciprocated, and when we'd finished our drinks, she suggested we get a bottle of something fizzy and retire to her hotel room. As it was a special occasion, I accepted. After all, it wasn't every day you got to see a man writhing around dying in agony, right there in front of you.

Speaking of which, there was no doubt in my mind that the sex Isabelle and I had together was massively enhanced by our brush with mortality. It was the kind of intense, slightly savage sex people have when they see someone randomly perish and they realise how easily it could have been them. It was 'we hang by a thread' sex. It was 'barbaric yawp' sex. It was YOLO sex, and it was amazingly, life-affirmingly glorious.

Then, as they all do sooner or later, Isabelle left, and I went back to work, presuming, incorrectly as it happened, that nothing had changed.

1.8

By the end of the next night's Red Light, the news that I'd accidentally killed a man with a wasp had spread all the way to Paris. Obviously, I'd told everyone I met at the square the next afternoon, which included Henk and Monica and a couple of other guides, and obviously, that's the kind of news that gets passed around quickly. It is genuine news after all. "Did you hear about Wesley? He killed a man with a wasp!" It was also no surprise that someone had mentioned it to Nix, fellow guide, rising stand-up comedy star and my flatmate, who at that moment was spending a few days in Paris with one of his paramours. I can't deny I found it kind of thrilling that the news had crossed the Channel. I imagined the French dropping their baguettes in alarm. *Oh la la! Avec une guêpe?!*

"So you finally got to kill a man," said Nix in a WhatsApp message. "How was it?'

I'd been sharing a flat with Nix — full name Marnix de Wit — for four months by this point and our friendship had ripened like a first-class cheese. Both naturally confessional, and both huge fans of recreational slash medicinal drug use, there was little we hadn't shared. I knew his origin story, for example, which in many ways was far worse than mine — my mum got eaten away by cancer; his was a former junkie and lifelong white supremacist. Which was why at 13 he started calling himself Nix, because Nix meant nothing and at 13, nihilism was all he had.

Equally, Nix knew pretty much everything about me, including the fact that once or twice in the past, I had expressed a desire to kill a man. In my defence, it was always a very abstract desire, a philosophical game really, a thought experiment, usually voiced under the influence of various intoxicants and in the same breath and very much in the same vein as my desire to smoke crack and be anally penetrated. I'd say things like, "What a shame it must be to reach the end of one's life knowing that one has neither killed a man, nor been violently penetrated by one." So you see, it was just a vague, tongue-in-cheek, dark bucket-list conversation. But I'd definitely said it, and Nix had remembered.

"It didn't feel great," I replied. "But it didn't feel terrible. To be fair, and as I'm sure you're aware, it was a complete accident. Hardly your classic murder. Having said that: it couldn't have happened to a nicer person."

That night, before falling into a deep, disturbingly dream-filled sleep, I gave more thought to Nix's question: How was it? How did it actually feel? And the more I thought about it, the more I realised — if I was perfectly honest — I was genuinely unmoved by Osmotherley Man's passing, and his consequent absence from human society. I wasn't in any way glad it had happened. That would clearly have been a step too far. But I wasn't upset.

In our ten-minute pre-tour chat the following afternoon, Monica had been kind enough to suggest that if I'd performed CPR on Osmotherley Man, I might have been able to save his life. When I told her that I didn't know CPR, she was shocked. "How can you be so old and not know CPR?"

It amuses Monica to remind me how old I am at every possible opportunity. I find it devastating of course, but I rise above it with an eye-roll and a barely audible "fuck you".

When I say I'm in love with Monica, I should probably clarify. What I mean to say is, having struggled through infatuation, besottedness, obsession and worship — I really love her, both genuinely and begrudgingly, as a friend. She's intelligent, sensitive, generous, wise and sometimes outrageously funny. It just so happens that I'm also bewitched by her face. And her body.

There's a photograph of us on Facebook, at some social gathering, smiling and posing with our arms around each other, looking, to all intents and purposes, like a couple. I must have wasted hours of my life staring at that photograph, imagining what it must be like to actually be with Monica; to wake up next to her, and burrow into her sticky sleep like an incubus.

The fact is, aside from her wonderful personality, Monica Gandolfo is — in my most humble opinion — the perfect human female. Women of her type are the primary reason I ended up in Italy for a couple of years, and Monica is the most bewitching of her type I have ever seen. She has long, thick, slightly curled, shiny jet black hair, and dark, impenetrable eyes. Her lips are plump and voluptuous and when they aren't stretched across her teeth to accommodate a dazzling smile, they tend to lounge in slightly downturned, sweetly petulant repose. Occasionally, when she's angry or frustrated, they bunch up in a sexy sullen huddle. Her nose has a tiny hump halfway down the slope, her front teeth protrude ever so slightly and she has a small scar at the end of her right eyebrow where the hair no longer grows. Without these putative imperfections, it's possible her beauty might somehow be a little hollow, but as it is, as far as I'm concerned, her flaws make her utterly flawless.

Sometimes when I pass her in the street addressing a group of tourists, she reminds me of a dragonfly, or a hummingbird. She seems to just hover there, pulsating, her hair seducing the sunshine and emitting unnameable colours. Sometimes when I see her, I hear myself sigh, involuntarily, with painful, palpable longing.

She is, quite simply, a consummation of exquisiteness and I, to my eternal regret, am condemned forever to be her friend.

"I don't think of you that way," she told me after my first ham-fisted attempts at seduction.

30

"You mean you don't fancy me," I said, clarifying.

"No."

My heart fluttered hopefully. "No, you don't mean that?"

"No, I don't fancy," she said, clarifying. "You are too old," she said. "For me," she added, thoughtfully.

Of course I knew she was right. I was 46 at the time, just over a year ago. She was 27. And according to the international rule of age gap acceptability, she needs to be at least half my age, plus seven. She's two years too young.

"And you are too pale," she added. "And too ginger."

"OK, OK, you've made your point."

"And your chin…"

"Oh do fuck off, Monica."

She smiled platonically. "Beside, I told you, we have a special relation."

"*Ship*," I added, for the thousandth time.

This is true, and despite my instinctive belly-aching, I remain enormously appreciative of our special relation. We are very close. We tell each other all our secrets and when she needs one, I am her translator.

Monica has written the bulk of a book about her six years as a fashion model on Milan catwalks and various private beaches around the world. The book details the exploitation at the heart of the fashion industry, as well as touching on the sex and the drugs and the overall deep-rooted venality and glamourlessness of it all. My Italian is good enough for me to turn Italian into English, so I translated her first three chapters and she sent them off to various publishers and agents. I have experience with publishers and agents, plus I know that what Monica has written is not great, so I advised her — sweetly, mind you — not to get her hopes up.

31

As I lay in bed that night, recalling our conversation, I wondered if CPR really might have saved Osmotherley Man. I didn't think so, under the circumstances, but of course I'd never know for sure.

I thought about the tour again, about how obnoxious Osmotherley Man had been and how much the world might actually benefit from his absence. But then — what if he was just an ordinary man having a very bad day? What if the shit-stirring, nit-picking prick he presented yesterday was actually extremely out of character? What if ordinarily he was a warm and loving man who danced with children, crossed the street to stroke stray cats and brought laughter and joy into the lives of others? Although this seemed highly unlikely — after all, this was him on holiday, for God's sake; this was probably him at his best — it was still possible. Therefore, if I was really toying with the idea of his death being a positive for the planet, then suddenly it seemed like the least I could do was to find out for sure.

The next morning at 8, I awoke abruptly from a dream in which I was back at the scene of the incident, bent over Osmotherley Man's face as he lay on his back, death-rattling. I took hold of his nose, placed my mouth over his and blew. As I did so, worried that I might vomit into his disgusting maw and choke him to death, I felt the wasp as it passed, from Osmotherley Man's throat, to my own.

I got out of bed laughing.

Less than an hour later, I was at the hospital on Spuistraat, telling terrible lies.

1.9

I really don't know where it came from, but when the kindly receptionist told me that she wasn't permitted to give me the name of the man who'd died on my tour, I burst into tears.

"We just really hit it off," I sobbed. "You know when you meet someone and you just know you're gonna be friends for the rest of your life? Then a couple of hours later… he was gone!"

Aside from the fact that the lies came so easily, the strangest thing was that the tears felt real. I'm no actor but the second I started faking it, I did feel genuine remorse. It felt like Osmotherley Man's death — in all of its random finality — hit me all at once and overwhelmed me with grief.

"I just wanted to go on his Facebook page…" I'd noticed during the break in the tour that he was using Facebook on his phone. "…and let everyone know what a lovely guy he was. And let them know that his last couple of hours were filled with joy. And laughter."

Thankfully, rather than say, "Well, if you were that goddamn close, how come he didn't tell you his name?", the receptionist's face crinkled with miraculous empathy and she asked me to wait. A minute later, she returned to her post with a name on a piece of paper. She slid it across the counter to me. "There you go," she said quietly. "I'm really sorry for your loss."

"Thank you." I wiped my eyes with the fingers of my left hand. "Thank you so much."

I took the slip of paper and walked out of the hospital. Only when I was outside in the blaring sunlight did I read the name she had written.

His name… was Matty Sutcliffe.

Back home and online, I tracked down his Facebook page. Turns out he had no family, just an ex-wife he occasionally, rather bitterly disparaged on his timeline. Also, to what I realised was my considerable relief, all of my worst suspicions concerning Matty's character were quickly confirmed.

A slow perusal of the last year of his online life left me feeling considerably relieved that my fatal wasp-batting hadn't inadvertently deprived the world of a cancer cure or a Nobel Prize winner. Or even of what anyone could reasonably describe as "a nice guy".

Matty's primary passions in life were darts, Leeds United, real ale, muscular dogs, Jason Statham, the *Fast & Furious* franchise and Keith Lemon. He was also a proud and fully paid-up member of the Brexit Party, a huge fan of the military and a vocal advocate of the All Lives Matter hashtag. Did that mean he deserved to die? Absolutely not. Well, not necessarily. Did it mean he deserved to live? Again, not necessarily. All it really meant was that I wasn't going to feel bad about what had happened. The man was a towering arsehole, with undeniable, easily identifiable sociopathic tendencies.

I fell to wondering, therefore, what such a man might have been doing in Amsterdam, what possible pleasure this bastion of liberalism might have afforded him. It certainly wasn't 800 years of history, if his sneering reaction to my tour had been anything to go by. Neither did he strike me as a typical weed smoker. My most likely guess — bolstered significantly by Facebook photos of a previous summer spent in the Philippines — was sex tourism. I shuddered.

Then, just as I was about to close down his page, I noticed a post from March 2018 in which Matty posed the question: "Why are there so many fucking benders in comedy shows these days?"

When one of his friends highlighted the homophobia in his remark, Matty responded as follows: "Even the very word 'homophobic' is a bullshit made-up rhetorical ploy invented by gay activists pushing their own autocratic agenda. People who 'hate' gays are not afraid of them. Our opposition has nothing to do with sex." And so on.

I'd seen enough, and what's more, I'd changed my mind. I *was* glad he was dead after all. And it pissed me off that he'd made me feel that way. I was a fucking Buddhist for god's sake! Granted, I hadn't chanted for a while, and I hadn't been to a meeting in years, but I still held firm to all the principles. I still believed wholeheartedly in the absolute potential of every human being to love and care and show compassion to others. Except sociopaths of course, who were not, strictly speaking, human. If I was totally honest though, maybe it wasn't just sociopaths at whom I drew the line. After all, only a fortnight before Waspgate, I'd come within a whisker of breaking my seven-year fist-fast…

1.10

After a night out with friends from an old Dutch course, I was walking south on Warmoesstraat at two in the morning.

De Wallen was still loud and full of the debris — human and otherwise — from an earlier televised football match. One particular group of eight white Englishmen in Liverpool shirts were staggering about and bellowing football songs at one another. Ordinarily and individually, they may well have been harmless, but foreign travel mixed with an excess of alcohol and weed had transformed them into a gang of raging, rampaging monsters of disregard.

A window opened two floors above and a resident shushed them, reasonably pointing out, in English, that "people are trying to sleep". Rather than becalm them, however, this interjection merely urged them on to greater heights of anti-social behaviour and they jeered at the woman like drunks in the House of Lords. The woman closed her window, presumably exasperated, and the men cheered, as if celebrating some well-deserved and hard-won victory.

I passed them at this point, walking in the opposite direction, then, irked, I slowed to watch, tension creeping into my jaw. *These are the ones*, I was thinking. *These are precisely the kind of scumbag devil-men who destroy everything that's good.*

I watched as the most extroverted of them — the one with the curly, fluorescent green wig — picked up a half-brick from behind a right-angle of red and white plastic roadworks barriers and hurled it up towards the window of the complaining woman. I watched as the brick bounced off the front of the building less than halfway towards its intended destination, then descended, its fall eventually broken by the head of an oblivious passer-by. The passer-by collapsed into the street, blood instantly seeping through his fingers and down his face.

Meanwhile, the Englishman responsible for the bloodshed reacted as if he'd observed a wide-brimmed hat being blown from the head of its owner and across the street by a particularly strong gust of wind, only to land squarely on the head of a stranger. He pointed and laughed like it was the most hilarious, the most insanely capricious thing he had ever seen. Then he ran to catch up with his friends. Nobody stopped or admonished him.

In the shadow of a shop doorway, I watched, twitching with the urge to make amends, drunkenly wondering if I should do something, because surely to God, something had to be done.

Surrounded by a small circle of concerned passers-by, the injured man's face was a mask of streaked blood and sodden tissues. He'd been helped to his feet and was insisting that no one call the police. I assumed there were issues with his legal status. He looked terrified.

My head was shaking side to side, incredulous. I refused to accept that this careless cretinous human being was able to commit a casual assault — potentially ruining another human's life — and then stagger off into the night unpunished. So, without thinking of the consequences, I went after him.

It was a suicide mission. I'm an accomplished fighter but I'm not Chuck Norris and eight drunken Scousers would certainly be more than I could handle. I would therefore focus on the brick-tosser. I picked up my pace, knowing that one well-aimed punch would be enough to knock him out. I wondered if he'd possess the wherewithal to connect his punishment to his wicked behaviour. Did it matter? Not to me in that moment. I was drunk, I was vengeful, and I was in motion.

I was within ten metres of the guy in the wig when I started to run, slowly, silently, but intently towards him. My fists were clenched and my trajectory was set. What would happen after I'd landed my first punch was irrelevant. It was happening.

Then, milliseconds before I reached St Olaf's Chapel and launched my right arm, two policemen on bicycles rolled silently out of a side-street and descended directly upon the perp.

I stopped moving instantly and dropped back into the shadows of another doorway. The woman at the window must have called them, presumably describing the ring-leader and his unmissably crass hairpiece. His friends, in an act of supreme disloyalty, bolted, some of them staggering and falling to the ground in their eagerness to escape, wholly unaware of the police van that was pulling quietly to a stop a short way ahead.

Never more relieved to see the police, I made my way home, trembling like a guilty child.

The urge to fight back against the inconsiderate and aggressive had been building for a while — probably since I'd last succumbed, seven years previously. On this particular night I came painfully close, and it felt awful. Two weeks later came Waspgate, and although it did not feature a deliberate act of violence, it felt like a stepping stone and there could be no doubt, it changed me. I was scared. Scared of what I might become if I slipped back into old habits. Scared of what might happen this time around. I felt I needed guidance. So I called my guardian angel, Bryson.

1.11

Bryson Bowyer is a 65-year-old Canadian gay Buddhist and Vipassana practitioner, with a penchant for politeness, playfulness and punching racists in the face. He also makes challenging short films with the help of the multitude of friends he's collected during his 35 years in Amsterdam. In my first year in the city, I lived in his spare room. After which, unusually, we stayed in touch. Now, every couple of months, Bryson cooks amazing food, and I turn up and eat it. I bring wine of course, and in our own peculiar way, we set the table on a modest roar.

"Wesley!"

He stepped out into the street in front of his house and took a hold of me. His hugs are always very physical, very bearlike, lots of patting and dominating and growling. They're also deliberately overlong. Apparently, during one of our early hugs, I'd conveyed some instinctive physical awkwardness, and having observed that, Bryson had instantaneously decided that every subsequent hug must result in a similar if not greater amount of awkwardness. For a wonderful man, he could be quite an ass.

"How's the book?" I asked, as I wriggled free and made my way through to the kitchen. "And the leg. How's the leg?"

His grin lit up his beard. "Both amazing. I just spent a month in Greece on the advance. Definitely broke the back of the book. And guess what happened two days ago."

I got to work on a bottle.

"Tell me."

"I won my first game of tennis on Dexter."

"No way."

"I'm back, baby!"

We clinked fancy wine glasses and drank. Dexter was the name Bryson gave to his lower right leg, which was prosthetic.

Bryson had been extraordinarily active before the accident in 2017. Tennis two or three times a week, a couple of marathons a year, then, wholly out of the blue, whilst cycling home one Sunday morning, an unnecessarily large SUV hit him from behind. Trapped under its back wheel with his legs still either side of his bicycle, he was dragged for fifty metres before the vehicle came to a halt. The driver, on his way home from a club and six times over the legal limit, had dozed off at the wheel. As a consequence, he lost his licence, and for a short while, his freedom. Bryson lost two pints of blood and half a leg. His tennis-playing, marathon-running days were over. At least for a while.

For a while he struggled, understandably, with anger and self-pity. Then, like a goddamn golden phoenix, he rose, and rejoiced in his good fortune. Decades of Buddhist training had him accentuating the positive and generating the necessary compassion, and within six months he'd started saying — because it was true — that losing his leg was the best thing that had ever happened to him. "It taught me how lucky I am," he'd say. "I found reserves of strength and positivity I never knew I had, and the benefits far outweigh the downsides." Most people shook their heads instinctively, but Bryson convinced them. Seeing was believing.

I'd known Bryson virtually since 2015, having interviewed him for an article I was writing about Vipassana for *Psychologies* magazine. I'd done the 10-day silent meditation retreat that spring and it had changed my life, for at least a fortnight, then — as I always, always seemed to — I drifted back into old, self-destructive habits.

I finally met him in the flesh when I moved to Amsterdam in 2016. The following year, I moved in for six months. Bryson was good for me. He was good for everyone.

Over a butternut soup starter, he talked some more about the book, which had started out as an online diary of his convalescence. A handful of early readers shared links on social media and his readership quickly grew. People were charmed by his combination of practical mindfulness and no-nonsense, occasionally biting social commentary. A couple of months in, he was contacted by a UK publisher, and a couple of Skype meetings later, he was commissioned to write a book entitled *Blessed Foot Forward: Adventures in Buddhism and Brain Chemistry*. His first draft deadline was not till the end of the year.

"Which gives me heaps of time," he twinkled, "to make the next film."

I laughed.

It was ridiculous how much Bryson managed to pack into every day of his life. Aside from the books and the films, he meditated for at least two hours daily; he volunteered for half a dozen local initiatives and political campaigns; he still did at least an hour of physio every day as part of his ongoing convalescence; he baked cakes, cooked meals and made kombucha; he even had a more active sex life than me, which frankly, considering his age, I found galling. Oh and he also found the time for physical violence.

Bryson had been in his mid-40s when he started punching racists in the face. His spontaneous, end-of-tether test-case was his brother-in-law, who, in response, beat the shit out of him. Then weeks later, Bryson received a letter of apology, in which — though it pained him to admit it and though he still had certain reservations — his brother-in-law confessed that he had begun to understand Bryson's point of view. Bryson was thrilled. This was much further than reasoning had ever got him. It was a turning point.

From that day forth, he promised that whenever he heard racist guff coming out of anyone's mouth, he would first seek confirmation of their putative prejudice, then, once confirmed, he would punch them squarely in the face. He knew it wasn't strict Buddhist practice, but sometimes you had to trust your gut and see where it got you. So far it had earned him two very short detentions in police stations in both London and Amsterdam, one £200 fine, and at last count, three solid renunciations of massively racist guff.

"You're a goddamn inspiration," I told him.

"I know it. But what about you? You've told me nothing. How's tour guiding? Are you happy?"

"I… yeah. I mean, yeah, sure, frequently. Something happened though. Something pretty weird actually."

"The weirder, the better. Hit me."

So I told him the story of Waspgate, and Matty Sutcliffe, in all its gory detail, from the first spiky exchange to the last spiky exchange, from the glorious bonus of post-mortem sex to the weird manipulative weeping in the hospital. I even showed him the dead man's Facebook page and his "gay agenda" bullshit. Bryson laughed.

"I feel bad," I explained, "because I don't feel bad. You know?"

Bryson shrugged. "Everything's allowed."

"Is it though? Surely I shouldn't be pleased that someone died in agony. Even if he did totally get what was coming to him."

"We all get what's coming to us, Wesley. That's the Mystic Law. Cause and effect, baby. You know that."

"I guess. I just… I'm getting some dark thoughts these days, you know." I told him what had happened on Warmoesstraat, how

I'd been seconds away from a physical intervention. "I'm afraid that I'm going to get overwhelmed by anger."

Bryson held my gaze, nodding slowly, smiling compassionately. "Are you meditating?"

In response I let rip with a massive, juddering sigh.

Bryson chuckled. "That sounds like a no."

I wasn't meditating. I wasn't chanting. I wasn't exercising. I wasn't writing. I wasn't really doing anything that might reasonably be described as a healthy habit. I took another glug of wine and shook my head.

Bryson stood up from the table. "There's someone I want you to meet. I think he might be good for you."

"OK." I looked around the kitchen, confused. "Who is he?"

"His name is Spas Daskalov." He smiled like just saying the name gave him pleasure. "He's in my closet. Stay where you are. I'll go fetch him."

1.12

Moments later, Bryson returned from his bedroom with what looked like a large pile of human hair in his hands. "Here."

"Here hair here," I replied.

He ignored me. "Try these on for size."

There were two items. One was an old wig, with real human hair attached to a Caucasian flesh-coloured skullcap. One was a large unruly beard made from synthetic hair. Both had apparently enjoyed an illustrious career, mostly in theatre, and both had wound up in Bryson's possession.

I took the wig from him, gingerly, and sniffed at it. "Was this stolen from a corpse?"

"Just try it on. See how you look. Humour me."

I pulled on the skullcap, squishing up my forehead and ripping out hair. "It's maybe a tad small."

"Come here." Bryson removed and replaced the wig in a slightly more professional manner. "It's gotta be tight, otherwise it looks fake. If you're gonna be a Bulgarian mystic, you're gonna wanna be a *convincing* Bulgarian mystic. Am I right?"

"I guess so." This was the first I'd heard of it.

Once Bryson was happy with the hair, he started on the beard. "This has seen better days, I admit." He picked bits from it as he talked. "I think maybe it's got one more shoot in it. What do you think?"

"Whatever you say, Bryson."

He gave the beard a shake before placing it over my face and smiling. "I say this is made for you. Ima glue it." So saying, he whizzed from the kitchen, returning seconds later with a small brown bottle. "We won't do the whole beard. Just enough to hold it so that you too can see how you were just born to play this role."

"What role, Bryson?"

"You'll see."

As Bryson brushed my face with adhesive, I thought of my Bulgarian friend and fellow guide Krastyo, who generally went by Kras, but was anything but. Kras already had a beard. If Bryson needed a Bulgarian mystic, surely Kras was his man. "You should meet my Bulgarian friend."

"I'd love to!" cried Bryson. "Bring him round!"

"I should. I will. Next time."

Bryson continued to fiddle, smiling and nodding maniacally.

The beard was extraordinary, just about clinging to the edges of plausibility. It was not a tidy beard, such as a TV newsreader might wear, but a wild beard, a boisterous beard, a beard befitting a Bulgarian mystic.

Bryson stopped fiddling, admired his handiwork and laughed.

When I pulled out my phone to take a look, he cried, "Wait! You're not ready."

With that he scampered back to his bedroom, this time returning with a long, not quite white hooded robe, like a cross between a klansman's robe and something Obi-Wan Kenobi might wear in the desert. The colour, Bryson informed me, was bone. He lowered it slowly over my head and once I'd managed to get my arms in the holes, he made some final adjustments to the wig and beard.

"Now you're golden." He laughed. "And you look — and this is not a word I use lightly — *magnificent*. Like Suleiman!" He laughed again. "Come. Come into my parlour."

I followed Bryson into his bedroom and approached his full-length mirror with some trepidation. Then I saw myself. Only... it wasn't me. Instead it was some ridiculously hirsute and undeniably mystical stranger. It was eerily convincing. "Whoa." I gawped. "That is amazing. I genuinely don't recognise myself."

Bryson chuckled. "Hey, maybe this is the real you."

I narrowed my eyes and lifted my chin like Mussolini. "Maybe."

"Anyhow, you'll just have a few lines. Nothing to worry about."

"I'm not an actor though, Bryson. What are you…."

"*Actor*." Bryson spat the word out like it was poison. "I'm not interested in *acting*. Look," he insisted. "Look in the mirror."

I was looking.

"Who is that there? Is that you?"

I shook my hairy head. "It doesn't look like me."

"It's not you, Wesley. That is Spas Daskalov, Bulgarian mystic, medic and folk musician." He nodded reverentially to Spas Daskalov.

Spas looked confused. "*Spas* as in *spastic*?"

Bryson laughed. "*Spas* as in *salvation*. I'll send you the script later. We shoot in November."

"Nazdrave," I said, in my best generic Eastern European accent. It was something I'd picked up from Kras, who said it before drinking alcohol, which he did only at parties and never to excess. Although it was hardly appropriate in this moment, Bryson took my *Nazdrave* as further evidence that I *was* Spas Daskalov.

"OK, take it off and leave it on the bed. We don't want you getting risotto in your beard." And with that he sauntered back through to the kitchen to serve the main course.

As we ate, we revisited my concerns over my anger management and Bryson said three words in which I think he probably had more faith than I did. He said: "Follow your heart."

I nodded, dubious.

46

"You've a good heart, kid. Follow it and you'll be fine. I promise."

That night in bed, my heart told me to send a message to Kras, who'd been on my mind on and off throughout the whole evening. "Hope you're well," I wrote. "I just got a part in a movie playing a Bulgarian mystic. Any tips gratefully received."

Kras wrote back immediately. "I'm in Sofia! Let's meet when I get back next week. I have news." Seconds later, he sent another message. "Life-changing news!"

"Tell me now!" I replied.

"Next week," he insisted. "Good things come to those who wait."

"Bad things too," I typed. Then, afraid of tempting fate, I deleted it.

1.13

It was maybe three weeks after Waspgate. I rocked up at the monument at 1.15 and greeted Henk and the other slaves who were holding umbrellas and drumming up business. I call them *slaves* because, unlike the guides, who were all freelancers making good money from tips, the MPMs and brolly-holders were tied to Beachams zero-hour contracts, paid very poorly and treated like dirt. Hence the alarmingly high turnover. I took Henk's umbrella, so that he might more easily do his job, and we chatted.

We were still very much in the high season, but it was unusually quiet. I was guide number three. The other two guides had yet to show. Hardly surprising, as the other two guides were sociopaths. Do I exaggerate? Maybe. One was a sociopath, for sure; one was probably just a gargantuan tool. Whatever. Neither ever turned up till the last minute, because neither gave a shit about anyone but themselves. One was Sam Lewis (sociopath); one was Hamish Brannigan (tool).

When Henk wasn't processing tourists, he spent much of his spare time having sex with anonymous men in dark rooms. He also enjoyed regaling me with unnecessarily pornographic details of these encounters. It was during one such repugnant tale of rimming gone wrong — delivered *sotto voce* in between handing out tickets — that Monica strolled up eating a cone of messy war-fries. A Dutch culinary speciality, war-fries are fries topped with chopped onion, mayonnaise and in this case, lots of satay sauce. It was like Henk's horrific sexploit come to life.

Monica was heading back for her bike after an earlier tour and had just popped by to say hi. As she fell into conversation with Henk, I glanced between the two of them, my eyes involuntarily lingering on Monica as she listened and laughed and chewed on her chips. Microseconds before my lingering became a creepy case of out-and-out staring, I tore my guilty gaze away and sighed. I didn't want to be that guy. Even if Monica was wholly unaware of it, my ever-present desire for her felt like an affront. It felt inappropriate, disrespectful and absolutely not part of the friendship contract. It felt like having a pet you adored, maybe a golden retriever, who was your most faithful and trusted companion and yet, every time you looked into his eyes, you imagined his balls resting on your chin.

My phone buzzed. A message from Milton Pacey, crazy old Yank friend and fellow ex-journo. "I've come home to watch America burn," he wrote. Attached to the message was the first ever photo of his new son, or daughter, apparently only thirteen weeks old and still living in his new wife's belly. This was typical Milton. I didn't even know he had a girlfriend.

Milton was the reason I moved to Amsterdam in the first place. Back in the UK after five years on the move, I'd posted something online about feeling restless again. Milton saw it and wrote, "Come to Amsterdam! There's a mattress with your name on it."

So I came to Amsterdam, and within a fortnight, Milton had moved to Bora Bora. That would always make me smile. That was so Milton.

Milton was a maniac, of sorts. He lived his entire life like he had six months left and if anything occurred to him — something he'd like to do before he died — he wouldn't write it down on a bucket list; he'd go do it. He was heroically unpredictable. We worked at the slowly perishing *Evening Standard* in the late 90s and shared a one-bedroom flat in Clapham. Milton had the bedroom and I had a mattress on the living room floor. There was damp and mice and lots of LSD. That's how it was in those days. Sometimes I missed him terribly.

I looked back at Milton's baby and shook my head. It shocked me that even Milton was growing up and taking responsibility. I thought about the last time I'd seen him, his last day in Amsterdam, him shoving a small bag of drugs into my hand — pills mostly, and liquid LSD — making me promise to keep it safe for him in case things didn't work out in Bora Bora. I promised. Of course, ultimately, things didn't work out in Bora Bora, but rather than come back to Amsterdam, Milton moved on. Milton always moves on. Except now maybe. I replied to his message.

"You've changed, Mil. Congratulations! I love you. I'm at work."

"Hey, muchacho!" Henk clicked his fingers next to my left ear. "It doesn't look like you'll be running."

With only a couple of minutes to go, there were only 26 tourists — two small groups or one large, to be determined by the guides, once they bothered to actually show up.

"You can go home if you like," said Henk.

"Thanks," I said. But I didn't move. I was keen to see how poorly the other guides were going to comport themselves, so that I could sneer at them behind their backs and feel superior.

At that precise moment, Hamish, guide number two, turned up, with his fist-bumps and his thick, borderline impenetrable Belfast accent. "Alright, guys and gals. How's about yuz?" Expensive sunglasses couldn't hide the fact that he looked like a speedfreak, with his pimply complexion, a greasy fringe that screamed Hitler and white bits in his lip-hinge.

"Who is number one?" asked Monica.

"Sam," said Henk, before making a kind of guttural rolling *R* sound somewhere in the back of his throat. It was the sound of lust. Monica laughed. My teeth ground.

It was 1.31. The sociopath Sam Lewis was now officially late. As he invariably was. Generally he arrived either on the dot or just after the dot, full of kisses and hugs and creepy little Joe Biden shoulder-rubs for the female slaves, but he never turned up early to help.

Sure enough, just as Henk picked up his phone to call him, the sociopath appeared, swooping up the steps of the monument like butter wouldn't melt. He took hold of Monica's shoulders and kissed her full on both cheeks. He shook Henk's hand, firmly, then Hamish's, then finally mine. He looked back at Monica, licked his lips and said: "Mmm, I got some of your mayonnaise when I kissed you. Look at you, you've got it all over you. Come here..." He lifted a finger to Monica's face and wiped her cheek and bottom lip, before sucking it clean in his own mouth. Then, whilst maintaining eye contact with Monica, he asked Henk for the tourist count.

My mouth, meanwhile, had dropped open, like a hanged man. My entire body was clenched. I was glaring at Monica, as if at a snuff movie. What the fuck was she doing? Why was she simpering like a Japanese schoolgirl when she should have been spraying pepper in his eyes and screaming, "Me too! Fucking me too!" Instead, she was positively glowing, shyly popping chips in her gob like she'd just been sexted by Ryan Gosling.

Within a matter of seconds, Sam had corralled the tourists and taken them across the street with Hamish, and I was standing beneath the giant purple Beachams umbrella staring at Monica like she'd just spat toothpaste on my best black shirt.

"What?"

I shook my head and looked away, embarrassed by the sheer magnitude of my jealousy. "How could you?"

Monica seemed genuinely confused. "What are you saying?"

"How could you let… *him* touch you like that and you just stand there grinning like…." I ran out of words. "Jesus, Monica."

Her face darkened. "Number one," she said, "Sam is fucking gorgeous and I would let him do much more than touch my face. Number two, it's my face. Who touches it is my choice and number three, you don't even have the right to an opinion."

Even if two of her points were identical, she was of course right and I should've just apologised and begged forgiveness. But no. Apparently, I was committed to the scene.

"Fine," I snapped. Then, expertly ignoring Henk's expression of petrified embarrassment, I thrust the giant umbrella towards him, and with a peremptory but unintentionally high-pitched "Goodbye!", I marched down the steps of the National Monument like a petulant butthurt teen. It was only after stomping off in one direction that I remembered my bicycle was parked in entirely the other direction. Instinctively, I stopped stomping and stood still in the street. Like a statue. Of course, I should've just butched it out and kept on walking like a proper man, picked up my bike later or maybe taken a different route. But now it was too late. So I shook my head, changed my direction and stomped off again. Then I compounded my shame by glancing back at Monica and Henk, who were both visibly amused. Henk was also turning a finger in the air next to his head.

I don't know how bad this seems to you, dear juror, in terms of social embarrassment. Maybe you'd shrug it off. Maybe you'd even laugh it off. I couldn't do that. I was mortified that I'd allowed my jealousy to ooze out in such a petty, infantile manner.

So mortified was I that I cried out in anguish all the way home, remembering Monica's contempt and Henk's visible cringe. I also knew immediately, and for a fact: this — was a keeper. This moment of shame would repeat on me for a long time to come, like the existential equivalent of a garlic smoothie. It would trigger a tsunami of shame that would manifest itself in twitches and shivers and embarrassing, often extremely offensive, verbal tics, probably for the rest of my life, albeit in ever less intensive waves.

So mortified was I that later that night, I would commit my first act of physical violence in seven whole years, and believe me when I say this:

I could not feel sorrier;

I could not feel more ashamed.

1.14

On the rough housing estate of my Sunderland childhood, violence was pretty much a way of life. It started for me around aged four, when the older brothers of close friends would make us fight, like dogs or cocks, sometimes for money, but mostly just for fun. It was either fight or be labelled a coward, and because I *was* a coward — afraid of the stigma and shame of being labelled as such — I fought. Public ridicule was always much more painful to me than actual physical pain, which was nothing, like blood off a seal pup's back. Part of me maybe even liked it, or at least felt I deserved it, because of my mum. My mum died of cancer when I was three, and my dad was worse than useless, so I channelled the pain of my loss into violence. Fighting felt good. Partly it was winning, which I almost invariably did, but mostly it was the feeling of liberation.

I still remember the first time I drove my fist into someone's face. It felt like my brain had been removed and tossed out to sea — for the first time ever, I forgot that I was hurting. So naturally, I became addicted.

Plus I really was good at it. I was driven, whilst fighting, by the imagined desire to incapacitate or kill my opponent. I would scream too, for the first year or so, like a little kamikaze warrior, and I always had to be dragged away from the fight. I wouldn't stop, even when my opposite number offered no more resistance. Frankly, I was terrifying.

As I grew older, I fought less frequently but more intensely, and by the time I was in my teens, I had quite the reputation. I was feared, and like so many violent men before me, I decided fear was a good thing. It was basically respect, minus love.

I fought, in a nutshell, because it was easier than talking. I took after my father in this regard. And it was only after I'd left

Sunderland that I made a conscious effort to curtail the violence. Later still, with my first therapy, I came to realise that like all brawlers, I was only really fighting myself. It was a tough habit to break though, and I continued to relapse long after I knew how harmful and futile it was.

In my thirties, I discovered that I'd hit a man so hard that I'd blinded him in one eye, and although I felt genuine antipathy towards the treacherous fiend in question, I also knew that blinding him was probably a bit much. Mortified, I swore off violence entirely and forever.

Two years later, however, I saw a man in Mexico City beating a dog in the street with his fists and I flew into a rage. In the heat of the moment, avenging the mistreatment of an innocent animal seemed like a good reason to fight, but then there was *always* a good reason. I made sure of that. As an adult, when it came to fighting, I always managed to convince myself I was doing the right thing. I was always the good guy. But at the same time, I knew in my heart that good guys didn't hit people. There had to be a better way.

Six months after the incident of the dog on the dirt road, I drank some plant medicine in the heart of a Peruvian rainforest and made a solemn vow that I would never again physically harm another living creature — no matter what. Excepting mosquitoes, ticks and, in an emergency, snakes. I was just about to turn 40.

In my early 40s, I discovered Nichiren Buddhism, and I chanted daily for eighteen months. Then I stopped. Then I dedicated two years of my life to the study of judo, with a view to mastering de-escalation. Then I stopped. Then I found Vipassana meditation, which I only practised for a few months before, inevitably, I stopped. All of these things helped me maintain my commitment to pacifism, however, which lasted, as I have mentioned, for seven years.

For seven years I never raised a hand in anger — no matter what. There were challenges along the way of course. Frequent challenges. But I prevailed. And when violence did erupt or threatened to erupt around me, sometimes I just turned the other cheek, like Jesus, but often I would step in and diffuse it, like a roaring bodhisattva.

Something, however, was building inside me, and that evening, after reliving my hissy fit at the square for the hundredth time, I lost control of my self-loathing, and I glassed myself.

Writing these words is difficult for me. Even if I am the only one who ever reads them, I find it embarrassing to admit that I was so angry with myself, so ashamed of myself, that I slammed an empty glass into my forehead. I mean… who *does* that?

It was a small glass beaker that broke into four pieces on impact, cutting a deep gash between my eyebrows. I was shocked. Despite having spent most of the day cringing and shouting out self-hating obscenities, the attack took me by surprise. It really shook me up.

Examining the wound in the bathroom mirror as the blood dripped from my nose and splashed into the sink, I was concerned I might need stitches. I was also concerned it might leave a scar in the shape of an inverted crucifix. I groaned. What a colossal freak.

I took a shower. Under the hot spray I closed my eyes and had a little weep. Although it was nowhere near as bad as attacking another human, this was not a good sign.

Instinctively, I wanted to blame Sam for what had happened, but that would have been insane. Sam was barely aware of my existence.

The next day, thankfully, I had no tours. At some point, Nix shouted my name up the stairs but I kept out of his way. I still hadn't figured out how to explain the self-harm crucifix between my eyes. It looked like I'd been fighting. I was really embarrassed.

I sent a message to Monica, apologising: "I'm really sorry for yesterday. I was just jealous. I know I've got no right to be jealous. I'm an imbecile. Please accept my most sincere apologies." Praying hands emoji.

I reread what I'd written, then pressed send.

Then I wrote another. "I'm not usually jealous of your sexploits. No, that's not true. But I can usually handle it. It's just Sam. He's not a good man, Monica. If you ever do sleep with him, please don't tell me about it, or I may have to go on a murderous rampage."

This one didn't stand up so well on reread, so I was about to delete it when I impulsively added two random emojis and pressed send.

Within a couple of hours, the messages were blue-ticked, so Monica had seen them. But she didn't reply. I checked my phone for the rest of the day. Nothing.

This was really bad. I didn't mind humiliating myself. Not really. I didn't even mind hating myself and attacking myself with a glass. But losing Monica's friendship would be unforgivable.

The next morning she still hadn't responded and I felt sick with shame. Back in the bathroom mirror, I fingered my Satan scar and in a crude impersonation of the old lady in the Zuiderkerk courtyard, I said, "I want you to *die*." I narrowed my eyes. "You should be *ashamed* of yourself." I took a deep breath. "You are dis*gus*ting."

I felt terrible, with no idea whatsoever how to make myself feel better.

Then, as if by magic, up popped Kras with the remedy.

1.15

We'd plumped for De Prael on the south-west edge of *de Wallen*.
We met at the bar. We hugged hello.

"Kraskolnikov. My man."

"Hey Wes. How are you, m- Whoa."

Kras clocked my cut.

"What the fuck did you do to your face, man?"

"I glassed myself." I gave a quick angry mime.

Kras took me at my word and his face clouded over. The
slightly hooded eyes that always painted him haunted, narrowed
with tender empathy. He had a sad face, Kras, there were no two
ways about it. Even when he smiled or laughed, something broken-
hearted always seemed to loiter there in the peripheries. "Man, are
you serious?"

Before he'd even got the question out, however, I was laughing
and denying it. I didn't want to burden him with my tomfoolery.
"No, no, no, I fell — drunk — fell forward, up the stairs, glass in
my hand, smash."

He winced. "You're lucky you didn't blind yourself, man."

I agreed.

When our drinks arrived, Kras, his cheeks high on his face like
something on a vine, said, "It finally happened, man. With Donka."

"You had sex?"

He tutted. "No, man. It's not about…" His face immediately
lost most of its ebullience. "She loves me, Wes." The ebullience
returned! Cheek berries aflame! "She told me she loves me!"

"That's fantastic! That's everything. I'm so happy for you!"

"She's going to move in with me."

"Even better!" I felt a wave of genuine joy and relief.

"Then at end of summer, we move back to Sofia."

"Oh." I felt a wave of disappointment. It didn't wash away the first two emotions, but by dint of its very existence, it diluted them.

In the summer of 2018, Kras had been guiding a large group of tourists down the main road in *de Wallen*, when he tripped over a raised paving stone and fell on his hands and knees in the dirt. Glancing to his right as he climbed to his feet, he saw a beautiful woman, naked but for the skimpiest of underwear, pointing at him through a full-length window, and laughing. Kras bowed — to the woman, to his tourists, to the group of laughing men across the street — and he moved on, already smitten.

Next time he saw her, he'd just finished a tour. Her eyes lit up, he said — he swore — and when she asked him through the glass if he wanted to join her inside, he shook his head no. And then when he didn't move away, Donka opened up and Kras introduced himself, as Krastyo. When he heard that Donka was not only Bulgarian, but also from his neck of the woods — Varna Province — he knew it was Destiny, so he asked her to meet him sometime for a coffee. They could speak Bulgarian, he said. She could help him with his homesickness. Donka agreed and took his number. To his surprise, she texted a week later and they met for midday coffee.

After that, they started meeting once every few weeks and even though Kras was telling his closest friends he was already in love with her, he never told Donka how he felt. She must have known though; Kras had one of those faces — it was all in the eyes and forehead. But he never put it into words, for fear of frightening her off, and also because her profession and her living situation made things difficult. This was all new territory.

Despite everything, or because of everything, they grew closer. Donka opened up about her shitty childhood, in and out of foster homes, and later shop doorways on the streets of Sofia. She told Kras that when she was picked up by two Hungarian businessmen who offered her a passport and a new life in Amsterdam as a personal secretary in some unnamed business collective, she knew it was dodgy. She just figured, why not? It had to be better than begging for change in Sofia. Amsterdam sounded cool, and whatever happened didn't have to be forever. Then, suddenly she was 25, and she'd been a sex worker for six years.

Nobody knows how many of the women who sell sex in Amsterdam work for pimps. Some of the women claim it's not even as many as one in ten. Some government employees and members of Christian organisations claim it's as many as nine in ten. Whatever the real number happens to be, Donka was one of them.

Once in Amsterdam, she was purchased outright by a couple of Albanian pimps, one of whom, name of Fisnik, took a shine to her and moved her into his flat. I believe Fisnik was what's known as a *loverboy*. So, as well as making Donka sleep with men for money that he would keep, he also slept with her himself, bought her nice things to wear and told her that he loved her and wanted a better life for her. Eventually, as a sign of his affection, he would only send her out to work four nights a week. As I understood it, Donka was never under any illusions where Fisnik was concerned, but aside from the whoring out, which she mostly buried beneath vast quantities of weed, she still preferred Amsterdam to Sofia. She knew she was essentially a sex slave, but for the first time in her life, she had necklaces and Netflix, and she ate well.

After six months or so, at one of their midday coffee meetings, Kras confessed to Donka that he was in love with her. He couldn't keep it in any longer, he said. He'd literally fallen for her that first day in the street. Donka was upset. She told him he'd compromised their friendship and now she'd feel guilty whenever she looked at

61

him. So she broke it off and Kras was authentically heartbroken. Then, when she texted him a fortnight later saying she missed him, they started back up, but it was different now; now Kras was convinced that she couldn't live without him.

Sometime in July, Donka informed him she'd be going clubbing with a group of friends. Fisnik would be there too, but not for the whole night, so if Kras happened to be there… maybe they could see each other.

They knew they were taking a risk but Kras didn't care. He had to see her. So he went along and they ended up meeting in a gloomy nook away from prying eyes, and Kras took a chance and he kissed her. She reciprocated. They kissed for as long as they dared and Kras kept a lid on the love stuff even though it was coursing through his body like amphetamines.

Kras confessed that after that, he got scared. "I was sure that evil fucking bastard was going to find out and… you know, do something."

But that evil fucking bastard didn't find out and when they next met for coffee, Kras told her again that he loved her — "not in a desperate way," he insisted, "but totally no emotion. I said I love her and if she wants to leave her window and start a new life with me, then I would help." He took a deep breath and let it out slowly. There were tears in his eyes. "She said she loves me too, man. She said she wants to be with me. But she's too afraid to stay in Amsterdam. So…."

There were tears in my eyes too. "So when are you going?"

"Hopefully within two months."

Kras had come to study in Amsterdam seven years previously. Like many students, he'd grown attached and had never left. I was slightly surprised by how casual he was at the prospect of going home.

"But you love Amsterdam. Won't you miss it?"

Kras shrugged. "It's just a place. It's not a person. I love Donka."

I nodded slowly. "I guess so."

"Don't guess." Kras smiled. "It's a fact."

"No, I mean, I understand," I clarified. "I guess loving someone is the best reason to do anything."

"Don't guess," Kras repeated. "It's the only reason."

"I guess so."

Kras rolled his eyes. "Anyway, before that, she has to get her passport back."

"How will she do that?"

"She's smart." Pride mingled with concern in his forehead. "She has a plan."

1.16

When Monica still hadn't replied by the following morning, I became emotional. Hurt turned quickly to anger but I checked myself because anger is a gateway drug and if we can, we give it short shrift. We say, *thank you very much, Mister Shouty McButthurt but we don't have need of your particular brand of assistance right now.* That used to work quite well. All I had to do was acknowledge and dismiss my angry side, my *beast*, using the moniker *Mister Shouty McButthurt,* and all the tension would leave me. I was able to relax, and feel comfortably vulnerable. I read self-help books for a year too and they also helped. Well, some of them. One of them made me punch a wall.

My forehead was healing nicely, thankfully, so I treated myself to a new meditation cushion. Bright yellow, the colour of hope; hope, the fermented pus of desperation. I knew I was drifting into a bad place. I knew I needed to head it off at the pass with tried and trusted techniques. I knew I needed, at the very least, to instil good habits. It really was as easy as that. So I meditated for the first time in six months or so, and I went for a long restorative cycle ride up the Amstel. When it started to rain, I stepped into a bar by the river and drank a cappuccino by the window.

Then I sent the following text to Monica: "Oh come on, Monica. Please don't torture me with your silence. I'm a good egg, aren't I? I'm sorry I've been a dick. I'm sorry I said I'd go on a murderous rampage if you slept with Sam. That was stupid. I probably won't. It's not my business, I appreciate that. Sleep with who you want to sleep with. Obviously. I just want to be your friend. Please don't stop being my friend."

I added a modest number of emojis, before removing them one by one. Then I pressed send and stopped looking at my phone.

I was the only customer in the bar. *Almost Blue* by Chet Baker was weeping from a pair of dusty speakers. The rain outside was like machine gun fire. Like steel pipes. I watched it drumming on the roofs of nearby cars, hypnotised. The patron closed what windows were open and said something relevant in Dutch. I agreed. "It's biblical."

My phone buzzed to life on the bar, like a giant hornet throwing a fit. Number withheld. I answered, tentative.

"What the fuck is wrong with you?" screamed Monica.

"Oh. Really? I mean…."

"You are so far up in your own ass, minchia."

"I'm sorry."

Monica laughed. She was in Palermo.

"Why are you in Palermo?"

"I told you."

I was pretty sure she hadn't. But maybe she had. Sometimes I drift off.

"I definitely told you."

Monica was in Palermo seeing family. Her younger sister still wasn't fully recovered from her bike accident on Monica's birthday and Monica still felt guilty.

"Oh, did that really happen?"

"Of course it fucking happened!" She was yelling so loudly that I had to move the phone away from my ear. "You think I'm a liar? I never lie."

"Really?" I was smiling, happy to hear my friend's screeching voice. "Everybody lies sometimes."

"I *never* lie," she repeated. "I'm sorry I didn't answer your stupid message. I was travelling. I came a day early because the airline is lame."

"That's fine. I thought you were pissed off with me, that's all."

"Fly the fuck down, Wesley Bell. Why would I spend any time thinking of your neurotic bullshit, ah? I'm spending time with my family, with my friends, with real problems. I have bigger fish in the sea."

"Of course." I was grateful. "I'm sorry."

"It's not your fault. You can't help being you."

"I'm trying," I told her. "I bought a new cushion. It's yellow."

"Idiota."

Precisely as I was re-establishing my special sweet and sour relation with Monica, I received a message from my English friend and former employer, the landscape gardener Malcolm Fitch. We'd first met in Italy at the party of a mutual friend, six months after Fitch had lost his four-months-pregnant wife in a multi-vehicle pile-up on the M23. His trip to Italy had been his first social occasion since her death. We hit it off and stayed in touch, then years later, just before I moved to Amsterdam, I ended up working for him in Brighton. For six months I slept in a spare room in Fitch's house, racing around the suburbs in the daytime, pimping rich people's back gardens with timber decking, tumbled travertine and trellis.

Fitch often sent me links to news stories I might have missed. The latest was just a cropped screenshot from an online news story, with a familiar but unflattering headshot and the following headline: "Local man in tragic wasp death linked to Amsterdam drugs ring."

I gasped. I read on.

As well as all the other stuff — all the sleepy creeping evil of his political beliefs — turns out Osmotherley Man had been in Amsterdam trying to buy €50,000 worth of uncut coke. When alerted to the presence of a small brick of cocaine in his hotel room, police trawled his phone and found months of messages incriminating half a dozen people, including one very foolish Amsterdam bar owner. The bar owner had been arrested, as had a couple of small-fry dealers in Leeds, who were also implicated in funding the deal and sending Matty the Mule over here to pick up the gear. The police also found, sitting alongside the cocaine on his hotel room desk, a couple of bags of Dutch flour. Apparently his plan had been to simply refill an empty flour bag with cocaine and then carry it home on the Eurostar.

He might have gotten away with it too, I thought, if it wasn't for that pesky wasp.

The article also confirmed his lack of family. Just an ex-wife and an allergy to wasp venom he never knew he had. The story confirmed he died from asphyxiation following anaphylactic shock after being repeatedly stung in the throat.

"That was me!" I texted back, before filling in Fitch on the details.

Fitch was shocked and perhaps strangely excited by the story. "We hang by a thread!" he exclaimed. Then: "What are you doing for Halloween? Week before more like. Middle of October. You got any plans?" When I said I had none, he booked himself in. "Keep it free. I'm coming for a visit."

"Nice," I replied, with only mild reservations. Fitch was always welcome and I was happy he knew that. It was just, some of his friends….

"If that's OK," he added.

"Of course." I waited a sec then typed: "By yourself?"

"Three of us, I reckon. Me, Rich and Damo."

I felt myself physically deflate. There was no thunder in that moment, but goddammit, there should have been.

"We can get an Airbnb if you don't have space for the three of us," wrote Fitch, as if reading my thoughts. He knew that Damo rubbed me up the wrong way. Rich was a damn fine egg, but Damo I kind of disdained.

I'd met him on three separate occasions by this point, all when I was working with Fitch in Brighton, and each time found him cocky, toxic and hateful, like a Fox News anchor. Indeed, if Tucker Carlson were a British plasterer, he'd be Damo. Even aside from the whole toxicity thing, there's the whole *Damo* thing. I mean, seriously, anyone who stoops to adding an *o* to the first syllable of their name in such an artless manner can only be capable of terrible things.

"No, don't be silly," I replied. "We've got a couple of sofas and a blow-up thing. Plenty room."

"Superb," typed Fitch.

I was curious. "How is Damo these days?"

"Yeah, he's good. Nothing to worry about, I promise. I know you two have had your ups and downs before. Is that fair to say? Anyway, no worries. Having another kid has really mellowed him out I reckon."

"Good," I wrote. "Thank god for that."

I would like the jury to take special note of Fitch's assurance regarding Damo's character. I don't want it stricken from the record. On the contrary, I want it engraved on the record, a hundred times, in letters ten feet tall. Then highlighted. Because it'll be important later, and — spoiler alert — it isn't fucking true.

II

September 2019

2.1

When my father paid a surprise visit to Amsterdam during the first weekend of September, I must admit, I was both relieved and disappointed that he had no intention of staying with me. He hadn't even asked. He'd just booked himself a hotel room opposite Central Station. I wasn't surprised. Like many desperately insecure men, rather than admitting to his terrible fear of rejection, my father prided himself on his fierce independence. He needed no one. I was exactly the same, sadly, but I was working on it.

It had been three years since we'd seen each other, nine months since we'd last spoken, and within five minutes of our meeting, I was already incensed by what I considered his utter obnoxiousness.

We were walking towards the Red Light District in the late afternoon, catching up. When I told him, apparently for the first time, that I gave tours of the area, he said, "D'ya shite." When I insisted it was true, he said, "Yulafta pick uz out a canny whore like."

"Sex worker," I said.

"Fuckin reet ah will."

"What? What does that even mean?"

"Yael see."

My father pushed buttons, consistently, and for sport. Not just mine; everyone's. It's what he did. He was — in my opinion — an odious, spiteful, potentially sociopathic child who delighted in the discomfort of others. Of course I should have laughed it off, but I simply couldn't. I was programmed to be incensed.

We had never got along. Everything about my father seemed, to my eyes, an unpolished reflection of his more or less omnipresent aggressiveness and ignorance, which I disdained.

70

Everything, from his physical aspect — his denim, his boots, his skinhead and scowl — to the words that came out of his mouth, I disdained. Consequently, my *ad hominem* disdain for my father also bled into a topographical disdain for the North East of England, particularly for Sunderland. Or, as the natives boiled it down: *Sunlun.*

My father loved the place. He basked in his Makem identity like a kitten in a shaft of sunlight. Meanwhile, I, like a dog eating grapefruit, disdained it. And I think we both got worse when we moved away.

I moved to Southampton, literally as far away as I could get whilst remaining in the UK. There I became both a lacklustre student and a disproportionately extravagant belittler of the dirty North. Also, within two years of my escape, I had entirely neutralised my accent, eradicating a large part of my childhood in the process. It felt good. Sunderland was dead to me.

My father meanwhile, moved South out of necessity, seeking work. Like Jesus before him, he worked as a carpenter. Also like Jesus, he turned over the occasional table in a rage, but that's where the similarities ended. Once in London, perhaps in fear of the creeping poncification of the South, my father ramped up the Sunderland to eleventy-stupid. He wanted the world to know how much he loved his home town, so he declared it with badges, with sportswear and tattoos. And of course, every time he opened his mouth… *Sunlun.* Like the beat of a drum, or an endless deluge of calloused fists…

Sunlun. Sunlun. Sunlun.

"Will you *please* put your fucking phone away? Jesus."

I'd already told him twice, quite emphatically, that he was *not allowed to photograph the sex workers.* Yet he persisted. Eventually a sex worker clocked him, clacked her rings on the glass and yanked the curtain across her window. I stopped walking and grabbed hold of his arm.

"I'm not joking. Put your phone away or I'm gone. That's it."

My dad laughed. He didn't laugh a lot, but when he did, it tended to be at someone's expense. Eventually he pocketed his phone and said: "Y'gunna hafta settle down man, son. Am serious. Y'gunna hava fuckin stroke man. Haway let's gan in hiyah."

Imagine if I kept that up the whole time — the phonetic transcription of his accent I mean; now be thankful I'm not going to. Even if you're not quite as regionally prejudiced as I am, it's clearly in no way conducive to a smooth read. So from now on, we'll just pretend he could speak properly.

So, fizzing with tension, I followed him into a pub on the Oudezijds Achterburgwal. It was one of the nasty ones against which I always advised my tourists. It catered predominantly for hens, stags, ignorant tourists, indifferent drunks and football fans who didn't care who was playing, so long as they were playing on a massive screen.

We were sat at the bar with a couple of pints of Heineken. My dad asked me again how I was.

"Good," I replied. "Great. Things are working out pretty well." I decided against sharing the wasp incident.

He asked me if I was seeing anyone.

I sighed and shook my head. "Not for ages. I'm actually beginning to think all that may be over."

He laughed, short and sharp. "Stupid little bugger." He knocked back more than half of his pint and wiped his chin. "Don't tell me you don't go with the whores."

"Sex workers. No, I don't."

"Why not? What's wrong with you? Or can you not afford it?"

I told him it was nothing to do with money. "I've just got this weird idea that if I get intimate with a woman, I want her to actually *like* me. I want her to *want* to be with me, and ideally not despise me or... pity me at best."

My dad's face contorted with utter dismay, like he'd just woken up in a Bollywood musical. "Sometimes — I'm not joking — I've got absolutely no idea who you are. What the fuck are you on about man?"

"What's not clear? I have to like a woman in order to...."

"It's got fuck all to do with *likin'* anybody man," he interrupted. "It's about fuckin' *fuckin'*. It's about gettin' in there and emptyin' your nads, man. Whores don't want to be *liked*. It's their fuckin' job to get that spunk out of your cock as quick as they can. That's it. That's what you're payin' for. It's not fuckin' brain science."

He drank the rest of his pint before ordering another. I watched him in silence, seething.

"That's *exactly* why I don't pay for sex," I said. "Because for me it's never just about *emptyin' me nads*."

My dad shook his head again. "Are you absolutely positive you're not a fuckin' puff like?" He laughed.

I considered sharing the fact that often when I went to bed with a woman, I didn't even manage to *empty me nads*. How would he respond, I wondered, to the news that I had to feel really comfortable with someone before I could climax? That I generally needed at least three or four attempts before the apparent anxiety of unfamiliarity went away? I suspected that once again, my father would feel compelled to impeach my heterosexuality.

He then told me he had every intention of availing himself of the services of a sex worker while he was here, so I told him how it worked, how much he would be expected to pay and what he'd get for that. Then we continued to drink and as best we could, to converse.

At around 8pm, after at least eight pints of lager, my dad took a blue pill from one of the pockets of his denim jacket and swallowed it with another half pint of lager. He gave me a wink. "Got to be fuckin' sure like." Then at around 8.30, on Oudekennissteeg, he stopped at a window and began cursing lustily in front of a tall, blonde sex worker. "Look at this one! She's the fuckin' spit of Pamela Anderson!" I nodded. She was also the antithesis of the kind of women to whom I was attracted, but that was irrelevant, so I didn't share it.

When she saw that she had a potential customer, the sex worker in question opened her door and began to negotiate. I stepped forward at that point, gestured to the pub at the end of the street and told my father I'd wait for him in there. I then walked in that direction and when I turned back to check on his progress, I saw my father stepping into the brothel, and the door closing behind him.

2.2

I changed my mind about the pub. Instead I stood on the bridge between the window in question and the Old Church behind me. I thought about what was likely happening inside. I thought about my father — my dad — and the young woman he was with, probably Eastern European, probably young enough to be his granddaughter. I imagined myself in my father's place. I knew I'd be asking her questions. I'd ask her name for sure, where she was from, how long she'd been in Amsterdam. I might even ask her if she'd ever made it out to see the tulip fields. I remembered my father's words: "Whores don't wanna be *liked*." There was no way *he'd* be asking her questions. And yeah, maybe she'd prefer it that way. Strictly business. Cock out and washed. Condom on. Suck it for a minute while looking in his eyes and moaning fake pleasure. Then if that doesn't work, in it goes with a handful of lube, more fake moaning and there it is. Nads emptied. Business done. Next!

I'd done a lot of research for my Red Light walking tours. I'd done just about everything in fact except visit a sex worker myself. I'd read books, blogs and articles. I'd gone on tours with sex workers, with former drug addicts, and with other less exotic guides. In one documentary I'd found online, a young Eastern European sex worker talks about the fact that many of the Johns are horrible to the women. They look into their eyes while they're fucking them and call them horrible names, abusing them, trying to shame them. I could imagine my father doing that and it turned my stomach.

What the hell was that all about?

I could only guess it was some Neanderthal attempt to try and claw back some semblance of power and control. They knew they were powerless, these men. That's why they were there. Women had something they craved, something they felt they needed, and that very fact refuted their dominance. So they tried to take back their power by overcompensating with vileness and aggression. *I have the power*, they were saying. *Do you hear me, you filthy slut? I HAVE THE POWER.*

I thought about my mum, and all the terrible shit she must have had to endure. No wonder she…. I took a deep breath and closed my eyes.

I was three when she died, so I never really knew her. But I'd heard stories. Mostly they came from my mum's younger sister, my Aunt Jo, who helped bring me up. Jo idolised my mum, so I never really trusted her rose-tinted recollections. For Jo, my mum was basically a Makem Maria Von Trapp. Part irrepressible tomboy, unable to keep her mouth shut, always getting into scrapes and standing up to bullies; part salt of the earth, heart of gold, do anything for anyone, common or garden saint. And I couldn't really get on board with her. So when I did think about my mum, which I did from time to time, I was under no illusions. I knew she wasn't real. I knew she was merely an amalgam of other people's wishful thinking and half-invented memories, no more real to me than Santa or Jesus. Which was how I liked it, because if she was any more real, I knew I'd never stop crying.

I was in my twenties when I found out, from my Aunt Jo, that my mum had been just about to leave my dad — once and for all — when she found out she was pregnant. Then of course, my dad begged her to stay, swore he'd turned over a new leaf. My mum knew it would be hard if she stayed, but maybe even harder if she left. So she stayed with a man who made her miserable, for the baby. For me.

If I'm honest, that was information I could have lived without.

Even before I knew *I* was the reason she stayed, however, I used to fantasise about an alternative universe in which my pregnant mum had walked out on my dad, without saying a word. In my fantasies, she moved somewhere far away, brought me up on her own and never, ever died.

The death and deification of my mum and the banal brutality of my dad was a large part of the reason I prefer women to men. I have been accused on more than one occasion and by more than one person of rather putting women on a pedestal. I don't deny it. I also put men *beneath* a pedestal. I disdain them. Not *all* of them of course, but certainly the kind I grew up with, and the kind I've always observed, all around me, making trouble and spoiling things.

Perched on the railing with my back to the Old Church, I glared at a random pack of the usual suspects staggering by — drunk, loud, obnoxious men. And just as my abhorrence began to properly take hold, then — thank God — came the shame.

All at once I saw the horrible arrogance within me swollen and all-consuming. Of course I was no better than any one of those men. And of course I could just as easily be drunk and loud and obnoxious, just as easily as they could be kind and warm and loving and good. My hatred of Sunderland too, was equally shameful. Of course the men of Sunderland were no better and no worse than the men of Istanbul or Timbuktu or Penge. Probably. I took a deep breath and told myself it was OK. I was only human.

I glanced back down Oudekennissteeg and saw my dad stepping out through the glass door and back onto the street, a look of unwavering pride on his face. He stood still for a moment, tucking his black tee-shirt into position over his belt buckle and adjusting his faded blue denim jacket. People walked around him. A couple of tourists sniggered, amused and maybe a little shocked or disgusted by the sight of an old man — or indeed any man — leaving a brothel. He then waved to the sex worker and set off up the alley.

It was at that moment that I experienced something wholly unfathomable. A wave of affection rose up in my chest and completely took my breath away. It made me want to run up to this freaky old shambles of a man, wrap my arms around his red neck and weep. I couldn't think of a single thing we had in common, outside of DNA, but he was my dad, and whether I liked it or not, that meant something. Something unfathomable, for sure. But something.

I watched him march into the pub, having not spotted me staring with this doubtless rather peculiar expression on my face. I jumped down from the railing and ran across the street to fetch him. When I suggested we retire for some food, he agreed.

As we made our way to the restaurant, I asked, "So how was it?"

"Aye," he began, "it was… ehhh. It was fuckin' alright that, like." He suddenly seemed quite shy, which was something I don't think I'd ever seen before. "Aye, that was quality."

"Do you like Thai food?"

He didn't know. I caught my breath. He was in his 70s and he'd never eaten Thai. The fact that I was warmed rather than irked by this revelation made me think that maybe there was hope for us yet.

So I took him to a nearby restaurant and watched him taking it all in, the typical Thai blend of twee opulence and comical kitsch. The elephants, the prayer hands, the fresh flowers, the ostentatious wall hangings in gold and red. Being a carpenter, he was especially interested in the fixtures and fittings, fashioned as they were from the darkest and most intricately carved wood. Then he clocked a photo of the Thai royal family. He pulled a face. "Who are those fuckin' idiots?"

I laughed and advised he watch his mouth where the royals were concerned. When I told him I'd been to Thailand a couple of times, he was shocked. He then asked me where else I'd been and I felt bad that he didn't already know.

Once our food arrived, he asked me if I still followed Sunderland football team. I told him I hadn't been interested in football since I left home, almost thirty years ago. He asked me if I remembered going with him to the matches when I was a kid. As it was one of the very few things we shared, I remembered it well.

We then took a quick mooch down memory lane. He reminded me that aside from Roker Park, there'd been more relatively normal times — kicking a ball in St George's Park, eating chips at Jackie White's Market, watching the motorbikes on Westgate Road in Newcastle of a Saturday afternoon. Of course, none of those things happened without a pub being involved at some point, but that's how it is with alcoholics.

I told my dad about my secret life as a teenage arsonist and petty thief, which he found amusing. I also told him about my years of seeing a therapist to finally try to come to terms with mum dying. Which was when he clammed up.

"I guess you don't want to talk about… *her*."

He shrugged. "There's nowt to say." His face twitched aggressively. "She died. I didn't."

Then a very effeminate Thai waiter came to collect our plates and my dad said something indelicate and far too loud about ladyboys. The moment had passed, the intimacy was gone, and once again, I felt ashamed, of my father, and by extension, of myself.

Ultimately, I had to accept that there simply wasn't very much to him. He was a simple, selfish, fairly small-minded man-child, and all I had to do was make sure I didn't follow in his footsteps.

Outside in the street after the food, he gurned at another blonde woman in a window and declared himself ready for a rematch. I sighed.

We said our goodbyes and I cycled slowly home, only slightly trepidatious about him coming on my tours the next day.

2.3

The next morning I awoke from a dream about the death-wish lady, only this time she was my mum. And rather than, "I want you to die", she said, "I wanted to die, Wesley. It's OK, son." I guess she was trying to comfort me. Or I was trying to comfort myself. Either way, it was appreciated. I considered telling my dad about it. I decided against it.

When I arrived at 1.15 and he wasn't there waiting, I wondered if he'd show. I hoped he would. Monica's replacement was already there, however, and it filled me with so much joy to observe that it was Lizzie Visser, that I let out a big cheer and gave her an enthusiastic hug.

Alongside Monica, Nix and Kras, Lizzie was the fourth Beachams guide I considered a close friend. She tended to work mornings, however, so I rarely saw her at the square. Hence my enthusiasm.

I told her how good it was to see her. "You know something, you are — hands down — the nicest person I know."

Lizzie laughed generously. "I am pretty great, I'll give you that."

"You are such a creepy little weasel," said Henk. "That's such a weaselly thing to say."

"Weaselly Bell!" Lizzie laughed.

I smiled. I once broke a boy's jaw for calling me that. In a different lifetime of course. I scanned the square for my dad — always quietly proud of my childhood violence — but he was still nowhere to be seen. Instead, happily, my gaze returned to Lizzie.

Lizzie was tall with a soft round helmet of shiny brown hair, large green eyes and a near-constant beaming smile. She was like the opposite of those cartoon characters plagued by their own rain cloud. Lizzie seemed drenched in her own permanent sunny spell. She was sweetness and light personified, but somehow never annoying with it. She sang a lot too, almost constantly, like her brain was set to music. Sometimes she'd even converse in song. She did so now, to a jaunty improvised melody.

"Would you like a coffee, Wesley Bell, Wesley Bell?"

She held up the thermos she seemed always to have about her person. When I accepted, she poured me out a cardboard cupful.

"Would you like some cream in your coffee, Wesley Bell?"

Lizzie often joked that her half-Scottish, half-Dutch heritage genetically predisposed her towards tightfistedness, but she confounded the stereotypes and was never less than remarkably generous. Not only did she always turn up to help out a full fifteen minutes before kick-off, but also, she invariably had treats for all in her backpack.

"Would you like a cookie with your coffee, Wesley Bell?"

She was also the only guide I knew for whom tour guiding wasn't merely a stopgap. She wasn't just killing time before making it big as an actress or a singer or a stand-up. Tour guiding was like, her calling. I loved her for that too.

In fact, I think it's safe to say that I loved absolutely everything about Lizzie, apart from her English boyfriend, Doug. And the only reason I didn't care for Doug — as was almost invariably the case with people for whom I didn't care — was that he seemed not to care for me. In fact, I rarely saw him, but whenever I did, his antipathy towards me was always made, to my mind, abundantly clear. I assumed he was just one of those people who find me rather grating, so I never questioned his antipathy. Consequently, I wouldn't discover the real reason behind it for quite some time. All I knew for now was that Lizzie and Doug had just moved in together, taking on a monster mortgage and apparently willingly plumping for proper adulthood — impending marriage, kids and all.

When I asked Lizzie how the move had gone, by way of reply, she burst into song.

"High on a hill was a lonely goatherd! Layee odelayee odelay hee hoo!"

There then followed, in the shadow of the National Monument, an instantaneous outbreak of localised joy.

"Please stop," I said.

"Never stop!" beamed Henk.

"Loud was the voice of the lonely goatherd."

This time Henk and a surprisingly large number of the nearby tourists joined in with the yodelling. "Layee odelayee odeloo."

And they were off. In my memory now, I see Lizzie dancing around the monument with a fat conga-cum-chorus line of tourists in her wake, all yodelling in unison, some of them high-kicking. I'm sure it wasn't *precisely* like that but it was quite a moment. So much so that a few minutes later, when we split the tourists into two groups, I could not fail to discern some conspicuous disappointment within my flock. I addressed the elephant on the square. "I'm afraid I have to confirm," I laughed, "that you are indeed stuck with me. I know you'd rather go on a tour with the wonderful lady with the beautiful voice. Believe me, you are not alone. I'd give anything to go on Lizzie's tour, but if we all go with her, then I don't get paid. Which is not to say that I'm in it for the money, because I'm not, ladies and gentlemen. I'm in it for the love! For the love, I say. What am I in it for?"

As I spoke the question, I raised my hands like a cheap warm-up man, ushering forth enthusiasm. Three of my 24-strong congregation responded. "The love!" they cried.

I smiled. "And don't you forget it."

At which point, my dad showed up and attached himself to the back of the group. I was glad to see him.

Minutes into the tour, I got a text from Lizzie. It said: "You got time for a drink after?" When I texted back that I could do tomorrow, she responded: "Better still! I'm so fucking depressed!"

2.4

My dad was quiet on my tours today. He'd been drinking, of course, but it was barely noticeable. After the Red Light, we returned to the main drag for our last few hours together and he said, "Aye, you're canny funny like." Whilst not the most glowing or fulsome review I'd ever received, this was still very possibly the nicest thing he'd ever said to me. I thanked him.

By 9pm, however, our conversation had almost entirely petered out and I could feel myself becoming tetchy again. Thankfully, my father had become transfixed by a football match showing on a giant screen, and had fallen into conversation with another British guy at the bar. As this seemed like the perfect opportunity, I told him I had to nip out for some food. By the time I returned just before 11, he'd made a few more friends.

"This is Davo," he began. There was also a Kev, a Davey, a Spuggie and a Daz, all from Sunderland or thereabouts. They'd turned up just after I left, my dad had spotted their accents and together, like birds of a dialectical feather, they had flocked.

After we'd shaken hands, a couple of them expressed surprise that I was my father's son, mostly on account of my lack of regional accent. "Aye, I've totally betrayed me roots like," I squawked, momentarily affecting the Makem tongue. Nobody laughed. I even caught my dad looking slightly embarrassed on my behalf, which was an interesting experience. It had never occurred to me that my shame for him might be reciprocated. I wasn't sure how that made me feel. All I felt in that moment was that I had a choice: I could either try my hardest to blend in; or I could revel in my opposition. In reality I knew: there was no choice.

Having heard that I gave tours of the Red Light District, one of my father's new associates wondered — with a devilishly impudent smirk — whether one of the perks of my position might be *gratis fellatio*. He even did a brief mime of the act in question, causing his cohorts much delight. Indeed, his salacious inquiry did fair set the table on a far from modest roar, and it was with some considerable woe that I had to inform him that no, no I was not the grateful recipient of "loads of free blowies like".

"He doesn't even fuckin' pay for them man!" my father pointed out, his voice strained with incredulity.

Father's companions, equally dumbfounded by this disclosure, were aghast.

"Fuck *off*," barked Davo, clearly speaking for the group.

"Fuckin' hell, man," interposed Kev or Daz or, perchance, Spuggie. "If I lived here, I'd be fuckin' a new one every fuckin' night man."

Davo concurred enthusiastically.

Indeed, unless I was sorely mistaken, there seemed to be a tacit implication that my reluctance to engage in intimate acts with sex workers somehow bespoke a lack of masculinity on my part. Consequently, very much despite myself, I could feel rising within me a desire to defend myself to these barbarians. Before I could frame my response, however, a cheer rang out across the bar.

A goal had been scored onscreen and within seconds, to the accompaniment of heavy boots stomping on wooden floors, a chant had been taken up. Only seven or eight voices combined — my father's amongst them — but oh, what sweet music they made!

It was a sporting incantation I had heard many times on the streets of Sunderland and the terraces of Roker Park on my occasionally harrowing journey towards adulthood. The melody was from *You Are My Sunshine*, a song that first appeared in Louisiana in the late 1930s, but this particular libretto, repeated *ad nauseam*, was presumably the invention of the Roker Park hive mind:

"We are the Sunlun — the Sunlun Bootboys.
Oh we are mental. And we are mad.
We are the loyalest football supporters
That the world has ever had…"

Tempted though I was to quibble over "loyalest" versus "most loyal", I decided instead to take my leave. My father seemed slightly disappointed, which made me feel guilty. But not guilty enough to stay.

"Are you not coming to the strip club?"

They were planning a trip to the Theatre Casa Rosso, the oldest, largest and most expensive sex club in Amsterdam. I had been there once as part of my tour research at the beginning of the previous summer, and without wishing to appear haughty, I'd decided pretty much immediately, that once was enough.

I told my dad I had to be up really early for a private tour. This was untrue. I actually had the day off. Although I didn't enjoy lying to make my desertion more palatable, it felt like a necessary evil.

So we said our farewells with a brief handshake and the most cursory of man-hugs, then I made my way through the packed Saturday night bar, feeling immediately relieved. At the doorway, I glanced back into the bar to see my dad with one hand in the air, lost in a rousing rendition of *We Love You Sunlun, We Do*. I smiled, shook my head and went home.

My dad was flying back first thing the next morning, so we wouldn't see each other again before he left. He was 75 years old too, so realistically, considering how close we were, there was a good chance we'd never see each other again. And although I knew I wouldn't exactly miss him when he died, and might even feel a soupçon of relief, I also knew — mostly because of moments like this — I'd feel profoundly guilty.

2.5

It's always the people you least suspect. Well, not always. Sometimes the person has a face tattoo or bloody knuckles, and your instincts are bang on. In Lizzie's case, however, I was shocked to hear her using the D-word.

As we settled at a corner table in In't Aepjen, the old wooden pub with the monkey legends and the funky museum vibe, I told her, "I didn't think you got depressed."

"Of course I get depressed." Her forehead creased. "Thank God, eh? Imagine if I spent my whole life yodelling. I'd be fucking unbearable."

Turns out Lizzie had had a miscarriage. Much worse than losing the baby, however, was the fact that on some level, she was actually slightly relieved it had happened, and she was having trouble reconciling that.

"I just don't think I'm ready," she said. "But it's time, right? I'm 36 this year. It's already long past time if you listen to my mum, but I'm just not feeling it. You've not got kids, have you?"

I shook my head. "I'm not ready. Plus, I am very selfish and destined to die alone."

"Jesus. Sorry I asked." She sipped at her beer. "Speaking of dying, have you killed any more tourists lately?"

I laughed.

"Nah, not yet. He really did have it coming though, I swear." I told her what he was like, the late Mr Sutcliffe. I used the word "sociopath", as I so often do.

Lizzie laughed.

"What?"

"You know."

In the year we'd known one another, Lizzie and I had had variations on this conversation maybe half a dozen times. And we always disagreed.

Lizzie hadn't always been a tour guide. She'd trained as a doctor and had spent most of her twenties working in oncology. So she knew a lot about death, and about the darkness that lurks — potentially — in all of us. What's more, she considered said darkness a necessary evil. "No darkness," she would say, palms up like perfectly balanced scales, "no light." When I likened sociopathy to cancer and argued that it was equally important to cut out both, she pooh-poohed me. When I argued that it was our duty, if we could, to try and lead those who dwelt primarily in darkness towards the light, she called me arrogant.

"But don't you believe," I said, "that we should try and help people become less toxic members of society?"

"No, I think we *need* toxic members of society. No toxicity, no non-toxicity. We need to embrace it."

"Hold on a minute." I pointed a finger at her. "What do you think about empathy?"

"Big fan." She gave me a thumbs-up.

"So you agree we should try to empathise with each other, even…"

"It's what it is to be human," she interrupted. "Without empathy, we're nothing — we're not human."

"Great! So you agree that it's our duty to empathise with even the darkest of humans in their darkest of hours. Like Hector Black. You remember Hector Black?"

"How could I forget?"

Hector Black was the man whose adopted daughter was raped and murdered by a man called Ivan Simpson. When Ivan was in prison, serving a life sentence without parole, Hector wrote to him.

He wanted to understand why Ivan had done what he'd done, so rather than give in to instinctive hatred and vengeance, Hector chose instead to extend compassion and empathy. Ultimately, because of Hector's overwhelming, impregnable sense of empathy, he and Ivan became pen-pals, and eventually, against all odds, friends. It's the most profound real-life example of empathy and forgiveness of which I am aware.

Though Lizzie agreed that empathising with people who have wronged us was admirable and something towards which we should all strive, she had zero interest in actually changing those people's behaviour.

I told her I could not agree less. "Connecting to people who feel no empathy — people who harm other people because they feel no connection to them — and leading them to a point where they do feel a connection to other humans, and therefore no longer desire to harm anyone... that's the meaning of life, in my opinion. It's why we exist."

Lizzie smiled her sweetest smile. "You see, to me that just seems incredibly patronising. We need people without empathy. They are part of life. If everyone was totally empathetic and looking out for each other's interests all the time, can you imagine how boring that would be?"

"What are you *talking* about?" I shrieked. "It would be amazing! We'd just spend all our time laughing and loving and rubbing oil into each other's buttocks. How could that be anything other than fantastic?"

"It would get boring pretty quickly," Lizzie insisted. "We need conflict. We need drama and darkness and we need for things to go wrong. All stories, all books and films, all human drama, Wesley — all of it has conflict at the heart of it."

I was gobsmacked. "But that's because books and films reflect the real world! And the real world is fucked up by sociopaths doing horrible shit. What I'm talking about is a world *without* these people, either because they've been cured by sitting down and talking to trained professionals, or, as a last resort, because they've been executed. Doesn't really matter. What I'm talking about is a world *without* sociopaths and all the other malevolent egomaniacs. A world where nobody is looking to hurt anybody or fuck anybody over. A world where everybody just sits around kissing, playing Scrabble and eating plant-based trifle all day long."

Lizzie continued to shake her head and smile as if what I was saying were not only impossible, but also undesirable. I couldn't believe she was turning her nose up at Utopia. She just kept saying things like, "Life without suffering is life at a standstill," and, "How can I develop if I don't suffer?" Then she said, "Leonard Cohen said: 'There is a crack in everything. That's how the light gets in.'"

That was a quote I happened to love and I didn't much care to have it thrown back in my face like that.

I was exasperated. "What if your kid was being raped?" I flinched from my own example, but it had to be done.

"I don't have a kid," said Lizzie pointedly. "As you know."

"I know, I know, I'm sorry." Fleeting prayer hands accompanied an empathetic bow. "But you will one day though, right? Fingers crossed, if no more of your beloved dark shit happens to you. So imagine that day has come, you've got your kid and you go into their room in the middle of the night, just to check on them, and there's a man in there and he's doing something hideous to your... baby girl or baby boy or baby non-binary being." I pushed my right fist slowly into my left fist. Lizzie recoiled. "No, no, come on, Lizzie. Embrace the jarring darkness. So — what do

92

you do? Do you just let the abuse continue because that's how life is and without abuse, there is no love? Or, do you try and stop that person hurting someone you love?"

"Of course I stop him and protect my child," she said. "And of course I do try and stop people hurting people when I see it happening in my life. On a personal level, I do what I can to stop bad things happening to people…"

"Then how can you not extend that to the rest of the world? Surely you want to stop all bad things happening to all people?"

"Meh. Not so much."

I shook my head, giving up. "You're insane."

Lizzie laughed and started singing. "There is a crack," she crooned, "a crack, in everything." Beat. "That's how the light gets in."

We went around in circles for a while longer, then we stopped and went home, Lizzie to her oven-ready boyfriend; me to a bout of suffocating futility and self-disgust. I spoke of wanting to make the world a better place but I was doing nothing to make that happen. And I was nearly 50, for God's sake. I had to accept — admittedly in the face of a great deal of resistance — that my window for world-improvement had almost certainly passed.

Then Monica came home and a couple of days later, in another pub just a little further up the street, two weeping women broke both of our hearts.

2.6

I know it diminishes my feminist credentials and makes me seem like I'm not a serious person at all, so I really hate to mention it, but when I saw Monica in Café 't Mandje, when she looked up from her phone and into my eyes, I was — once again — almost literally bowled over by how outrageously, supernaturally attractive she is. As a feminist, it diminishes me, yes, but as a reporter, I feels it's my duty to try to do her beauty justice. So, for just a moment, indulge me.

Monica's beauty is a force of nature, like a waterfall or a meteor shower. It's impossible when you glimpse her not to gasp and gawp like a slack-jawed simpleton. It's like if you saw a cheetah take down a giraffe in your local high street, you'd be entranced and captivated. You wouldn't be able to stop thinking about, or talking about what you'd seen. Well, Monica's beauty is that cheetah. And every time I see her afresh, I am that doomed giraffe, bleeding out in a Lidl carpark.

I ordered a drink and sat down beside her. She kissed me hello and spoke quietly: "See the two women at the table opposite." I saw. One in her mid-20s, the other in her 50s, chatting and laughing over a bottle of champagne. They were clearly mother and daughter. They shared the same mischievous smile, the same high cheekbones and crinkly, twinkly eyes. "The mother is dying," said Monica.

As she spoke these words, the mother laughed uproariously, rounding out a melodious peal with a wicked short squeal and a hard slap across her daughter's upper arm. Then she dabbed her eyes with a tissue and took another swig of bubbly.

"They've been laughing and crying," Monica continued. "Then the girl said, 'I don't want you to die.' It's the most tender thing I ever saw." Monica sipped at her beer and wiped a tear from her cheek. My heart did a little flip.

When I glanced back across, the mum was stroking her daughter's hair and wiping tears from her cheeks. I wondered if my dad had ever stroked my hair or dried my tears. I doubted it.

Don't Leave Me This Way by The Communards provided unnecessarily pointed background.

"That's so sad," I said.

"It's horrendous," said Monica.

"You're very tanned," I said.

"It's still summer in Palermo."

As we hadn't really seen one another in August, she asked me about Waspgate and when I got to the happy ending and showed her Isabelle's Facebook profile, she exclaimed, with far, far, *far* too much surprise, "Ma è propria bella!"

"What did you expect, a fucking warthog?"

"Fucking what?"

"Un cinghiale."

She laughed. "No, ma…." She clicked through to more photos. "She's really pretty. You won the lottery, ah?"

I shrugged. "I won the lottery for one night. And I'm exceedingly grateful, don't get me wrong, but ideally, I'd like more than one night."

"Well, you have to make a fort."

It took me a moment to decipher her Itanglish. "You mean I have to make *effort. An* effort. Yeah, awesome, thanks."

"But it's true! You can't expect a woman to fall out of the sky. *Cazzo.*"

While I had Facebook open, I decided to show Monica Matty Sutcliffe. Her face twisted. "He is not so pretty. He looks like what you said, ah? Like an egg."

"A bad egg."

"Certo. I have to pee."

Once she'd left, I glanced back across the room as another bottle of champagne was requested, supplied, opened and two fresh glasses poured. I thought about my mum. I tried to imagine how she might have been if she'd lived; how I might have been if she'd lived. I ordered another beer.

By the time Monica returned, there was a Village People song playing and I was thinking again about Matty Sutcliffe. I imagined him here, in this bar when it was busy, surrounded predominantly by overtly gay or gender fluid humans. In my imagination, he suddenly let go, threw his arms in the air and started dancing in amongst the throng. I sighed, feeling bad for the fun-loving Matty in my mind.

"What's up?"

I laughed because Monica had caught me, mid-doubt. I told her what I'd been thinking, that maybe Matty wasn't such a hideous person after all. "I mean, maybe there was good inside him, you know?"

"So what?" she snapped. "You didn't kill him. It was an accident."

"Yeah, I know, but I was convincing myself I was glad he was dead because he was so awful. But that feels wrong, you know? I mean, maybe he was learning. Maybe he was on the road to becoming a good person."

Monica's face made it clear she didn't buy it.

"Can you keep a secret?"

"Sure," I replied. "Why not."

She looked around the bar. There were only half a dozen other people spread about the place. "I'm serious, ah? You can't tell to no one."

I crossed my heart.

"I did it one time too," she said. "In Istanbul. Ten years ago."

"You did what one time too?"

Again, she cast a furtive glance around the bar. Then she leant in close and I breathed her in as one might breathe in a herb garden in a convent, which is to say, respectfully, reverently… quiet as a mouse.

"I killed a man," she said.

2.7

Adnan met Monica in 2010, on the set of a Turkish Vogue shoot in Istanbul. He shot fashion for high-end glossies and Monica fell so hard that she walked out on a lucrative modelling contract, and moved into his apartment. "I was 18," she stressed. "I was a child. But I loved him."

They had eight months. Which is not to be sneezed at.

Adnan's step-mum from a previous marriage was Patricia, an expat Berliner who'd been in Istanbul for 25 years. Very blonde and very beautiful, Patricia got a lot of unwelcome attention from certain Turkish men — *maganda*, she called them. The maganda would touch or grope her in the street or on the bus, and she got angry and would shout and scream and swear. Sometimes she'd even lash out herself but the molesters would never own up to what they'd done. They'd call her crazy, or a liar, and walk away laughing. So when Patricia found out that some women in Izmir had taken to defending themselves against molestation by using hijab pins, she thought... *ja*.

"She told me she stabbed maybe fifty men in total," Monica said. "This was before, in the 80s and 90s. Imagine. It will be even worse then. But even in 2010, it happened maybe six times that I had a bad experience with men grabbing. It pissed me off."

So she took a couple of simple silver pins, three inches long, from Patricia, and she practised pulling them from the cuffs of her long winter coat in the mirror. "Aim for the butt," Patricia had told her. "Don't go too deep." Patricia knew one woman who'd actually gone to prison for sticking a man who grabbed hold of her breasts in a train station in Izmir. Monica pulled another pin on her reflection, stabbing it towards herself and hissing like a cat. She hoped she wouldn't need it, but if they continued to push her… then she was going to push back.

Her eyes started to tear up. "You don't say nothing to no one, ah?"

"Omertà." I promised.

She flared her nostrils, then told me how it happened.

It was her final night in the city and she'd been walking back to Adnan's apartment in Karaköy. She'd spent the early evening with friends and would spend the last part of it with Adnan. She was sad that they'd split, but really happy they'd managed to remain on friendly terms. The next day she'd make her way back to Italy and find out what was left of her career.

Within five minutes of Adnan's apartment, she turned onto a steep narrow street with expensive cars down one side. The buildings were a mishmash: shops, apartments, offices, garages. Monica noticed a man up ahead closing the boot of an expensive car in the dark. She entertained the idea that he might want to do her harm, as they so often did, but dismissed it. Examining her reasons for the dismissal, she realised she considered him less dangerous than she otherwise might, solely on account of his conspicuous wealth. She felt bad. With her head down and her heavy winter coat wrapped tight around her, she walked briskly, her brow furrowed. She was still examining her implicit biases when the man with the expensive car wrapped his hands around her face and mouth from behind, dragged her a short way along the street, up three crumbling stone steps and in through the large open doorway of a residential building.

2.8

"He kept his hand over my mouth," she said. "I could hardly breathe. It was the most terrifying thing that ever happened."

He slammed the door shut and pushed Monica face-first against the hard hallway wall. With one arm pinning her in place, his other hand found its way between her legs, up under her skirt. Then, suddenly, he was crying out in pain and springing back across the floor, with a pin sticking in his right thigh. Freed from his grasp, Monica made for the door and just managed to open it a crack before he was back again, kicking it shut while landing a vicious punch to Monica's kidneys.

Bent double on the hallway floor, choking, coughing and crying out in pain, Monica managed to retrieve the second pin from her right cuff, and when her assailant pushed her back against the wall and resumed his assault, she let him have it.

Still conscious of not wanting to cause lasting damage, she pricked him three times in quick succession, in his belly and chest. Once more he sprang back, this time hitting the wall behind him and landing in a heap on the floor. Monica bolted. Through the front door and away.

Once inside Adnan's apartment, she set about washing her hands. Adnan was on a call in his bedroom. She thought about interrupting him, and wondered how he'd react. Would he want to go to the scene of the crime? Would he beat the shit out of the guy? What if he went to the police? Would Monica go to jail like the woman in Izmir? She was stressed. And she resented it.

Adnan finished his call and when she told him what had happened, he grabbed hold of Monica and hugged her. When she led him back to the doorway, the car was gone, the door was closed and the hallway behind it was steeped in darkness. When she checked for spots of blood, there were none. Adnan suggested calling the police but they both knew no good would come of it.

So Monica pretended nothing had happened and went back to Rome the next day as planned.

Two weeks later she received an email from Adnan with a link to an English Turkish news site. The story told of a man, a professional footballer, whose heart had been punctured by a woman with a pin in an unprovoked attack near the Galata Tower. The man made it home to his wife before collapsing and being rushed to hospital, where he remained in a coma for a week, and then died. Police were keen to speak to witnesses and were treating the incident as a murder enquiry. Monica focused on two words only: *unprovoked attack*.

"I recognised him at once," she said. "He was a very big football player." She brushed the palms of her hands together twice, brusquely. "That's that. I killed him. I didn't mean but… the result is the same."

I watched her for a second. Her face was hard.

"So how did it make you feel?"

She shrugged. "He attacked me. I attacked back. I'm not here to fuck spiders."

The equivalent of "I'm not messing about" or "I mean business", "I'm not here to fuck spiders" was one of Monica's favourite expressions. She'd picked it up from an Australian ex.

"Plus he had also a wife and new baby. Which type of fucking pig does that? I'm not sorry I defended myself. I don't want to be raped."

My whole body was tensed with anguish for Monica. I felt sick at the thought of someone hurting her and of course she was right: her assailant was absolutely responsible for his own death, and any man attempting to rape any woman absolutely deserves to have all of his internal organs punctured in return.

Across the room, the daughter was now kneeling on the floor with her head in her mum's lap. Her mum was stroking her hair and singing softly.

"You never feel guilty then?"

Monica's lips puckered in distasteful contemplation. "Honestly, no. Everything I ever felt was anger. He had every intention to rape me, Wesley. He was schifoso. I'm glad actually that he's dead." As I gasped at her audacity, she radiated defiance and doubled down. "I'm glad I killed him."

"Really? You're actively glad?"

"Why not? If somebody can't arrive to the end of the day without trying to rape another person, then I don't think they deserve to be alive."

"Wow."

"No, not *wow*, Wesley," Monica countered. "You have to understand, I love my life and I love my family and my friends and I don't waste my time on... *shit* people, hai capito?"

"But we're all shit once in a while, right?"

Monica shook her head and looked exasperated. "Like *this?*" she cried. "Have you attacked somebody? Have you raped somebody?"

"Of course not!" I hissed, glancing guiltily around the bar. "Well, not... the second one. Not the R-word." I twitched. "But you know I used to fight a lot. I do have a bit of a violent past."

Monica narrowed her eyes at me, maybe wondering just how much of a dick I used to be.

I had sworn to Monica once that I only ever fought bigots and idiots and violent people. I told her I was like Bryson, who only ever punched racists. But it wasn't quite true. Then one drunken

102

night of shame purging, I admitted that I used to fight at football matches in my teens. Monica was genuinely shocked by that. That was maybe a confession too far.

"Don't look at me like that," I whimpered. "I used to have a short temper, I admit it. But I've changed, Monica. People do change."

"OK, OK, calmati. I'm just saying that not everybody deserves… to even be alive. Ecco. You don't agree?"

I blew out my cheeks. "I honestly don't know anymore, Monica. I used to believe in infinite potential, for everyone…"

"You are too idealistic," she cut me off. "If we were only maybe ten thousand people, I would agree. But we are nearly eight billion, Wesley. So." She gave a little shrug. "There is literally no space for forgiving everybody. Sorry." She finished her beer with a flourish. "Not sorry. Let's have one more."

We had one more and were just about done with that when the women opposite finished their champagne and started readying to leave. Immediately Monica jumped up and approached them. She spoke to them in Dutch quickly and quietly. The younger woman shook her head. Monica spoke some more and then the old lady hugged her. Monica hugged her back and they held on to one another for the longest time. Then the young woman hugged Monica too, they all spoke together some more and the mother and daughter left.

Back at our table, I asked her what she'd said.

"I just told that I heard what they were saying and that I was very moved by their relation. I wished the best possible experience for them both and asked if I could pay for their champagne, as a gift to them. I said it would be an honour for me to do that. The mother agreed to let me pay."

"Wow." I was impressed.

"Wow what?"

"That's… I dunno. That's… that's really lovely."

Monica shrugged. "I told you. I'm not here to fuck spiders."

2.9

As I compile this confession, I am frequently assailed by the urge to censor myself. Certain episodes, like the one I'm about to relate, feel like a shoo-in, psych evaluation-wise... but at the same time they cannot fail to paint me in a distinctly unflattering light. I could easily pretend they never happened, of course. No one would know. But I'd know. And that would sour the whole deal. Corny as it may seem, the truth is important to me, because it's beautiful, cracks and all. Plus, I'm genetically predisposed to bare all. So with that in mind, I must confess to an act of moral terrorism.

But first, an excuse.

Above all else, the two main things that always upset me about 30-year-old Californian guide Madison Clay — and they're clearly connected — were her self-righteousness and her superciliousness. No one was ever *right* like Madison Clay.

If Madison disagreed with someone, which she very frequently did, her disapproval would first manifest itself in the tiniest modifications of certain facial features — top lip, left eyebrow, angle of neck. She'd then become sarcastic and mildly pugnacious, making it clear that the person to whom she was talking was her intellectual and moral inferior, or simply didn't care about whatever was being discussed as passionately as she did.

Madison was a hardcore intersectional feminist eco-warrior who despised animal cruelty, sex trafficking, homophobia, racism and the excesses of capitalism in equal measure. I agreed with her entirely. I just didn't yammer on about it *ad*-fucking-*nauseam*, or cover myself in badges to prove it.

I kept out of Madison's way.

At the September guide meeting in the empty ballroom of the HoHoHostel, Nix and Madison had a minor disagreement over the marketing fee increase.

Every Beachams guide pays Beachams for every tourist we take on a free walking tour. Beachams call it a marketing fee and that's how they make their money. Most guides are OK with it, or else they leave and set up their own company. Happens all the time. Unless you organise it all yourself, you pay for your tourists. Obviously. Well, Madison Clay didn't like it.

The latest increase was a large one — another twenty cents per tourist — but also the first in almost two years. Most guides accepted it with a passing grumble. Madison, however, seemed particularly upset. When her grievances were ridiculed by a couple of fellow guides, Madison grew prickly. When she began to repeat herself, Nix calmly interjected: "If you don't like it, why not set up on your own? Then you won't have to pay any marketing fee at all. It's pretty simple."

Intakes of breath ricocheted around the two rectangular tables at which 13 guides and two members of the management team were gathered.

"Well, that was extremely aggressive," said Madison, her bottom lip pursed self-righteously.

Nix laughed. "It honestly wasn't, Madison. You're just really fucking cheap. Try not being so cheap and everything will be fine."

Madison's entire face puckered. Like a dog growling in a library, she said, "You have no right to talk to me like that. If you use offensive language again, I'll have no choice but to make an official complaint."

Nix laughed a fine free laugh. "Really? You'll have no choice?"

"It is bullying and it is completely unacceptable in the workplace." Both lips had now entirely disappeared.

106

Nix held out his hands in a placatory manner. "I'm so sorry. I really never meant to bully you. I just don't agree with you. I think the raise in the marketing fee is reasonable. Is there anybody else here who feels that twenty cents is too much?"

"I would prefer fifteen," said Lizzie, "but you know… fuck it."

"To be honest," said second-in-command Elvira, "it's not up for debate. That's the increase. It's come down from Garry Beacham himself, so, take it or leave it. Sorry to be so blunt, but that's how it is."

"You see, that feels more like bullying to me," said Nix.

"That's it." Madison pushed back her chair. "I can't stay in a room with so much toxic masculinity." And with that, she bolted, and was gone.

"That ain't me," said Nix. "I'm toxic. And I'm masculine. But never at the same time."

"Shall we move on?"

Elvira took control and for most of the rest of the meeting, we discussed the Beachams strategy for the coming year. As far as anyone could see — even in our perfect ignorance of the fermenting pandemic — 2020 was going to be a make-or-break year for Amsterdam tour companies. New legislation was going to choke them hard, maybe to death. So Beachams were expanding their offering, replacing the doomed Red Lights with food tours, pub tours, coffeeshop tours, alternative lifestyle tours, Second World War tours and of course, canal tours — a tour for every tourist's taste! I was loath to learn anything new, frankly, on account of instinctive laziness and issues surrounding a fundamental fear of failure, but needs must — or would, soon enough — so I signed up to learn the canal cruise.

All of which — the identification of Madison as a neurotic, self-aggrandising creature of very little charm — that's my excuse for what follows. And yes, I'm already perfectly well aware that, as excuses for bad behaviour go, it's down there with skin colour and genitals.

2.10

Madison Clay had a morbid fear of pigeons. Or so she claimed. It's true that whenever pigeons were massing on the square, she would freak out and cower behind another guide, but I for one called bullshit.

So…

It was a surprisingly cold afternoon in late September, miserable and drizzly, winter coats on. I was guide number two for the 1.30 but it was eerily quiet and highly unlikely that two tours would run. Madison, guide number one, was another of those selfish pig guides who never turned up early to help. It irked me. And because it irked me, and because I happened to be thinking about it when I spied the Grim Reaper chatting to one of the Seed Guys in front of the Royal Palace, I had a terrible idea.

The Grim Reapers were street performers, of a sort, who dressed up as Death, with robes, skull-masks and scythes. They would then loiter by the Palace, especially when the sun deigned to shine, and tourists would sidle up and be photographed alongside them for a bob or two. I once saw a couple of proud parents meticulously posing their twin daughters between two towering Reapers like it was a proper photoshoot, scythes positioned overhead like a bloodless rainbow. I loved the Grim Reapers. As well as a kooky, morbid souvenir, I saw them as striking a blow against the tyranny of Death. For when we point and laugh and tweak the beard of Death, do we not remove some of its sting? Do we not, in a sense, become immortal? OK, OK, too far. But by laughing into the void, I'm sure we at least begin to come to terms with our own mortality. And enough people seem to agree with me to warrant at least one lone Reaper on the square on all but the most inhospitable of days.

The Seed Guys, meanwhile, sold seed, and sometimes rice, for tourists to toss to pigeons. Sometimes Seed Guys would seed the heads and shoulders of tourists, and their shrieking friends would commemorate the subsequent mayhem for Instagram, or what-have-you.

I glanced up at the Palace clock. Sixteen minutes past one. I peered across the street to the monument, checking to see if Madison had — against all odds — turned up early to help. Of course, she had not.

So I gave her four more minutes, during which time, had she appeared, I would have done nothing. Then, when she didn't appear, I approached the Seed Guy. "You see that purple umbrella across the street?" I gave him ten euros and a rough idea of what I wanted him to do in exchange, then I waltzed across the street and joined MPM Elise by the monument.

Elise was a perfect example of Dutch womanhood. Every time I saw her, I found myself empathising with the Nazis' eagerness to embrace the Dutch as honorary Aryans. They were so gleaming, beaming and healthy. We kissed hello and I took the umbrella, apologising for my relative tardiness.

"No Madison yet?" I asked, archly.

Elise took the bait. "Well, you don't get paid for helping out."

Yes! We were bitching!

As we bitched on, I observed the Seed Guy ambling casually across the street and around the back of the monument. He stopped a few metres behind us, and began to sow.

By the time Madison arrived — at 1.26pm — the back of the National Monument was awash with hundreds of hungry pigeons. The Seed Guy had succeeded admirably. He'd seduced a group of four Japanese students, each of whom screeched and squawked like banshees as the dirty birds fluttered, pecked and scratched all

110

around them. He then popped a cheeky handful into one of their hoods, which instantly became a screaming chaotic flurry of hood-fur and pigeon-feather.

Madison's horror blanched and lengthened her face like pizza dough. Anxiety rippled across her cheeks, keeping time with the shrill squeals of hysterical adolescents and the vicious heckling of errant gulls.

"Why are they here?" Her voice was a tremulous whisper.

Instinctively she'd taken hold of my arm, gripping tightly like a little girl in a hurricane. Tears formed on her eyelids and threatened to spill over her cheeks like tiny barrels of grief. My heart, meanwhile, fell apart like an overcooked lamb. What the fuck had I done?

"Please get rid of them," she hissed.

Knowing it would have little if any positive effect, I freed myself from Madison's terror-grip and stepped towards the feathered melee, opening and closing the Beachams umbrella like Sean Connery in that film, whilst simultaneously shouting like a drunk.

The pigeons took off in all directions, cooing and colliding in mid-air, potentially creating in the process even more chaos than that which had gone before. Worse still, I'd mentioned to the Seed Guy that if I happened to make the pigeons disperse, and even if I happened to appear to try and get him to stop — as I did now — he should double down, scattering twice as much seed, so that hopefully twice as many pigeons would return. This he did. And this they did.

As the pigeons circled the monument and came back in for a second course, Madison began to properly lose it. Jumping in front of Elise to shield herself, she inadvertently trod on the foot of an old lady tourist, who cried out in pain. I apologised to her before chastising Madison. "*Don't* step on our tourists!"

At which point, Madison, now in tears, declared "I can't stay here!" and fled.

Elise was shocked. "She can't do that."

"She did do that," countered the old lady.

I gave her a look. "She really doesn't like pigeons."

Elise couldn't get over it. "But she can't do that."

"It's OK," I told her. "I can take these guys."

Elise was grateful. I was ashamed.

I heard later that Madison had received a verbal warning for her behaviour. Elvira had informed her that running out on a tour without assuring adequate cover, no matter what the reason, was unacceptable.

Meanwhile, I was baffled by my behaviour, and repulsed by my recklessness. What the fuck had I been thinking? I guess I was hoping she'd freak out *slightly* before then admitting, begrudgingly but with a warm smile, that she had been rather exaggerating her pigeon phobia for attention. Like I do whenever someone calls me on my fear of buttons.

I found myself wondering what must have happened, to create such a mania of fear. I imagined an abusive pigeon-fancying uncle, and one especially horrible encounter in a loft.

I was appalled that I'd pulled such a small-minded, mean-spirited, and potentially damaging prank. I *hate* pranks. And so covert, so cowardly. Punching her in the face would have been more honest. I felt like punching myself in the face. My forehead throbbed at the thought.

As we were working together the next day too, I made a vow there and then to make amends.

2.11

Madison turned up at 1.17 the next day. A less charitable person might think she'd only turned up early to piss and moan, but not me. I thought she made some really interesting points about the culture of bullying and intolerance at Beachams, especially with reference to what some (me) were already calling Feathergate.

"At least they didn't fire you," I observed, once she'd detailed her dressing-down.

"They wouldn't dare," she replied, "I'd sue."

I sympathised. "You don't have a contract though, so.…"

"Well, this is exactly why we need to unionise. We need a tour guides union, in English, for English-speaking guides."

"You could set one up." I was about to offer to help when Madison tutted and jutted her lower jaw. Instead I said: "Have you ever thought of seeing a hypnotist?"

Elise turned to face us and said, "I have a friend who's a hypnotherapist. But she's in Spain. You mean for the pigeons? Is that the problem?"

"There's no problem," said Madison.

"Except an irrational fear of pigeons," Elise corrected her.

I tutted.

"It's not irrational," said Madison. "They are vermin. They carry disease. It's a known fact."

I nodded.

Elise laughed. "When was the last time you heard of someone catching a disease from a pigeon?"

Madison shook her head. "That's irrelevant. Just because you don't hear about it doesn't mean it isn't real. You don't hear about women being sex-trafficked or bees being raped. Doesn't mean it doesn't happen."

Elise looked confused. "Who is raping the bees?"

"Honey farmers," said Madison.

Elise laughed.

Madison's face knotted. "I don't think it's funny."

"No, I know," said Elise, still smiling. "It's just your face — you look so serious. And I couldn't help thinking of the farmers raping the bees with their tiny little piemeltjes."

I laughed, despite myself.

But Madison was not going to let it lie. She never did.

"It's not that kind of rape. It's artificial insemination and it's a serious issue. Countless thousands of bees are raped and murdered every year by large-scale honey producers."

Elise smiled a conciliatory smile. "Oh come on, Madison. Don't you think maybe there are more important things to get mad about?"

I wasn't so sure. "No bees, no people. Isn't that what Einstein said?"

Elise turned back to a cluster of tourists.

"I don't believe any one creature is more or less important than any other," said Madison.

"What about pigeons?" said Elise over her shoulder.

Madison pursed her lips humourlessly. "Pigeons are vermin."

I gasped at her hypocrisy.

"Look, all I'm saying is, pigeons spread disease. If pigeons were raped for their milk, then I'd be upset about that too, but they're not, so...."

"What about racing pigeons?" I really didn't want to argue with her but she made it impossible. "They're exploited, right? No doubt treated badly. What about their rights?"

"Look...."

"Yeah!" cried Elise. "Pigeon rights!"

114

"Yeah, I'm sure pigeons are exploited and of course, that's not right, but I just…."

"Don't care?" That was me. It slipped out.

"No, I just…."

"Hate them?" This was Elise.

"Will you let me finish please?!" cried Madison.

Elise and I both made meek faces. "Sorry," we said.

"You have to choose your issues, don't you? You can't give time and energy to everything. I'm already overcommitted as it is. I can't bring myself to care about the plight of the racing pigeon."

"Plus you do hate them," I said, smiling.

"Well, yeah," she admitted, smiling back. And that was all it took.

I'd been finding it hard if I'm honest, what with her tone, her attitude, her micro-aggressions, but the second she smiled, I felt something flutter inside — something much like a pigeon wing in fact, in something much like a heart.

"Why do you hate them so?" I asked, softly, hoping for a way in. "Did something terrible happen?"

Madison shook her head, short and sharp, closing down the conversation. "They're vermin. They spread disease."

I laughed. "I give up! Elise, how many do we have?"

There were 27 tourists: two shitty groups or one good 'un. As it was literally the absolute least I could do, I offered them to Madison.

She seemed suspicious at first, but accepted my offer with thanks. Then I went home feeling lonely and small, with naturally no idea that the Universe (capital U) was about to reward me amply. For what, I don't know, but I was grateful. My god, was I grateful.

2.12

A short, dark, exceedingly fashionable lady marched up to me on the square one bright afternoon and came to an abrupt halt in front of me. I saluted her, military-style, as that seemed appropriate. In response she offered a Nazi salute, or something very similar. I guffawed instinctively, glancing guiltily around. "Don't do Nazi stuff! Jesus."

Her head flew back in a roar at this, her mirrored sunglasses held in place with panicking hands.

"You're a wild one," I said. "What's yer name and where yer from?"

"Beronica!" she cried. "Buenos Aires!"

"No, no," I corrected her. "Veronica. *Vvv*. With a vee."

Again her huge mouth burst into life with delirious laughter and I, I admit, was entranced. "Veronica," she repeated, licking her cushiony lips and concentrating on the correct pronunciation. I wondered how old she was and decided there and then I wouldn't ask.

After taking a purple ticket from Elise, Veronica walked past me to wait with the other tourists. I watched her for a moment, baffled by the power of her pulchritude. She was hypnotic, like a panther. She was a kaleidoscope of vivacity and voluptuousness. Red lipstick, mirrored shades, kinky little leather handbag. She was miles out of my league. Although, having said that, with this job you never knew. A good tour was oftentimes an aphrodisiac. We already clicked on humour. If there were any hope at all, a good performance could turn that hope into gravy. Sex gravy.

Eventually I noticed Elise, staring at me as I stared at Veronica. Reading my mind, she rolled her eyes, her expression quite pained. "Please don't turn into one of *those* guides."

"One of *what* guides?"

"You know, like Nix and Sam and Hamish. They're always sleeping with the tourists."

"What?" I was shocked. "*Hamish*? Really?"

"You'd be surprised."

"I'd be *amazed*."

Elise nodded archly. "He's always coming on to his tourists — I mean, *a lot*." I winced. More than one of his online reviews had complained of predatory or lecherous behaviour. "It stands to reason," Elise continued, "if he asks enough times, he's bound to get lucky sooner or later, right?"

"He spits when he talks though." I couldn't let it go. "He looks like he sleeps in his clothes like, *every* night."

"I guess some girls go for that rough edge stuff. I'm just saying though, you don't wanna be like those guys."

"Don't I? I bloody do," I squeaked. "Not *Hamish*, but…." Elise sneered. "What?! Why shouldn't I? I'm lonely. Why can't I have some company once in a while?"

"So find yourself a girlfriend, Wesley!"

"I would love to!" I screeched, increasingly high-pitched.

"So what's the problem?"

I shook my head and shrugged. "I'm old. And I'm weird."

"Hmm." Elise nodded, apparently convinced. "OK."

Veronica was the model walking tour tourist. Not only did she laugh at my jokes and make jokes of her own, infecting the rest of the group with her overall *joie de vivre*, but also, she brought out the best in me. In the break, she bought a ticket for my Red Light, then after the Red Light, when she went for a drink with another single lady tourist, I invited myself along.

Veronica was an actress in her heart and, completely confounding all my expectations, "something like a trader" in her real life. She bought and sold money.

When the other lady tourist went back to her hostel, I kissed Veronica on the Oudezijds Voorburgwal, and was overjoyed when she responded. We kissed a lot over the next hour or two and before she returned to Haarlem, where she was staying, she promised to see me again the next evening. She decided to extend her stay in the Netherlands. "I hab my own personal guide," she said. "I feel I am blessed."

The next morning, I received a series of voice messages from Veronica. And I quote: "I hope you don't mind, but right now, I'm not fucking anyone." She laughed. She reminded me she was still wounded from a recent split from an eighteen-month relationship. "I am so broking heart that I'm in therapy and I agreed in therapy that I don't wanna have an affair with nobody until I feel OK, because when I fuck a person without any feelings... I feel really empty, despite the sex it's so good and all that, but really, really I feel really empty and sad and..." — with deliberate emphasis, as if this was something that had been repeated more than once in therapy — "...we don't want that. So I hope you don't mind that. I like you and you can like me and all that stuff but I want to let you know that we're not fucking." The message ended with another peal of delicious laughter and an abrupt click.

I was touched by the simple sweet honesty of her message, as well as the truth of her concerns. She was right. Empty and sad. I felt the same after a one-night stand, once the self-satisfied glow had worn off. Although, on closer inspection, I actually feel empty and sad at least 75% of the time. When I'm not working, I mean; when I'm left to my own devices. In fact, the only time I don't suffer the most crushing emptiness is when I'm consumed with the pursuit or continued captivation of a woman. Hmm.

I loved that Veronica had given me the option to bail, although I had no intention of doing so. I wanted her of course, but if sex was off the table, fuck it: I'd still like to hang out, especially if there was kissing involved, which, thank God, there was.

The next evening, we ended up in a dark corner in the Waterhole and when we weren't kissing, Veronica was torturing me with her Instagram profile, insisting I tell her which of her pictures I found the most alluring. Fucking millennials.

When she was hungry, I took her to a pizzeria on the Amstel, then up to my bedroom. She didn't object. As we ate pizza, I asked her questions about her past, and the more she told me, the more she surprised me.

The only reason she'd ditched her dream of drama and retrained in finance was because her engineer father was made redundant and her parents needed money. Not only that, but she'd also stolen $35,000 from a dead Kuwaiti businessman and had given most of the money to charity. "And I bought myself some nice clothes," she added. "And a car."

I was impressed. "The people you meet on a walking tour."

By 10pm, the wind outside was making a terrible fuss. I closed the window. "Looks like a storm's a'coming," I said, fully expecting Veronica to take that as her cue to leave. She said nothing.

I tidied up the pizza stuff from the bed and lay down next to her. We kissed a little more but I sensed some distance. I guessed she didn't want to encourage me right there on the bed. She didn't know me after all. I might be the type to take a mile. So, in order to put her mind at rest and show her that I was a man of honour, I kissed her on the forehead. Veronica smiled and closed her eyes.

A short while later, when it looked like she might be drifting off to sleep, I turned off the bedside lamp so that just a couple of candles were illuminating the room. Beyond the room, muffled light flashed silently across the nebulous night sky. When lightning came, it came not in sticks or forks, but in brief flashes of fire, exploding softly behind cloud. I imagined God as a junkie, squirrelled away in a corner of the sky, struggling to light his crack pipe.

When Veronica began to snore lightly, I stripped to my undies and got under the delicate duvet upon which she was lying. I watched her bafflingly beautiful face in the candlelight for a while as the storm raged at the windows all around. I imagined her waking up and screaming.

She was still fully clothed: black woolly jumper over green and white floral summer dress, black leggings and provocative black leather boots. I crept carefully from under the duvet and removed the boots. Then I removed her socks and saw that her toenails were painted a dark bloody red. I lowered my head and very briefly took one of her big toes in my mouth. She let out a small, single-syllable moan.

That was probably assault.

How good am I really? I wondered. More importantly, how bad am I?

It was time to find out.

2.13

Bad enough to suck a sleeping toe, for sure, but good enough to stop at once and creep guiltily back under the duvet.

With the room flashing white like a horror film basement, heavy rain hammered at the roof and windows, driven in all directions by an increasingly berserk wind. The wind worried me. My room was at the top of a 300-year-old house, with time-weakened windows on either side. The wilder the wind became, the more I feared that one of the windows would give way and the entire contents of the room would be sucked into a giant shard-filled vortex and carried off into the night. Eventually I closed my eyes and drifted off.

Veronica woke around 1am with pressing toilet needs. On her return, she was hot and sweaty so she took off her jumper and leggings before she lay back down. I kissed her. She kissed me back. Lightning flashed. Thunder rumbled. Fucking was off the table. I accepted that. But what else, I wondered, aside from kissing, was still on there?

I moved a hand down her body, onto her buttocks and under her dress. All good. I stroked her thighs and between her legs. Some moans of seeming encouragement. Thus encouraged, seemingly, I inched down her body and began to nose around. As I went to work, the storm outside continued unabated, wild and loud and violent. This was augmented by the sound of sirens as emergency vehicles screamed around the city on damage control. Slowly I removed Veronica's undergarments and proceeded to make love to her with my mouth and fingers.

I took my time. I lost myself in it, thinking, *This… is special*. It's not often you get to worship a woman in a thunderstorm.

When it comes to my feelings concerning women, many people — male people primarily but not exclusively — find my ideas to be somewhat extreme. Of course I disagree. I believe — not to put too fine a point on it — in Female Supremacy. Some women are fucking idiots of course, just as some men are absolute angels, but generally speaking, I feel that women are kinder and have more emotional intelligence and greater empathy than men. These are the qualities I prize above all others, and sometimes, to my eternal shame, find lacking in myself.

Also, my mum died, didn't she? So yeah. That may have had some subconscious influence. I couldn't rule it out.

I feel very strongly, however, that women's role as mothers — incubators and bearers of life — probably plays a part in their superior intelligence. Their increased capacity for sexual pleasure, meanwhile, is almost certainly their reward for having to put up with the blinkered bile and raging bullshit of so many men. I figure women have evolved superior pleasure themselves, out of necessity. Furthermore, I sincerely believe it's only a matter of time before women figure out how to dispense with men entirely. I only wish I could be around to see it.

I say a lot of this kind of thing in certain online chatrooms, not just because I believe it to be true, but also because it seems to really upset a lot of the kind of men I very actively dislike. I get a lot of abuse online. 'Cuck' and 'soy boy' are increasingly popular epithets. I embrace them.

When it comes to sexual pleasure, I consider women's capabilities, when compared to those of men, to be in entirely another dimension. Certainly if my own fleeting localised eruptions are anything to go by. Therefore, when I'm given the opportunity to make physical contact with a woman to whom I am drawn, especially if I'm privileged enough to gain access to her engine room, as it were, I take it seriously.

In such moments, I am an artist. A concert pianist perhaps, attempting to master the Rach 3, or else some wild-eyed experimental artist plucking out gabba on the world's tiniest harp. It's hard work for sure, but without doubt the most rewarding I have ever performed. I'm diligent too, and I do whatever is required. I feel myself in these moments incredibly focused, like a surgeon or a watchmaker, painstaking and serious, unflinching and tenacious. My ego, irrelevant and unnecessary, melts away. I am at one with my partner's pleasure, lost in it. I am never happier.

The noise of the storm absorbed Veronica's moaning and cursing, and her final climax, an appropriately liquescent affair, coincided perfectly with the sound of an enormous crash outside and the mangled bleating of a battered car alarm. It was a beautiful, baptismal moment wherein Veronica seemed almost to meld with the storm, losing herself wholeheartedly in divine, diluvian abandon.

When we were done, and my pants were still very much on, I kissed her passionately then whispered into her ear, "I care for you. OK? So don't feel empty. Now go to sleep." She did so.

In the calm after the storm, with the cold September sun shining brightly on the bed and the drone of impromptu chainsaws drowning out the usual dawn chorus, I gave a repeat performance and Veronica was very, very pleased with me.

"Am I good?" I asked.

"Better than good. Magic. You can be paid money for doing that."

I shook my head, because that was sadly untrue, but still I was flushed with satisfaction. Did I want to fuck her? Fuck, yes. Very much indeed. Did I want her to break down and start begging me to fuck her? Fuck, yes. Very much indeed. Was I satisfied with what had passed between us? Fuck, yes. A million times yes and goddammit, yes again.

Then I leapt from the bed like a gazelle, looked through the skylight at the Amstel and gasped. "Come," I said. "Come see the end of the world."

2.14

Last time I'd looked, seven tall trees had been lined up along the river's edge, each almost as tall as the five-storey houses that looked out upon them. Now there were none. Whether they'd fallen one after the other like huge unruly dominoes, or whether it had been a more gradual process, I would never know. All I could see was the subsequent devastation. You don't realise how big trees are, until they come down.

Veronica stood next to me and gasped. "Dios mío."

There were crushed vehicles in various states of annihilation everywhere. One white Toyota Sequoia had taken some serious trunk to its back half, and its front wheels were up in the air like it was begging for mercy.

The Gemeente — the local council — were out in force. In order to clear the street and get the traffic moving again, Gemeente employees in luminous gilets were dismantling massive portions of trunk with hefty chainsaws. There were also cranes, emergency vehicles, a pair of wood chippers, and a bunch of uniformed police, poking about.

Back in bed an hour later, propped up like a peacock on a pile of pillows, I slapped my laptop onto my belly and wrote Veronica an email. "Here are the names of the music and dance places you should maybe try and catch in London." London was the next stop on her European tour. As I wrote, Veronica buried her face in my chest. When she looked up at the screen, she read the following words, capitalised for maximum impact:

> "DON'T EVER FORGET THAT THE TIME WE
> HAVE SPENT TOGETHER MEANS A LOT TO ME.
> THIS IS NOT AN EMPTY EXPERIENCE FOR ME. I

HOPE YOU NEVER THINK OF IT THAT WAY EITHER. I CARE FOR YOU VERY MUCH INDEED, EVEN THOUGH WE HAVE ONLY JUST MET EACH OTHER, AND I WISH YOU THE MOST AMAZING THINGS FOR THE REST OF YOUR LONG AND WONDERFUL LIFE."

Her shoulders moved like she was sniggering softly. I closed and set aside my laptop, then lay down facing her. "Why are you crying?"

She laughed through her tears and hugged me.

Eighteen months she'd been with her ex, she said, and he'd never said that. Or anything like it.

Now I didn't know the guy's story, obviously, but really, eighteen months and he'd never once said, "I care for you and wish for you wonderful things"? What kind of emotional midget was he? Just be nice, for fucksake. I felt bad for Veronica. So I soothed her, *sotto la vita*, one final time.

Downstairs on the Amstel, we kissed goodbye, and she held on tight for a nice long time. As we were hugging, I glimpsed our reflection in the windows of a police van parked opposite. We made an interesting couple, objectively, and I knew that if I didn't know us personally and I happened to be passing us in the street — this middle-aged white man with boring hair and balding legs in an IKEA dressing gown and slippers; and this smoking-hot different-league mixed-race South American miracle hanging off his neck, looking just fucking resplendent in her mirrored shades and kickass leather boots — I'd assume the guy was loaded. A broker maybe, or a tech billionaire. Why else would such a woman be hanging out with this no-mark schlub?

Before she sashayed off to the station, she had me take a few shots of her posing in front of the messed-up Sequoia for her Instagram. Then she kissed me one final time, looked into my eyes and said, "Thank you for everything. I lo— I kind of love you."

I laughed at the self-correction, which was absolutely appropriate.

"I kind of love you too," I said, very much meaning it. "Enjoy London."

I watched her go. After ten steps or so, she turned her head to check, laughed and gave one final wave. Only when she'd passed out of sight by the Munttoren did I finally turn away. Back across the street, a policewoman and a tree surgeon were watching, arms folded, grinning.

I grinned back. I knew what they were thinking. Alas, no. I was no tech billionaire. Just some lucky schlub with a good job and a quick tongue. Heck, on a good day, it was the greatest goddamn job in the world. I gave a little wave and went back upstairs, where Nix, cooking defiantly non-vegan sausages, had had enough of my shit.

2.15

According to Nix, I have low self-esteem and zero self-respect. "Just imagine this situation," he said, by way of illustration. "I'm with a woman. We have sex. I come three or four times and she doesn't come at all." He raised his hands like he was lifting a shelf. "What do you think of that?"

"Well, yeah. That doesn't sound... fair. It sounds like bad sex."

Nix shrugged. "Need I say more?"

My brow furrowed. "She said 'We're not fucking.' I've told you. I've told you this more than once. 'We're not fucking.' I could play you the message. It was important to her. 'We're not fucking.' So we didn't fuck. What are you not understanding?"

Nix bristled. "She said you weren't fucking but then she let you go down on her like a fucking... rat on biscuits."

His colourful simile amused me but I blocked it. "Yeah, she *let* me," I countered. "Exactly. She let me put my tongue in her arse too. What's your point?"

"Then why didn't she let you fuck her? Does that seem fair to you?"

"It seems perfectly fair to me. What's *not* fair is you trying to find something to blame her for. I'm absolutely certain that if I'd just taken off my pants, we would've ended up fucking, but I didn't want to because I knew that — deep down — she didn't want to. And — more importantly — I'd *agreed* that we weren't going to fuck. I wanted to be true to my word. You know? Can't you see that? It's about *honour*, motherfucker. I wanted to show her that not all men are... *savages*. I wanted to show her that not all men are DJ fucking Khaled."

I was at that time slightly obsessed by DJ Khaled, following the resurfacing of an infamous interview he'd given in 2015. In the interview, the DJ-slash-music producer states, with not one scintilla of shame, that he never has given, nor will he ever give, oral pleasure to a woman. His reason for this is simple: "the man is the king" and it's the woman's job to praise him, literally and orally. Furthermore, she must do so without the expectation of reciprocation. "It's different rules for men," says Khaled.

Needless to say, I don't agree with this primitive evaluation of gender relations. Indeed, in my most humble opinion, DJ Khaled is a misogynistic cocktard and a spineless, confused little turd of a man. Not a man at all, in fact. Being a real man means doing everything within your power to make the world a better place, doing everything within your power to improve the lives of your fellow humans, in all situations and in all environments. In the context of intimate physical relationships, this means getting your face into your partner's groin, finding out how that shit works and making it sing.

I've seen that interview twenty times maybe, and every time I laugh and despair in equal measure. "The man is the king," says DJ Khaled.

What a poor reading of humanity.

The woman is the queen.

Equally flawed perhaps — well, not equally. Either way, I say it a lot, not just in internet chatrooms but in any conversation regarding sex and gender. It's my retaliation against DJ Khaled and a tribute to his poor neglected wife. *May she take many lovers.*

"But if the woman is the queen," Nix argued, pleased with himself, "it still follows that you're her king, right?"

I smirked and shook my head. "No, man, it's like bees. One queen and an endless supply of drones."

"*Aha!*" He snapped his fingers loudly, like he was breaking a leprechaun's back. "*This* is the problem. You see yourself as a drone. If that's not low self-esteem, I don't know what is."

Another small smirk flashed across my jowls. "I have low *gender*-esteem. There's a difference."

Nix raised an eyebrow.

"OK, OK." The eyebrow had a valid point. "I have low self-esteem too. Fine. But at least I know how to treat a woman."

"Ah, but do you? Nobody likes a spineless cuck."

I laughed. "If it's spineless to find most of your pleasure in the pleasure of others, then… fine. I have no spine."

Nix rolled his eyes. "*Cuck*-a-doodle-doo."

"I don't get why that's such an insult anyway. Every man should be a cuckold, if that's what his queen requires."

"Oh, you'd be happy with that, would you? Your woman fucking other guys behind your back?"

"*Your woman,*" I repeated, witheringly. "Look, if I failed to satisfy my queen, then she'd be insane not to fuck other guys, but she wouldn't have to do it behind my back. On the contrary, I would fully endorse it. Hopefully it would never come to that though, because I would devote myself — do you understand? *I would devote myself* — to satisfying her. That is my role in any relationship after all. I live to please. Whatever. My queen. Requires."

Nix stared blankly for a moment. "Exactly when *was* your last relationship?"

I took a deep breath and let it go very, very slowly.

"Have you ever actually *been* in a relationship?" He raised one particularly challenging eyebrow. "It's fine if you haven't. Just… be real, man."

Of course I *had* been in relationships. There was the first, when I was really just a child, Bronwen in Hay on Wye, who used me up, spat me out and broke my heart, all within a week. There was Stephanie at Uni — 18 months. There was Lindsay at Sky — my longest at two years. Then a year with Zuhrah reviewing restaurants in London, and another 18 turbulent months with Anna in Italy. And aside from those relatively long-term relationships, I'd had quite a few shorter and much, much shorter flings, but nothing since…

"Violet," said Nix, crippling another leprechaun.

"Oooooooooh," I said. With her loud, proud laugh and her loose and fluid tongue; with her restless, often aggressively tangential conversation, and that overkill of energy that had her bouncing and hopping about the place like a Beyblade… how could I forget about Violet? Probably because I was, as Nix phrased it at the time, *her Old Jew in the Cellar*. "I've got to go to work."

Nix laughed. I mounted the stairs to my room like a goat. He shouted after me: "See you later, Cuckleberry Finn."

I laughed. *More Tom Soy boy*, I thought, but not till two days later. By which time, Kras had cried in a wardrobe and once again, wholly inadvertently, another wretched man-demon was dead, because of me.

2.16

It was a tough day for tour guides. All over the city, streets were shut down as burly men continued to take control of the dead wood situation. Shit was shook up. You had to be on your toes, improvising new routes, like a ninja. I did good, if I say so myself. I was on good form, psyched by the city in recovery, thrilled by the power of the weather to fuck up so much shit in just a few short hours. The ebb, the flow, the yin, the yang, the rain, the sun, the impermanence, in perpetuity — sometimes it all just seems to harmonise perfectly. I was also full of bouncy beans, of course I was, from my time with Veronica. And I'd meant every word of my conversation with Nix. About honour. And if I sound like a self-righteous berk, then take me to a court of law and sue me, but it will still be true: it's *always* a question of honour.

So I cut short my Red Light, giving the main square a miss on account of the chaos — the wood-chippers, the foliage-mincers, the chainsaws. Then I wandered back into the Old Church Square in the heart of *de Wallen*, just to check out the damage, which was extensive. Between the 5D Porn cinema and The Caressed Breast, five more giant Dutch elms had been ripped out of the ground by the wind.

Wandering slack-jawed through the ruined space, I was amazed that there was so little damage to things of genuine consequence. The only building to have been hit by a falling tree was the Old Church itself. None of the brothels or residences seemed to have been touched at all. And neither, most importantly, had Belle.

Belle is a metre-high bronze statue of a sex worker standing in a window. "RESPECT SEX WORKERS ALL OVER THE WORLD" reads her plaque. She is a brilliant, vibrant, meaningful piece of public art that was always one of the highlights of any tour of the area. The night of the storms, she came within a metre of being flattened. Literally an arm's length to Belle's left, an ornate lantern-style streetlamp had taken a direct hit, its once proud head crushed and hanging loose, its neck broken. I tried to imagine the moment of impact in the eye of the storm: branches ceaselessly thrashing, the trunk of the tree closest to Belle moving side to side, lifting the ground as the shallowest roots snap, the tree finally losing its grip on the earth and… over it goes, taking the head of the streetlamp with it. I pictured each of the four small panes of glass and the bulb itself exploding simultaneously. Would there have been sparks? Sure. Why not. I even threw in a thunderclap for good measure.

I walked on, observing the damage, reverse imagineering. Motorbikes trashed and crumpled. Bicycles compacted into their racks. Benches written off entirely. Amputated tree bases uprooted and exposed, like dead Gorgons, secret parts laid bare. It was indecent. One of my favourite spots in Amsterdam, destroyed.

But it would be back. And there were other places.

Back at Belle, I rubbed and squeezed her shoulder paternally, reverentially, and I watched as one real life sex worker took to her stool in her window, because it was business as usual and nothing had really changed.

When Donka came into my head, I texted Kras. "How's tricks? Any progress?"

He called me. I picked up.

"I want to fucking kill him," he said.

2.17

Kras was home alone, so I went to see him and he caught me up. Donka had taken her first step towards freedom and her pimp had not taken it well.

In order to prevent coerced sex workers escaping on the next plane, one of the first things pimps do when they take possession of a woman, is to confiscate her passport. One method employed to prevent this, is the pre-shift passport mandate — sex workers must show their passport to the people who rent them the rooms every time they go to work. Unfortunately, Donka's pimp found a clever way around this: he let her have her passport; and then he took it back. Apparently, when he first put Donka to work, he would literally stand across the street when she checked in, so there was no chance she'd run off. Then, as she settled into her life with him, seemingly without complaint or dissatisfaction, he started to give her a little more leeway, usually picking up her passport a couple of hours into her shift.

She'd been considering escape for a while apparently. She'd been putting a little money aside, occasional tips she kept from Fisnik, and she'd worked out a plan. Falling for Kras had given her the impetus to put that plan into action.

So, one evening around 9.30, when Fisnik popped by to pick up her passport, Donka couldn't find it.

"He knew," said Kras. "She's too smart to lose her passport."

So Fisnik beat her up. He hit her mostly in the stomach and the kidneys. He must have figured she'd be so terrified by the violence that she'd confess immediately and hand over the passport he was instinctively convinced she still had. But Donka didn't waver.

Her bag had been open, she told him. Between the offices and the cigarette shop, someone must have dipped in and taken it. She urged Fisnik to check the shop's security camera footage. She stared into his eyes and she held onto the collars of his shirt and she swore on her mother's life she was telling him the truth. And when he hit her, she took it.

Kras couldn't take it. He wanted to kill Fisnik. He wanted to organise a posse and weapons, but Donka made him promise not to. She was afraid of Fisnik and what he might be capable of. Fisnik had made her aware from the very beginning that if she ever did anything stupid, like going to the police or trying to run away, Fisnik's cohorts would find her, and they would kill her. And Donka believed him.

We were seated at a table in his living room, and Kras had his head in his hands. So often he seemed steeped in sadness — and I mean, long before Donka. As long as I'd known him, Kras had always been tethered to the pain of his childhood.

Krastyo's origin story, like Nix's, was way worse than mine. My mum got eaten away by cancer; Krastyo's mum got on a bus. She chose to leave, not just Kras, but his father and three older brothers. Being the youngest — just five years old at the time — it was inevitable that on some level and for the rest of his life, Kras would blame himself for his mum's departure. He was only human. Perhaps it was also inevitable that his adult relationships would be something of a car-crash. The second he got close to a woman, he started fretting over her imminent departure. He was, therefore, by default, intense, and a little dour. Sometimes I just wanted to shake some positivity into him.

"So what's next?" I asked. "Eh? Come on, Kraskolnikov! Things are moving! Let's look on the bright side! What's the plan?"

The plan was in action. The game was afoot.

Ultimately, Fisnik had no alternative but to accept Donka's version of events. Which meant he was left with a choice. He could either put her to work unlawfully, on the streets or in a private apartment, which was rife with complications, both logistical and legal. *Or* he could just get her to apply for a new passport and in the interim, put her to work on a temporary document supplied by the immigration people. When he plumped for the latter, Donka was pleased. Part one of her plan was accomplished.

Part two of her plan was to bide her time till the passport arrived, then wait a few more weeks till any suspicion on Fisnik's part died down, and then, probably when one of Fisnik's less observant cohorts was on passport duty, fob him off with the old document, and fly off into the night with the new. The big switcheroo. Kras was a mess of anxiety.

"Let me show you," he said. "Come."

I followed him into his bedroom. He opened his wardrobe. On one side of the rail hung a row of dresses and fluffy coloured jumpers. "These are things she wants to keep." He took hold of a fluffy sleeve and fondled it. "She throws them in the street when she finishes work, disguised like they're rubbish, and I go and collect them, and I bring them here. She's slowly moving in." He smiled. Then he leaned inside the wardrobe, and with his eyes closed, started to whine.

"Kras." I spoke softly, my hand on his shoulder, my chest heaving. "Come on, man. Come out of the wardrobe. You can't be crying in a wardrobe, Kras. At your age." I laughed. "Come on, mate. Pull yourself together. Fucksake."

Kras managed a smile. I led him back through to the living room.

"It's happening, man," I told him. "There's a lot to be grateful for here. Donka knows what she's doing. It's all good."

I believed it too.

I really did.

2.18

The very next morning, I was cycling west on the Herengracht wondering, as it happens, how my father was, when without signalling or inching forward to check for cyclists, the fat front end of a shiny black Mercedes with tinted windows pulled right out in front of me, blocking the road entirely. I had to brake and skid violently to avoid impact. Without stopping, I took evasive action, hopping onto the empty pavement for a stretch, before dropping back down into the road, ahead of the Mercedes, which was still manoeuvring itself out into the traffic. Instinctively, I raised my left hand, and without looking back, I extended the middle finger high into the air behind me. By the time I lowered it again, seconds later, I'd reached a line of cars and bikes at a traffic light. The moment I came to a standstill, I heard somewhere behind me a loud, vengeful screech of tyres. I cursed.

The pavements were now blocked with pedestrians, so I had to wait in line, and take my punishment. So be it. The Mercedes pulled up alongside.

An overweight, dark-skinned Asian-looking man in a tight suit was glowering out of the open window. His arm was outside the car, his right hand splayed out on the perfect paintwork, knuckles pulsing. Before the car had even come to a standstill, he'd already started screaming in Dutch. His eyes were popping and spit was jumping from his lips. Immediately I felt terribly sorry for him.

"*Langzaam*," I said, not comprehending. *Slowly*.

"Oh, you don't speak Dutch. What a surprise."

I began to speak. I wanted to explain to the angry man, "Well, I do actually speak Dutch — I've had a year's worth of lessons and I'm making adequate progress — but the fact is you're just screaming much too quickly for me." I got as far as "W-".

137

I was not allowed to speak. Instead the angry man ranted at me, non-stop, in quite heavily accented, profoundly furious English. "You show me your finger! You *dare* to show me your finger!" He banged the outside of his door as he spoke. "You arrogant son of a bitch. You fucking white prick. You think you can show me your finger and ride off without facing the consequences?"

I bristled at the *white* thing, as anyone might, but I rose above it and started to say, "You pulled right out in front of me!" I got as far as "Y-". I was becoming frustrated. I was happy to debate the rights and wrongs of the situation and was absolutely ready to share some of the blame, but not even allowing me to contribute at all was just childish.

The lights ahead changed to green and the stalled traffic in front began slowly to move off. I had to yell angrily in order to be heard. "Are you going to let me speak?"

"No, I'm fucking not!" he roared. "You have to learn, you arrogant Imperialist fuck! The moment you show your finger, you lose the right to speak. And you have lost that fucking right." Cars behind began beeping their frustration. "Fuck you and welcome to Amsterdam!" He pulled forward dramatically, clearly desperate to speed off into the sunset, but it was ten o'clock in the morning, and the lights were back on red. So he squealed to a halt again, just ten metres ahead, first in line.

I cycled past him and stopped my bike a couple of metres ahead. Instinctively I turned to face him. Then I lifted both of my fists as if I were curling a barbell. Then I unfurled my two middle fingers and began to thrust them meaningfully into the air, as if repeatedly violating two invisible angels.

As soon as I began my mime, the driver of the car made a move to advance upon me physically. His door opened but, much to my relief, he became entangled in his seatbelt and was momentarily stuck. So I had time to finish my fingering with a flourish, take off through the red light and dart right, fast into the sporadic oncoming traffic on the Vijzelgracht.

I laughed as I rode. I was feeling pleased with myself, I'll admit, and my heart was beating like bongos. What a day this was turning into! I'd only come out for an English breakfast.

Then I heard the screeching of tyres again. Whether the lights had changed or he'd jumped them too, I did not know. All I knew was, he was giving chase.

"Fuck."

I checked up ahead. A tram was coming towards me. If I got in front of it and pulled a U-turn, there was no way he'd be able to keep up. I checked briefly behind. Nothing coming but the mad bastard in the Merc.

I picked my moment and pulled a sharp left in front of the tram. I had a good five metres to spare but the tram driver still went ape with her bell. Thankfully there'd been nothing on the other side of the tram or I might have been in trouble. As it was, I was OK. I took a deep breath but before I could let it out there came a loud crash of metal on metal and the screams of shocked passers-by. I stopped and looked back. The Mercedes appeared to be stuck to the end of the tram, side on, but I had no idea how much damage had been done.

Should I go back and implicate myself?

What was the right thing to do?

What was the sensible thing to do?

I took off.

I turned back onto the Keizersgracht, made my way to Greenwoods, and ordered my gourmet English breakfast, as planned. That was why I'd been thinking about my dad. He loved a fry-up.

"Are you OK?"

The waitress, back with my coffee, was clearly disconcerted by my anxious distance-staring. I looked into her eyes. She was a vision, a black-haired tulip. How wonderful it would be, I thought, if I came clean about my altercation with the angry man and somehow, for reasons neither of us would ever fully understand, she became enchanted by me.

"I'm fine, thanks."

She smiled. "Your food will be right out."

Twenty minutes later, I received a message from Monica.

"Pick a night," she wrote. "I'm moving on. I owe it all to you. Well not all. I'll cook for you. On my new boat!"

I understood precisely two sevenths of her message.

"Thursday," I replied. "Please don't cook."

2.19

I checked the Dutch-English newspapers in the coming days to see if the tram incident had been deemed substantially newsworthy. It had not.

Although I didn't think I'd broken the law, aside from jumping a red light, which is not really a thing for cyclists in Amsterdam, I felt bad about what had happened. Of course I did. I'd acted rashly. Even if it had been provoked by a dangerously inconsiderate act, repeatedly fingering a stranger was hardly my best self. And my ignorance of the stranger's impulsivity didn't change that. I definitely bore some responsibility.

Still, I put it out of my head and on Thursday went to meet Monica on her new boat. Lizzie and Doug were there too, to my surprise, but only one of them seemed pleased to see me. Indeed, pretty much as soon as I'd taken off my jacket, Doug stood up and readied to leave.

"Was it something I said?"

"Huh?"

"Don't leave on my account," I clarified.

"Nah, mate, don't flatter yourself," he replied, flashing a cold handsome smile to take the sting out of his words. "I got football."

And with that, he hugged the ladies goodbye, gave me a half-hearted thumbs-up and was accompanied by Monica off the boat.

I asked Lizzie outright: "Why does your boyfriend hate me?"

"Ah, don't mind him. He's a grouchy so-and-so at the best of times."

I shrugged, refusing to get worked up about it. "So how are things with you? You feeling better?"

Lizzie blew out her cheeks as if to say *not particularly*, but then Monica returned and said, "Ah? What do you think of my new home?"

"It's amazing," I told her. "Now — what the fuck is going on?"

Before she became a tour guide, Monica worked for a guy named Remi, helping flog luxury boats to luxury tourists. It was soulless work, ultimately, so she quit, but Remi kept in touch, always inviting her to parties and trying to lure her back into the fold. "Gay but creepy," was how she described him. Then, eventually, he made her an offer she couldn't refuse.

The rather crappily named Miss Adventure was a recent acquisition, a brand new luxury vessel moored in front of the Science Museum. Four of its five cabins would be rented out throughout the year to wealthy Londoners, sourced by Remi via an associate in Canary Wharf. Each cabin contained a double bed, a large TV, a shower, a toilet and a kitchenette, all for the ludicrous price of €400 a night, or a little less in the low season.

Monica's job was to manage the boat, troubleshooting problems and liaising with guests. She'd be available from 8 till 1.30 every day and more or less always on emergency call. It was a three-month contract from October 1. She'd also live onboard, rent-free in the fifth room, and she'd be paid €2,250 per month, after tax.

"It's perfect for me," she said, after a brief tour of the cabins. She'd carry on doing Red Lights and the occasional late afternoon tour for Beachams, and she'd live off that money. The boat money would go directly into her 2020 Travel the World fund. "Also I can work on my book."

"What book?"

"This is my other news." She'd received a letter. "They want to publish my book!" She squealed and shook her fists in the air. Lizzie immediately jumped up and hugged her.

Milliseconds before my astonishment began to look like unkindness, I followed suit. "That is absolutely fucking amazing. Are you sure?"

She showed me the letter, which began, "I am delighted to let you know that your book proposal has been accepted for publication by Melody Penguin, subject to approval of the final manuscript."

"Tomorrow I go to meet the editors in London. They paid for my flight." She squeaked her excitement again.

Based on Monica's experiences as a teenage supermodel, the book is basically a guide to fashion modelling for the #MeToo generation. A tale of old men exploiting young women. A tale as old as time itself.

"I want to thank you for your help," she said.

"My pleasure," I replied. And of course it was. But I was also envious. Bryson had a book deal. Monica had a book deal. Where the hell was my book deal? Then I remembered. I hadn't written a book, and I didn't have any ideas.

After we'd eaten, I brought up Veronica, and Monica and Lizzie both agreed with Nix that basically, I'd been a bit of a sap. I couldn't tell if they were being serious. "Anyway," I confessed, "the whole one-night stand thing just makes me feel empty and sad. And we don't want that."

"Are you not on Tinder?" asked Lizzie.

I groaned. "Tinder's no place for a poet."

Monica rolled her eyes and in an effort to change my mind by demonstrating how many people were out there looking for love, she showed me her Tinder profile, with her hundreds of matches and thousands and thousands of likes. I was genuinely enraged. I glared at her.

"Yeah, but you're fucking gorgeous, you insensitive cow. I'm like an old cinnamon stick at the back of a spice cupboard."

Lizzie laughed and Monica grimaced. Neither contradicted me.

"Idiota," Monica muttered.

"But it's true!" I cried. "You're the Taj Mahal. I'm an old shed with no windows, graffiti on the walls and a large pile of human shit in one corner."

Lizzie laughed but Monica seemed angry. "Your attitude really sucks, Wesley. There are men who are much more ugly than you that get lots of girls just because they have confidence."

This was frustrating because I did have confidence, just not in my appearance. When I was giving a tour, I was charming, ebullient, perfectly comfortable in my own skin. I was a riot. The rest of the time, however, if women saw me at all, they saw a chinless douche and they instinctively swiped left. Or so I believed. And that was enough. So all I had were words, and on a dating platform plagued by illiterates, words were worthless.

Monica ran out of patience. "Look, you need to meet some women, no? So you go online, you meet them and boom — Bob is your uncle."

Lizzie concurred. "If you don't try, you'll never know."

As I wavered, remembering the disaster that arose from my last Tinder profile, Monica and Lizzie set about writing me a new one. Monica took the lead and Lizzie corrected her English. She wrote it quickly, seemingly without having to try too hard. I didn't say anything, but I was very touched.

"Wesley is a good man," she wrote. "Very funny and very kind. Much better than he looks. He works as a tour guide. He is one of the best. Smart, lovely and very hilarious. If he was ten years

144

younger and had more chin, I would take him for myself. Also, he really cares about women. He is a proud feminist and from what I hear, a good lover. Catch him while you can! — Wesley's friend Monica."

"Who told you I was a good lover?"

"You told!" she cried. "If it's not true, we can take it out, ah?"

We left it in, and within minutes we were all gathered around my phone judging women's faces.

"Maybe try not to be so fussy," Monica said after a few minutes. "What's wrong with this one?"

"She looks like a scarecrow, Monica."

Monica laughed. "Eh Wesley, remember what they say about the people in the glass house, ah?"

"Oh come on, I still have to find someone attractive, no? It's not like my lack of chin disqualifies me from having an opinion regarding who I get to kiss. I still get to choose. No? Everybody gets to choose, Monica."

"OK, OK. Take it easy. Ah, guarda, what about this one?"

"Thin lips."

"Ma *dai*, Wesley!"

"What? I can't pretend. Look at her! She's almost translucent. She looks like a lychee rolled in dog-hair."

Another wore a crucifix; another looked too angry; another had had the temerity to write "lol" in her profile. Meanwhile, the women I actually liked were laughably attractive and generally far too young.

"As much fun as this is," Lizzie eventually said, "it's time to go."

There was a club night at OT301, one of the few squats to have survived the ongoing gentrification of Amsterdam. Monica's DJ friends were playing. Doug was meeting Lizzie there. Did I fancy it? Of course I didn't fancy it but, just like with Tinder, I was prepared to give faking it another go. So I went along and watched the attractive young people moving their bodies without a care in the world; I watched Lizzie and Doug become embroiled in an intense and clearly private conversation; I watched men hovering around Monica like giant wasps around a bin full of ice cream. Then I crept out of the club and made my way home in a pretty rank mood.

As I was passing the Torture Museum, I noticed a group of six Scots women dressed in identical French maid outfits. One had a pink sash bearing the word BRIDE, and a can of squirty cream that she aimed into the mouths of her friends and passing strangers. She also squirted some into her cleavage for some passing drunken men to lick from her chest. She ended up violently snogging one of them.

I shook my head. While a part of me certainly looked down my nose at these wanton debauchers, another part yearned to be one of them. I knew, however, that if I were one of them, brain blurry with Big Buddha Cheese and Jägerbombs, face sticky with Glasgow hen cleavage-cream, I wouldn't be happy. The fact was, I expected more of myself. If I was perfectly honest, I still desperately wanted — somehow — to make the world a better place. How, I had no idea. The Universe knew though, which is why it had sent the mad bugger in the Mercedes, to give me a little nudge.

2.20

It was the third day after the accident when one of my news alerts — "tram crash" — came up trumps. I clicked through to an English-Dutch news site and gawped. There was the Mercedes, in the mouth of the tram. Beneath it the following headline: "Man, 82, dies in Amsterdam tram crash". My first thought — bolstered by the picture of an old man I'd never seen before — was that some poor sod on the tram had died. A complete innocent. Feeling all at once breathless and physically sick, I began to read.

Kusal Sivaram, 56, had been driving his father to the airport, on his way back to Sri Lanka. His father had been in Amsterdam for a week, spending quality time with his businessman son. They'd just left their hotel, however, when they were the victims of a vicious racist assault by a passing cyclist. It was whilst chasing the racist to bring him to justice that the Mercedes was hit by a tram and the old man in the backseat suffered a fatal heart attack.

The words *vicious racist assault* hypnotised me, much as the words *unprovoked attack* must have hypnotised Monica a decade earlier.

It was unlikely, concluded the article, that Sivaram would face any criminal charges related to dangerous driving. The police were very keen, however, to speak to the cyclist who'd launched the verbal attack.

I was appalled. And concerned. The article clearly implied that the racist cyclist had killed the old man. Had I been caught on CCTV? Would the police be tracking my whereabouts at that very moment? Mostly, however, I was pissed off that this psychotic fucker had lied about his motivation. Vicious racist assault! Me! If anyone had been racist….

I took a deep breath and pasted "Kusal Sivaram" into a new search window. Half a dozen more versions of the same story popped up, along with lots more unrelated hits. One story that caught my eye had a very different headline: "Sri Lankan ex-General killed in Amsterdam incident". I clicked through and discovered with astonishment that the old man in the back seat — Kusal Sivaram Senior — had once been a big cheese in the Sri Lankan military. More investigation revealed that Sivaram Senior was a hugely controversial figure, repeatedly accused of running secret detention camps that were notorious for the systematic torture of Tamil political prisoners.

My mouth opened slowly like a mechanical toy, my heart pounding in my ears and neck. I felt very much like I was in a dream.

I found a site with photographs of Tamils who'd allegedly been raped, branded and brutally beaten in Sivaram's camps. My forehead creased and strained as I forced my eyes to stay open and observe.

Sivaram had always denied that any torture had taken place in his camps, but an awful lot of evidence seemed to suggest he was lying. I quickly dug up large dossiers of hundreds of sworn testimonies from grieving relatives and survivors begging for Sivaram to be brought to justice. I held up my hands in disbelief, brought them together in front of my face, and smiled. Then I laughed, for quite a while.

Then, fully satisfied that the second person I'd inadvertently helped to die in just under two months was also a sickening monster who had it coming, I closed my laptop and lay on my bed.

I don't believe in God. I should make that clear. I don't believe in any kind of predestination — I don't even really believe in the

148

Universe (not even when it starts planting so many cosmic messages that it begins to feel, frankly, like bullying).

Having said all that, things were becoming undeniably bizarre.

I was reminded of an interview I'd once heard in which the writer Paolo Coelho was challenged on his ridiculous belief in signs — he won't, for example, embark upon another novel until he chances upon a white feather. The loon. The interviewer suggested that to exist in a world where every mundane thing was loaded with significance was to risk going insane. Paolo's response was that obviously, you pick and choose your signs. You weigh up what significance any given sign might have, and if it feels right to you, then bingo: it's a motherfucking sign.

Buddhist ideas also came to mind. I had heard, and I had seen, that if you're making good causes, living your best life, everything begins to harmonise. You fall into rhythm with the Universe; you start to notice things and, even though they don't exist, coincidences proliferate. Maybe it's a sign, or maybe you're just seeing life more clearly now. The Universe begins to feel like an old poem you're finally beginning to understand. (I know I just said I didn't believe in the Universe, but if what Coelho says is right, then clearly my concept of the Universe is really merely an extension of my own brain. So… I guess I *am* the Universe. Oh, I don't know. Consciousness is confusing.)

However, the fact that Kusal Sivaram Senior was a torturer of Tamils felt enormously significant to me. It felt like a massive flashing sign that I was going in the right direction. Even if I didn't feel like I'd been making particularly good causes of late… maybe I had. The Universe was on board. The Universe was saying, *Keep doing what you're doing, Wesley. As long as your heart is good, you cannot fail to make the world a better place.*

I prepared my cushion, set my timer and began to meditate.

149

My mind, however, was restless with images: tortured prisoners; Matty Sutcliffe falling to his knees; Kusal Sivaram spitting venom at the lights; his father, the old torturer, staring blankly out from the newspaper. A sudden sensation of falling passed abruptly through my torso. I opened my eyes and brought a hand up to my chest with concern. I couldn't catch my breath. I gulped for air, wondered briefly if I was having a heart attack and realised no, not quite. Rather, for the first time in maybe fifteen years, I was having a panic attack.

III/1

October 2019

3.1

I'm not sure why I didn't tell anyone about my involvement in the death of alleged Sri Lankan torturer and murderer, ex-General Kusal Sivaram. I was afraid, I think. Coming so soon after my involvement in the death of belligerent bigot and very petty criminal Matty Sutcliffe, I think I was afraid people might get the wrong idea. I was also afraid they might get the right idea. So I blocked it out and concentrated on the living, some of whom were making excellent progress.

Donka, for example, had moved in with Kras. The big switcheroo had gone off without a hitch, the old passport had been passed off as new and Donka had left her old life in what sounded like fairly spectacular style. Rather than work another shift and sneak away in the dead of morning, she wanted it over with, so she'd prepared. There was nothing left in the apartment she needed or wanted, so when the coast was clear, and more importantly, when the roads were clear, she texted Kras and waited. Ten minutes later, Kras arrived on the street, the Oudezijds Voorburgwal, at the top of Donka's alleyway. He was dressed head to foot in black leathers and riding a large motorbike he'd borrowed from a friend. Wearing a long coat, carrying a small bag, Donka stepped through her window for the very last time and hurried up the alleyway towards him. I can't begin to imagine the excitement she must have felt as she squeezed her head into the helmet Kras gave her and climbed onto the bike, or even better, holding tight to Kras as she sped across the city with years and years of depression and slavery behind her. But it must have felt fucking good.

Nix and I went for dinner and met her for the first time.

Kras cooked a risotto and Donka made a cheesecake for dessert. It was all delicious but what was especially beautiful was just how couply they were. I couldn't stop smiling and poking Nix in the ribs like a proud father. They were so loved up. I knew from Kras that they'd been waiting till they'd moved in together to make love for the first time, and you could see it had gone well. I'd never seen Kras so happy. He was transformed.

And Donka was wonderful. Very shy at first but when she opened up, she was sharp, funny, everything you could hope for. A first class human.

She looked familiar too. I was sure I recognised her smile from a year of wandering past the windows. I always smiled if I made eye contact with a sex worker, and I always loved and tended to remember the ones who smiled back. She'd chopped off her long blonde hair though, the night she gained her freedom, and she'd dyed what was left of it very dark brown, so my brain was thrown out of whack. Now she looked like an actress in a French New Wave film.

She didn't recognise me.

"So what's the plan?" asked Nix. "How long have you got left? Will you have a party?"

The plan was as follows: head to Haarlem the next morning and hide out there till the last week of October, then pop back to Amsterdam, spend a day doing last minute in-person admin and financial stuff, then fly to Sofia. They were pretty sure they were safe, they said, but there was no point hanging around in Amsterdam tempting fate. Their flight was booked for the 27th of October.

As for a party, this was probably it.

Once in Sofia, they'd move in with Krastyo's great aunt. There was a huge double room that was theirs for as long as they needed it. Kras had money though, so it needn't be long. He'd been working flat-out and saving hard all summer. Plus he had his coins.

Tour guides get a lot of shrapnel. Tourists keen to ditch the Euros that are about to become redundant are ten-a-penny. And it's not like Amsterdam is London, where every doorway has its own homeless person. So rather than get stuck with a pocketful of heavy trash that it's weirdly immoral to throw away, many of those coins get passed along to the tour guides. And many of the tour guides collect them in jars.

Kras had three two-litre glass demijohns he'd found in a second-hand shop. Last time Nix and I had been at his place, sometime in the summer, we'd been wondering how much one full jar might be worth. Kras had promised to count them one day soon.

"So?" I asked. "Did you count them yet?"

Krastyo's plan had always been to bank his coins only when he had something, or — he was always hopeful — someone, to spend them on. They were his rainy day coins. Now that day, and indeed that someone, had come. In three weeks' time, the coins would be banked and Kras would be gone. Friends being what they are, or me being what I am, or a combination of the two, I knew I'd probably never see him again. It was the story of my life; the story of life. People came. People went. People moved. People changed. People — increasingly — died.

"Man, didn't I tell you?" His excited smile flipped a switch and his cheeks came on. "I counted one jar. Guess how much." Without leaving time for anyone to guess, which was actually quite annoying, he said: "Two-thousand six-hundred euros. Just one jar! So I've probably got maybe seven, eight thousand in total. Can you believe it?"

I barely could.

"How does it work with the bank?" asked Nix.

"They've got a giant counting machine," I said, with a gleam in my eye. My own collection was hopefully going to get me to Vietnam in January. Suddenly a thought occurred to me. "Ooh, what are you going to do with your demijohns?"

Donka looked shocked.

"You want them?" said Kras. "No problem."

"Yeah, I'd love them. I'll pay you too. I give you good price."

"Nah, man. You can have them. I'm not gonna need 'em."

Donka and Kras shared something urgent in Bulgarian and Donka dissolved into giggles. "She thought you wanted my long johns, man."

"I'll take your long johns too!" I cried. "You know I have no shame. And at the same time, nothing but."

"I'll send you a message as soon as I empty them," Kras said. "The demijohns I mean. Or how about this, man? Why don't you come with me to the bank? If you're free of course."

"I have the whole week off!" I cheered. "It's destiny!"

I'd been thinking I might go somewhere to recover after the nightmare that a visit from Damo was sure to be, but seeing Kras one final time would be even better. "It's a date," I told him. "You can bank on it," I added, to little enthusiasm.

At the end of the evening, which went swimmingly well and far too quickly, we all started getting a little misty-eyed about missing each other.

"Come for Christmas!" cried Donka. "Come to Sofia! You will be both very welcome."

Kras seconded the offer with gusto and Nix and I looked at each other with the same expression. It was an expression that only two single humans estranged from lone parents can share. Such humans are always looking for some reason to make Christmas special. We agreed instantly that this was the greatest idea we'd ever heard. So Kras poured more walnut liqueur and we each raised our glasses in a toast:

"Christmas in Bulgaria!"

But first, of course, I had to deal with Damo...

3.2

When I arrived at Central Station on a Thursday morning halfway through October to meet Fitch, Rich and Damo, the first thing I noticed was that Rich was not present. Apparently he had "a last minute family thing". This was not good news as I'd been counting on Rich to dilute Damo. But still, I vowed to keep an open mind, and when Fitch and Damo both expressed the desire for a Full English Breakfast, I judged them not.

Fitch was on fine form. With small features and black murine eyes, he always reminded me of an Edward Gorey drawing. There wasn't a lot of furniture on his face but what he had was expressive and alert. He was also very excited to be in Amsterdam, having not visited for more than ten years.

Damo was initially rather quiet. I was relieved. Maybe fatherhood really had tamed the raging oik. I began to think that perhaps we'd have a charmingly modest time of it while they were in town, possibly taking in a few museums and a nice sedate canal cruise. The fact that Damo had not demanded alcohol with his breakfast was also a very good sign. It was only 11am of course, but I understood only too well the urgency with which certain English people tended to set about becoming intoxicated in Amsterdam, and I was pleased to observe this early sign of restraint.

Our coffees came.

"So how's it going, Damo? You enjoying family life?"

In response, Damo looked at me, then he looked at Fitch. Then he reached wordlessly into the inside pocket of his heavy black jacket, took out a silver hip flask and poured the remaining contents into his coffee cup.

Fitch laughed. "He's finding it a little... how shall I put it? Testing? Is that fair? Testing? *Trying*, is maybe a better word."

I then watched, appalled, as Damo reached into his rucksack and pulled out a half-empty bottle of Jack Daniels — presumably purchased at Schiphol when they got off the plane — and refilled his hip flask. I glanced around the café to see if Damo's unseemly behaviour had been observed. I then turned to Fitch, hoping for some sign of reciprocated disapproval. Instead Fitch just winked at me for some reason and held out his coffee cup for Damo to spike with whiskey.

When I refused the proffered flask, Damo grimaced before finally getting round to my question: "It's a fucking nightmare if you want the truth. Having a second kid was the second-biggest mistake I ever made. First-biggest was having a first. They suck the life out of you. They're like tumours with hair. Cheers."

He lifted his coffee cup to Fitch, who clinked it with his own and they both drank.

Damo made a toast. "Here's to a couple of days of total fucking debauchery."

I sighed. He was such a cliché.

After their breakfast of black pudding and Jack Daniels, Damo and Fitch decided they should "break the weed seal". In an effort to put off the inevitable demise in sensible conversation, I suggested we hire a couple of bicycles first. "It's by far the best w-"

"Yeah yeah," Damo cut in. "Bicycles schmicycles."

"Excuse me?"

"Maybe tomorrow?" said Fitch. "We were thinking today we might just relax and, you know…."

"Get totally fucking mashed," Damo suggested.

Fitch twinkled. "Yeah, exactly. What do you think?"

I glared. "It doesn't really matter what I think, does it?"

"Yeah, of course it does." Clearly able to observe the horror in my eyes, Fitch put his hand on my shoulder and held my gaze. "We don't wanna be a problem for you, Wesley. We really appreciate you putting us up and looking after us while we're here. Don't we, Damo?"

"Yeah, yeah, course, mate. Fucking...."

"And we don't just wanna, you know, storm in and take over. We wanna be respectful and considerate, you know?"

"Alright." I was appreciative. "Good."

"But also," Fitch continued. "At least today, we wanna just chill out and..."

"Get totally fucking mashed," Damo repeated.

So I walked them in the direction of Siberië, which I knew to be a nearby coffeeshop of considerable charm and quality. On the way, we passed one of Amsterdam's many Bulldog outlets and as soon as he saw the snarling teeth of the cartoon dog, Damo started to head towards the door.

"This'll do," he chirruped.

"Alright, but they're not the cheapest," I pointed out, "and not exactly renowned for their quality."

"Quality schmality," said Damo.

I tensed. A rush of fury made me stop in the street to gather myself. They'd been in Amsterdam for an hour and already I was getting bad ideas about Damo. Fitch noticed and once again placed a hand on my shoulder. "Don't worry, Wesley. He's still a bit wound up. He'll calm down in a minute, I promise."

"He'd fucking better."

"He will." Fitch gave me another wink and followed Damo into the Bulldog Rock Shop with its laboured 70s vibe.

A very attractive female server greeted us as we entered. I said good morning in Dutch, hoping with my resigned expression to distance myself from Damo. The server, however, blanked me entirely and to my gut-wrenching disgust, seemed almost to light up when Damo spoke to her and thrust his hand across the bar to introduce himself.

Irritatingly, Damo was undeniably attractive to women. Aside from a comely face, he was also a plasterer who spent lots of time in the gym, so he had a very muscular, undeniably enticing physique. Hell, even I was enticed by his physique. To add insult to injury, he then had the temerity to bear a striking resemblance to Matt Damon around the time of *Good Will Hunting*, with pretty green eyes and a dazzling smile that wholly disguised the devil-man that lurked just beneath the surface.

Damo held on to the server's hand much longer than I would ever have dared. He let go once she'd told him her name, which was Loes.

"Loose?" repeated Damo. "I'm very glad to hear it, darling."

Loes laughed and even in the relative dark of the bar, I could see her blush. I sighed and checked my phone. It was just gone noon. If I'd known how much worse the day was going to get, I'd almost certainly have sneaked out of the coffeeshop there and then, and surreptitiously disappeared.

3.3

Out on the street at a large covered table, Damo and Fitch rolled joints and started smoking, occasionally taking furtive nips from Damo's hip flask.

"This is the life," said Fitch.

"I don't know how Dutch people ever manage to get anything done," said Damo.

I rolled my eyes. This was not the first time I'd heard an English person make the rather small-minded assumption that because marijuana is tolerated in the Netherlands, all Dutch people must therefore be stoned from morning till night.

"Actually, Dutch people don't smoke much at all," I pointed out.

"That's bullshit, mate," said Damo.

"It's not bullshit, Damo." I tensed. "And can I ask you something? While you're here, while we're spending time together — do you mind trying not to be quite so incredibly rude all the time?"

Damo was nonplussed. He made an innocent face and looked at Fitch like he couldn't quite believe his ears. "Am I rude?" he asked Fitch.

"Well, you are a little bit... I don't know if *rude* is the right word."

"No, it definitely is," I interjected. "In fact, I'm going to stick with *incredibly rude*, as I said."

Fitch and Damo both giggled like stoned people.

"Like telling me what I'm saying is bullshit or dismissing everything I say with the Yiddish schmiddish thing. That's *really* fucking aggravating."

161

"Aggravating schmaggravating," said Fitch. They both cracked up.

"Oh, *et tu*, Fitch." I shook my head. "Brilliant."

"Sorry, Wesley." He slapped Damo's arm. "Yeah, come on, you. Stop being a dick. Wesley's been here for — how many years now? Three years?"

"Almost three."

"So it stands to reason he might just know a bit more about what goes on here than you do, yeah?"

"Yeah, I'm sorry, man. I was just winding you up."

"He's just a bit overexcited," said Fitch. "Aren't you?"

"I am," Damo agreed, holding out his hand as a peace offering. "I'm overexcited."

I took his hand. Damo squeezed it too hard and handed me a joint. I smoked for a moment and passed the joint to Fitch. Then I said: "It's about ten per cent, of the Dutch population, that smoke weed. About half as many as in the States and the UK."

"Isn't that interesting?" said Fitch.

"Dutch people are pretty conservative on the whole. And they have no problem getting stuff done."

"Well, there you go," said Fitch. "Spoken like a true tour guide. You hear that, Damo? Makes you think, doesn't it?"

But Damo wasn't interested. Instead he was initiating a conversation with two younger Dutch guys who were sitting further down the table.

"Any idea where I could get something a little bit stronger?" That had been his opener.

"What did you have in mind?" said one of the young Dutch guys in an American accent. Damo tapped an index finger on the side of his nose. "How much?" Damo showed him two fingers.

162

"Two grams?" Damo nodded. "One hundred." Damo nodded again. "Give me ten minutes."

"I'm going nowhere," said Damo and both Dutch guys got up from the table and slinked off around the Brouwersgracht. Then Damo looked at me and said: "You gonna tell me there's not a lot of coke here and all?"

I rolled my eyes and drank the last of my cold coffee. I was trying to relax, trying not to shake my head and get pissed off with Damo because it was barely noon and apparently Jack Daniels and weed were not enough for him. It wasn't my business. I took a slow deep breath.

"Oh he knows about the coke business in Amsterdam," said Fitch with a gleam. "Don't ya?"

I was confused. "Do I?"

"Oh don't be so coy. Tell him about the coke dealer you murdered."

The penny dropped. "*Ohhhh*. Well, I didn't know he was a coke dealer at the time, to be fair."

"Whoa whoa whoa whoa whoa," said Damo. "Back up a sec. Who murdered a coke dealer? *Him?*" He hooked a thumb at me.

"Don't say it like that," I cried, instinctively, suddenly very stoned. "Like I'm so shit I couldn't murder a man. I murder men. Alright?"

Fitch started giggling.

"Oh yeah?" said Damo. "What men d'you murder?"

"I murdered a man just a couple of weeks ago as it goes," I said, regretting it immediately.

Fitch looked into my eyes and stopped giggling.

"I didn't mean to," I said.

I told the story of the angry Sri Lankan for the first time. Fitch looked it up online to confirm it.

"Respect," said Damo. "You fucking… ultimate revenge, mate. You owned him."

"No!" I cried. "I don't… you can't be happy that somebody died — somebody's dad, and his son's in the front seat. That's horrible!"

Damo shrugged. "You taught him a lesson, mate. Cunt cut you up. You killed his dad. End of."

I was speechless.

"So anyway, that's not even the first person he's killed this year," Fitch pointed out. "Tell him about the wasp, dude."

I sighed. I didn't want it to seem like I was boasting, because I definitely wasn't. However, when I told him the story, Damo was clearly impressed. I'd obviously gone up in his estimations.

"So you've killed two people in the space of a couple of months?"

"I think the word *kill* implies a certain amount of intent," I said. "At best I involuntarily manslaughtered them."

"Yeah whatever," said Damo. Then: "Thing is, he probably had an EpiPen on him. If you'd maybe searched him for his EpiPen, you probably could have saved his life." As he spoke, he opened up the bum-bag that was always wrapped around his waist and produced a pair of fat EpiPens.

"I appreciate you trying to make me feel guilty," I said. "But he had no history of allergies, so he didn't have an EpiPen on him. Why have you got those?"

"Why do you think?"

"You can't just answer a simple question, can you?"

"Can I not?"

"He's got food allergies," said Fitch.

"*Violent* food allergies," Damo added.

I smiled.

"I can't be in the same room as a nut."

I laughed. A lot. I was *delighted* by this news. "What? A big strong lad like you, afraid of a little peanut?"

"Yeah, it's far from fucking funny," he insisted. "I've nearly died like, half a dozen times."

"Trust me," I said. "It's *hilarious*."

Fitch laughed. "It *is* pretty funny," he admitted. I took a joint from him and laughed *uproariously*. Fitch joined in. "Actually, I'd forgotten just how funny it is."

Damo took another furtive nip of whiskey, his lack of amusement adding fuel to what had become for me a veritable fit of giggling. Eventually I settled down and asked, "So what are you allergic to?"

He didn't look pleased. "Pretty much every type of nut."

Once again, I was destroyed by laughter.

Damo glared at me and shook his head. "Dick."

"You're allergic to dick too? That must make your sex life difficult."

For that remark, Fitch followed up a high five of appreciation with a fist-bump of appreciation. Grinning wildly, I accepted both.

"What else though?" I asked. "Anything else?"

"Yeah, as it happens. Shellfish, latex and red wine. Alright? Happy now?"

I gave a silent thumbs-up, cheeks puffed and mouth tight shut, just about holding in smoke and laughter. When I finally, slowly exhaled, one of the two Dutchmen returned and sidled up next to Damo.

"So how's tour guiding?" Fitch asked me. "You still loving it?"

As Fitch and I caught up, Damo took his purchase inside to the coffeeshop toilet, emerging moments later looking satisfied. Back at the table. he delved into his bum-bag and passed over a couple of fifties. Then he took out his phone and swapped details with his new friend.

"Damo," said Damo. "D - A - M - O."

And I believe it was in that precise moment that I first imagined pouring a packet of peanuts into Damo's open mouth.

3.4

Half an hour later we were back at mine. I led them through to the large living room with the two sofas. Fitch pointed. "We can kip there."

"Deal," I said. Nix's room was also available as Nix was away for the weekend, but no, sofas would suffice. "Right. There: toilet. There: kitchen. There…" I gestured to the view: "Amstel Bay. There…" I glanced down at Damo, who was already emptying a wrap of coke onto the glass coffee table in the middle of the room. "…barbarian."

"I do like Amstel Bay," said Fitch, staring across the street at the bulging belly of water at the base of the Amstel. "You've done well for yourself."

"Yeah, I guess so." I thanked him, grateful for the moment of mindfulness. I had done well for myself. I was doing a job I loved in a city I adored and I was paying a relative pittance for an apartment in a place that didn't even exist. Nix had invented Amstel Bay almost a decade previously. Whenever he was required to use his postal address, he would end it with Amstel Bay, Amsterdam. When one day he received an Amstel Bay letter from the Gemeente, he knew he'd done it. He'd invented a place.

"'Ere," said Damo, "fucking… get your snorting gear round that."

I sighed. I do not care for cocaine. For me, it's an ego drug rather than an empathy drug, and for that reason I disdain it. I also rather disdain cocaine-and-lager-fuelled conversation. If more than two people are involved, it's basically Hungry Hippos with spit and empty words. However, I am also a hopelessly weak man who finds it impossible not to partake of whatever narcotic is being offered. Would I smoke crack cocaine if it were offered? A very

167

large part of me would definitely not want to, but if I had the day off, of course I would. To be sociable, I'd say, but really it was morbid, chronic, pathological FOMO.

So we gathered around the low coffee table and Damo proceeded to rack up line after line of cocaine, followed by reason after reason why I should absolutely hide his EpiPens, fill his pockets with nuts and crab, wrap him up in latex and leave him in a pool of red wine to swell up and die.

I learned, for example, that Damo had been in a relationship with his girlfriend (and the mother of two of his children) for four years, and in that time he'd slept with around "twenty or thirty" other women. His girlfriend knew about a couple of them but he promised her each time, it would never happen again. "I honestly think she believes me." He laughed.

I learned that Damo was 30 years old and had slept with at least fifty sex workers, or, as Damo, just like my dear father, insisted upon calling them, "whores".

I learned that Damo had come to Amsterdam with but three principle goals in mind: the first was to become intoxicated in as many ways as humanly possible; the second was to "fuck a couple of whores"; and the third was… Damo's little joke. He had but two goals.

To my mind, Damo was another example of the tourist who everybody hates, the archetypal bad traveller — bad non-traveller too. His travel status was irrelevant. He was just bad. A wrong 'un.

A short way into this session — I think it was when he said something about immigrants — I decided I should start surreptitiously recording our conversations. I just wanted proof that Damo was real and I wasn't actually having a horrible nightmare.

On that first afternoon he expressed hateful opinions on immigrants — who perhaps unsurprisingly, he thought were treated far too well by the British government, to the point that "all the homeless people in Brighton are English, when most of the plastering jobs I've got these days are for Indians. How is that fair?"; Donald Trump — "I much prefer him to any of those other cunts — at least you get a laugh with Trump"; and Anne Frank. The conversation about Anne Frank, however, deserves a chapter all of its own.

3.5

Here you go. A short one-act play: *The Barbarian*. We open in an Amsterdam living room, October 17, 2019. Although he won't realise it for months to come, the Tour Guide (Me) is offering the Barbarian (Damo) salvation. Fitch (Fitch) is also present.

> **Me**: So you don't want to do anything else while you're here? No museums, for example? You know Amsterdam has got like, seventy-five museums?
>
> **Damo**: Jog on. What the fuck?
>
> **Me**: [stoical] What about the Anne Frank House? Have you got no interest…?
>
> **Damo**: [to Fitch] Is he winding me up or what? You're having a fucking laugh, mate. I couldn't give a bollocks.
>
> **Me**: You've seriously got zero interest in the Anne Frank House?
>
> **Damo**: What?
>
> **Me**: You've read the book though, right? *The Diary of Anne Frank*? You probably read it when you were a kid?
>
> **Damo**: No, mate.
>
> **Me**: You do know the story though? I mean, you know who Anne Frank was, right?
>
> **Damo**: Nope.
>
> **Me**: [After a genuinely shocked pause] You don't know who Anne Frank is?
>
> **Fitch**: Yes, you do. You know Anne Frank. He's winding you up, Wesley.

Damo: I'm fucking not! I don't know no fucking Anne fucking Frank and I've told you I don't give a flying fuck!

Me: Whoa, whoa, say that again. I gotta write that down. [grabbing a pen] "I don't know no fucking Anne fucking Frank..." What was the rest?

Damo: Yeah, yeah, yeah. Who the fuck is she?

Me: Damo, Anne Frank was the teenage girl who was in hiding from the Nazis because she was Jewish. Here in Amsterdam, this was, in a house just twenty minutes away. Her and her entire family, hiding in a few rooms for two years during the Second World War. [Beat] Damo, have you heard of the Second World War? [Beat as Damo silently raises a middle finger] For *two years*, they never left the house. Eight of them were living in these secret rooms behind a wall, in tiny cramped conditions, terrified of even making a noise, not even able to see daylight, for *two full years* — and then, just a few weeks before the war ended, someone told the Nazis where they were, and they were all taken away, and seven of them were killed in concentration camps.

Damo: [taking a break from rolling a joint to rub together a thumb and forefinger] You see this? World's smallest violin, mate. [Fitch laughed; I shot him daggers]

Me: [to Damo] Seriously?

Damo: We've all got our fucking problems, mate.

Me: *You* certainly have.

171

Damo: Tell me about it. You don't know the fucking half of it.

Me: I can't believe you've got daughters.

Damo: Fuck's that supposed to mean?

Me: It just doesn't seem like you deserve them, or maybe I'm wrong. Maybe they'll teach you. Maybe they're a blessing.

Damo: Blessing? You *must* be joking. I was so fucked off when I found out they was girls, I tell you. Kim refused to find out. She was scared that if it *was* a girl I'da pushed her down the stairs. I fucking would've an all.

Me: [to Fitch] Are you...? Can you hear this? Are you alright with this?

Fitch: He's winding you up, Wesley. Honestly, don't take him seriously.

Damo: You know who I fucking hate?

Me: Everyone?

Damo: Fucking feminists.

Me: Oh, fuck off. Don't. Seriously. That's enough.

Damo: What? Don't tell me you *like* feminists?

Me: What are you *talking* about? I *am* a feminist. I proudly identify as a feminist and anyone who doesn't is quite clearly retarded. Fitch, for fucksake, tell him. You're a feminist, right?

Fitch: Well, I wouldn't say I was a *feminist*, exactly. I mean, obviously, I support equality for the sexes, but....

Me: But that's what feminism is!

Fitch: Well, hold on....

Damo: All feminists are blue-haired, man-hating cunts. End of.

Me: [Bewildered pause] How is this happening?

Curtain.

3.6

At around 2pm, we made for the Oudezijds Achterburgwal and sat in a nasty pub for a couple of hours, during which time I felt increasingly disappointed by Fitch and his lack of support. After which, Fitch and Damo went out to eat, and I went home for a lie down. Or so I said. In reality, I just had to get away. I said I'd join them later, but equally, I might not.

The walk home was a drunk and angry one. A thin drizzle fell across my face and I felt ashamed of myself for wasting time on such a gargantuan sack of human garbage. I was angry with Fitch too. I couldn't understand why he'd voluntarily spend time with someone so relentlessly hateful, when Fitch himself was anything but. I also felt a certain amount of responsibility for Amsterdam. Damo after all, was my guest, ostensibly, so I felt at least partially responsible. I felt that if Damo misbehaved, it was up to me, Wesley Bell, to knock him back into line.

At some point, I passed a FEBO, a Dutch fast food outlet that sold variations on the theme of tasty paste in breadcrumbs. One variation is the Satékroket. It looks exactly the same as all the other krokets, but it's packed full of peanut. I stopped.

Staring into the window of the FEBO, I replayed all the hideous things I'd heard thus far from Damo's mouth. I thought of the homeless person he'd teased by stopping close by and faking like he was going to make a contribution, before changing his mind and moving on. I'd given the guy a fiver to make amends, but Damo's wickedness remained.

I walked into the FEBO.

I thought about what I was doing. For longer than a minute, I stood and I thought. Then I bought one ordinary FEBO meat kroket and one potentially fatal Satékroket. I took them both home and examined them in the kitchen. They were identical, except for one thing: one of them could kill Damo. If he were to accidentally eat it, or even, by all accounts, brush up against it, and of course, not have access to one of his EpiPens....

I placed both krokets on a plate in the fridge and buried the wrapping at the bottom of the bin. If Damo was to help himself to something that was not his, without asking, then... that was just fate, right? That was the Universe doing its thing and Damo would have to suffer the consequences.

I went online and discovered that it was actually the protein in nuts that made the phobics swell up and die. I also found something called peanut protein concentrate, which must be like kryptonite for the likes of Damo.

I glanced around the living room. What if I planted a single peanut beneath each sofa cushion? This would test the veracity of Damo's claim that he couldn't be in the same room as a nut. It would be like a real-life update of *The Princess and the Pea*.

The Plasterer and the Peanut.

Then I suffered an enormous wave of doubt and shame and *Oh my God what on earth am I doing?*

I stood up and went to the kitchen fridge. I took out both krokets and ate them, one after the other, making wholly involuntary noises of appreciation as I did so.

I then cleared my search history, closed my laptop and shook my head violently. I berated myself. What if I did actually hide Damo's EpiPens and somehow get him to ingest peanut protein? Then what? If he did swell up and die, would I be happy with that? That would, after all, be murder. Technically. And if it all came to light, along with Matty Sutcliffe, they might start calling me The Anaphylactic Shocker.

That thought made me smile, and I relaxed.

Everything was fine. Nothing had happened. Sure I'd come closer than ever before to altering my stance on the fundamental question of the perceived value of human life, but I'd resisted. Sure I'd bought a nutty snack, but I'd eaten it, and washed my hands. I'd wavered, and no one could blame me for that, but then I'd made a conscious decision not to go down that road. For that is not who I was.

I breathed a sigh of relief. It was only two nights. I could survive 48 hours of infantile fascist pronouncements, and so could Amsterdam. We'd both be fine. Damo would be fine too. He'd get fucked up, and then he'd be on his way. Just so long as he didn't say anything else to prove his utter, utter worthlessness. Because if he did that, I'd probably kill him.

3.7

The first night ended in a club where the music was so unspeakably soulless that I lasted only twenty minutes. Leaving the club, however, and stepping out into the relative quiet of the Leidseplein gave rise to such feelings of almost overwhelming euphoria that I actually considered paying the ten-euro entry fee a second time, just to experience leaving all over again. But I'm not *quite* that mad. So I went home.

On hearing the first signs of life around 10 the next morning, I descended to the living room, expecting the worst. I saw Fitch, flicking through an Amsterdam guide book and smoking his first joint of the day, but Damo was nowhere to be seen.

"He copped off with someone," Fitch explained. "Went back to some bird's house."

"Copped off? Some bird? What are you, from the twentieth century?"

"I am," said Fitch, who'd be forty in three weeks. "I'm an old man, man."

"Do you dare eat a peach?"

"Oooh, I could murder a peach."

In lieu of a peach, we went out for coffee and croissants on the Spuistraat. Pleased to have some time alone with him, I asked Fitch if he'd met anyone recently, potential partner-wise. He said he'd had a couple of flings but nothing significant. He blamed himself. "I'll never meet anyone who shines a light on Nathalie. Is that the expression? And I'm not even sure I want to, to be honest. I've kind of given up."

"No!" I cried. "Come on, man. You've no idea what the future holds. I command you not to give up on it."

He laughed and agreed, in theory. "I just don't see it. That's all."

"You don't need to see it, Fitch. It'll see you." I nodded smugly, like I'd said something awfully clever. "Speaking of seeing things, what on earth do you see in Damo?"

"Aww, he's a good lad deep down," he replied. "People like you bring out the worst in him."

I bristled at that. "What, you mean people who give a shit?"

"Yeah, basically."

Fitch insisted that Damo was generous and decent and on balance, a good person. He said he didn't agree with most of his opinions on immigration and gender relations, for example, but he didn't think that Damo really held those opinions anyway. "He's a contrary person," he explained. "Like Jeremy Clarkson. But he's alright, I swear."

I was not convinced.

"He's an amazing plasterer," he added.

"That may be true," I conceded. "But is he good enough to plaster over the cracks in his own personality? Eh? Eh?"

Fitch's phone began to vibrate against his coffee cup. He picked it up. "Speak of the Devil." There then followed a concise and functional back and forth. "He's on his way."

"Awesome," I intoned.

"Oh come on, Wesley."

I sighed. "I know, I know. I don't wanna be a twat about it, I just…. Don't you wish he was a little bit nicer?"

Fitch started nodding before the words came. He admitted that he did. He admitted he'd been embarrassed by many of Damo's utterances so far on this trip. When he slagged his own family off, for example, Fitch felt particularly aggrieved. "I'd give my right arm for what he's got." He even admitted that once or twice he wished he'd come alone.

Feeling incredibly relieved, I thanked him. "Seriously, that's gonna make the rest of today a lot easier for me to get through. Just knowing I'm not alone. I appreciate it, Fitch. Now…" I slapped the table. "…what's all this about you not being a feminist?"

Fitch laughed and we got into it slightly, dropping it deftly as Damo arrived.

At Damo's suggestion, we adjourned to a nearby coffeeshop. As I was working at 1.30, I refused the joint when it was offered. I knew from experience that marijuana was not at all conducive to the focus required by tour guiding.

"You're such a woman," Damo told me.

"Thank you," I said. "That's the nicest thing you've said since you arrived."

"Let's have it then," said Fitch. "The juicy details."

"A gentleman never tells." Damo smirked. "Me on the other hand, what do you wanna know?" He guffawed.

I checked the time. My plan was to leave after my coffee to run some imaginary errands. Until then, I found myself silently beseeching Damo not to say anything too hideous. Of course, even if Damo could somehow have picked up on my silent entreaties, he would never have complied. Indeed, there was every chance he'd have doubled down, daring me to take him on.

There then followed some common or garden infantile sex boasting as Damo, with unnecessary crudeness and not so much as a scintilla of respect, compared his girlfriend, 32 years old and the mother of two of his children, to his latest conquest, 19 years old and childless. Unsurprisingly, the focus of his comparative analysis was anatomical and deeply personal. He spoke in laddish euphemism, which at times took on an almost poetic quality. Even

179

at its most inventive, however — even when he invoked the ears of mice, the eyes of Japanese soldiers, pelicans yawning and toothpicks floating through space — nothing could paper over the misogyny. So I blocked it out. It was not my problem. It was almost over.

It was just gone 11 when Damo went to the loo and I told Fitch: "OK, that's my cue. I'm off to work. I'll come find you around 8, OK?"

"Oh come on, Wesley, stay a little longer. We'll talk about something else, I promise. You haven't got to be at work till 1.30. Come on, mate." He made a face. "Please?"

I laughed.

It was a moment. A freeze-frame. If the whole of my life had been captured on CCTV and pored over by social historians, they would isolate this particular moment and discuss it at length. It was significant.

For had Fitch not been quite so persuasive; had he just let me leave the bar and forget all about Damo, things would have been very different.

3.8

"I'm gonna ask you one more thing about last night," said Fitch on Damo's return, "then we'll change the subject."

"Change the subject now if you want, mate. You're the one banging on about it."

"Alright, spiky, keep your hair on. I just wanna know: were you safe?"

Damo laughed. "Jog on, mate. What do you reckon? I'm allergic to latex, innit. It's bareback with me, or don't bother, mate."

"Oh, *Damo.*" Fitch was disappointed. "There are non-latex condoms. You know that, right?"

"*I* do, yeah. They usually don't."

"What about pregnancy and disease?" I asked.

"Not my problem."

"Well… *yeah*," I insisted. "How could they not be your problem?"

"Alright, if I caught a disease, that'd be problematic, I grant you. I'd get round it though. Kim'd never leave me. I wouldn't let her. Anyway, I'm not gonna catch anything 'cause I don't go with skanks."

I was paying close attention, the list in my mind, the justification list, growing longer and longer. On the back of this conversation, I found myself wondering if Damo really had allergies. I started to suspect he'd feigned the latex allergy just to get out of using condoms. Nuts, red wine and seafood were probably just three things he didn't like, so he'd invented a story to make himself seem human. He probably stole the EpiPens.

"How is an unwanted pregnancy not your problem?"

"Well, I'll never see them again, will I? I never make any connections. No Facebook, none of that shit. And I make damn fucking sure they don't know my name."

"What do you mean?" said Fitch. "You introduce yourself as Damo. I've heard you."

"Yeah, *Damo* short for *Damon* innit. *Damon* as in *Matt Damon*." He gave a broad smile.

Fitch laughed. "What? You tell them you're Matt Damon?"

"Not *the* Matt Damon obviously, although if they're dumb enough to believe I *am the* Matt Damon, I allow them that."

He did look disturbingly like Matt Damon. Fitch, however, was buying none of this. He laughed. "He's winding us up."

"Am I fuck," said Damo. "Have you never seen this?" He reached into his jacket pocket and handed over a folded piece of paper. "I've got a copy on my phone as well, but paper seems more official."

Fitch examined the document, shaking his head. Looking distraught, he handed it to me.

The document was addressed to Mr Matt Damon at a fictional address in London. It was from a fictional doctor on Harley Street confirming that Mr Damon's vasectomy operation had been a success and recommending various options for palliative care, including specific painkillers and emergency telephone numbers. It seemed very professional and was dated July 2018.

"Works a treat," said Damo. "Convinces them they're never gonna get pregnant and it's a piece of cake to convince someone you've got no diseases. Usually I tell them I haven't had sex since my wife died."

At which point, my sociopath divining rod burst into flames.

I'd previously had Damo pegged as a run-of-the-mill racist misogynist with narcissistic tendencies, but much of what I heard that morning stank to high heaven of weapons-grade sociopathy.

I wanted to be sure though, so I thought I'd run a final check. All I needed was just a trace, just a single solitary spore of common or garden humanity, and I swore I'd back off and do nothing.

"What if someone treated your daughters that way?"

It was the olive branch of empathy.

Take it, Damo. Please take it.

Damo shrugged. "More fool them for taking some dodgy cunt at his word, I'd say. If they don't have the mental equipment… yeah? If they're not on the ball enough to suss out the wankers, then they get what's coming to them, don't they? Survival of the fittest."

"So…." I was struggling to formulate my objections; there were just so many of them. "Don't you want to help protect your daughters from men — well, from men like you I suppose? Don't you want to educ-"

"That's Kim's job, mate. I'm not interested."

"But they're *your* kids!"

"They are my kids," said Damo, "but… fuck me, you are very tedious." My mouth, once again, fell open. "I never wanted them, mate. They're a pain in my fucking arse and they cost me an arm and a leg. To be honest, the only straight-up decent thing about them is, they're brilliant for pulling. You'd be surprised how many times Matt Damon has got his dick wet just by flashing a coupla photos of his kids." He pulled out his wallet. In the photo, Damo and his daughters, aged 2 and 3, both of them hanging onto his chest and laughing. Him also laughing. "Of course in this scenario, Kim's dead, which doesn't hurt, if I'm honest. They love a widower."

I felt sick. Fitch too, looked similarly dejected.

"Do you even love them?" I asked.

Take it, Damo.

He laughed again. "I fucking pay for 'em, mate. That's all you need to concern yourself with."

"Fair enough." I grabbed my jacket and tossed a fiver on the table to cover my coffee. "I've heard enough."

"We'll see you later, yeah?" Fitch was clearly concerned he'd never see me again after this latest hateful outburst. But he needn't have worried.

"You will, mate. I promise you. I'm working till 7. I'll come find you by 9 at the latest."

"You better had, yeah. We're back home tomorrow."

"Mate," I said, holding Fitch's gaze. "I wouldn't miss it for the world." Before I left the coffeeshop, I said: "Pace yourselves, yeah?"

Pace themselves, they did not.

Ultimately, it was impossible to say exactly what Damo had ingested by the end of the day. "Everything he could get his hands on" was accurate, certainly, but also, equally, the very height of ambiguity.

When he later came to replay the day, it being done, Fitch could recall the following with absolute clarity: one joint each in Kandinsky mid-morning, plus one piece of vanilla space-cake each before leaving; two pints of lager with burgers for lunch; two beers each with their post-prandial constitutional in the Vondelpark; half a pack of truffles each at around 4pm; an indistinct amount of MDMA each at 5.30, scraped from the paper wrap Damo had inadvertently smuggled over in his wallet. Then a haze began to descend in his memory.

184

He remembered Damo ordering a couple more grams of coke, "to straighten us out". The coke arrived just before I turned up at ten past nine. He remembered me saying: "You had one job: pace yourselves. Look at the state of you." He also remembered a row with a group of Moroccans but only really, really vaguely. After that, he remembered fighting with Damo because Damo "went nuts". Then Damo staggered off. That's all he could recall.

I on the other hand, remember everything.

I remember, for example, why the Moroccans were pissed off. It was because they'd overheard Damo using the word *jihad* in a loud and deliberately provocative manner. When challenged, Damo followed up by declaring with blithe belligerence that Islam was nothing more than "a paedophile death cult". This was outside the Waterhole on the Korte Leidsedwarsstraat and it was everything I could do to placate the Moroccans and drag Damo away and stick him in a chair.

I corralled them in a corner seat outside of Eijlders. I established that they were both *compos mentis*. "Fine, mate," snapped Damo. "Get 'em in."

"Good." I got 'em in.

I returned with a tray that had three small Dutch beers and three shots. I sat down and handed out the shots. "You probably shouldn't have this," I said to Damo. "State you're in, it might send you over the edge."

Damo gurned at me, holding up his shot at head height. "Up yours, mate." He necked it.

"He didn't wait for the toast," I said. "Allow me. Here's to a delightful weekend in Amsterdam, and what was it you said yesterday? Getting more cunted than ever before. Here's to that."

"Cunted!" said Fitch, and we downed our shots.

Idle conversation ensued. Spurred on by Fitch, I told a few stories about tour guiding. I was on good form, as I recall. Alas, my form, and indeed my peculiar excitability, were both wasted on Fitch and Damo.

Damo was starting to zone out when I glanced at my watch and nipped inside for a pee. Then, when I got back outside, neither Fitch nor Damo were anywhere to be seen.

3.9

I looked up and down the street and spotted them in conversation on the edge of the Leidseplein. Damo was swaying and gesticulating wildly. I took my seat. I felt a bit sick but… it was done. Now it was in the hands of Damo and the Universe.

When Fitch returned a few minutes later, he looked angry.

"He just went fucking nuts, man."

Apparently, as soon as I'd gone inside, Damo had suddenly stood up and declared, "This is fucking bullshit!" before storming off up the street. When Fitch caught him up and asked what was wrong, Damo slapped him hard across the face. With his instinct to protect his friend taking precedence over his instinct to retaliate, Fitch tried again to get through to him, but Damo was becoming more and more erratic. All Fitch remembered was that he couldn't make sense of their conversation and eventually Damo snapped, "How about you just fuck off and leave me alone?"

So he did. And Damo staggered off into the Leidseplein.

Protective to the end, Fitch shouted after him, "Don't lose your phone!"

Back at Eijlders, I tried to comfort him. "He just needs a bit of time to get his head together, I reckon. He's a big boy. He'll be fine."

"Yeah, I hope so. I've just never seen him that bad before."

Ten minutes later we heard a woman scream in the distance. We wondered if it might be Damo-related. Should we go check, or was that insane? It was a city after all, and a crazy one at that. People screamed all the time. When we heard another two screams in quick succession, however, we left our beers and quick-walked down to the Leidseplein.

A crowd of onlookers had formed around the front of a stalled tram. As we got closer, we noticed people crying and at least two vomiting into the street. The sound of approaching sirens was punctuated with fresh screams. Two plainclothes policemen were clearing the area, holding people back, but it was still very easy to see what had happened.

The first thing I noticed was that the front of the tram was slightly raised up into the air, as if something was trapped under the wheel. The second thing I noticed was Damo, trapped under the wheel.

After staring for a moment in absolute horror, I approached one of the young women I'd seen vomiting. I'd also noticed her boyfriend taking a crafty photo of Damo's dead body. They looked around 19 or 20. I asked the woman what she'd seen, realising immediately she'd been the perfect person to ask.

She was a Londoner, and was very happy to talk. "We was standin' literally two metres away from him when he just started screamin' at me an 'im." She cocked a thumb at her boyfriend behind her. "I couldn't make out much of what he was sayin' to be honest but he just sounded mental."

"He was shoutin', 'Keep away from me, keep the fuck away from me' at one point," the boyfriend chipped in.

"Then he walloped that girl over there." She gestured to a small Indian girl who was talking to one of the plainclothes officers. "Just cracked her one and ran face first into that tram." She pointed, slightly unnecessarily, at the tram. "Only it wasn't face first, was it? He went in wiv 'is bollocks."

"Yeah, he sort of tried to slide under it, like in *Watchmen*?"

"The Lube Man! Yeah, he was like the Lube Man!"

My heart was pounding. I felt like I was dreaming, or like it was me that was tripping.

More police arrived, but before I was moved on, I managed to get a good look at Damo's body, or what was left of it.

Giant glistening skidmarks of blood and squashed and smeared intestines clearly delineated the moment of impact. You could see that Damo had been trapped under the tram's iron wheels and dragged a couple of metres to a stop.

In that couple of metres, his entire body seemed to have been turned inside out at least once. One of his legs was off, as were his jeans. Only one bare leg and half of his face seemed intact. Most of his top half was reduced to an eviscerated torso, the bones of his ribcage, beautifully symmetrical, snapped and splayed apart like a battered Venus flytrap.

I saw that Fitch was crouched down behind a police cordon, his head in his hands. "Let's go," I said, helping him up and leading him away from the square. Fitch allowed himself to be led, very much in a daze, tears streaming down his cheeks. We blended in with the crowd — the tourists and gangs of morbid rubberneckers — wading through them, not looking back. We didn't say much. "I'm guessing you don't want to talk to the police yet," I said.

"God, no. I want a cup of tea."

So we went home and I made a big pot of soothing fennel tea, which we drank in the dark in the living room, not saying much, staring down at oblivious Amstel Bay.

"It's a beautiful city." Fitch's voice was a tear-sodden croak.

"Amen," I said. "And there's so much more to Amsterdam than drugs and sex."

"Is that something you say on your tour?"

I smiled. "Yep. Well spotted."

"Sorry we never found time to come on your tour today, man."

"That's alright. Maybe you'll come out another time."

"I will," said Fitch. "I definitely will."

3.10

First thing Sunday morning, Fitch found a seat on an evening flight, giving us ample time to make statements to the police and discuss what was going to happen with what remained of Damo's body. We also took his stuff to the morgue. Damo's dad and a couple of his uncles were flying in to Amsterdam the next day.

That didn't feel good.

Regarding what we should say to the police, Fitch and I had prepped beforehand. We agreed he should confess not only to alcohol, truffles and weed, all of which were tolerated, but also to cocaine, which was not. It was in Damo's pocket at the time of the accident, after all, along with Matt Damon's vasectomy confirmation, so if it had survived the devastation of the tram, it was knowledge they already had. May as well go in open. Or at least appear to.

I couldn't imagine they'd bother analysing tissue from his corpse. There were enough eye-witness accounts, as well as CCTV footage, to see what had happened. Some idiot tourist had taken too much of whatever, freaked out, punched an ethnic minority, then lost a reality fight with a tram. Open and shut case of death by misadventure. It was the go-to verdict for any death where substances were involved. Generally, I resented death by misadventure, as a verdict, because it solved nothing and it sounded like the name of a rather dark boat, but in this particular case, it felt right.

We had lunch at an Indonesian restaurant, because we had to eat, then we made our way to the airport in the late afternoon, leaving ample time for a goodbye drink in a sterile airport bar.

We were both still in something of a daze.

Over and over again Fitch said, "I still can't believe it." Then, lifting his watery Guinness to eye-level: "Let's drink a toast to him, Wesley."

I cleared my throat. "May his daughters prosper in his absence."

"Fucking hell, Wesley." Anger flashed across his face.

I apologised and tried again. "May his girlfriend find the kind of love she deserves, and may his daughters find an empathetic father, who can give them love and allow them to grow, flourish and thrive."

Fitch shook his head. "Why do you have to make it sound like you're glad to see him go?"

I blew air through my cheeks.

"You don't have to answer."

"No, I think I should. I think I owe it to both of us to own up to it. Getting to know him over the past twenty-four hours or whatever… frankly, if that's all there was to him… I am glad he's gone, yeah."

"Yeah, but that's not all there was, Wesley. That's what I've been saying. He was a decent bloke underneath all that bluster. You have to give me some credit, you know. Why would I spend time with him? Why would I bring him here if I wasn't prepared to vouch for him?"

"Maybe because he was playing you?" I felt bad saying it, but it felt like the truth. "People like him need their anchors in ordinary life to let them get away with the shit they pull. Why do you think he had a family? You heard him say he couldn't give a shit about them. So why bother? Because he's yet another sociopath playing yet another nasty little game. It only occurred to me yesterday morning, with the fake vasectomy letter. Now it seems obvious."

Fitch just sat shaking his head and breathing heavily for a few moments. Then he said: "Well, I'm not glad he's gone."

We both became quite tearful as we hugged goodbye and Fitch promised he'd visit again soon.

On my way back through the airport to the train station, I was searching for my travelcard when my heart missed a beat. The bottle — the little brown dropper bottle that had contained Milton's liquid acid — was still there in my pocket from the night before. Which meant I'd taken it with me into the police station that morning. A shiver of retrospective horror ran through my body and I tossed the bottle into the nearest bin.

Back home, no sign remained of Fitch and Damo, so, as best I could, I pretended nothing had happened, and looked forward to the rest of my life.

For the next week, I went to ground. When I wasn't at work, I stayed in my room. When Nix asked after me, I deflected his concerns lightly and kept him at a distance. I knew I couldn't admit what I'd done — not even to him. If we got chatting though, I was afraid I'd blurt it out like I'd blurted the story of the Tamil torturer to Fitch and Damo. It wasn't that I feared Nix would turn me in; there was little to no chance of that. It was more that I was simply too afraid of what I'd done, and what it might mean, which at that point, was still very unclear. I needed time and space to figure it all out.

I had — there was no denying it — deliberately caused another man's death. It wasn't like I'd pulled a trigger or pushed a blade into someone's guts, but I had been instrumental. And *intentional*. This was no random happenstance, like the incidents with the wasp or the fingers. I had made it happen. And although I genuinely believed — with substantial corroborative evidence — that Damo had been a malign influence in the world, I still had mixed feelings about the whole *murder* thing. After all, society said murder was wrong, and I had been a card-carrying member of society for almost five decades. It was therefore reasonable, after becoming so fully institutionalised, to expect a little resistance to the idea of moving beyond society's rules and expectations. I simply didn't think of myself as a murderer. *Murderer*, as far as I could see, had almost entirely negative connotations. I much preferred to think of what I'd done as a dark necessity and of myself as a positive influence.

Naturally I was assailed constantly with doubts. Whenever I felt guilty and ashamed of what I'd done, however, I simply remembered the conversation that had convinced me. I remembered everything Damo had said about unsafe sex and vasectomies and dead wives, and then once again his loss did not seem so grievous. The world, I felt, was indisputably less dark without him in it.

Therefore, after a week of moping, which I felt was commensurate with a visiting friend being killed in a freak accident, I made a concerted effort to move on. Nothing had changed really. I was still a good guy. I just wasn't necessarily going to put up with terrible behaviour anymore. Not if I didn't have to. We'd see. Life was a game. Love was the answer. And Henk was having a house party. So I decided to go.

I didn't really *want* to go, but… FOMO.

3.11

Henk held a lot of parties. He called them Henksgivings. He had a laughably large apartment on the western side of the Prinsengracht. Lots of space, three rooms, two balconies, bought by his dad in the Sixties, left to Henk, his only child, when Henk was in his early twenties.

"But you know what? If I could swap the apartment for just another couple of years with my dad?" Henk said this a lot. "Naaah. I'd keep the apartment." It was kind of his catchphrase.

Henk knew lots of people. Even if many or most of them might (rather self-importantly) object to the very notion of being labelled, the following types were almost always in evidence at his gatherings: guides, gays, queers, trans folk, non-binaries, actors, dancers, anarchists, activists, artists, theatre types and common or garden freaks. He moved in lots of different circles and his parties were always reliably entertaining.

It was, in fact, at one of Henk's soirees, in my first month at Beachams, that I first saw Sam Lewis in oily predator mode. (*Oily* is exactly the right word, by the way, for Sam has a luscious hipster beard, which he oils shamelessly.) At that point, I'd met him fewer than half a dozen times, but already I had him pegged as "a person of interest", having seen him sell to tourists at The Clurichaun.

At the halfway point of every history tour, Beachams guides would treat their tourists to a well-earned breather in The Clurichaun, a cavernous, yet peculiarly atmosphere-free Irish boozer with stone walls and not quite credible antiquities. It provided an opportunity for tourists to rest their feet and move fluids through their bodies; and for guides to try and catch them off-guard and sell them stuff. Now — Sam selling to tourists. That you should see.

He flits from one to the next, like a dilettante wasp, prying for gaps in itineraries before bullying his way in like a rowdy little truffle pig and washing the tourists' brains with his odious lies.

"Oh my god, you have to take the canal cruise — if you don't, I swear, you will regret it for the rest of your life." He plays it straight, with not a trace of humour, because he knows no other way. "I had a couple last week on a cruise, about the same age as you guys, and they were holding on to each other on the boat, weeping, moved to tears by the beauty of Amsterdam's canals at night. Sobbing with joy, they were. It is *the* single most romantic thing you can do in the whole of Europe. I'm just saying, if you truly love this beautiful woman here and want to treat her to a night you will both remember for the rest of your lives... Well, you know, it's your choice. Do you like art? For one week only, we have discounted tickets to the best modern art exhibition in the whole world. *The New York Times* described it as unmissable, a once-in-a-lifetime opportunity..." And on and on, grinding them down till more often than not, they cave. Sometimes he convinces them; sometimes they just want rid of him. Either way, the sale is his.

Then, at my first Henksgiving, I was standing with my back to Sam and a younger, Spanish-speaking woman, when I overheard the seduction-themed sell.

"My God, I'm not kidding, it's so rare for me to meet a woman who's as bright and interesting and funny as you are, and yet still so stunningly beautiful. I'm serious, I could fall for you in a heartbeat. Just looking at you now, looking into your eyes, the most beautiful, spellbinding, astonishing eyes I think I've ever seen — my God, what are you doing to me? And your hair is so shiny. Could I touch it? Would you mind?"

And that was that. Tiptoes, neck hands, tongues in throats, deeply entwined. As they do with all but the most super-zen pale

195

men with ginger complexions and weak chins, good-looking sociopaths really bring out the worst in me. There's just nothing more upsetting than seeing handsome con-men prosper.

I'd arrived around 10 to this latest Henksgiving, after sharing a bottle of red with myself at home. On arrival, I moved through the usual potpourri of people to the kitchen, where Hamish yelled inanities into my ear and drenched me in spittle. When I managed to escape to the main room, Hamish, like a barnacle, followed.

It was already very busy with upwards of a hundred and fifty people crammed in and bouncing along to what was — or at least it seemed to me — offensively loud music. I always have to physically restrain myself from turning down other people's music at parties.

Loitering at the threshold of the living room, I turned to deal with one of Hamish's indecipherable utterances when I saw Sam, drunk, manoeuvring his way through the packed dance floor, just as he manoeuvres his way through groups of tourists. I immediately became transfixed by him. I'd never seen him so shamelessly predatory before. He was shockingly bold, lurching from one woman to the next. When he found one he liked, he would dance in front of her, staring into her eyes and making sexy faces, which were preposterous to me but which clearly conveyed the intended message. If the woman in question didn't turn away in disgust, Sam would follow up his staring with physical contact. I watched in genuine alarm. I watched him stroking hair, caressing arms or taking hold of hands. I watched him snaking his own hands round women's waists and pulling them towards him. I was appalled. And somewhat confused. Was this normal behaviour? Was this acceptable? Within seconds of dancing next to someone, just grabbing at bits of their body?

Apparently it was, because not one of those women headbutted Sam into unconsciousness or drove a pin into his heart. To my fleeting gratification, however, I did observe two women pull back and totally cold-shoulder him. I saw another dance with him briefly before cutting him dead and leaving the room. Yet another pulled a face that conveyed unadulterated repulsion. Every time this happened, however, without even missing a beat, Sam would simply turn 180 degrees and zone in on the next female that took his fancy. Totally unfazed. Utterly shameless.

I looked away, infuriated. As Hamish had drifted off, I scanned the room for friends. There was no one. No Nix, no Lizzie, no Kras, no Monic— oh wait… Monica was there. With some relief, I spotted her by an open window on the other side of the living room, chatting with Elise. As I set out in her direction, the bodies between us reconfigured and I saw who else she was talking to. Not just Elise, but also… the sociopath Sam Lewis.

I stopped moving, watching in glimpses through the crush of dancers. I watched against my better judgement, as the sociopath took a joint from Monica. Like a begrudging voyeur, unable to stop, I moved my head when other people blocked my view, determined not to miss a second.

I saw Elise excuse herself and the sociopath Sam Lewis lean in and either whisper something into Monica's ear or… maybe even attempt to kiss her? I couldn't be sure. I held my breath.

In response to whatever he'd done or said, Monica wriggled away from him, giggling, one hand resting on his shoulder, either pushing him away or deliberately making flirtatious physical contact. The sociopath Sam Lewis then moved around behind her, swaying to the music, one hand eeling around her waist. Monica turned to face him again, her body moving in the opposite direction to his, seemingly dancing with him. Bodies blocked my

197

view for a second. I moved to get a better view and saw them separating. Had they kissed? Had Monica actually allowed this serpent to kiss her? Had she kissed him back?

Seconds later, all doubts were dispelled as they embarked on a passionate, profligate snog, right there in the living room.

"Oh, Monica."

I was mortified. I felt like I'd observed an erstwhile decent politician taking a bribe, or Noam Chomsky kerbing an infant.

I turned away and left the room and left the house and grabbed my bike and cycled home immediately. As I cycled, my disappointment with Monica turned to disgust. Had she not seen the sociopath? Had she not seen him circling for half an hour like a dog in the street, sniffing at the females' hind quarters and trying to mount them? How could she debase herself this way?

Back home I became a raging tsunami of jealousy and self-loathing. I had nothing in my emotional knapsack to help me deal with what I was feeling, let alone rise above it. So instead I wallowed, for a while, imagining them together and shouting out in terrible torment.

Not *Sam*. Please not Sam.

I lay tense on my bed and considered my options. I could carry on rage-weeping over Monica's betrayal, banging my fists on my knees and screaming about how unfair life is, *or*, I could take control of my emotions, take the bull by the horns, and run the fuck away.

3.12

Less than 24 hours later, I was in Pigneto, the rebel-hipster capital of Rome, rage-weeping over Monica's betrayal, banging my fists on my knees and so on. I'd booked some cheap last-minute flight-n-Airbnb package the night before, taken an inconspicuous rucksack on my morning tour, my last tour for a week, and then, like a thief in the night, I'd cabbed to the airport and disappeared.

By 8.30pm, I was laying tense on a stranger's bed in a city I didn't know, wondering what the fuck I was doing there. Then suddenly I jolted upright and let fly with a loud "Fuck it!" I'd forgotten about Kras! Coin Day. The Day of the Great Reckoning. I wouldn't be back in time.

I felt rotten. I sent a message. "Sorry I won't be able to go to the bank with you. I'm in Rome! I saw Monica kissing Sam and I fled the country. Please don't tell anyone. I hope everything goes super smooth and I'll see you at Christmas if not before. Love you man. Sorry again. I'm an imbecile."

I sent another message immediately afterwards: "The demijohns! Fuck my eyes, I'm worthless! Tell me. Tell me how I must punish myself."

When no immediate response came, I felt more wretched still.

The room was dark. I lay on my back with my hands covering my face, listening to the music of hectic, lively, distinctly self-important Pigneto. Through my open window, the hardiest of the year's cicadas rattled their hibernal deaths as cats, dogs and human families fought over dinner scraps. Plates clattered like brash birdsong, mopeds screeched and sirens wept and wailed. Just outside my window, a passer-by hawked up something of so much substance that it hit the ground like a piece of wet fruit.

Aaaaah, Rome.

Then I spent the entire week walking around and marvelling. Rome was both laughably beautiful and repulsively decrepit. If it seemed less devastated by tourism than Amsterdam, that was merely an illusion created by its size, and if you hung around the Colosseum or the Trevi Fountain, the illusion was quickly dispelled. Also, like any other populous modern city, the side effects of overpopulation and hysterical consumption were all on permanent display, on a daily, ever-worsening loop — air pollution, noise pollution, poverty and trash. Ceaseless tsunamis of trash.

I wandered through all of this aimlessly, losing myself deliberately, hopping on buses and trams at random, enjoying the lack of itinerary, the freedom of being a tourist without a guide. But I could not hide. Everywhere I went, women who looked like Monica plagued me, reminding me why I'd fled the Netherlands in such an infantile, butt-hurt hurry, forcing me to replay fifty times a day that which I could not forget.

I looked up an old journalist friend from London, decided I could love her and was then rejected by her.

I felt so lonely in restaurants that I could no longer chew my food.

On the third afternoon, I received a message from Monica, asking me if I fancied a beer after her Red Light. She didn't know I was in Rome. Nobody knew. Not even Nix, unless Kras had told him. All Nix knew was what I'd messaged on the second day: "I've gone on holiday by mistake. See you next week."

Monica had no idea I'd seen her kissing the sociopath, and that I was now in another country as a direct result. I typed the following message: "Why don't you go for a beer with your sociopath boyfriend?" I deleted it of course. I had to keep

200

reminding myself: *Monica is not my girlfriend. Monica owes me nothing. If Monica wants to sleep with sociopaths, that is entirely Monica's business.* In the end, I sent the following: "I'm in Rome. See you next week."

I spent my penultimate afternoon in Piazza Testaccio, a large public space where all kinds of local people gather and let themselves off the leash. I watched them with great warmth. Children having real-time, actual physical fun with balls and wheels; old men smoking and gossiping; young mums hiding out with their babies, smoking super-thin cigarettes away from prying eyes; people of all ages, transfixed by their handheld devices, both digital and analogue. I watched them all, equally transfixed.

As I watched, the sun moved slowly across the sky, illuminating the first casualties of autumn as they tumbled slowly down and drifted through the square en masse like refugees.

I'd enjoyed my spontaneous break from Amsterdam. Rome had been a tonic, even if I had spent most of my time there wallowing in disgust. I became obsessed by the idea that, unless someone intervenes to make it otherwise, sociopaths prosper. Was it not then one's duty to intervene? Why are we on the planet anyway? Surely it's our duty to make our mark and change the world, for right or wrong. Ideally for right, obviously, but as TS Eliot once said: "It is better to do evil than to do nothing. At least then we exist." Not that I'm pro-evil. On the contrary.

It was whilst pondering such thoughts in Piazza Testaccio that I finally heard back from Kras. "I know you don't need me to tell you how to punish yourself!" he wrote. "Don't do it, Wesley! It's all good. I'll take care of everything. You'll see. Take it easy man. Gotta rush. Busy like bees! See you in Sofia! LOVE!"

I smiled. I closed my eyes. It was all good. I loved that expression. I thought about Sofia. Maybe my wife was there, waiting.

The next day I flew back late into Amsterdam, feeling better, and calmer, and more positive, for having been away. Then the next morning, with a face like he'd just hit a child with his car, Nix tried to ruin it all.

"It's Kras," he said. "He's gone missing."

3.13

"No," I said, shaking my head. I held up my phone and showed him the message. "*All good… See you in Sofia!*"

"That was two days ago, Wesley. He was supposed to call me after that. About your fucking demijohns. I said I'd go pick 'em up for you."

"Awww."

"But then he didn't reply. I left a bunch of messages. He didn't get back to me. So I went round to his place and there was no reply."

The furrows in Nix's face stayed in place after he'd stopped talking.

"Do you have Donka's number?" I asked.

He did not.

"Instagram?"

Nope.

Concerned air whistled through my nose. "He was really busy though, look." I waved my phone. "Like bees."

"You think I'm being overly… whatever?"

I waggled my head. "Maybe?"

He nodded.

I placed a hand on his shoulder and smiled reassuringly. I always got the feeling that because he'd never had one of his own, Nix looked up to me as something of a father figure. Poor devil. All he'd ever had was his racist ex-junkie mum; a woman who didn't even know she was pregnant till it was far too late to abort; a woman who actually told her son to his face that the worst moment of her life was seeing him for the first time and discovering that he was black.

Oh wait... you didn't know he was black either, did you? Well, that's exactly how it was for Nix's mum. Hopefully your reaction was not the same as hers, but if you had been automatically picturing Nix as a white man... I don't know. Maybe just try to be aware of your implicit biases, if you can, and I'll try to be aware of mine.

"Maybe you're right," he said.

"Yeah, don't worry so much. Kras is shit at keeping in touch at the best of times. And he is busy." I waved my phone one last time. "Oh, wait. I got you something from Rome." With that, I ran back upstairs and returned with an ashtray in the shape of the Colosseum.

With a puzzled face, he thanked me and said, "What was in Rome?"

When I told him about Monica and Sam and my breakdown and impromptu decampment, he creased his face, shook his head and said, "Wesley. Wesley, Wesley, Wesley. What are we gonna do with you, eh?"

I shrugged. "Love me?"

That evening I met up with Monica and said, "Don't speak. Listen. I know it's not my business — I promise you, I do know that. I know it with all my heart. *But...* when I saw you kissing Sam at Henk's party last week, I just felt *terrible*." Monica tried to speak but I held out a palm towards her, between us, as if waiting for a high five that would never come. "Let me just try and explain why." I took a drink, to steel myself. "For me, Sam is everything that is despicable in a human being. He's the worst aspects of humanity, the worst aspects of masculinity, all wrapped up in one hideous, *hideous* human. He's your classic predatory male. You know what I mean? At Henk's party he was like a dog in a park, sniffing the arses of all the other dogs." Once more I raised my hand to stop Monica interrupting. "And no, I'm not saying that *you*, therefore, are also like a dog in a park. I know it sounded like that but.... *Au contraire*, Monica. That's why it hurt me so much to see you with him, because I love you." Tears came into my eyes. "You know I love you. You're one of my best friends in the world and one of my all-time favourite humans, and to see you with one of my all-time *least* favourite humans just... made me want to... I didn't know what to do, to be honest. Which is why I ran away to Rome for a week."

Monica laid a hand on my forearm and rubbed it affectionately for a moment. "What a person you are," she said. "How are you such a yuge mess, Wesley?"

One stupid tear rolled down my left cheek. "I don't know," I said. "But my heart's in the right place." I looked at her, desperate for her validation. "Right?"

She rubbed my arm again. "*Certo.*" She sighed and drank some wine. "For regarding Sam, look, I was really drunk and I thought, *fuck it*. You know, he's super-cute and I felt horny, so... why not? Believe me, it's not something I will do ever again."

"No?" Immediately I brightened. "Was he not... good?"

Monica pulled a sour face while shaking her head. "Not at *all*."

"Oh God, I'm so happy!" My mood was instantly, genuinely transformed. "Tell me *everything*."

Monica laughed. "You don't tell no one, ah?"

"Cross my heart." I crossed my heart.

His penis, she said, was of average size, but bent like the spout of a teapot — or *perhaps*, I suggested, "like one of the Devil's horns". She said it was also unusually waxy. I imagined a candle next to an open fire. The absolute worst thing about having sex with him, however, was the fact that all he was really interested in, was *fucking.* "Intense, but *strange.* Lots of staring, like he was looking through a window. No pleasure. No *fun. Proprio niente.*"

This almost made it all worthwhile. I was willing her not to stop.

"And so boring, like a… *come si dice…?*"

Jackhammer was what she wanted to say, but she dropped the aitch and bungled the stress so it ended up sounding like a private detective.

"…Jack 'Ammer?"

I was very taken with *Jack 'Ammer* and hooted it with considerable joy, twice.

"Did you come?"

She waggled both her head and index finger in the negative.

"Did he go down on you?"

"Not *really.* He had a look."

I sneered. "He didn't wash his face?"

Monica laughed. "No. It's obviously not something that he likes."

Oh, I was *so* overjoyed. You can't imagine. I swear, if I could have done cartwheels around the goddamn bar, I would have done cartwheels around the goddamn bar.

"You promise you don't say anything, ah?"

"No, no, I promise I won't say much at all. It's just… really good for me to know. Really. I'm so glad you had shit sex, Monica. And you'll never do it again, right?"

Another finger-waggle. "You don't touch two times the 'ot eye-ron."

I concurred. "Fuck me bad once, shame on you. Fuck me bad twice… won't get fucked again."

"Huh?"

206

That night I lay smiling in bed, thinking about all that I'd learned. I knew it might not reflect awfully well on me, how happy it made me to hear about Sam, and his piss-poor performance in the sack, but I didn't care. I was genuinely elated by his disgrace. I knew I would never defeat the sociopaths of the world; I knew they were in control; I knew they'd eventually usher in the breakdown of society and the extinction of the human species. However, at that particular moment, none of that mattered; none of that could diminish the unadulterated joy in my heart, just knowing that no matter how many thousands of conquests the sociopath Sam Lewis was able to stack up, he still had absolutely no idea how to make a woman feel good.

I was still feeling buoyant the next morning when Nix phoned Bulgaria Air and fucked everything up. Turns out he was right to be worried after all. Neither Kras nor Donka had made it out of Amsterdam.

Fuck.

III/2

November 2019

4.1

Right from the start, when Kras first mentioned helping to liberate Donka, Nix had been scared. He just felt that Kras was being too casual, and urged him to take more care. Kras *yeah-yeah*ed him, always defensive about Donka, and Nix felt stymied. It irked both Nix and I that Kras seemed to expect the same levels of boorishness from us as he got from certain other of our colleagues. As a consequence, there was often a sense of eggshells where Donka was concerned. "Just… be careful," said Nix. "Please."

Now that Kras was officially missing, Nix was inconsolable. "They've fucking killed him, man. What are we gonna do about it?"

"We don't know anything yet."

"We know, Wesley. What are we gonna do?"

First we went to the police, but we were neither of us under any illusions. "Bulgarians are tantamount to gypsies," said Nix. He was probably right. They were certainly a long way down the Dutch authorities' give-a-shit list. The Dutch would never admit to having such a list, but of course they do, and to paraphrase one of Nix's bits, it's just like the one the Nazis had.

"What else are we gonna do, Wesley?"

"OK," I said. "He's got to be somewhere, right? So… we find him."

So we drew up some flyers. Above a photo of Kras we wrote "MISSING PERSON". Below we wrote "HAVE YOU SEEN THIS MAN? IF SO, PLEASE CALL". Followed by Nix's number.

Then we took to the streets with a couple of rolls of tape and 300 A6-sized flyers. We posted them everywhere: Central Station to Leidseplein, Oosterpark to Westerpark and *de Wallen*. We also dipped into Krastyo's neighbourhood in Oud West. Then we did the same thing online, flyering all our socials and urging shares. It was an effective campaign, with a decent uptake. If Kras was still out there, we'd surely find him.

Then for two days we sat on our thumbs, fielding messages of support as we hunkered down and, begrudgingly, got on with our lives.

Meanwhile, Amsterdam grew dark, miserable and wet.

Usually when it rains in Amsterdam, it comes in showers, and the bright spells make it bearable. Occasionally, however, it rains incessantly, without a moment's respite, for days on end. And if you happen to be working as a walking tour guide during a stretch like that, it can really get you down. It was during one such stretch that Nix pulled an *if-not* on me.

The *if-not* was an eight-word motivational maxim. I'd first come across it on some Buddhist podcast, but then, typically, I'd seen it all over the place. It was beautiful and peculiarly striking in its simplicity. It was this: *If not you, who? If not now, when?*

When I first got into Buddhism, this thing drove me crazy. I was so excited about the idea of sending out positive vibrations into the universe, so electrified by the idea of being the change I wanted to see, that the *if-not* became my mantra. What a nightmare.

For the better part of a year, I couldn't leave a public toilet without cleaning up someone else's shit. Even if the answer to *if not you, who?* was *Er... the cleaner, whose job it is, in a couple of hours?* I'd still think *fuck it*, and start wiping. Don't get me wrong, I was an angel in that time, and my willingness to make everything better was much prized amongst my acquaintances. I was suddenly a much more popular dinner guest. But it was unsustainable. I was a bit manic back then, to be honest. Those were the wilderness years, between the *Incident of the Blinding of the Literary Agent* and my decision to start afresh in Amsterdam. I was still very much trying to make amends.

And then, just as spring follows winter, my mania passed, my Buddhist fever broke, and once again I became manageable. I stopped chanting, and the *if-not*, along with everything else, slipped into the background. But as it's always lurking just under the surface, it invariably comes up on drugs. So I shared it with Nix one time when we were fucked up, and Nix climbed aboard, with alacrity.

"Make us a cuppa coffee, would you, Wesley? If not you, who, Wesley? Who?"

"That's not how it works, Nix."

"I know, man."

Nix actually took to the *if-not* vibe like a duck to nectar and we began to use it to spur each other on whenever we felt we needed spurring.

Nix's first message read: "The police are doing nothing, man."

His second read: "If not now…."

He was right.

So that night, on the first night of November, when the autumn still seemed winter-bound and our intentions were as good as our hopes were fundamental, we went out to look for Donka.

De Wallen was especially grim in cold wet weather, and within fifteen minutes of traipsing round the windows, Nix and I felt dejected and depressed. It was super-quiet, many of the windows empty. "We should ask if anyone knows anything," said Nix. "As we're here."

"If not us," I replied.

"Precies."

The first three women we asked said they'd never heard of Donka, and we believed them. *Ish.* The fourth, a Dutch woman, followed suit, but seemed like she was lying. When Nix spoke to her in Dutch, she shook her head in silence and closed her window. We kept walking.

At around 11pm, we realised we were being followed. We were halfway along Bloedstraat when we heard footsteps behind us. We turned to see two stacked white humans with bald-looking heads moving with purpose in our direction. On seeing us turn, the men shouted something we didn't catch in what I assumed was an Eastern-European accent.

"This is getting dangerous," I remarked.

When we reached the end of Bloedstraat, which we did at that very moment, we turned right onto Nieuwmarkt and broke into a quick trot. We were followed no further. We walked home in silence.

Back at the flat, I set about making a pot of fennel tea. Eventually, Nix broke the silence. "I'm terrified that he's dead. That they're both dead."

Instinctively, I pooh-poohed him. "No, no, no, don't just assume the worst, Nix. Jesus. Look, all we know for sure is that Kras has disappeared. And Donka too. Maybe they've put her back in a window. Maybe they haven't."

"We have to keep looking," said Nix. "I know it's dangerous. And I know it could be pointless, but…." He ran out.

"I know." I nodded. "I'm with you."

"Just as soon as I get back." Nix was leaving the next morning for three short consecutive stand-up tours of Finland, Estonia and Ireland. He'd be gone for ten days. It was terrible timing. "Don't go out on your own," he said.

"I'll be careful," I replied.

Dark nights kicked in hard. I was working Beachams Red Lights most of the evenings Nix was gone and let me tell you, they were very tense tours. I couldn't stop thinking about Kras and Donka. I found myself straining to spot them in crowds. Sometimes I'd return to *de Wallen* in the wee small hours and cycle slowly past the windows in my parka with the hood up, like a junkie. I never saw Donka. But I never stopped looking.

It was in that same period too, with Nix on tour and Kras not yet resurfaced, that I did see one familiar face in the middle of a tour. It was the sex worker with whom my dad had transacted back in September. We made eye contact and I smiled. Responding to the recognition in my eyes, she instinctively smiled back, but of course she had no idea who I was.

That night I thought of my dad. We hadn't spoken since his visit, which was par for the course. Sometimes we didn't speak for years.

I also thought about Bryson, who sometime in October had shared with me his disappointment not to have met my father during his visit. He'd wanted to meet him, and I'd known that. When he asked me why it never happened, I told him, "You wouldn't have enjoyed it." And when he asked why, I said, "He's just embarrassing."

"But that's about you."

"What do you mean?"

"I mean there's no relationship between my enjoyment and your embarrassment. Or rather, there is a relationship, but it may be very different to the one you imagine."

"But he would've said something crass about your leg, or about your gay... *ness*," I said, trying to scramble back some credibility.

"I just think it might've been fun." He was disappointed. "And maybe even good for your dad, and for all of us."

It was only somewhat later I realised how right he was. It was actually easy to imagine Bryson and my dad bonding. Bryson could tame a rabid scorpion with his charm, and my dad, for all his faults, was nothing if not sociable.

So I called him. And we talked. And it was OK.

As the conversation was winding down, he said he was thinking he might come out again. I agreed that he should. When he suggested Christmas, I told him that hopefully I'd be in Sofia. I then explained that a close friend was missing and just saying it out loud caused my words to break apart. "Come out in the New Year," I said. "I want you to meet my friend, Bryson. You'll like him. He's got one leg. He plays tennis on it. And he punches racists."

My dad laughed, in all the right places, and my heart, seemingly just waiting for the opportunity, doubled in size and then shattered.

4.2

Two days later the rain stopped, the sun came out and, perhaps teaching us that there is nothing in this world on which we can rely, autumn transformed itself back into spring. At first, it seemed like a last-ditch attempt to prove something, like a painfully old man working out on the beach. But then, throughout the month, it kept coming back, like Rocky, ever stronger, ever more out of place. Waiting on the square for a 2pm I was splitting with Monica, I was doling out sun cream to tourists as Elise checked them in and gave them purple tickets. Monica was nowhere to be seen. I forgave her.

One of the tourists was a pretty blonde woman I recognised. "You look familiar," I told her. "Do you live in Amsterdam?" She said she did. "Yeah, I've seen you around, I'm sure of it."

"It's possible," she said. "I don't recognise you."

Elise laughed at the woman's directness and asked her to wait behind the purple umbrella. Then she said, deliberately loudly in an effort to embarrass me, "Stop hitting on the tourists!"

"I wasn't!" I squeaked. I turned to face the Dutch woman. "I swear I wasn't," I insisted, before adding, "What are you wearing?" The Dutch woman smiled, although not effusively. She was very attractive, if you liked tall blonde women with twinkly eyes, prominent cheekbones and perfect skin. I was curious to know why a single Dutch woman who already lived in Amsterdam was doing an Amsterdam walking tour. That wasn't common. I guessed I'd find out on the tour.

Then when Monica arrived and greeted everyone, the Dutch woman stepped forward and spoke to her. I tried and failed to eavesdrop, but as we escorted the tourists across Damstraat to share them out, Monica explained: "She's the woman from Café 't Mandje. The one with the dying mum. She's coming with me."

Two mornings later over an expensive cappuccino, Monica caught me up.

The Dutch woman's name was Sylvia, and ever since it had happened, she'd been thinking a lot about the beautiful Italian woman who'd paid for her mother's last champagne. That day in the bar had been the last day of her mum's life. The next morning, after five years of serious illness, she elected to put an end to her suffering. Ultimately, the overbearing, overbitching nature of constant pain — fighting it, fearing it, knocking herself out to avoid it — had simply been too much. So rather than face the creeping death of the senses, a process that had already begun, she made the choice to go out with her head held high, and Sylvia wholeheartedly supported her.

So that was the very last day of their life together, single mum and only daughter, and they made absolutely sure that it was perfect. As well as taking in the Rijksmuseum and the Van Gogh Museum one final time, they also had a swanky lunch at a posh hotel and rode around the city in a horse and carriage. In the late afternoon, they went to Sylvia's favourite pub and ordered champagne. In the early evening, they hired a large screening room at Sylvia's mother's favourite cinema, LAB 111, where they met up with around twenty of their closest friends and watched Sylvia's mother's favourite movie together: *Texas Chainsaw Massacre*. No, I'm joking. Sorry. I couldn't resist. They watched *Monty Python's Life of Brian*. That was her favourite film, and that was how she wanted to go out, always looking at the bright side of life. A woman after my own heart.

216

After which, half of the guests accompanied Sylvia and her mother home, and they played old records and danced and cried till they fell asleep together, one last time.

It must have been, in just about every way imaginable, the most emotional, the most meaningful day of Sylvia's life. And right there in the heart of it, with one of the greatest meet-cutes of all time, was Monica. So naturally, Monica's gesture had a huge impact on Sylvia, restoring her faith in human kindness, and giving her hope in an especially hopeless period.

She spoke with her mum about Monica too, in those final few hours. They'd even gone so far as to wonder if maybe Monica's intervention was somehow… significant. I perked up. "You mean like you were sent… by the *Universe*?"

"*Sì, ma… dai. Cazzo.*" She gathered all of her fingertips together on each hand and waved them at me. I took this to mean that she was no great believer in the Universe. "Anyway, she gave her blessing before she died." Monica smiled and tears rolled across her cheeks.

"Oh, sweetheart." My brow furrowed. I patted her awkwardly.

I can easily imagine them being bewitched by Monica, especially how she was in that moment, all shimmering from the joy of giving. Of course they thought she'd been sent by the Universe. It made perfect sense.

So Sylvia plunged herself full-time into her work, noble work, acclimatising refugees, helping them adjust to new life in the Netherlands. Then for two months she stayed home at night and drank wine and OK, look — obviously I have no idea how often or with what degree of fervour she thought about Monica in that time. Of course not. But I know human beings, and I know a little bit about her situation, so… come on. Of *course* she was thinking about Monica. *Constantly.*

Then sometime in October, she happened to be passing Dam Square when she saw her, leading a group of tourists through the Beurspoortje archway. Noting Monica's purple badge and the purple umbrella on the square, she found her way to the Beachams website, then from Monica's tour guide profile to her Facebook page, where she deduced she was straight but thought, *fuck it*. Then she phoned up Beachams and booked herself a place on Monica's next tour.

She followed the history tour with Monica's Red Light and after that, the two of them went back to Café 't Mandje, where they got to know one another properly. "She just asked me," said Monica, "totally direct — you know, Dutch-style — if I ever had sex before with a woman."

"And had you?"

"Not sex, no. I kissed before, obviously."

"Obviously. So what happened next?"

Monica smiled shyly. "Well, we kissed a little."

"Really?"

"What *really*? Why? You think she's not 'ot?"

"Of course, yeah, she's totally 'ot. I just didn't think you were very gay."

"Maybe not *very*, but a little bit for sure." She laughed. "Anyway, then we went back to the boat and… now I'm, *diciamo*, a little bit *more*." She blushed and raised her eyebrows.

"Well, well, well."

"Well, well, well, *what*, Wesley?" Suddenly she seemed all vulnerable.

"Nothing, no!" I laughed. "I'm happy for you!"

"*Grazie, fanciullo, ma… dai*. It's early. It's not serious… *yet*."

218

I laughed with over-popping joy and gave her a hug. I could feel it. That she could feel it. That something special was happening.

"And what about you, Wesley? It's about time, ah?" She pointed to a watch she didn't have.

I shrugged listlessly. "They say it's when you least expect it. Which I guess means..." I looked at a watch I didn't have, "...any moment... *now*."

4.3

Next morning the sun doubled down and I received a reminder from Elvira to learn the canal cruise. I didn't want to miss out next year, she said. She knew I was a hot mess, so she was looking out for me. I grasped the nettle. If there's a tour today, I said, sign me up. There was. She did. It was Madison's tour. Madison Clay.

I'd never seen Madison at work before. I'd only ever seen her moaning at meetings or guilting people on the square, so I had low expectations. When in the end I was very impressed, I hung around after the tour and told her so. "That was fucking amazing."

Madison was literally taken aback. As her features bunched up in a mask of suspicion, she actually stepped away from my compliment. "What do you mean?"

"I mean what I say! You were funny and charming and sociable… and you seemed to really enjoy it. You were everything a good guide should be. It was a pleasure to watch you at work. Thanks!"

I swear, I'd never before seen anyone react to a compliment as Madison did. She continued to glare at me suspiciously, her eyes twitched a couple of times and then her whole face started to contract into itself the way people do when they're becoming emotional. She became emotional.

"Oh God," I said. "Is that… are you sure?" My right hand instinctively alighted on her left shoulder and gave her a little squeeze. "Come now. What is all this?"

Madison was embarrassed. "I'm fine. I just…" Then she really let go. Her hands sprang up to hide her tears and I, always awkward in those moments, tried to comfort her, patting and stroking her like she was an unruly duvet. In the midst of this foolishness, she fell into my chest for a micro-sob, before pulling away and laughing. "I'm really sorry. I don't know what's wrong with me." She wiped at her eyes, looked at me and laughed. "You look horrified!"

"No! I'm concerned. Are you OK? Has something bad happened?"

"No!"

"Oh." There was a pause. "OK. Then I don't understand."

Madison looked down at the ground and said, "I haven't... I guess I'm not used to people being nice to me. I... yeah, that's... Now you know. I'm such a loser."

"Don't say that, Madison." My heart ached, pained by Madison's humility. "I bet it's not true." I wanted her to feel better. "Have you got plans? Do you wanna grab a drink somewhere? I feel like I need to make you feel better. I've made you cry. Now I feel I should cheer you up."

"No, you don't have to do that. I'm fine. Honestly."

"OK, no... no worries."

"Well, if you're sure you don't have anywhere you need to be, we could... I mean, why not? If you..."

"Absolutely! Let's do it."

So, at just after 8.30pm, I found myself sitting outside a Japanese restaurant on the East Dock, with one of my least favourite people in the world. Or so I thought.

Madison told me her stories. Sacramento upbringing by super-Liberal parents — militant hippy activists turned big cheese civil rights lawyers. Then Madison let them down by flunking law and becoming an English language teacher. "It wouldn't have been so bad if I was teaching refugees," she said. Instead she was teaching scoundrels in financial behemoths. "I was even at Lehman Brothers in 2008 when the shit hit the fan." Then a year later at the Climate

Camp in London, she was one of thousands of G20 protesters who were kettled by police. "There's nothing like being forced to publicly pee in a bottle to radicalise a person." That was the beginning. Then she started volunteering and marching and flyering for a large, large number of pressure groups, making up for lost time.

"I know what people think of me," she said. "That I'm all pious and preachy and basically a whingeing SJW with no sense of humour. And I am all those things, that's the annoying part of it. People are right. I hear myself sometimes and even I find myself boring."

I smiled. "I thought you were going to say mean."

Thankfully she laughed. "Oh God, I'm mean too. It's true. I'm so far up my own ass and I honestly don't know what to do about it. I'm thirty-fucking-five too. Aren't people supposed to know who they are by that age?"

"That's 38," I said. "It's in the post. In the meantime, what do you do to break the monotony? Do you take drugs?"

She shook her head. "I have control issues."

"Do you have sex?"

She raised an inscrutable eyebrow. "Not as much as I'd like." She sighed. "I live with a guy. He's quite a bit older and he has some physical issues, so we don't really… very often."

"Oh, I'm sorry to hear that."

"No, it's fine. We have an open relationship and I have a couple of eff-buddies I see now and then, when the pressure builds up."

"Eff-buddies eh? Splendid."

There followed a long, slightly awkward pause, eventually broken by Madison asking, "What about you?"

I waggled my head. "I have sex *occasionally*."

"No, I mean… how did you end up in Amsterdam?"

222

"Ah."

So I told my story, we ordered more drinks and the sky grew black.

"And if I do ever leave Amsterdam," I concluded, as heavy rain spots started punching the ground, "it'll be because of the fucking weather."

We were under a thin canvas awning, looking south across the East Dock. The sky was being eccentric. On the horizon was a strip of bright, mostly yellow and orange light, but above and around that, blocking out the rest of the sky was a massive bank of mostly grey and white cloud. What was particularly curious was how fast the cloud was moving.

Madison mentioned Extinction Rebellion. She'd been one of the 200 activists who staged a mock funeral for the city of Amsterdam in June, in an effort to pressure the Dutch government to declare a climate emergency. She was excited to be a part of this new movement and really believed they might actually make a difference.

I was worried they weren't going far enough. "Maybe instead of staging funerals and blocking roads, they should be targeting government buildings or actually going after the people who make decisions."

After a withering pause, Madison snapped, "Well, at least we're doing something."

"Of course! No, I know and I totally admire the effort. Sorry. I didn't mean to sound dismissive."

"No, I'm sorry, I'm just so fed up with people not caring. I actually had a real-life climate change denier on my tour last week. I nearly lost it."

I told her the bit I sometimes drop into my tour, regarding the recent weather extremes — frozen canals and heat waves, within weeks of one another. "Thank God global warming's a hoax," I quip. "Otherwise we'd all be dead in thirty years!"

"Holy shit!" cried Madison. "Look!"

I looked, up in the sky to the west. As well as moving quickly, the huge bank of cloud was now rolling and swirling like rising smoke.

"What the fuck...?"

Fellow alfresco diners picked up their phones and started filming as one section of cloud began to darken and thicken, freeing itself from the rest but still twirling and churning. I stared, agog, as the cloud continued to swirl and then one thin tendril, a little lighter in colour, formed at the base of the bank of dark cloud and grew longer, extending itself like an alien's tentacle.

A trayful of glasses exploded on a concrete floor somewhere inside the restaurant behind me, but I just kept watching, transfixed, as the alien's tentacle twisted its way towards the earth.

4.4

"It's a tornado," Madison hissed.

I caught my breath.

The tendril grew thicker and wider, pirouetting across the water towards us. Bits of whatever lay in its path were dragged into its vortex and spat out into the air. People had started screaming and laughing outrageously, unable to believe their eyes.

It moved closer, still heading directly towards us. Madison laid her hand on my forearm. Someone shouted for people to move inside but we stayed still and watched, bewitched.

The tornado then changed course slightly, dancing off to the east. Then it became wider but less intense, before disappearing behind the Conservatorium. Madison took back her hand.

The whole thing lasted no more than ninety seconds.

"Well, that was intense," I offered.

Madison made an *I-told-you-so* face and shook her head grimly. "It was almost a hundred degrees this morning," she said. "In November. What the fuck is that?"

I nodded earnestly. "Thirty trees blew down in September."

"Freak hailstorms too. Stones the size of human hearts."

I shook my head. "Thank God global warming's a hoax!"

We smiled. Then Madison finished her wine and said she was expected at home.

When we parted, she thanked me for the drink and nice chat. I reciprocated and we hugged. Then there was an awkward instant when one or both of us was definitely thinking about going for a kiss, either on the cheek or even on the mouth, but neither of us did.

Back home, twenty minutes later, I examined the tornado footage that was already online and I laughed like a man in a straitjacket. Tornadoes? Sworn enemies almost kissing? These were the end times.

By the end of the next day's Red Light, I'd received a message from Madison: "I'm free tonight and feel like letting off a little steam. You wanna help me?"

My first thought was that I'd just received an invitation to have sex with my former enemy. My second thought was that I shouldn't be so presumptuous. Sometimes a cigar is just a cigar. I told her I'd just finished work and asked her what she had in mind.

"Maybe I could come to yours for 8?"

My cigar twitched to life. I texted my address.

Madison arrived with a bottle of wine. We took it up to my room and after just a single mouthful, she pulled me towards her.

Her kissing style took me by surprise. She was ravenous, like a starving dog with a bowl of hot beef. Like she was trying to devour a giant over-succulent peach that might at any moment be confiscated. Concerned that any efforts to soothe her might cause offence, which might in turn lead to further violence, I just let myself be mauled.

Then came the biting. First my face and neck, which was mostly quite pleasant. Then she peeled off my t-shirt and like a late-stage Ophelia bobbing for apples, went feral, growling and bucking as she chomped on my chest. Then, as if it were the knot of a balloon, she brought her teeth down hard on one of my nipples. I cried out in pain. "Take it easy, Madison, Jesus!"

She laughed.

"*Please*," I begged. "I'd really like to survive this. Ideally."

She laughed again and bit into my belly. "Survival *not* guaranteed."

Then she moved downstairs, rubbing, groping and biting through my jeans. Frankly, I wasn't used to and didn't massively appreciate such relentlessly rough attention. However, despite my reservations and cuckish oversensitivity, despite the fact that the tenderness for which I longed was decidedly unforthcoming, my body responded.

Ach, get away with you. Who am I trying to fool? My body didn't act alone. She was hot. I was turned on. Her face transformed as she unbuckled my belt and unzipped my pants, eyes half-closed, mouth gaping like a gargoyle's, breath voiced like a demon's; her lust was infectious, and irresistible.

Easily the roughest, the most frantic and forceful lover I'd ever known, Madison set about my penis like a Tasmanian Devil with a choc-ice. In the end I had to push her away and demand she take it easy. She tried, but easy wasn't easy for Madison. I could see I was going to have to subvert the normally fairly prevalent female side of my sexuality and exert my physical dominance. So I got butch.

I took hold of Madison, pinned her to the bed and stripped her. At first, she seemed pleased with the new dynamic. Then, when I got down between her legs and went to work, things began to go awry. I did what I usually did, bringing to bear my usual smorgasbord of tantalising tactics, but I got nothing in response. Rather than wriggling and writhing in rapture, Madison grabbed my head and tried to pull me away. I shrugged her off and persisted, throwing in a little variation till she actually leant forward, lifted my head and said, "I'm ready for you. Put a condom on and fuck me."

"But…" I was upset. "I want to go down on you."

She made a face. "I don't really like it."

I gasped. "*What*?"

"Come and fuck me," she demanded.

I glared at her with my mouth open. I felt like a concert pianist who'd just been told, "I don't really like piano music. Here — here's a kazoo. Do something with that."

For a while, I just knelt between her legs, feeling discouraged and, some might say, a tad ungrateful. I suspect that many if not most red-blooded heterosexual men would be delighted with such a request. *Piece of cake*, they'd think. *No pressure, no strings, no fiddly bits. Straightforward fucking.* I did not feel that way. I felt burned. I wanted to play Chopin. *Please let me play Chopin!* But no. Madison did not care for Chopin. Madison preferred DJ Khaled.

So I put a condom on, and Madison rode me like a Sybian.

She was loud, and violent. As well as the usual, there was lots of extra-curricular physicality: slapping my chest, grabbing my face, pulling my body hair and pinching my skin till I cried out. It was quite an ordeal on the whole, and peculiarly antagonistic. Even though there'd always been a certain spikiness between us, I hadn't expected the sex to be so unrelentingly rough and wilfully phallocentric.

I tried not to sulk, but it just feels like such a crime to have a woman in your bed and not be going down on her a lot. That some men consciously elect not to participate bewilders me. And I know DJ Khaled is not alone. I've met other such men on my travels, men who recoil visibly from the very idea of feasting on a woman, men who find it *dirty*. Invariably religious men, in my experience. And that some will even go so far as to shun menstruating women is as baffling to me as it is obscene. It should be painfully, blindingly obvious: shame a bleeding woman and you slap the face of God. But balls to God — you also miss out on the pleasure, the blessed carnal rapture of sanguinary relations. You'll never know the joy of resurfacing, panting and glistening and gurning, like a freshly painted Aztec shield. You *idiot*. Also, if you absolutely must drag

228

religion into sex, then for God's sake do it right — get down on your knees and worship, *especially* during those sacred days of miraculous regeneration.

But no. Madison didn't like it. At *any* time of the month.

I was careful not to shame her, but I did find it galling. It was like having a Ferrari that you refused to take out of the garage.

Madison left just before 11pm. I showed her to the front door, where she bit me goodbye.

"Thanks for popping by."

"Thanks for having me."

The next day she messaged to say she'd enjoyed herself and would like to do it again. I could think of a number of reasons why I might *not* want to, but ultimately, I decided it was better to sit in a Ferrari and be lightly abused, than do nothing. *At least then, I exist.*

Madison's next message said: "I use contraception. You should go get yourself checked out. If you're clean, we can dispense with condoms."

I wrote back: "I'll get right on it."

4.5

Life went on. I was thinking about Kras and Donka all the time. Almost all the time. And I was still scouring the windows for Donka when I could, but there was only so much I could do and life just... kept going. Like it always does. It's heart-breaking like that.

"Have you noticed," asked Lizzie, "how Sam describes all of his ex-girlfriends as *batshit crazy*?"

I hadn't. But then, we didn't talk much. Lizzie tended to split the 10am tours with him, so she got to hear a lot more of his nonsense than I did. We were in De Prael after a Red Light and Lizzie was in sparkling form: bright, breezy and full of gossip.

"Do you know he has photos of newborn babies on his phone?"

"What?"

Lizzie explained that Sam would often mention how tired he was on his tour, having been up all night with his wife, who'd just given birth. He would then brandish photos of someone else's newborns — preferably with him holding them — and claim they were his own. He reckoned on a good day, being a brand new father could double his tips. It put me in mind of Damo using his daughters to pull. I didn't mention that to Lizzie though, in case it all came spilling out.

"Do you know that he just makes stuff up on tour?"

"What?"

She nodded. "He told me, 'Tourists are so fucking dumb they believe anything.' So he just makes up random shit."

Apparently he'll pick an old house and tell them Van Gogh lived there or cut off his ear there, or that Rembrandt had the world's first tattoo.

"And when I asked him why he does it, do you know what he said?"

"Tell me."

"He said, 'Just to fuck with people.' He said, 'if they're dumb enough to believe whatever they hear, then fuck 'em.'"

I shook my head. "Textbook. He should have the word *sociopath* burned into his forehead." Lizzie laughed. "I'm serious. Lying to tourists is like lying to children." After a pause, I continued, "Speaking of which, if you ever fancy telling me what I've done to offend your… *Doug*, I would appreciate it."

Lizzie blew out her cheeks and ordered another pair of beers from a passing bar-lady. "You really wanna know?"

"Of course I wanna know! I'm amazed you haven't told me already to be honest."

She shrugged. "I'm not a big fan of gossip, that's all. But if you insist… I need you to promise me you're not gonna flip out when I tell you."

"Really? If it's that bad, we should wait for the beer. I might want to toss it in your face."

Lizzie smiled but seemed nervous. "OK, so, Doug knows a guy in England and, he told Doug that you're, you know, basically, a psychopath."

"*What?*" Instinctive guilt moved my heart up a gear.

"Yeah, because of something that happened in London?"

"Oh, *London*." I swatted an imaginary fly.

"Something about you blinding a guy?"

"Aah." I nodded and held Lizzie's gaze.

She smiled. I smiled. The fresh beers arrived and wordlessly, we clinked glasses and drank. The more I got to know Lizzie, the more I liked her. With Doug, it was precisely the opposite. I really didn't think he was good enough for her. We continued to gaze at one another. Only when my groin twitched inappropriately did I look away and laugh.

"What's irks me most about this," I began, "is that he's just accepted this *tittle-tattle*, without having the balls to check in with me. And then he's so fucking obvious about it. Whenever he sees me, he's like a cat with a ghost."

Lizzie smiled. "Yep. That's Doug all over."

I loved that she had no intention of asking if it was true.

"Come to dinner," I said. "Both of you. Tell Doug to bring a written apology and I'll cook you both a lovely meal and tell you what happened."

Lizzie liked this idea very much and she said she'd set it up. I was pleased. Because it was a good story, and it deserved a decent build-up.

4.6

By the end of the same week, I'd been given the all-clear, sexual health-wise, and Madison and I arranged another evening. Half an hour in, however, I ran into a little trouble with my penis.

"Oh, what's wrong?" asked Madison.

I sighed. Mostly I suspected I was just a little bored by the rather monothematic lovemaking style Madison favoured. Treacherous boredom had then led to the fear that I might lose my erection, which — the very thought — had made it an inevitability. Confessing to boredom, however, seemed unnecessarily cruel. I considered maybe blaming Kras, and my nagging, distracting concerns for his safety. I'd feel bad using Kras as an excuse for my mousey little soft-cock, but rather that, than the inevitable upset of the truth. Because for all of her haughtiness and casual sexual violence, Madison was a sensitive soul prone to tearful outbursts, and I couldn't bear another one of those on my conscience.

Although boredom was certainly a factor, I couldn't rule out that my age may also be playing a part in my impotence. I'd noticed, as the years stacked up, a certain creeping depletion of potency. I wished it weren't so, but I was in my late 40s, and it rather came with the territory. So I accepted it. Occasionally it even seemed like a boon, considering how much of my youth I'd spent cowering on public transport, plagued by an unstoppable deluge of desire and concomitant bloodrush, daily risking public humiliation or scandal. Now, as an older, calmer, less virile man, I was free to think about other things. Should I choose to.

Ultimately, I said none of this to Madison, plumping instead for, "No, nothing, give me a sec." Then: "Kiss me." Kissing would usually do the trick in these moments. "*Softly.*"

"You wanna dick pill?" Madison had a weird glint in her eye.

This was a question I'd never heard. "You mean Viagra?"

"Cialis I think, but whatever. A dick pill is a dick pill is a dick pill."

"Why do you have *dick pills*, Madison?"

"Waldo uses them. Me too occasionally. I've got some in my bag. You wanna try?"

I shrugged. "Sure, OK."

As Madison rummaged in her bag, I asked, "What do you mean, *you too?* You don't have a penis, Madison. I'm pretty sure I'd have noticed."

"I don't need a penis. They're vasodilators. All they do is relax the muscles around your veins, so they expand and facilitate blood flow. That's all they do. They don't make you horny, like some people think." Returning to bed, Madison popped a pill from the strip and snapped it in half. "If you're not already aroused, nothing happens. If you are aroused, blood flows more easily to your genitals, whether you have a penis or not." She handed me half a pill and washed down her own half with water. "Increased blood flow makes it all more intense, especially orgasm. Not with all women, but it works pretty well with me."

I took my half and giggled. It had been a while since I'd tried a new drug. "Is your boyfriend impotent?"

"He has muscular dystrophy, Wesley." She said it sternly, like I should have known, but this was the first I'd heard.

"Oh God, I'm sorry."

Madison shrugged. "He's even older than you, so he's taken it for years. Not so much these days, but it used to be that a few milligrams of active ingredient sildenafil would make him worry less and enjoy it more. He used to say it made him feel young again."

"Well, that's *very* interesting." Who doesn't want to feel young again? "Get over here."

Fifteen minutes later, I could already feel the effects of the sildenafil. Madison was on top of me, slamming into me. I placed my hands on her upper arms and asked her to stop moving. She did so. "I just want to feel…." I ran out of words. My mouth was open, seemingly in rapture. I could feel myself, inside Madison, throbbing like a 19-year-old on a train.

"This is *amazing*." I gasped. "I have a young man's erection!" I laughed out loud. "And an old man's brain!"

Madison was smiling too. "May I?"

"Please." I was reborn, in pure cock form. "Fuck away."

4.7

The next day was yet another scorcher. We were in the midst of an Indian summer like none I'd ever known — a real slam-bang, honest-to-goodness, three-fisted, Armageddon-style heatwave. Nix was back from his stand-up tour so we headed out into *de Wallen* together and continued our search for Donka in vain. It was a Thursday night in mid-November, just after 10pm, twenty-three degrees Celsius. We were wearing shorts and tee-shirts.

We'd been walking for fifteen minutes and were back on the main drag, the Oudezijds Voorburgwal. We were about to head back into one of the side-streets and start asking around after Donka, when an Eastern European hardman appeared alongside us, all weird, wired, and amiable. "Hey guys, I wonder if you can help me." We stopped walking and both turned to face him. "I wonder if you can tell me what exactly it is that you're looking for. Maybe I can help you."

My eyes narrowed.

The hardman was half a metre shorter than Nix, but very well-built. He made me think immediately of that Danny Boyle quote: "Small psychos are the best." Was he a psycho? My instincts said fuck yes. He had indisputable charm and menace, in equal measure. He wore jeans and a t-shirt and a brown leather jacket zipped halfway up, as if to conceal things.

"Who wants to know?" I said, because someone had to.

The hardman gave a handsome, natural and entirely winning smile. "Well, I guess I want to know!" He was positively effervescent!

"Well, who are you?!" I mirrored his fizz.

The hardman continued to smile. "I'm maybe a guy who can help, depending what you're looking for."

"We're looking for Donka," said Nix, cutting to the bone.

The hardman stopped smiling. "You know that bitch?"

"Oy!" I snapped. "Don't use that word… about her."

After a tiny pause, the hardman relented. "Alright, man. Alright."

"Or any woman," I added. I looked to Nix for support.

"Sure," said the hardman. "Whatever, man. All I know is, Donka doesn't work here no more. Nobody seen her for weeks."

Nix and I traded glances.

"We might just keep looking if you don't mind," I said.

"Ah but I do mind, you see," said the hardman. "You're upsetting some of the girls."

"*Women*," I said.

The hardman's smile was gone. "What the fuck, man?"

I shrugged.

"So what happens if we just keep looking anyway?" said Nix.

The hardman laughed and looked left and right. "Do what you want, man. I'm just letting you know, if you continue to upset the girls, the *women*, whatfuckingever, then you know… we can't let that happen. It's on your head, man. Have a nice evening."

He walked off stiffly, briskly, business-like, towards the Old Church.

"Well, that was intense," said Nix.

"He's lying, right?"

"He's definitely lying."

"So what do we do?"

"We keep looking."

We kept looking. But after another ten minutes or so, Nix suggested we call it a night, and I have to say I was extremely relieved.

Back at the flat, I was cooking up a pot of restorative fennel tea when Madison messaged. She'd been in Rotterdam for a week with her partner and his family. Now she was back. "Tomorrow's the last day of the heatwave," she wrote. "You wanna do something special?"

I really wasn't sure. "Sure," I replied.

4.8

A temperature drop of fifteen degrees was forecast for the following day, so with a view to taking full advantage of the final moments of this most incongruous summer, Madison proposed a picnic. I agreed, but with reservations.

I didn't want to be Madison's eff-buddy, even with the game-changer of sildenafil. Sure, I was much more confident in the hammering away department now, but it was still just hammering away, which… meh. Then there was the undeniable fact of feeling especially empty and sad afterwards, and no, we really don't want that. And yet… I guess it's like a margherita pizza. Sure, it's the most uninspiringly bland pizza imaginable, but… it's still hot cheese. And we all get hungry. Even so, I had to break it off. She scared me. She was so masculine in bed. She reminded me of my dad. It was like being fucked by a chubby-cheeked woke lady version of my dad, which was exactly as weird as it sounds. So the picnic was to be our last date. I'd break the news once we'd eaten. It was a decision I'd made.

When we met in a supermarket around 2pm, however, Madison pushed an entire dick pill into my mouth and gave me water to wash it down.

"Oh," I said, only slightly freaked out. (Also turned on. Couldn't help it.) "Maybe I don't need it," I squeaked.

"Maybe I do," she parried.

Cycling south to Amstelpark, Madison did her usual slowing down for pigeons thing and I laughed openly, enjoying her foolishness. "You're not going to hit a pigeon, Madison. Just be cool, for God's sake." She laughed, thankfully, but the fear was hardwired into her.

Bikes ditched, we walked the always surprisingly ample public grounds of Amstelpark, with its peacocks, its red squirrels, its rabbits and its kangaroos. We found a lovely spot by a large tree, where we picnicked. The park was busy because of the dying heatwave, but we'd found a relatively isolated spot. The nearest people, maybe ten metres away, were two Spanish couples. Between us and them, their four kids played excitedly with a ball.

Madison was not a great drinker and I was surprised by how drunk she appeared after just two glasses of wine. As a consequence, she became very frisky, straddling me with way more abandon than was strictly appropriate, and moving back and forth on my hips like a stripper. With the encouragement of the dick pill fattening up my veins, my arousal felt powerfully, disconcertingly evident. I protested, but weakly.

Madison grabbed her phone meanwhile, and started playing a little salsa music so that — I presumed she presumed — she could dance around on my crotch without appearing quite so salacious. Because of the unseasonal heat, we were both wearing very few clothes. Me a pair of light cotton shorts, Madison a long summer dress that covered both of our groins. Despite the look of alarm on my face, I was very aroused. Madison seemed amused by my awkwardness. She leaned over and kissed me, whilst simultaneously reaching under her dress, brutally and painfully pulling down my shorts and forcing me inside of her.

"Whoooooooa," I cried. "And also… no? What the fuck?"

She straightened up again, laughing and dancing around to the music, feigning innocence, as I, inside her, throbbed like a bullfrog. It seemed to be Madison's view that so long as she continued to move her arms around in the air as if she were dancing, she could actually fuck me quite intensely, making short, sharp, shockingly fast oscillations with her pelvis.

240

This she did.

Supporting myself on my elbows, which seemed a much less carnal pose, I guiltily looked around. The children continued to play, oblivious, unblemished. Aside from the Spaniards, another couple of families were picnicking a similar distance away in different directions. All seemed fine. It was just another ordinary summer's day in the middle of autumn. The air was abuzz with unseasonal bees colliding drowsily mid-flight, and my mouth — clenched like a tragic theatre mask — was the window to my soul.

What Madison was doing was actually causing me some quite profound emotions. I was in pain, for sure — a great deal more pain than I was comfortable with — but I was also very, very turned on. My mouth had fallen open, my lips were drawn back across my teeth and I was trying not to make any noise. I was also trying to remain as still, and as casual, as possible. I was trying to pretend, as best I could, that nothing was happening. But the truth was gurning all over my face.

I noticed a couple of people glancing over. I had no idea what they were thinking. They could've suspected nothing, or equally they could've been thinking, "My God. That woman is quite clearly fucking that man in a public place with children playing very nearby." I lay back and put my hands over my eyes. *Fuck it*, I thought. *On with the dance.* The fact that I'd not given permission for this act was in a way, rather freeing; in a way, it was nothing to do with me.

Madison had started to make a little noise. I ignored her. I blocked her out. What I couldn't block out, however, was the sensation in my groin, which was building and intensifying and beginning to feel exactly like I might be about to—

Yep. It was happening. I was having an orgasm — an uproarious, outlandish, outrageous orgasm, in a public place —

and just as I let go, and lost myself fully within it, something soft made contact with my left elbow and automatically, I opened my eyes.

One side effect of not necessarily coming every time you have sex — at least in my experience — is that when you do come, especially if it hasn't happened in a while, your reaction might be a little overly enthusiastic, maybe even melodramatic. For some reason — who can say why? — this particular physical sensation with this particular woman in this particular moment, struck me in the very core of my viscera with the power of a meteor strike. Not literally. My orgasm didn't leave a fifty-mile-wide crater and kill 30,000 people, but believe me, it was powerful. More powerful, I maintain, than any that had come before.

On reflection, I can only presume that the power of my orgasm was also massively augmented by a combination of the public and therefore taboo nature of the coitus, coupled with the blood-rush of sildenafil. I had never had sex in such an exposed place before. Madison's efforts to disguise what we were up to were surely fooling no one. I was also excited by the fact that, from the first moment Madison had straddled me, I'd been fantasising that this was happening very much against my will. In my head I had a wife and six kids and I was being violently coerced by this crazy American woman in this public place. My God yes.

As a consequence of this perfect storm of factors, I had the kind of orgasm I've only really read about in *The Hite Report*. The kind that feels like the climax of a very expensive firework display, maybe one on the eve of a new millennium. In my case it was condensed into 10-15 seconds of absolute delirium, radiating out from my groin and reverberating through my entire body like an atomic explosion of joy, like an ayahuasca orgasm.

My hands were still clamped to my face when this tsunami of sensation made landfall in my brain and a prolonged ecstatic howl began to emanate from my opened mouth. Which was when something soft glanced against my elbow. When I moved my hands from my face, two Spanish children were standing over me, their large brown eyes stretched wide in alarm. Because I'd lifted my head and moved my hands, and then because I was staring at them, they were staring right back, absolutely bewildered. They were siblings by my reckoning, brother and sister, around six years old. They'd probably never seen anyone experiencing orgasm before. I assume they imagined that I was in terrific pain and they were naturally, instantly terrified. Unfortunately, I was able to stop neither my face contorting nor the terrible moan that was curdling and billowing out of my mouth. What I was able to do, however, was bat away their football with my left arm and take cover once more behind my hands.

This I did.

I also caught a glimpse of Madison, eyes closed and teeth clamped tight around a pack of pocket tissues. Her arms were still moving through the air like she was dancing, but her hips couldn't lie. She was clearly having intercourse. Fuck it. I was past caring.

The children, scarred for life, ran off in the direction of their ball and their family. I could hear their parents having a heated debate about something. I didn't know what was upsetting them but I could guess. Madison continued to jerk away spasmodically as the fingers of both of her hands clawed at my chest, under my t-shirt, like she was trying to tear the flesh from my ribcage. I arched my back and held my breath as a way of dealing with the pain. When Madison slumped onto me, I allowed myself to breathe again. Madison let the tissues fall from her mouth. She was gasping, and twitching.

243

The Spaniards were still bleating.

"I think we were spotted," I whispered.

Madison started chuckling, but she didn't move. We stayed for a moment in silence, breathing together. I could feel myself slowly dissolving. Madison could feel it too. Our cheeks were touching. My eyes were closed. We could have been anyone. We could have been anywhere.

"That was the best orgasm I've ever had."

"Mmmm," said Madison. "That's nice." She darted her tongue into my ear and tried to bite off the lobe. I moaned and stopped melting. Jesus. I was invincible. I wondered how much of my unquenchable libido was the sildenafil and how much was the taboo nature of the sex. I fleetingly pictured the pair of us, sometime in the future, arrested for sex in a kindergarten. Oh, shit. I suddenly remembered. I was supposed to be ending it.

"Come on," whispered Madison. "Let's go back to yours."

4.9

We extricated ourselves from one another and cleaned ourselves up, efficiently and relatively surreptitiously. Madison tossed back most of another glass of wine, we packed up the picnic and strode off, refusing to make eye contact with anyone, refusing to even acknowledge their scrutiny. I felt ashamed. Yet proud. Like an adolescent.

Riding home along the Amstel, I began to feel quite concerned by how reckless Madison suddenly seemed on her bike. Having said that, when we came upon the next couple of pigeons in our path, I couldn't help but encourage her in her newfound nonchalance. "Face your fears!" I shouted. And she rode towards the birds like Boudica, stretching a fist towards the heavens in bellicose abandon. When the pigeons scattered ahead of her, she almost lost her nerve, letting out a little scream and wobbling slightly on her bike. But she regained control and seemed pleased at her courage. After which, whenever she saw a pigeon in her path, she sped towards it screaming, "Begone, wingéd rat!" It was rather amusing and in those moments, I wondered if maybe I could love her.

We'd talked a little more about her relationship with her boyfriend, who was now planning to move back in with his parents. His deterioration was speeding up and neither he nor Madison envisioned her as a full-time carer. I thought about the orgasm I'd experienced. Aside from the unsavoury moment with the infants, it had been truly astonishing. I wanted to do it again. I wanted to see Madison again. I suddenly felt strongly attracted to her.

Five minutes from home under the Toronto bridge, there was a single pigeon in Madison's path and once again, she sped towards it, now utterly convinced that it was a physical impossibility for a pigeon and the wheel of a bicycle to make contact.

I don't know quite what to say. I guess even pigeons have their off days. Maybe this particular bird was sick or injured and its senses and reactions were not as sharp as they usually were. Or maybe it was a suicide. How should I know what goes on in a pigeon's head? All I know is, this poor little fucker failed to get out of the way of Madison's front wheel, and Madison, in her newfound drunken confidence, left it far too late to brake.

Consequently, on becoming entangled in her rapidly slowing spokes, the pigeon was then presumably dragged around with the wheel rim towards Madison's body. Presumably, what happened then — and the very brief splatter analysis I was able to perform at the scene bore this out — was that the bird's body made full contact with Madison's front mudguard, and exploded on impact.

Losing control of her bicycle, Madison crashed into the tunnel wall and fell in a crumpled heap. The crash was not so serious, but her reaction to being sprayed with the blood and guts of her most despised creature was quite something.

I dismounted just ahead of her and immediately crouched down to tend to her. I helped disentangle her from her bike and tried to get her to stand. Which was when she noticed the blood up her right leg. Then, on further examination, she realised there was more blood, all over her dress. Then she saw the twitching mess of what was left of the pigeon a metre to her left. She lifted her hands to her face — also wet with bird innards — and let rip with a short but piercing scream.

Meanwhile, I had located serviettes and water and was attempting to wipe the blood from her face. She pushed my hands away and hissed at me to get the fuck away from her. A middle-aged woman on a bicycle stopped to see what was going on.

"She hit a pigeon," I explained. "She's fine."

"I am *not* fine!" Madison screamed.

The woman scowled and rode off.

"Madison, really, it's OK."

"It is *not* fucking OK! It's totally not OK."

She was shaking and gasping. Tears turned pink on her cheeks and tiny white feathers clung to her hair and dress. I offered her clean tissues, which she ignored. Then quite suddenly, she froze and looked down at the ground, stepping back slightly and moving her feet apart. I followed her gaze and grimaced as something in amongst the avian remains glistened, something that wasn't blood. Oh God, no. It only became clear why Madison was looking so repulsed when fresh globules of bubbling sperm dripped onto her blood-spattered calf.

I tried offering tissues again, but she really wasn't interested.

Instead she hissed, "I will never, ever forgive you for this."

I gasped. *Me?* Before I could figure out how I felt about taking responsibility for what had happened, Madison was back on her bike and riding away.

I watched her go, then glanced down at what was left of the pigeon. It had definitely got the worst of it. Guts, blood and feathers were everywhere. One wing was completely off. A vision of Damo, eviscerated, flashed into my mind. I sighed, and crossed myself, for both of them.

Back home, I messaged Madison. "I'm so sorry for what happened, Madison. I know I encouraged you to face your pigeon fear and be brave but I really don't think I can be blamed for what happened today. It seems to me like it was complete chance. I hope once you've got over the shock, we can be friends again. I hope you're feeling better soon."

She wrote back almost immediately: "Delete my number."

And that was that.

When Nix heard the story, he shook his head solemnly and looked at me with concern. "Did you ever think you might have some bad juju?"

"What do you mean?"

"There's just a lot of weird shit happening around you, Wesley — exploding pigeons, killer wasps. Do you want me to get you some crystals?"

I laughed.

Jesus.

He didn't know the half of it.

4.10

Two weeks after Nix first told the police about Kras, they called back. Nix wandered out of the kitchen to take the call. Of course we feared the worst. Staring down at Amstel Bay through closed wet windows, I realised that the latest clot of crazy weather — the tornado, the heatwave — had all kicked in the moment we found out Kras was missing. The previous night, as predicted, the heatwave broke and we woke up this morning in the cold.

Nix wandered back through from his bedroom and said, "Kras is dead." His voice was not much more than a whisper. He made it as far as the kitchen doorway, where he sagged against the jamb. "They found him in a canal by his house. They reckon he was drunk and fell in." He shook his head. "When was the last time you saw Kras drunk?" He slipped slowly down the jamb till he was sitting on the kitchen floor. "They killed him, Wesley. And they got away with it."

My mouth was open. FOLLOW YOUR DREAMS was emblazoned on the mug in my right hand. Kras had been following his dreams. And they killed him for it. I put down the mug and my face made its way into my hands. "This is awful," I eventually said. "I can't believe this is happening."

"They killed him, Wesley," Nix repeated. "What are we gonna do about it? Are we gonna do anything about it?"

"Like what? You mean go after them? Violence? Violence begets violence, Nix. Nothing would change."

"Ah, but it would though," he hissed. "It would stop them."

A deep, deep breath juddered through me.

"It would stop them doing it again," he added. "Wouldn't it."

We went to the police station together, and the police were singularly unhelpful. They wouldn't let us see Kras because we

249

weren't relatives. When Nix explained that Kras had no relatives in the Netherlands, they told us to leave it to them. When he told them about Donka and the fact that Kras was in the process of trying to help repatriate her, they made a note, and they insisted we leave it to them.

We were a couple of hours at the station, mostly just waiting around. Eventually they asked Nix lots of pertinent, as well as lots of wholly impertinent questions, and then they sent us both home. They said they'd be in touch when they knew something.

Back in De Prael, sitting over the bar in adjacent armchairs, the small beer glass in Nix's right hand looked like it might crack under pressure. His entire face was furrowed. "They couldn't give a fuck, man. It's not a little blonde girl, is it? It's a fucking full-bearded Bulgarian. He may as well be a burned-out car. He may as well be black." He was convinced they wouldn't bother looking for Donka either. "It's just Slav-on-Slav shit. They don't care, Wesley."

When he started to cry, I squeezed his shoulder and he snapped himself out of it.

"OK," he said. "Fuck this. We can't do nothing. What we gonna do?"

I shrugged, shook my head. "I don't know, man. We're talking about dangerous people. We can't just…" I ran out.

"We can though. We have to, Wesley. Seriously. And if you won't help me, I'll do it myself."

"Aw, come on, man. Nix, please. Don't say that."

He shrugged. "That's how it is."

I shook my head at him, pissed off. "If you're gonna push me on it, fuck you. Count me in, but I hate you for it, and I want you to know that."

We hatched a plan. We'd track down Krastyo's Bulgarian buddies and with their help, take bloody revenge. It was vague as fuck and frankly, I was against it. I was convinced that violence was not the way to go, and this was not merely my audacious pacifism talking. It was also my audacious pragmatism. The Red Light District was not a good place to go seeking revenge. It was not neutral territory. Nix and I knew it better than most, but beneath the surface it was still a dark and dangerous place and only an insane person would go barging in there mob-handed without a meticulously detailed plan. And what we had was the exact opposite of a meticulously detailed plan.

We wanted to find the people who'd killed Kras, but we had no idea where or indeed who they were. We'd met one guy in the street and he'd be a very good place to start, but as he'd already threatened us, seeking him out would be asking for trouble. Our plan was terrible. But it was all we had.

So we set up a Facebook group, *Friends of Kras Mikhaylov*, and invited everyone who knew him. The page read: "We're especially sorry if this is news to you, but Krastyo was found dead in the Admiralengracht not far from his home on October 18th. The police say he was drunk when he fell in. If you knew Kras at all, you'll know that's not true.

"This here is a private forum for friends of Kras to grieve and share stories and information about our wonderful departed friend. There will be a proper party too, very soon, to celebrate his life and give him the send-off he deserves."

Nix knew a couple of Krastyo's Bulgarian buddies, one of whom connected us with Zlato and his brother Radko, old friends from Bulgaria who'd basically followed him out here. Nix fixed up a meeting. Zlato suggested the back room at Zest, a Bulgarian bar on the Bilderdijkstraat.

Krastyo's father would arrive on Sunday. On Monday morning he had a meeting with the Bulgarian Ambassador in the Hague. A translator would be appointed. The next day, along with his son's body, he'd fly home.

"We want to thank you for everything you've done," said Zlato.

"Of course," said Nix. "We loved him very much."

We drank to Kras. He was the nicest guy any of us knew. You probably think that's an exaggeration, but I don't think it is. He was naturally warm and sensitive — over-sensitive for sure, but just the sweetest, loveliest man. A man who'd always open his arms to you.

Nix asked the Bulgarians if they knew about Donka. Without saying a word, they made it clear that they did. They listened solemnly as Nix spelled out everything he knew about Kras and Donka, including our recent impromptu head to head with the handsome hardman.

I really couldn't blame the Bulgarians for not wanting in on our plan.

They agreed that Kras had "almost certainly" been murdered, but they spoke like they were resigned to it. "We told him not to get involved with those people," Radko said at one point. Nix was sorely disappointed.

"What about Donka?" he asked. "Did you meet her?"

Zlato had met her.

"And?" demanded Nix. "What did you think of her?"

"She was very nice girl, for sure."

"So don't you think we should try and help her?"

"Where is she?" asked Zlato, exasperated, fed up I think with Nix's bluntness. "How can we help if we don't know where is she?"

"I would like to help her also," said Radko, "but how? I have family here. I am happy to talk to police, but anything more…." He tightened his hoodie round his head.

Ultimately, they wanted no part of that world, and even Nix couldn't really blame them. But for the rest of the evening, he said little.

At home that night, before he went to bed, he turned to me and said: "It's not fair, is it?"

I shook my head. "It's not, man. I'm sorry. Come and have a hug."

We posted the following message on the *Friends of Krastyo* page:

TUESDAY NIGHT / 7PM / DE PRAEL
WE WILL BE DRINKING HEAVILY TO THE
MEMORY OF OUR VERY DEAR FRIEND
KRASTYO MIKHAYLOV.
PLEASE COME AND HELP US SAY GOODBYE.
NIX & WESLEY

Tuesday was the same day that Krastyo's body would be leaving Amsterdam.

In the end, almost everyone I'd ever met at Beachams was there, with two notable exceptions. Madison, who was at home in the States, thank God; and Garry Beacham himself, who was doubtless too busy expanding his markets to really have even the first idea who Kras was. Their absence aside, the evening was very well attended and as send-offs go, it was a roaring and beautifully moving success. Krastyo's life and his personality was on everybody's mind and lips. Nix had prepared a playlist of Krastyo's favourite bands and Zlato and Radko had added recommendations from their shared past. At one point a

253

microphone was passed around and people talked about their friend and why they loved him. It felt like an unofficial funeral service. It was very poignant. There were lots of tears.

"Donka should have been here," said Nix at one point.

"Kras should have been here," I said.

Nix tutted. "Well... *duh.*"

We laughed. We cried.

Nazdrave.

Then a couple of days later on the Facebook page, someone linked to a YouTube video that made everything ten times worse.

4.11

Magnet fishing is big in Amsterdam. It's basically next-level metal detecting and all you need is a rope, and a powerful neodymium magnet, which you can pick up online for less than fifty euros. Then you lower your magnet on the end of your rope into any one of the city's 165 canals and you pull up whatever your magnet attracts, more often than not a stash of keys, cans, cutlery, bottle tops and bicycles, all old, rusted and useless. Or sometimes you might get lucky and bring up something of genuine interest or value. Very occasionally, you might discover exotic weapons, such as swords, guns and — more often than you'd imagine — hand grenades. These finds usually make the local news.

When I came downstairs for breakfast on Thursday morning, Nix was sitting at the kitchen table behind his laptop. He looked up at me, his face wet with tears. "You need to see this."

I took a seat alongside him and he replayed the video he'd been watching.

The film opens on the Admiralengracht in the west of the city. On the left side of a low concrete bridge with iron railings, one 20-something Dutch guy is pulling on a length of rope which disappears into the canal. He knows he has something substantial because of the weight, and he can't fail to hide his excitement.

Suddenly there is a cut in the film and the one guy on the bridge becomes two. They explain in the video description that they'd had to wait for a friend to arrive to take over filming duties, as hauling their catch to the surface was a two-man job.

Having wrapped the end of the rope around the top of the railing, the two men start to pull together and eventually their catch comes into view.

It's difficult at first to make out what it is. For a moment it seems like just another old bicycle. You see a bent and rusted wheel with the tyre rotted away. Then the rest of the bicycle comes into view and you realise its dead frame is just a kind of garnish for the main event, the really heavy thing that's proving so difficult to hoist up out of the water.

With another heave, it becomes clear that beneath the bike is a black canvas bag of some sort, and the magnet is stuck fast to its contents.

What makes neodymium magnets particularly interesting, aside from their strength, is the fact that, unlike ordinary magnets, they also attract coins. And in this particular case, the rucksack attached to the end of the magnet contained an awful lot of coins. Thousands of euros worth.

With the next heave, the rucksack comes fully into view, as does the torso of the person to whom the rucksack is still attached.

The film shakes and goes momentarily out of focus as the person holding the camera realises what's afoot and yells out to his friends in Dutch, "It's a person! It's a person! Keep pulling!" He then zooms in on the weird discoloured monster that Krastyo's swollen body has become.

The coins in the rucksack are stuck fast to the magnet. The rucksack is attached to Krastyo's shoulders, chest and waist. His head, arms and legs are hanging from the magnet like a bouquet of dead sunflowers. As his body is yanked free of the water, it begins to spin and his face, greenish-black and bloated with methane and hydrogen sulfide, comes briefly into view. Water is cascading out of his clothes.

At which point, the film ends, presumably because the person holding the camera joined in the efforts to get Kras onto dry land.

I was crying. "Why is this online?"

Nix told me he'd already messaged the owners of the channel, demanding that they take down the video at once.

The video description meanwhile, explained that the drowned guy's rucksack had been full of coins, and that of course the police had been informed.

"I can't believe they didn't tell us about the coins," said Nix.

It's true that the police had neglected to mention that Kras was found with his coin collection strapped to his back. This news was particularly distressing for me. I began to sob. "It was my fault. It was my fucking fault. If I'd been there like I promised…." I broke down.

Nix laid a hand across my shoulders and squeezed. "You don't know that, Wesley. Don't… don't do that to yourself."

When I'd calmed down a little, we tried to figure out what must have happened. We guessed that maybe they'd grabbed Kras on his way to the bank and taken him back to his flat, where presumably Donka was waiting. Then they probably took Donka away and kept Kras captive till the dead of night, before tossing him into the canal.

That was one possibility, but we knew we'd never know for sure.

Had he been alive when they threw him in? Or had they already killed him? I kept breaking down as we tried to piece it together.

Ultimately, the only thing I knew for sure was that every day for the rest of my life, the possibility that Kras might still be alive today if I'd been a better friend, would tear strips from my heart. And rightly so.

4.12

Regardless. Life goes on.

So it was that I found myself in a room, feeling nervous. Of the five people present, two were giggling, one was taking photographs, but all eyes were fixed firmly on me. I held my hands together, as if in prayer, and gave a short bow to the assembled persons. They mirrored my movements in response. I then turned and moved slowly — because, I had intuited, that was how *he* moved — out of the apartment, down the narrow stone staircase and out onto the bridge.

At first I was embarrassed. I imagined people thinking, "Why is that silly Englishman dressed like a Bulgarian mystic?" After five, maybe ten minutes, however, I no longer gave a damn what anyone thought. I was focused, standing tall in the half-smiling sun, giving out hugs to strangers.

That was the plan for the morning session. Bryson was filming with a static camera from his friend Sanne's apartment on the Bloemgracht, where I'd just changed into my costume. It was situated in the heart of the Jordaan and overlooked the Kees de Jongenbrug on the Prinsengracht, where Spas Daskalov now stood, arms outstretched.

On a piece of string around his neck was a square of white card with large letters in black and red marker pen declaring: FREE HUGS. Around his body the large, slightly itchy bone-coloured robe. On his feet, sandals and thick woollen socks. And up top — of course — the wild wig and beard.

The disguise had been perfected by another of Bryson's friends, a professional make-up artist called Charlotte. Thanks to her help and expertise, I felt like an almost entirely new man. I felt... like Spas Daskalov.

I got away with it too. In the one hour I stood there, no one called me a fraud or spat in my face, and seventeen people hugged me. It was like being at church. Most of the huggers were clearly tourists, mostly women in small groups. Only one was alone: a bleached blonde woman in red jeans carrying an old-fashioned typewriter. She glanced at me in passing, stopped in her tracks, placed her typewriter on the ground and wrapped her arms around me. I reciprocated, soft-rubbing her spine with my knuckles.

In an American accent, she said, "Never say no to a hug," before ending with a hard squeeze and adding, "That's my motto."

"Nazdrave," I said. "That is mine."

As the woman stooped to pick up her typewriter, I found myself really wanting to know why she had it. But Spas Daskalov didn't. "It is not my story," thought the mystic. "If I must know, she will tell me." She didn't tell him. Instead she told him he smelled good, and off she marched. This was true. He smelled far better than he looked, in fact, because Bryson had washed his robe in frankincense and lavender.

I was grateful for that. I was also grateful, more generally, for the hugs. Each hug I received seemed to insulate me just a touch further against the creeping all-pervasiveness of death. It was all I could do to let go.

A few people stopped to take photographs. Some photographed their friends hugging me. One middle-aged Australian woman said, "We've just come out of the Anne Frank House and a hug from a stranger is exactly what I need."

"Nazdrave."

When the Westerkerk's bells tolled 11.30, I lowered my aching arms and performed a few salubrious half-stretches. When I returned to Sanne's apartment, I was greeted with rapturous applause by the nine people now in attendance. I replied with prayer-hands, my signature move.

"How did it feel?" asked Bryson.

"Apart from pain and prickly heat," Spas replied in halting English, "feel pretty good. Maybe I do every day from now."

It had indeed felt good. It warmed my heart that complete strangers were willing to take time out of their lives and even if just for a few seconds, share their compassion and humanity, openly and boldly, just for the joy of it. The fact that most of them were tourists touched me too. Amsterdammers are always slagging tourists off but the good ones are some of the loveliest people out there — they're instinctively predisposed to having a good time.

In the afternoon, I had my speaking scene, where Spas is approached by main character Felix, and as they're hugging, Felix starts weeping into his chest. Spas holds him tight and says, "*Ssshhhhh. Ne plachi*, my friend. *Ne plachi*. Everything is fine."

"Do you promise?" asks Felix.

"I promise," says Spas Daskalov. "Why not."

At the end of the day, most of the crew went for a drink in a nearby bar. I wore Spas Daskalov's beard, but not his wig. I got a lot of admiring glances, and people kept buying me shots. *Nazdrave!*

Towards the end of the night, Bryson told me he was looking into adopting kids. I was surprised, and foresaw on his behalf some fairly substantial obstacles. I counted them out on the digits of my left hand.

"Bryson, you're 65 years old. You're down a leg — I know that has absolutely zero impact on your ability to parent — *I* know that, but to the people who give out kids, it's bound to be another black mark." I shrugged. Bryson nodded, and bade me continue. "Also, while I appreciate you must be fairly expert by now, you are still, in the eyes of the law, a practising homosexual. You observe a religion that some people do refer to, as a cult. And you have a known history of physical violence. How do you plead?"

"Guilty." He smiled. "It's worth a shot though, right?"

When it was time to go home, I made a move to remove my beard and Bryson objected. "Don't you dare! That's your beard now, Wesley! I never wanna see you without it. Here, take the gum too. And what about the wig? You want the wig?"

"Really?" I was feeling incredibly moved. "Are you sure?"

"Sure I'm sure. For all your help today. You were wonderful! What about the robe? You want the robe? Sure you do. It suits you so well, Wesley. So well. Like I said, you were born to be a Bulgarian mystic."

With tears moistening my beard, I gathered my new identity together and smiled, mystically. "Nazdrave."

4.13

The Mystic Law. That's how Nichiren Buddhists explain the transcendent insanity of existence. Sometimes referred to as the Mystic Law of Cause and Effect, it underpins *everything*. If you ask me, as attempts to make sense of existence go, *The Mystic Law* makes a damn decent fist of it. Although if I'm entirely honest, it's not a million miles from *The Universe*. Either way, on the eve of Thanksgiving this year, it was very much in evidence, and, as it often tends to, it was fucking with me.

I'd accepted an invitation to a dinner party at Bryson's place, where I was honoured to sit around a table with a bunch of people I'd never met before, many of them Buddhists of one stripe or another. It was an American as opposed to a Canadian Thanksgiving and at some point between courses, we took turns to verbalise that for which we were most thankful. When it came to my turn, I immediately became emotional.

"I'm thankful for my friends," I said, "Bryson being one of the best." I paused for the smattering of *awwwws*. "And I'm thankful that I'm a little bit closer to my dad than I ever was. We're still not what you'd call *close* and I still kind of despise him for everything he did and didn't do, but we made a little progress this year. And, Bryson, he's coming out again in the new year. And this time I'd really like for you to meet him."

"Bravo, Wesley!"

At the end of the night, I had my coat on ready to leave when Bryson took me to one side and asked me if I was alright. He knew about Kras and Damo and he was worried that losing two close friends in such a short space of time might all be a little too much for me. With my tongue loosened by alcohol, I told him plainly that Damo was not my friend. Then I asked him outright: "Is it wrong to rejoice in the death of an evil man? What's the Buddhist perspective on that?"

"Well it's not very compassionate," he said, "and compassion without exception is pretty much at the heart of all Buddhist teaching."

"Really? Without exception?"

I posited that because the sociopath's sole purpose in life was to torture and torment his fellow humans, then surely one's duty of compassion lay with the rest of society, for the greater good of whom, the sociopath must be vanquished.

Bryson posited that there was goodness, or at least the potential for goodness, inside every living being; he posited that, goodness aside, every living being had a purpose — from the ugliest bugs to the mightiest mammals, from the sweetest of caregivers to the most hateful of psychopaths — that they all had their purpose and their part to play in the endless dance of cause and effect, karma, benefits, and compassion without exception.

Seeing that I was struggling with this idea, he said, "If it's hard to feel compassion for some people, try at least to wish them peace. That's a kind of compassion too. And remember, everyone can be redeemed."

I didn't agree, as everything I'd read and heard suggested that sociopaths were incurable, but I appreciated the sentiment. I thanked him, hugged him, and told him that I loved him.

On the ride home, I mulled over Bryson's words. I was reminded of Lizzie's theory that we need darkness — from cancer and psychosis to torture porn and wasps — to balance out the universe. We need to suffer, in short, so that we may learn to understand and appreciate the absence of suffering. If that were true, however, if evildoers really were necessary, then surely, people like me were necessary too.

Back home I went straight upstairs to bed, noticing on the way that I'd received a voice message from my Aunt Jo.

"Ohhhhh fuck," I said out loud. "Really? Now?"

It had to be.

And I swear, I'd just been thinking, for the first time in my life, now that Sofia was off, I should invite him over for Christmas. I shook my head. There was no other reason she'd call. Possibly Peter. But she hates talking on the phone as much as I do. I listened to the message.

"Hello? Wesley, are you there? He's not answerin'. Wesley, pet, give us a call when you get this. Or should we just...? I mean, you've probably already guessed like, so we might as well... Wesley, your dad's not well." I could hear Uncle Paul spluttering in the background. "Well, yes, more specifically, he's dead... but he's still not well, technically." Jo laughed. "Sorry, son, I know it's not funny. We just found out, half an hour ago. We might be in shock. Let us know if you want to come back for the funeral, son. We'll totally understand if you want nothing to do with it though. Just let us know, chuck. I hope everything's good in Amsterdam. Lots of love, Wesley! Ta-ra for now!"

I was smiling. I wished I made more of an effort with Jo and Paul. Especially Jo. She always made me laugh. I sent a message.

"Thanks for your message, Jo. Of course I'll come back for the funeral. I wouldn't miss it for the world. I'll arrange work cover and I'll see you soon. It'll be nice to catch up. Every cloud. Love, Wesley."

I put my phone aside and lay silently in the dark.

Nothing had really changed. The me that lay on my bed now, after the news that my father was dead, was more or less identical to the me cycling across town ten minutes previously, when my father — as far as my awareness was concerned — had still been alive. Nothing had changed. But I swear I felt something move inside. It was like a door that had always been locked had suddenly been flung open and after almost fifty years of trying and failing to get through this big rusty mysterious old door and into the room beyond, suddenly, in one fell swoop, I'd gained access. And the room beyond was empty, and infinite. And I was at the heart of it, floating in space — no spacesuit, no umbilical cord, just

4.14

My dad had been dead, at home, for around 36 hours before he was missed by alcoholic friends. Which is not too shabby. I'd be happy with that.

The funeral was not till the following Friday, so I arranged cover for the tours I'd miss and booked tickets on the Eurostar.

In Peckham, I caught up with my Aunt Jo and Uncle Paul. I talked about my dad's visit, about how irritated I'd been; about that unexpected wave of affection. They talked about their intermittent interactions with him over the previous forty years, about how he'd ring up drunk on my mum's birthday or at Christmas, and end up weeping down the phone, begging forgiveness. Jo resented him for making her feel sorry for him. She didn't believe he deserved her forgiveness, especially for his cowardice in the face of my mum's illness.

I also heard — for the first time — about the time he nearly died. Apparently I'd been abroad when it happened and they hadn't wanted to bother me. The gist of the story was this: out in Finchley late one night my dad saw a man pushing a woman hard against a bus-stop shelter, his hand wrapped around her neck. So he waded in and a fight ensued, with my dad getting the upper hand. Apparently he had the guy on the ground and was administering a sound kicking when the woman stopped him. Then when he relented, the other guy scrambled to his feet, whipped out a blade, cheffed him up and left him for dead.

In hospital, convinced he was dying, he asked a friend to get word to Jo, so she could let me know. When he didn't die, the friend informed Jo anyway. She was glad he did.

"I used to say I wished he'd never been born," she said. "But then maybe that lass at the bus shelter wouldn't be alive today.

And of course, you wouldn't be here." I smiled. "And I'm really glad you're here, Wesley. It's lovely to see you, son."

As soon as she saw I was crying, my Auntie Jo gathered me up and with a "poor little bugger", she rocked me back and forth like a baby.

On the morning of my father's funeral, I noticed everyone on television calling the day Black Friday. Not in honour of my father alas, but because it was the day Americans shot each other for cheap TVs (as opposed to just… *ennui*). It was a pleasing coincidence.

I arrived with Jo and Paul at the St Marylebone Crematorium around 11.30am and I was shocked to see so many mourners. At least a hundred. Is that a lot? I know it's not Lady Di numbers but it seems like a lot for a man who drank his wife to death. Objection. Sustained.

The cremation had been organised by a man called Kev Pinder. Kev was slight with — to my jaded eye — the physical bearing of a suffering junkie. What was even more surprising, however, was that he was clearly mixed race and I knew from bitter, uncomfortable experience that my father was a practised racist. Or at least, he used the language of the practised racist. His everyday conversation, for example, especially after having moved from the very white north-east to multicultural London, was positively littered with Pakis, niggers, darkies, coons, nips, chinks and jungle bunnies. See also frogs, wogs, spicks, wops, micks, jocks and pikey cunts. (Not to mention puffs and raspberries.) My dad was your classic northern bigot. A shameless bigot. Maybe even a proud bigot. Yet here was this swarthy man not only going to great lengths to arrange this racist man's send-off, but also readying himself to say a few words.

I'd also been given the opportunity to contribute to the eulogy, or to say a few words of my own if I wished, but I passed on both counts. I couldn't pretend, and saw no point making waves.

Taking my seat in the front row of a packed hall with Jo and Paul to my right, I felt sick with tension. I didn't want to feel like I was sitting in judgement over my father, but I was. I definitely was.

"The first thing I learned about Gordon," said the humanist minister, "was that he lived his life in his own unique way."

Hmm. I was pretty sure belligerent drunken chippies were ten a penny throughout the British Isles, but no matter.

"It's very clear that he had a strong personality."

Sure. Strong personality. Basically a euphemism for colossal twat.

"Not much is known of Gordon's childhood, or of his life before he moved to London."

Jo and Paul had also elected to take no part in the post-mortem, electing instead to "let sleeping dogs lie".

"His marriage to Karen ended in tragedy when Karen lost her life after a short battle with cancer in her late twenties, leaving Gordon devastated and the single parent to their three-year-old son Wesley. It can't have been easy for Gordon bringing up a son on his own, but he never shirked from that responsibility, and he did the best he could, always making sure that Wesley was provided for, both materially and emotionally."

"Ha!"

A mutter ran through the congregation. The minister paused and glanced towards me, twitched, then continued, waxing significant about my dad's less than mediocre life, bigging up and rose-tinting, frustrating the fuck out of me frankly.

Then came Kev Pinder.

Kev began by thanking everyone for coming and read nervously from the scrap of paper in his hands. "I first met Gordon a couple of years after he moved down south. Probably like most of you here, I met him in a pub."

Some titters here, for alcoholism.

"First time I met him he asked me if I was a camel jockey."

Some chortles here, for racism.

"I told him I was half camel jockey, half jock, and from then on we became great mates. And Gordon was just that… a really great mate. Most of you are here today because, although he was not always an easy man to get along with, he was always a generous and protective friend who would do anything for the people he cared for.

"Gordon was a real character and as we all know, he liked a drink, and he liked a fight. One of the things that made him special was that almost every time after he lost his temper and did something regrettable, he would always send a bunch of flowers the next day to say he was sorry. I know there's a couple of florists here today who'll miss him more than most.

"Gordon had his faults and he wasn't always a good boy, but lots of people loved him. You've only got to look around this room to see how much he was loved. He will be missed by everybody here today and… it breaks my heart… that he's gone." Kev started crying, keeping it together enough to finish. "Thanks again for coming today… to celebrate Gordon's life."

Kev took his seat to warm applause and the minister retook the lectern and spoke about the end of Gordon's life. "Although Gordon suffered from ill health quite a bit in the last few years of his life, he was a stubborn man with a will of iron, and if he wasn't ready to go, he wasn't going to go. But eventually, the incoming tide did catch up with him. And so, whatever the different beliefs of those gathered here today, we can all share in the comforting knowledge… that he is now at peace."

Maybe because I didn't know. Maybe because I felt guilty because we weren't close enough for me to have known he was ill. Maybe that. Maybe everything else. But whatever the reason, I broke down.

My head slumped forward on my chest, my hands rose up to my face and I started sobbing. I was embarrassed, and I was angry, and I was confused. The minister, who had a job to do, kept going...

"We're going to end with another piece of music that meant a lot to Gordon. Apparently this will be familiar to any of you who ended up in a lock-in with him. Gordon's favourite song and one he would regale his fellow drinkers with, whether they liked it or not."

By the end of *Streams of Whiskey* by The Pogues — a song that contains the immortal lines: "*When the world is too dark and I need the light inside of me, I'll walk into a bar, and drink fifteen pints of beer*" — I had pulled myself together.

The minister continued: "We think of this building and others like it as places of death, but really they're not. We might be here because of a death, but once we're gathered together here, we talk about life. The life we have known and shared, and will treasure into the future. As a consequence of that, these buildings hold more love than many places in the world.

"In parting, I would like to thank you once again for your time. The fact is, your very presence here today speaks louder than all of our words."

I knew this to be true and it made me — despite myself — re-evaluate my opinion of my father.

The minister finished with a poem about birds in the mist returning to the sun, and people filed out of the crematorium to the sounds of Louis Jordan and his Orchestra singing *What's the Use of Getting Sober (When You're Going to Get Drunk Again)?*

4.15

The wake was in one of my dad's favourite bars. I stayed for a couple of hours and had a couple of borderline belligerent conversations wherein I refused to share my dad's friends' opinions that Gordon was "the salt of the earth". My feeling that their friend was a weak and ignoble man who hit women, was afraid of everything, gave a shit about nobody but himself and totally, one hundred percent wasted his life, was met with resistance. Respectful resistance for the most part — I was Gordon's son after all — but resistance nonetheless. Kev Pinder said, "Maybe your family never really gets to know the true you."

I laughed, not unkindly but not with warmth. "That may be so, man. I dunno." My head shook. "I think maybe the man you knew, and the man I knew, were two very different men." On that note we shook hands and I left around 4pm.

Later that evening I picked up my stuff from Jo and Paul, vowed to see them again soon under more cheerful circumstances, and made my way to London Bridge, walking in from Elephant & Castle, rather than getting the tube, because of terrorism.

That night I spent with old friends, and as old friends have, since the beginning of time, we talked about death and the end of the world.

I also met, for the first time, a guy called Simon, who looked like he knew his way around an ashram. He was Welsh and older than me, with an unkempt beard and piercings in his eyebrows. It's OK, you don't need to remember him. He's not staying. But he'll say something in a moment that impressed me at the time, and I wanted to make sure it was on record.

It was Simon who told me the news that, only a few hours previously, just fifty metres from where we were sitting, two people had been stabbed to death by a convicted terrorist who was then disarmed by a tour guide (of all people) and two other members of the public. One used a fire extinguisher. The other a narwhal tusk. Then the police shot the terrorist dead.

I do hope the strangeness of this day is coming across. I did say *narwhal tusk*, yes. Meanwhile, at exactly the same time, America was reliving *The Night of the Living Dead* yet again, because… cheap stuff.

You know?

"I don't think we've got long left," said Simon.

And so we turned to the end of humankind.

Simon said: "I know lots of people who were absolutely *convinced* that the world was going to end on December 31st, 1999. There were also loads of prophecies and astrological shifts that suggested this might be the case, so a lot of people were expecting some cataclysmic finale. Conflagrations in the sky, you know. Mountains crumbling. Sodom and Gomorrah. Fire and brimstone. Yadda yadda yadda. Obviously that didn't happen. But that never happens, right? Or rarely. It's much more nuanced than that, isn't it? More commonly, what we actually have is more of a slow, gradual, creeping apocalypse. We inch towards Armageddon, a little closer with every earthquake, every war, every terrorist atrocity, every psychopathic politician. And next week when Boris Johnson becomes the next Prime Minister, we will have entered the final stretch, I think. Gloves off. Anything goes. Last days of Rome. Fuck and eat *everything*." He shrugged, smiled and took a drink of his craft ale. "Now who would like some ketamine?"

I gasped. "You're my actual hero."

What a day. Funeral, wake, terrorist atrocity, apocalyptic prophecy, drugs in a pub. Classic.

And so we got high, danced in the backroom of a South London boozer till four in the morning and forgot. And in that delicious forgetting... *life*.

IV & V

December 2019

5.1

December came in like a frozen goldfish. In the first days, fresh from father's funeral, I felt like I was unravelling. I was a mess of intense and contradictory emotions. Whenever I felt guilt connected to my father, it was followed immediately by terrible rage. *So what? So what if one time he'd intervened in a domestic dispute? What was that compared to the countless number he'd initiated?* And yet… a packed crematorium does not lie. And if people were crying for my father, didn't that mean he was a decent guy? Didn't that mean I was wrong about him? And if I was wrong about my father, whom I'd known for many long years, wasn't it almost a certainty that I was also wrong about Damo, whom I'd known, all told, for just a handful of days?

I thought a lot about the killing of Damo. Aside from the time I spent squabbling with myself about semantics — *killed* still seemed a bit strong, frankly — I struggled with guilt. I visited his Facebook page, poring over the messages of shock and condolence. I thought about the tears of Damo's wife and daughters and I felt sick. Sometimes I'd get a flash of him, crushed and eviscerated, and I'd be hit with such a sharp sensation of falling that I'd have to stop whatever I was doing and take a moment.

Then I'd remember everything Damo said about women, and I'd listen to the vile recorded conversations I still had on my laptop, and I'd think, fuck that. He was the Devil. He had to go.

So, clinging hard to the fact that I'd done an *Objectively Good Thing,* I looked to the future. I heard back from Lizzie and started planning our confessional dinner, and I booked a one-way ticket to Da Nang, leaving on January 4th, 2020. That felt particularly good.

Meanwhile, I carried on working as many shifts as I could. When I worked, I forgot. I got lost in my tours. The second I jumped onto the concrete bench at the foot of the Rokin, the me that was preoccupied and guilty was immediately replaced by the me that was irrepressible and borderline vaudevillian. Guiding gave me something in which to lose myself and I was extremely grateful.

So I trudged through the first half of December with perpetually ice-cold feet, working hard and deferring gratification. I also started meditating again. I seem to start four or five times a year. Then, on December 13, rampaging sociopath Boris Johnson was voted into power in the UK, in something of a landslide, and I sent a message to my new friend Simon. "What was that?" I wrote. "That was the point of no return, mate. Enjoy the end days!"

Then, on December 14, completely by chance, I came across something called *An Essay on the Principle of Population* by the Reverend Thomas Robert Malthus, and I read it in a few days. It was a bit of a slog but fascinating, and gobsmackingly pertinent. I was just in the final stretch when Monica popped up in my WhatsApp. "Biertje?"

Cheered by the invitation, which didn't happen quite so much since she'd got together with Sylvia, we met at In't Aepjen and snagged the corner table by the radiator. After her first sip of beer, Monica sighed with satisfaction and declared, "Aaaah, gezellig." In response, my mouth made an unusual shape and I started sobbing. Violently too, but only for a moment.

I have no idea why. Grief? Guilt? Overdose of gezelligheid? The resilience of Monica's friendship? A delicious cocktail of all of the above? I genuinely couldn't say.

Monica comforted me but I laughed it off. "I'm just a bit burned out. I've been working like a slave. How've you been?"

Monica had been well. Things were going great with Sylvia and her free time was spent mostly writing her book and planning her cruise. She'd be away for eight months, partially on her own, partially with Sylvia. She'd finish her book by March 2020 and set sail in April. Nothing could stop her.

After we'd caught up, I told her about the Reverend Malthus, explaining that he was way ahead of his time, writing in 1798 about the inevitability of humans one day running out of food.

Monica shrugged.

"He was a dick about poor people though. Thought they were animals, more or less, and if it wasn't for rich people teaching them how to suffer, they'd just lie around drinking and fucking all day."

"That doesn't sound so bad."

"I know, right? He also reckons that the point of evil is to give good people something to do. Listen to this."

I pulled a notebook from my jacket pocket and located my favourite passage. I read it aloud to Monica.

"'Evil exists in the world not to create despair but activity... It is not only the interest but the duty of every individual to use his utmost efforts to remove evil from himself and from as large a circle as he can influence, and the more he exercises himself in this duty... the more completely does he appear to fulfil the will of his Creator.'"

Monica shook her head. "Let me see." She took the paper from me and took the time to process the quote. "But he doesn't say that evil is good, no?"

"No, more that it serves a positive function, I think, in that it gives the rest of us something to fight against."

"So even Trump, per esempio, has a function?"

"Yeah. He shows us what we need to get rid of."

"So how do we get rid?"

"Well," I said. "Obviously, voting him out at the next election won't stop him being a malign influence on the planet, so..." I went

278

back to the relevant quote. "'It is not only the interest but the *duty* of every individual to use his utmost efforts to remove evil from himself and from as large a circle as he can influence.' So it's our duty to remove him, however we see fit. And not just Trump but every evil fucker. I mean, evil's everywhere, right? It's not just your Trumps and your Putins, and your Borises and your Epsteins. It's also your ordinary, everyday monsters." Like Damo and Matty, I thought. And Sam. "I'm convinced that if we got rid of all the sociopaths, we'd be able to survive. You know, as a species. We could work together for the benefit of all. We could solve the fossil fuels issue and the dead soil issue. All the issues. We're fucking amazing! We could build another planet! We could colonise the whole universe! We could *evolve*, Monica!"

"And how many of these sociopaths there are?"

"By my reckoning, if Dr Martha Stout PhD is correct, there are probably forty to fifty million sociopaths."

Monica shook her head. "So how do we get rid fifty million?"

I gave a massive defeated sigh. "I don't know for sure, Monica, but I'm pretty sure we have to kill them. All fifty million. It'd be a sociopath holocaust. It'd make Hitler look like a toddler throwing rocks."

"You want to kill fifty million human beings?"

"God, no." I was shocked at the thought. "Human beings feel empathy. Sociopaths don't. For the sake of seven billion or so human beings, I want to kill fifty million sociopaths."

"Va bene ma… how do we know who is the true sociopath?"

"Well." I sighed. "That's where it gets tricky. There are tests, but as we know, sociopaths cheat. And who's gonna do the killing?"

Monica shrugged. "That's the easy part. If you are sure you are helping the world. I would do, for sure. You no? I have to pee." She went to pee.

Left alone, I tried to imagine it. Administering the gas, like a dentist, then pressing a small metal rod against the forehead or temple of the soon to be eradicated sociopath in question, then delivering the fatal charge and watching as the living monster became a lifeless, harmless hunk of meat.

I knew it wouldn't feel good.

Even inadvertent killing didn't feel good. Of course it didn't — I wasn't a psychopath. Even finishing off a mouse when cats had left them twitching in agony upset me quite considerably. Shit, I even crossed myself after murdering mosquitoes.

However.

Just because it might not feel good didn't mean it wasn't good. In my head, there were two very distinct kinds of murder. There was *bad murder*, which was murder for personal gain or petty, personal dislike. And then, there was *good murder*.

The moment Monica returned from the loo, I said, "Yes. I'd do it too."

5.2

December 16 was my birthday. I was 48. I told no one and I received two completely unrelated messages. The first was from Monica. It said: "What are you doing for Christmas Day? Come to the boat if you have no plans. I will have a small number of my favourite people. I'd like you to come too."

I wasn't sure if I'd been insulted or not. I told her I'd definitely come, unless something hideous happened.

The second message was from Madison. I'd seen her on the square a couple of times since Feathergate II and it had been mostly silent and extremely awkward. So much so that a couple of weeks previously, I sent her an olive branch message, the crux of which was: "I could never have imagined such a horrible thing would happen, and I'm really sorry it did. I was hoping we could be friends again. But if that's not possible, I hope all is well with you, and I wish you nothing but good things. Love, Wesley." A couple of weeks later, she replied: "Hey Wesley. I don't hate you anymore. I don't want to have sex with you anymore either though. Goodbye!"

Ha! The arrogance of the woman!

I didn't respond. I considered it. But I rose above it. Like a pigeon. Then a few days after that, I saw Elvira in the Beachams office and she was behaving strangely, regarding me with an extremely curious expression.

"OK," I demanded. "What's going on?"

"Nothing!" She laughed and told me she'd been talking to Madison.

"Oh yeah?"

"So you and her had a thing, huh?"

"A small thing."

"So I hear." Elvira smiled.

I wasn't sure whether or not she was deriding my penis.

"Are you deriding my penis?"

"No!" She laughed some more. "I mean, I heard it wasn't very long — just a few weeks! And then you made her kill a pigeon?"

"Are you serious?" I bristled. "Is that what she's saying?"

"No, I'm just fucking with you. She said you encouraged her and she was a bit drunk and she hit a pigeon and then freaked out and blamed you. She even said she feels embarrassed about the whole thing."

"Really?" I told her about the message. "Like I was angling for sex!"

Elvira sympathised. "She's a bit crazy, for sure. Like all the guides."

"Right? I think I'm the only sane one here."

Elvira laughed heartily. "Very funny, Wesley. For sure, you are one of the worst."

"Oh, come on. At least I'm not afraid of pigeons."

Elvira stopped smiling and asked me if I knew why Madison was afraid of pigeons. I said I didn't but I'd love to know. She screwed up her face. "You didn't hear it from me, OK?"

Madison was 12 years old; her kid sister was 10. They were playing together across the street from their home. Madison had a bag of popcorn and she tossed some to a passing pigeon. More pigeons arrived. Lots more, and her kid sister began freaking out. Finding her sister's fear amusing, Madison scattered popcorn all around. When her sister started squealing and waving her hands around, the pigeons took flight and her sister made a run for it, straight into the path of a passing motorbike. She was killed instantly.

Madison never forgave herself. Worse still, she feared her parents never forgave her either. Also, for the rest of her life, she never ate popcorn, she never dated boys with motorbikes and she was terrified of pigeons.

I was horrified, and felt incredibly guilty. Not about the pigeon-splattering incident but about paying the Seed Guy. What a horrible thing to have put her through. My ignorance of her trauma didn't make it any easier to forgive. I knew there was *something* and I'd deliberately put her in an uncomfortable situation. I was disgusted with myself. Afresh.

That night at home I told Nix about the Seed Guy prank and the source of Madison's trauma. He shrugged. "Don't beat yourself up over it. Or better still, do something good to make amends."

"I am," I said. "Tomorrow. I'm making dinner."

5.3

Lizzie had a mischievous twinkle and smelled, for some reason, probably strawberry-related, of strawberries. Doug was dour as always but his gruffness was somewhat subdued by his having to accept my hospitality. He handed me wine at the front door, I shook his huge hand and ushered him in.

As I was bringing the starter together, Lizzie and Doug chatted at table with Nix. Doug liked Nix. Once I'd served the roasted asparagus starter, I cleared my throat and said: "OK, let's get this out of the way, shall we? Then hopefully we can enjoy the rest of the evening and who knows? Maybe it will be the first of many."

"Can I just say," Doug interjected, "I didn't ask for this."

"Oh, I know you didn't," I replied, holding off from adding, "That's the whole fucking problem, you big, dumb, shit-talking clown", and instead adding, "I asked for this. I know you've heard some rumours about me and I could have just left it, but I wanted to clear the air and clarify that what you've heard is not true. Not quite. So don't worry. It's all good."

It was too. I was looking forward to unburdening myself. So far in Amsterdam I'd told only Nix, Monica, Kras and Bryson. It would be good to add a couple more to the list. So I poured some more wine and began.

"In 2004, I was working as a journalist in London and I had an idea for a book. It was basically a compilation of people's most embarrassing and shameful moments. So I collected a bunch of these stories online, stitched them together and called it *The Little Book of Shame*."

"Sounds like that TV show," said Lizzie. "What's it called? *A Little Show of Shame*?"

"Well spotted, Lizzie." I smiled. This was a good story. "The book did well immediately and through that I got an agent, a guy called Jim Bates. Over the next few years, I published a couple of other little stocking fillers — the same kind of stuff, worst break-ups, sex-fails. Not good books by any stretch, but they sold well and made money and I had a good relationship with Jim and everything was rosy in the garden.

"Then I had an idea for a novel. It was about a woman with a weird kind of superpower — basically every time she stimulated someone to orgasm, that person died and the life she'd inadvertently taken from them, in the act of killing them, then became hers. So as long as she kept making people come, she was pretty much immortal. I pitched it to Jim and he wasn't sure. He told me to write it though and he'd take a look. Fast forward to eighteen months later. I'd been writing pretty much every night in my spare time and I was coming to the end of the first draft, when a novel called *The Good Murderess* was published. It was the story of a woman with a weird kind of superpower and… well, you get the idea. It was my idea, and someone else had written it.

"I'd never heard of the author, a woman called Jessie Finn. So I did a little investigating and discovered that she also had Jim as an agent. Then I found out that Jim and Jessie were actually an item. Jim had left his wife and kids and moved in with this much younger writer.

"So I called him — Jim, my agent — and he didn't answer. So I left a message, and he didn't return it. So I sent him an email, and he didn't reply. So one day I waited outside his office at the end of the day and I stopped him in the street. I had a copy of the book, *The Good Murderess*, with me."

"Did you read it?" asked Lizzie.

"Yes."

"And?"

"It was actually very good, yeah, but not how I saw it and… *it was my idea,*" I growled. "Unfortunately, as my agent was very keen to point out, there is no copyright on ideas. I asked him if he thought it was part of his job to take certain of his clients' ideas and share them with other clients of his that he happened to be fucking. 'It just came up,' he said. 'And she really liked the idea.' I told him I'd just spent a substantial chunk of my life writing a book that was now useless, but he didn't care. He said it was a woman's book anyway — it had to be written by a woman. When I asked why he hadn't returned my calls, he said, and I quote, 'To be honest, I was hoping you'd just sort of, disappear.' And that was when I lost my temper. And this is the bit I'm not proud of, obviously. I grabbed hold of his neck and punched him three times in the face. Pretty hard. I had a lot of rage. Then I just walked away. I left him doubled over in the street.

"The next night he called me from hospital and told me the news, that I'd blinded him in one eye. He'd already spoken to his lawyer and basically, if I didn't give him everything he wanted, he was gonna press charges and he reckoned, for Grievous Bodily Harm with intent, I'd go to jail for five years.

"So I gave him what he wanted, which was… basically everything. He took the money I'd saved up, or most of it. He took my car. And he took the rights to the three books I'd published so far, including *The Little Book of Shame*, which as you pointed out, was later adapted into a hugely successful international TV panel show franchise. I don't know if there was already an offer on the table for the TV rights when we had our little *contretemps*, but… yeah. Of course there was. He was a devious fucker. Oh, and to add insult to injury, *The Good Murderess* was recently optioned by fucking Netflix, so you can imagine how thrilled I am about that."

I took a sip of Prosecco.

"So, in a nutshell, that's what happened. And apart from feeling that I'd been punished rather excessively, I also felt that I totally, one hundred percent deserved it. I was completely depressed by my behaviour. I didn't want to be a person who went round blinding people, no matter how awful they were. It affected me really badly — it was basically a culmination of years of self-loathing. Everything changed in that moment. I gave up everything I had, which amounted to a decent job and an apartment I really loved, and I ran away, first to South America. I had about a grand that I'd managed to keep back from Jim, so I used that to get going and I basically travelled the world for five years, working in bars and hostels. I also vowed to change my ways. I devoted myself to a life of non-violence and even became a Buddhist for a couple of years."

I placed my hands together, Spas Daskalov style, and bowed.

"So there we have it."

Then, just as Nix was about to break the silence and potentially give away the twist, I raised my hand instinctively to silence him; equally instinctively, he stabbed my hand with his fork. I laughed. "Except!" I continued. "There is one more detail. A bombshell, if you will." I raised my eyebrows at Doug and Lizzie. I was pleased with how I'd unfolded the story. I had them in the palm of my hand. Structure had never been my strong point but this time I'd nailed it. I milked it for a second longer, then it was time to devastate them. "Something I didn't find out until five years after it had happened was… *he lied*. My agent. He wasn't blind at all."

Lizzie gasped.

"Exactly." I folded my arms, dramatically. "He made the whole thing up! And like a fucking sap, I took him at his word."

"That's fucked up," said Doug.

"So what did you do?" asked Lizzie.

I shook my head. "I killed him." I left a second to see if either of them bought it, and neither looked entirely sure. "I'm *joking,* of course."

Doug and Nix laughed.

"You arse," said Lizzie.

"I didn't do anything. Ultimately, I think his lie was the best thing that ever happened to me. It started me on the path to pacifism. It got me to give up journalism — which never really suited me anyway — and it got me to see a lot more of the world. All I really lost was money, a career as a writer, and happiness."

"That's really awful," said Lizzie. "I'm so sorry that happened."

"No, really, I had it coming. Karma, innit. Buddhist revenge. I mean, what had you heard, Doug? That I'd hit a guy and blinded him?"

Doug nodded. "Pretty much. And that you then went on the run."

"Well, yeah, that's mostly true."

"No, but... you changed, right?" said Lizzie. "I mean, that's the point. People change."

"Lizzie's right," said Doug. "You changed your ways and that's a good thing. And I'm sorry I was... I think maybe I've been a bit of a prick. I'm sorry." He offered his hand across the table and I shook it.

"Thank you."

Then he reached into his jacket on the back of his chair and handed me an envelope. I opened it up and read the words on the slip of paper inside. "Dear Wesley. Please accept this my written apology. Doug." I laughed. Short and to the point. "Written apology accepted."

Nix made a toast. "To changed ways."

"Changed ways."

Which of course, is like a bloody red rag to the Universe.

Am I right?

5.4

Just as dry alcoholics may — for various reasons — frequently imagine themselves drinking a nice cold beer, so have I, throughout my seven years of physical sobriety, habitually and instinctively visualised punching people in the face. I don't just mean that knee-jerk way you might trip a running child — mentally, I mean. I'm talking about relishing the fantasy; staring at someone who's annoyed me and beating their face to a bloody pulp in my head. Is that weird? It didn't happen a lot. But it happened.

Occasionally I'd also wonder if any situation might arise in which I'd willingly violate my code; in which I'd jump rather than fall off the fist-wagon; in which I'd give myself a pass because, well... Nazis. And of course, less than 24 hours after we'd all fellated me silly for being such a changed man, it happened.

I was finishing up a Red Light, standing over De Gestreelde Borst, the bronze breast that rests unobtrusively between the cobbles near the front of the Old Church, when I was interrupted by two arse-faced enforcers demanding to see my licence.

Also known as Handhaving or Special Investigation Officers, enforcers tend to ooze so much self-importance and cold authoritarianism that I swear, they're even worse than police. They have that same superiority complex that every uniform bequeaths, but also, the fact that they lack the muscle of proper police clearly sticks in their collective craw. It gives them something to butt against, something to prove, ultimately making them pettier and more obnoxious than their pistol-toting cousins.

They do have some authority, however. At the time in question, they had the power of enforcement. Mostly this consisted of handing out fines for fare dodging, pavement befoulment and, God forbid, public consumption of alcohol. These fines were a major source of revenue for the Gemeente. For example, if a tour guide in the Red Light District failed to produce a valid licence, they could be fined as much as €950. And there were few things an enforcer enjoyed more than handing out fines. It really was their raison d'être. They relished it. You could see it in their eyes.

Even better than handing out fines, however, was the power of arrest, which came into effect when the enforcers' authority was called into question, and which was enforced with various tools of enforcement.

At first they just had handcuffs, so they demanded batons, pepper spray and bodycams. Like the police. When they were refused, they had the temerity to go on strike, thus cutting off a valuable revenue supply for the Gemeente. So, in a move which seemed like the very definition of negotiating with terrorists, Amsterdam mayor Femke Halsema immediately backed down and gave them bodycams. No pepper spray or batons though. On that she remained absolutely firm — until halfway through May 2019, when the fuckers went on strike again. One more week of whining about needing "the right tools" and Halsema relented, agreeing to the pepper spray. But absolutely no batons.

It was clear to anyone paying attention that all the enforcers had to do was step on the money hose every few months, and within a couple of years, they'd be a bona fide paramilitary unit.

Incidentally, this was only the second time I'd ever been checked. In the same period, Nix — a black man, you may remember — was in double figures. You do the math.

So I opened my bag and looked around for my licence. Instinctively I pretended I didn't have it, just so I could enjoy the relish in their eyes. Then, as they began to twinkle, I said, "Oh no — here it is."

"Let's see some ID."

This was the first enforcer, a middle-aged blonde woman with a sharp, angular face reminiscent of vacuum-packed supermarket parmesan. Worse still, she didn't say please. That really pissed me off. If I hadn't still been giving a tour, I'd most likely have made something of it. Instead, I pulled out a plastic cardholder filled with bank cards and photo ID for cinemas and museums. They shook their heads, unsuppressed glee seeping onto their faces. Only a driving licence or a passport would suffice. I had both of course, but carried neither, because one: fear of losing them, and two: celebration of the fact that I didn't live in a totalitarian regime. Or did I?

"You do know it's against the law to not carry official ID?"

"We could fine you and hold you in prison for up to six hours," added the second enforcer, a man maybe half my age, a man who barely had call to shave the bumfluff from his dormant spiteful face.

My jaw stiffened. I instinctively began speed-chewing the inside of my lower lip. "Can I just finish my tour? Is that OK? It'll take two minutes."

For a moment the enforcers said nothing, then the boy, Bumfluff, in a moment of grudging magnanimousness, consented.

I finished the tour. I wound it up quickly and apologetically, with a wildly unprofessional amount of eye-rolling. By the time I eventually turned back to the enforcers, however, something had occurred to me. "Actually, I do have my passport with me."

I took out my phone and located a photograph of my passport.

"That's no good," said Parmesan.

"We don't accept digital ID," said Bumfluff.

I laughed. "Bend a little for God's sake. I've got my tour guide's licence. I've got my bank cards. I've got a photo of my passport. I could show you all of my social media accounts and my website. I could phone up my family or any of my friends and they could confirm that I am who I say I am, but you're telling me that none of that is enough?"

For a moment they just stared at me, dead-eyed, like I was a game of cricket.

Then Parmesan said, "We'll give you a warning for not having ID. If you get stopped again and you don't have it, you'll receive a €60 fine."

"Are you serious?"

"Or," countered Parmesan, "if you prefer, you can pay the fine now."

"It's entirely up to you, *Sir*." Bumfluff clearly couldn't be happier with how much his *sir* had sounded like *kankerhoer*.

And that was when it happened. Something inside me just snapped.

For a full ten seconds, I stared in simmering silence, my teeth rapidly clenching and unclenching. And as I stared, vicious words flooded my brain, taking the place of the fists I was desperate to throw at this odious boy Nazi. I wondered how much of a ragu I could make of his hairless face before I was pepper sprayed, handcuffed and carted off. Was it worth it? Seven years down the drain and a criminal record to boot? My rage was suddenly so profound that I thought… yes, on balance, it probably was. Just one more word was enough. Go on, enforcer. Give me an excuse. One. More…

"Wesley."

It was Lizzie. She'd just finished a Red Light. She grabbed my left arm and I snapped out of it. I turned back to the enforcers. "Yes, thank you," I said. "A warning is great." I smiled. I nodded. I was good. I was over it. I was incredibly relieved. Lizzie had saved me.

A note was made on my official record. If at any point in the future I failed to produce official ID — originals, mind you — I would be fined €60. I thanked the enforcers for their understanding and wished them a pleasant evening. Then I turned back to Lizzie and hugged her.

"You OK? You looked like you were about to lamp that fucker."

I caught my breath and looked into Lizzie's eyes. The words *changed ways* floated between us, mocking me. I was trembling. I was extremely grateful, but also ashamed I'd been observed on the brink of a meltdown. "She didn't say *please*." I blinked a couple of tears onto my right cheek.

"Oh my God, come here, you silly sod!"

Lizzie grabbed hold of me again. She had a Scottish face, but a Dutch body, so she was a good six centimetres taller than me, meaning my head fell nicely onto one of her shoulders. The hug made me emotional. I held on tight and whispered into her ear, "I don't know who I am, Lizzie."

"Awww, sweetheart, it's OK. You'll be OK. Just follow your heart."

With a soft gasp at the repetition of Bryson's words, I tried to pull away but Lizzie held on. I didn't complain. Lizzie said nothing. She just held me, quite firmly, with a little gentle patting from her right hand. When after a while I attempted to withdraw a second time, she held on still and I laughed, settling back in. Lizzie didn't laugh. She held on fast. Then, with an extra little squeeze, she hissed, right into my ear, "Follow your heart!" and she released me, with gusto, like she was giving a pigeon its freedom. I sprang backwards, laughing again because she was insane and I loved her for it. Even when she'd been holding onto me, I was conscious that I was laughing, when only moments ago

I'd been on the brink of berserk. *That's* what friends are for. Then as I stepped back, full of the joys of Lizzie, my right foot hit something solid and I fell over backwards onto the ground, ending up on my back in the middle of a big icy puddle. Lizzie instinctively exploded into such loud, screeching laughter that anyone in the Red Light District who hadn't seen me fall, must surely then have turned toward the laughter and seen me scrambling back to my feet.

Actually I didn't scramble. I jumped up in a second, as one tends to when one lands in a winter puddle. The crouching tourist over whom I'd tripped had been taking a close-up of the bronze breast. He was a jovial Irishman, laughing and apologising, insisting on wiping down the back of my long winter coat. A Dutch woman joined him and both were laughing as they dried me off, then laughing even harder as their tissues fell apart and covered the back of my coat with tissue fibre. Lizzie was still bent double, with nary a flicker of remorse, still visibly and vigorously enjoying the impromptu theatre she'd created.

"It's coming off now," said the Irishman. "We'll have you right as rain in a moment."

Then a third person arrived at my back. "I can't leave you two alone for a minute, can I?" said an unmistakable voice.

5.5

Amsterdam is so small that if there's anyone you don't want to bump into — don't leave the house. And don't answer the front door. Especially if the Universe is fucking with you.

The woman to whom the voice belonged was the reason I'd deleted Tinder the previous year. At the time I tried to blame Monica for the whole debacle because when I asked her if I should upgrade to Tinder Plus so I could lie about my age, she said "Why not?" — like it was all a bloody big game and none of it really mattered a tuppenny fuck.

So I pretended to be 36. Ten years sounds like a lot to take off but I have coal-miner's skin so I got away with it. Probably. Either way, the whole idea of starting out on such a big stupid lie sickened me, and of *course* it was doomed to come back and kick me in the balls. It's all I deserved. But always there was the voice that said *hold on* — *what if you click?* That fibre-thin possibility is ultimately what tipped the scales, because it was true. What if you did manage to laugh at the lie and find love in spite of it? Then that big stupid lie would become the masterstroke of a love genius. That's the thing about lies. You never know which ones are worth telling till you've told them.

Violet was a 32-year-old Dubliner. Three or four days a week, she commuted from Haarlem to Amsterdam to waitress in the Hermitage museum restaurant. My Tinder profile made her laugh so she swiped right and we met at the zoo. Violet's idea. I'd asked her what she fancied and she'd replied: "So I love animals and I can't stand the idea of zoos but I've never been to one. So I want to go, even though I know I'm going to hate it."

"Well, you know what they say," I replied. "First date? Do something you hate."

Ultimately, the zoo far exceeded Violet's expectations. She just kept muttering, "What a fucking *atrocity*." Then in the monkey enclosure: "How is this allowed? It's just torture. Slavery and torture."

The elephants were the worst. Three of them — father, mother and child at an uneducated guess — lined up behind a giant wire fence, staring out at the humans, the mother in the middle, dancing. A simple side-step-and-kick routine with her two front legs, over and over as the families cheered and pointed and shared the atrocity on social media. It was all so far beneath the elephants' dignity, that Violet's heart just cracked apart and tears spilled over her cheeks.

When I saw that she was crying, I instinctively laid a consoling hand on her shoulder. In response, she laid her head against my chest and wrapped an arm around my waist. It was very intimate. It stirred me.

"Shall we get out of here?" I said softly.

She looked up at me. "Are you not wanting to see the rest of it?"

"Nah, it's making you sad. Let's do something less depressing."

Violet smiled. "OK, thank you."

"What about the Holocaust Museum?"

She laughed and wiped her eyes. "You're a daft bollocks."

As it was a hot day in July, we went for a picnic in Twiske. There, on a picnic blanket in the sun, we kissed for the first time, wonderfully well. Just as we were becoming quite heated, Violet broke it off suddenly and said, "OK listen, I've got a bit of a confession to make."

"Uh-oh."

"Bless me, father, for I have sinned. Don't worry like, it's nothing *really* bad. I mean I'm not like, a child-murderer or anything."

I shrugged. That might not have been a dealbreaker at this point.

"I told a bit of a lie, that's all. On my Tinder profile."

I held my breath.

Through a tight-lipped smile, Violet said, "I lied about me age."

An expression of seeming disapproval alighted instinctively upon my face. I removed it at once. "So how old are you really?" I was expecting, maybe 35, at the absolute most. But really, she barely looked 32.

"I'm 22."

My mouth opened of its own accord. "That's not... the direction I was expecting you to go in."

"You think I look *older*?!"

"No!" I cried, as quickly and forcefully as I reasonably could.

She did look young, but then some women do. It certainly didn't occur to me to question her youthfulness. I knew she was younger than me. It didn't matter how much younger. Besides, I'd been too much taken by her general allure to even consider her age. Online she'd been attractive, but in real life she was almost offensively so, and clearly, *ridiculously* out of my league — as they all were, let's face it. She had that horny savage rustic thing — milky-white skin, autumn-leaf hair and spellbinding, bestial turquoise eyes, with which she frequently made brazen, occasionally slightly disturbing contact.

"On the contrary," I cried. "It makes sense that you're younger. It's just..." *Uh-oh.* "It's usually the other way round, right? People usually pretend to be younger." *So*, it obviously occurred to me. *Now would be the ideal time. Come on, Wesley. Confession for confession.*

298

Truth for truth. Do it now, you lily-livered fuck. Show some moral courage. Woman up. "So why did you pretend to be ten years older, Violet?"

Violet explained that men her age were "proper fuckin spanners" and she was tired of them. Neither was she keen on older men who were consciously seeking out women half their age. "So I thought this'd be a way of bypassing all the creepy auld fellas. Are you pissed off with me?"

"No! Heaven forfend! That actually shows great initiative. And at least you confessed, right? Before anything serious happened. Which is the thing to do, obviously, if you're sitting on a big lie."

Obviously. *And…?*

So *that* was the moment. The perfect moment.

All I had to say was: "Speaking of which…"

But to my shame, I did not confess my lie. I did not grant Violet the same respect she had so maturely and courageously granted me. Instead, if I was perfectly honest, I made a simple calculation and figured that, if I told her the truth now, the chances that we'd go to bed together would go from *pretty much certain* to *massively unlikely*. And after kissing her for half an hour, I wanted nothing more than to go to bed with her. So I said nothing. And later that night, we went to bed together.

If I could lie about anything, I'd lie about this episode. Because now that I'm writing it down, I don't think I come out of it smelling especially charming. But it is what it is, right? I never said I *always* did the right thing. And a lot of joy came out of it too. For both of us. Before it turned to shit.

5.6

When a post-coital conversation about what can only be described as *pop music* revealed an ignorance on my part that Violet found both remarkable and amusing in the extreme, she said to me, with evident glee, "My God, you're like a proper auld fella!" Now, if I were a genuine bad man, as opposed to just an opportunistic shitbag, I'd have let it slide. I'd have gone on being 36 till I turned 37. And so on. But instead, I took this as my cue.

"Actually, I've also got something of a confession to make."

"Uh-oh."

"You're um...." I chortled. "You're gonna love this... turns out you're not the only one who um... lied about their age."

Stretched out by my right side, Violet propped herself up on an elbow, her eyes popping. "No. Way."

"Way."

"Go on."

"Well, a lot of people put 40 as their upper limit, don't they, when they're searching, so I thought it might be... to my favour... I thought I might meet more women and have more chance of, you know, finding someone to love, and to devote myself to, and to please for all eternity, and so on and so forth, if I claimed to be under 40."

She gasped. "You're 40?"

"God, no." I shook my head.

"Thank fuck for that."

"I'm 46."

Violet sprang up into a sitting position, gathering her knees to her chest. Her mouth was open like a doughnut that's just heard some very distressing news. She looked genuinely shocked.

"You're fuckin' what?"

"Yeah. Is that… are you pissed off?"

She was staring. She looked extremely pissed off. Her once seductive turquoise eyes now looked like the eyes of some piqued demon. She grabbed the corner of my duvet and pulled it up to her neck to cover her naked top half, like she was suddenly in bed with a stranger.

"You're older than me da."

I shrugged, laying on, relying on, the nonchalance. "Does it matter?"

"Fuckin' yes, it matters!"

I shuffled up the bed towards the pillows and sat with my legs crossed, facing her. I was naked. I looked OK. "Why does it matter?"

The fact that she didn't have a readily available answer came as a slight relief. She scoured my room in silence, as if searching for one.

"I should have told you earlier…."

"Yes! Why didn't you tell me earlier?"

"That was cowardly of me, I admit. But…" I ran dry. I needed to deflect, like a politician. "Let's not forget that you also lied, and when I found out, I congratulated you on your initiative."

"Oh, is that what you're after now? Being congratulated?"

"Well, look. What's changed really? We just had a fantastic day. You had a lovely time with me; I had a lovely time with you. We had a really good time in bed. With the kissing and the… sexy stuff, and you with the *Exorcist* eye-rolling and the shaking." I performed a very quick, and to my mind eerily accurate, imitation. Laughter was fundamental at this point. "I mean, come on now, Violet. Body don't lie. Powerful deadly orgasms. You said so yourself." I moved a little closer to her. I lay down in front of her trying to look young.

(Eyes wide, expression like a simpleton.) I kissed her left knee. "And you have to admit, I do know my way around a vagina."

She laughed. "That is so not the point!"

"Isn't it though?" I carried on kissing her knees. "And the fact that I'm good at this stuff… this is the upside, the consolation prize. This is what comes of being a little bit older."

"A little bit," she scoffed.

"But it's experience that comes with age." With my mouth, I moved over her left knee slowly, and super slowly worked my way along the inside of her thigh. Violet accommodated me, seemingly despite herself. "You know what men your age are like," I continued, teasing her for a fraction of a second with the tip of my tongue. "And men in their 30s… are often not much better." I became slightly more involved. Imagine cleaning the spout of a gravy jug, concentrating on the stubborn underlip. "They just barge in, don't they? Like a SWAT team… raiding the flat… of an al-Qaeda suspect." I rolled onto my elbows and with various digits set to work with a little localised micro-massage, adjusting and attuning according to Violet's reaction. "No finesse. Like a boxer doing origami. Gloves on."

"Stop talking now."

I stopped talking.

I was honoured.

5.7

I was honoured again the following morning and then, just as I was starting to feel we might be onto something, Violet broke it off. I was just too old, she said. It had been a fucking great day. And that would never change. Now goodbye. And I was fine with that. It had been a genuine honour and I wished her all the best, figuring I'd probably got off lightly. No one had got hurt. We'd had fun.

Then a week later, she was back in touch, drunk and horny.

And so it began.

In the end, I was honoured once every couple of weeks — on average — for the better part of a year. And let me tell you this: it was never, *ever* enough.

Sometimes it was frenzied and carnal, sometimes loving and intimate, but always, from the very beginning, it was transformative. You know? You know *sex?* When it works, it's fucking… *ineffable*. I had forgotten. Violet reminded me, and fairly swiftly, our little fuck forays became the highlight of my existence, and Violet herself — and her exquisite pleasure — became my *honzon*, my object of fundamental devotion. Word to the wise: you should never make a person your *honzon*. But I did it all so thoughtlessly, carried along by the profundity of the intensity of our lovemaking. I swear, we really managed to strip away the ego and move into realms of pure cosmic interconnectedness. Plus, she made me come. Whether she was riding me like a wincing Sybian, or moving sweetly over my body like a suit of dying eels, she made me come nearly every time, and I'd forgotten just how incredibly good that felt. So there was this delicious combination at play — this slow dance with God on the one hand and my festering nads being gloriously emptied on the other. It became for me enormously addictive.

Violet would always stay over and sometimes we'd pop out for breakfast, but never too near to her work. I knew she was embarrassed by the thought of being seen with me and I pretended I found it amusing. In reality of course, I found it humiliating and depressing. It made me feel like a shameful hobby. A human gimp suit. But we joked about it, which helped a little.

Plus, she always made it crystal clear, I'd never be a part of her life beyond my bedroom. I'd always be too old. "It is," she had a habit of explaining, with slow and deliciously cruel inevitability, "what it is."

So I was her *bit of old*, her grey bit on the side, and yes, aside from the wounded pride, which maybe on some level I actually got off on, I found the whole thing utterly irresistible.

"If I was black," I told her once, "and your Irish friends were all like, 'Ah, bejesus, can you not find yourself a nice wee white fella there like, our Violet?' and in the end you just kept me in the cellar because you couldn't handle your friends' disapproval... It's the same, right? You're a racist."

To my surprise, Violet agreed that she could indeed see a correlation between ageism and racism. "It's not just my friends though. It's me too. I've never denied it."

"And you're OK with that?"

She became exasperated. "Wesley. What do you want from me? I can only give what I can give and I can't give anything more. If you can't accept that, then, you know, bugger off. But don't pick at me for not being enough."

She was right, of course, but it stung. It didn't seem fair that someone who'd never heard of Billy Bragg got to have so much power.

"Ageism is the last taboo," I would rail. "We don't discriminate against people's skin colour or sexual orientation anymore — or at least not openly."

"You say that like you're disappointed."

I tutted. "I'm saying we've made a lot of progress. You can't even take the piss out of dwarves these days. Fucking dwarves! And midgets. None of that. Yet age is still fair game. Check out what passes for satirical comedy in the States and you'll rarely see Bernie Sanders mentioned without some crack about his age. And nobody bats an eyelid."

Violet didn't bat an eyelid. "I don't know who that is."

I sighed.

It was what it was.

On one level of course it was shameful and ridiculous of me to be fawning and straining to please a woman who was embarrassed to be seen with me in public, and who was, let's not forget, far too fucking young for me. But fuck that — she was mostly adorable and sometimes it felt like love. And I hadn't felt that for many years. I was desperate for love. Looking for it everywhere. And when I looked for it in Violet's eyes — because she too, was such an intimacy junkie — I found it, often. From right at the beginning till right at the end.

Finally, there was the validation Violet gave me. Not just the tacit legitimisation that all women confer when they disrobe in my proximity, but the validation of feeling that I was doing a good job. She was always very fulsome in her praise and that meant a lot to me. I always liked to do a good job, whether it was painting a staircase, guiding a large group of tourists through busy city streets, or teasing a vagina.

I loved it all.

Except the end. The end I didn't love one bit.

5.8

One day my 1.30 didn't run and as was my occasional wont, I decided to take in a museum. For no greater reason than that I'd never been there and it popped into my head, I decided to go to the Hermitage. At least, that's what I tell myself.

So I went, and for half an hour I rolled my eyes at the jewellery and the costumes and the portraits, shaking my head at the egregiousness of the opulence, finding it garish and pointless in equal measure. After half an hour or so, worn out by all the eye-rolling and head-shaking, I made my way to the restaurant area for respite and refreshment. I had no idea if Violet would be working or not. I reckoned there was a fifty-fifty chance.

Approaching the serving island in the middle of what turned out to be a fairly vast and rather swanky dining area, I ordered a glass of red wine and a large cookie. I felt tense. Violet was nowhere to be seen.

The place was surprisingly busy. As well as a clutch of couples and a handful of singletons, there were also a couple of large groups of what I guessed were fashion students. I reckoned in total there were at least thirty of them, all 18 or 19 years old, all female, all working on laptops, spread out around the restaurant on various tables. A high-pitched buzz of conversation was peppered with tinkling teaspoons and the occasional hiss from a coffee machine. I gathered my stuff and took a seat at the only free window table.

There I then sat, nibbling my cookie and watching the waitresses, half-expecting to see Violet pop up from behind a serving hatch. All of the serving staff in that moment were women, and they all wore the same uniform of black shoes, black trousers and white shirts with black ties. I imagined Violet popping up in the same uniform and pretending I was her uncle visiting from Ireland. Then, on some brilliantly believable pretext or other, she'd take me through to some storage room where they kept old exhibits, she'd put on one of Catherine the Great's dresses and bounce up and down on me like a giant taffeta jellyfish. Maybe she'd shove a ruby up my arse. I was smiling and just about to adjust myself when it happened. She appeared.

She came through the same door I'd come through. She was carrying a large cardboard box full of napkins. She didn't see me. She delivered the napkins to the serving island and then, glancing around the restaurant to see what needed doing, her eyes reached the table where I was sitting. I gave her a tiny wave. Like I was tickling an invisible fairy.

Initially, confusion at seeing a familiar face in an unfamiliar environment alighted upon her. Then, when the penny dropped, I was rewarded with neither the sweet smile of recognition, nor the reciprocated fairy-tickling I'd have preferred; rather there came a deep creasing of the forehead and full facial pulsing erubescence. Indeed, her face turned crimson so quickly and so entirely that for a second, I genuinely thought she might go pop. She walked across the floor to me, fuming. A few of the students stopped talking and watched her, so frighteningly serious and single-minded was her gait. A smile, half-wilted, clung to my face.

"What the fuck do you think you're doing here?" Her voice was a quiet but distinctly unwelcoming hiss.

The buzz of chat had become more of a whisper and I was very close to speechless. After an astonished pause, I managed, "What do you mean? Nothing."

"You've got no right to be here."

Immediately, I felt so deeply, painfully hurt that my instinct was to lash out. My right hand twitched with the almost

307

overwhelming desire to throw my red wine all over her dazzling white shirt. I felt devastated.

"My tour didn't run." My voice became cold and measured. "I've been to the museum."

Her lips were pursed like Madison's. "You shouldn't have come here." Then she turned away and joined her colleagues at the serving area. I felt like every woman in the room was staring at me like I was Harvey Weinstein. My blood turned cold. I was broken. And confused. What was going on? Had something horrendous happened? Had I lost my temper and been given a restraining order? Was I insane enough to do and then entirely forget something so hideous? Of course I was not. I knew, in reality, I was forgetting nothing. All I'd ever done for this woman was make her come and buy her breakfast. And if that's a crime, then string me up.

No. Violet was simply embarrassed and ashamed because I was old enough to be her da. I could have been her da though, for all anyone knew. Or her uncle, or her friend, or anyone at all. I don't know why she didn't just pretend I was nobody and say hello like a normal human being.

I glanced around the restaurant. Various condemnatory gazes were quickly averted. Then I drank back my wine in one gulp, stood up slowly and walked out of the restaurant without looking back. My entire body was inundated with adrenaline. I felt every muscle tensing, ready to scream itself into action. Somewhere within me was the instinct to go berserk and do what my father was famous for, which was overturning every table he could find and headbutting and punching as many people as he could till they dragged him off to a waiting police cell. Instead, I inhaled deeply, deliberately, and with my chest puffed up and out, I walked steadily, quickly, down the stairs, out into the grounds and out onto the street.

Not punching myself in the face was the hardest part of the next few days. I felt incredibly humiliated. My skin burned. Every time I replayed the scene, I felt fresh waves of humiliation and rage rolling over me.

Back home in the immediate aftermath, I grabbed my laptop.

"I'm sorry my presence today upset you so much. You made me feel absolutely worthless, but hey, that's on me I guess. It was fun making love with you, even though, evidently, it meant absolutely nothing. As soon as I've sent this message, I'm going to block you across all platforms. If I see you in the street, I will acknowledge your presence with a nod. You, if this afternoon's experience is anything to go by, will scowl at me like you've just fallen face first into a vat of human excrement. You ruined a lot of wonderful memories today. I don't think I deserved that treatment. In the future, please try to be nicer to people. Goodbye."

I pressed send. I blocked her across all platforms. I deleted Tinder. Done with Tinder. Done with inappropriately aged women. Done with love.

This was July 2019.

Then in December 2019, with two strangers picking tissue off my cold wet back, I heard her voice for the first time since she said, "You shouldn't have come here." I considered just walking away, without turning to face her, but that would have been cowardly. And nowhere near as much fun. So I turned, and I faced her.

5.9

For a second I thought I'd made a mistake. But no, it was definitely Violet — she'd just got rid of all her hair. Currently her neck and the back of her head were hidden away within the coils of a giant winter scarf, but the top of her head showed a pretty severe crew cut. And it suited her very well. The very front of her fringe had been styled into a slight point that drew even more attention to her bright turquoise eyes. She looked like an electric elf. Like she'd escaped from Santa's grotto and was up to no good.

When she recognised me, her face registered a split second of neutral alarm, long enough for her to spit out "Wes—", then the neutrality was replaced by absolute horror and she cut short my name in case her easy remembrance gave way to the truth, and it all came tumbling out in front of the man I understood, from the moment I'd heard Violet's voice, to be her *da*.

And it never even occurred to me to make things difficult for her. Well, OK, it occurred to me. But I didn't seriously entertain it for a second. You see? Good to the bone.

"That's right!" I cried, warmly, "Wesley! You remembered my name! I'm honoured." Her face at this point, was a picture of tempered terror. It was there in her eyes, genuine terror, as the rest of her face tried to produce something akin to blithe confusion. I let her stew for a second, then I made up an awful lot of lies. I turned to her father and said, "She remembers my name but she doesn't know where from. Which is fair enough. So I met...." I turned back to Violet for a second. "I wanna say *Vanessa*?"

"*Violet*," her father corrected me.

"*Violet*. Of course. So yeah, I met Violet when I came to the Hermitage with, I think it was 25 fashion students?"

"Oh yeah, of course!" Violet was tentative, but she saw where I was going and allowed herself to relax a little.

I turned back to her father: "I'm a lecturer at the fashion… thing. *Academy*. We take the kids to the museum."

Violet's father was enormously amused by the coincidence. He shook my hand, heartily. "I'm Violet's father. My name's Brendan, this is my wife Hanneke."

"Oh, I know who you are. I heard lots of tales about you while I was lying naked next to this thing! Funnily enough, you'd often pop up in post-coital conversation, you and your violent past. I often used to think we'd probably have um… quite a lot in common, from all the stories I heard."

I didn't say any of that, obviously. I said, "Well, it's an absolute pleasure to meet you."

Violet shook my hand too. She looked relieved. Still cautious but I think at this point she knew that her worst fear was not going to come to fruition. Her worst fear, as far as I could tell, was that her father would know that she and I had had a thing, and that he'd therefore have to imagine what we'd done together. And if he knew we were at it for almost a year, he'd know that in that time, we did *everything*. And she didn't want him to feel that disappointment and that disgust. "How could you?" he'd say. "He's older than me, and I'm yer *da*!" He might not say it out loud, but he'd say it with his eyes, every time he looked at her, for the rest of his life. And that now seemed to have been averted. So we were out of the woods, but not quite home and dry.

"How *are* you?" asked Violet, because it seemed like the natural thing to do. "You haven't been to the museum for a while."

"Ah well…"

There's always that moment, isn't there, any time anyone asks you how you are, when you must decide how honestly you wish

311

to answer. Will you just *fine, thanks* it? Or will you drop a couple of impromptu truth bombs? It should really come down to whether you think the other person actually gives a damn how you are, or whether they're just making necessary but hopefully incredibly brief conversation.

I made my choice.

"My dad died actually, so I've been a bit down about that. And my friend Kras was found dead in a canal, and I'm pretty sure he was murdered. And another friend, well — associate, Damo. He went under a tram. Balls first... Sorry? No, no. He died. Then there was a guy on my tour — he died from a wasp sting. Then there was an old man in the back of a car that chased me when I fingered the driver. Not like that. Anyway, he died as well. So it's been a bit of a weird few months actually. And there's definitely an argument to suggest that it all started when you were so unnecessarily mean to me back in July."

I didn't say any of that, obviously. I said, "I'm fine, thanks. Really well. Oh, this is my friend Lizzie by the way..." Lizzie, now recovered from her giggle-bout and watching this new exchange with a look of absolute wonder, waved a giant mitt. "...and we're just off to see a man about a coconut, so... lovely to see you, lovely to meet you guys. Have an amazing Christmas and a fantastic New Year!"

They reciprocated my good wishes, Brendan apologised again for tripping me into a puddle and we all laughed one more time and parted ways.

When we'd walked a few metres in the direction of Dam Square, Lizzie said to me, "What the *fuck* was all that about?"

We stopped into a bar and I explained everything. Except the coconut. That had just popped in there and as far as I was aware, it meant nothing.

"I do see what you mean now," she said at one point, "about not knowing who you are." I laughed. "You're full of surprises, eh?"

The next day, I received a message from a number I didn't recognise and Lizzie was proved right yet again. I was full of surprises.

The message said: "Hey Wesley! This is Violet. It was really good to see you last night. I really appreciate what you did. Thank you. Also, I know I owe you a huge apology from before. I am really sorry. I acted like such a freak. I know it wasn't that long ago, but I've changed a lot since then. I'm not proud of how I was with you. I hope I can make it up to you one day. I'm living in Amsterdam now by the way! So yeah, let me know if you want to hang out over Christmas."

I got so aroused reading that message, just remembering how good it had been, and imagining how good it would be again…. But I knew it would be a mistake. And life is about learning lessons, for god's sake. It's about becoming a better person, a stronger person. So, as I was intent on doing just that, I said thank you, you extraordinary electric elf you, but no. And of course it felt rotten. Transformative sex danced before me like a slinky hot goddess and I said *no*. It was one of the hardest decisions I'd ever made, but of course, one of the absolute best. Probably. But before I had the chance to really regret my decision, it was Christmas, and the Devil turned up to celebrate.

5.10

On December 23, Monica called, panicking. She was running out of time and needed help organising Christmas. So the next afternoon, I borrowed Nix's car and drove her out of town, where we picked up an IKEA order and did a massive shop for Christmas Day.

Back at the boat we were still unpacking when the Americans arrived. Rupert and Russell, from Austin, Texas, both of whom currently worked for JP Morgan in London and had come to Amsterdam for a finance conference at the Stock Exchange on the 29th. Together with Trevor, an English colleague who'd be joining them on Christmas Day morning, they'd booked out the entire boat — all four cabins — for six days, for a total cost of €12,000. (Prices were a little higher than normal, what with it being the season of goodwill.)

Having Ubered in from the airport, they'd been dropped off at the end of the jetty and Monica had gone out to meet them. I waited in her cabin, staring at the flickering footage of the communal area on her laptop.

The communal area was basically a sunken living room with a couple of luxury sofas and a very low glass table for communal dining. It was positioned in the middle of the lower deck, between the four rentable rooms. At the back end of this room was a small security camera, hidden in a small but ornate analogue clock, high on the wall. The footage from the camera streamed live online and was of course recorded.

First I heard their voices and tried not to sneer at how loud they were. Then they appeared on Monica's laptop, and slightly grainy though the footage was, you could still tell, they were incredibly well-to-do.

They followed Monica into one of the cabins, only to re-emerge seconds later, divested of their luggage and duty-free carriers. I watched as Monica checked them in, took photographs of their passports and ran through a few essentials, including the various remotes for onboard heating and entertainment. When that was done, one of the bankers popped back into the cabin and reappeared with a bottle and a small stack of glasses. I watched as they all sat at the table and drank together. Shortly one of the bankers fetched a laptop and Monica showed them something online before finishing her drink and returning to her cabin.

"So?" I was curious. "What are they like?"

She shrugged. "They seem OK."

She told me what they'd talked about. They'd had a good year, they said, so as well as the conference element of their trip, they were intent on celebrating their hard work with "a little party". One of them asked Monica if they could bring women back to the boat. Monica told them of course — they'd paid for the rooms, they could do whatever they wanted, so long as it was legal.

"Then they say they are looking for 'quality women'." She pulled a face, but as it happened, she knew a guy called Job who ran an upmarket escort agency called Seraphim. That's what they'd been checking online. Satisfied with the Seraphim website, they tipped Monica twenty euros and invited her to dinner.

I sneered. "I bet they did."

She told them she had other plans and left them to it. If they needed anything, they had her number and in case of emergency, she was just at the front of the boat.

A half hour later, as I was readying to leave, the sound of very loud, disconcertingly unmelodious electronic music began to thump its way through the boat. I raised an eyebrow at Monica.

"They asked if they could play loud music. I said yes."

I nodded slowly, tight-lipped. "That may have been a mistake."

Monica clicked her fingers and said, "Baileys."

From the moment we'd got back in the car after our mammoth shop, we'd been making a list of things we'd forgotten. I took out my phone and added Baileys to the list. I'd agreed to pick up the forgotten items before my Red Light at 5 and then return to the boat afterwards. Sylvia was going to cook something in the evening and Monica said I could stay for dinner if I didn't have other plans.

Riding my bike down the jetty a little later, I passed two extraordinarily glamorous women walking in the direction of the boat. From the way they looked and smelled, I assumed they must have been two of Seraphim's €250-an-hour sex workers. I cycled on, managing not to turn and stare.

Four hours later I was back at the boat. The dance music was still playing, but it was mostly drowned out by some salsa music in Monica's kitchen. I said hello to Sylvia, who was elbow deep in a large bowl of filo pastry, and once I'd unpacked the final haul of provisions, I joined Monica at the laptop.

She pointed. "They have cocaine."

Sure enough, back in the communal space, as one of the bankers slow-danced with the two women I'd passed on the jetty, the other was crouched over the table in the middle of the room racking up lines. One of the women was totally naked. Another wore stockings and suspenders. One began performing oral sex on the banker sandwiched between them.

"God, they don't give a shit, do they?" I was a little shocked. Bless me. "Why aren't they in their rooms?"

Sylvia laughed. "They're rich!"

"I have to let them know that I know," Monica explained.

This was something Remi had told her right at the start: if anything illegal happens, always make sure to get evidence. This — thanks to the hidden camera — they had. Then: "Always make sure they know that you know."

"It's a power move," said Monica. "This is what Remi says, ah? I'm just waiting for the right moment."

I set about pouring Baileys. Just as I finished and handed Monica a glass, she jumped up. "OK, I go!" On her way up the short flight of narrow stairs leading out of her cabin to the rest of the boat, she grabbed a swish upright Dyson vacuum cleaner and said, "Wish me luck!"

The Dyson was her excuse for the interruption.

Sylvia dried her hands and joined me at the laptop. We clinked glasses and watched as Monica knock-wandered into the communal area and acted all shocked at the sight of everyone doing coke at the table.

One of the women automatically jumped up and ran into one of the cabins and the other covered herself with a cushion. The two bankers, however, were completely unfazed. One of them even gestured to Monica to join them. She told us later he'd said, "Hey Monica! Come and have a toot!" Aaah, the nonchalant bravado of the wealthy. A poorer man would have been quaking and stammering like an orphan.

Back in the kitchen, Monica filled us in on the conversation. She'd told them in no uncertain terms that cocaine was not allowed on the boat. She told them she could lose her job. The bankers reiterated that they'd had a really rough year and they just wanted to kick back and relax. "Like cocaine helps you to relax," she said with a brief eye-roll. "Then he says maybe I can just look the other way, just this one time. Then he comes with his wallet and gives me fifty euros. He says, 'What do you think? Can you look the other way?' I go like…" Monica blew out her cheeks. "You know, like, I'm thinking, 'I don't know'. So then he takes another fifty and says, 'Pleeeeease', so I took the money and I say, 'Just this one time.'" She shook her head, still clearly baffled by such wilful extravagance. "One hundred euro. For nothing."

"You should have held out for more," I said.

Monica shrugged. "I don't want to be greedy."

Sylvia laughed at this and declared Monica terribly cute in Dutch, which like so many sweet things in Dutch, sounded like she was coughing something up. Then we forgot about the bankers, gathered round the dining table and ate.

I got to know Sylvia a little over the course of the evening and naturally, I was completely won over. She was fun and funny, and she seemed insanely happy. And who could blame her? She'd won the lottery, as Monica might say. It was clear from the attention they paid one another how enormously loved up they were. Was I envious? Of course I was. But I figured she deserved it, after losing her mum. Actually, death aside, they both deserved it. They were lovely people. I was very happy they'd found one another.

As I cycled home that night, I counted my own blessings. I was going to be spending Christmas with lovely people. What could possibly go wrong?

5.11

Back on the boat the next day, there were ten of us packed around the kitchen table, which was heaving with unseasonal vegan goodies, mostly prepared by Sylvia. Nix had joined us. As had Lizzie and Doug, Henk and his partner Felix, and Elvira and Cristina, who were not romantically linked. By 2.30pm, we were all assembled and ready to eat.

"OK, before we start," said Monica, "I want to say grace. Please, put your hands…" We linked hands around the table. I closed my eyes. Monica spoke. "Oh my God. First thing — happy birthday to your son Jesus. We hope you guys are having a good day. Maybe you are also having some lovely food with friends — maybe the Holy Spirit is with you. Sorry to interrupt — just to say thanks to you for this food today and these friends and please make sure that nobody in any part the world is missing this good stuff… especially the children, *cazzo*. For the heathens around the table, we say thank you to Albert Heijn and even more than that, we say thanks to Sylvia, for cooking all this amazing food."

We toasted Sylvia. We feasted.

Halfway through the meal came a tentative knock at the door to Monica's quarters and with a dramatic eye-roll, Monica rose.

Standing in the doorway was one of the Seraphim women, wearing a short black dress. She was looking for lemons. Monica invited her in. As she climbed down the stairs, greetings and yuletide felicitations pinged back and forth before Monica handed over lemons in a nylon net. "Is three enough?"

"For sure, thanks," said the woman, her accent Eastern European. She thrust a twenty-euro note towards Monica. "They said to give you this."

Monica shook her head. "It's really no need."

"Take it, Monica!"

We all of us yelled those words at her, repeatedly, like traders in a money pit. The young woman grinned and continued to hold out the note. "They've got lots."

So Monica took the note and the young woman returned to her clients. I watched her go, not inadvertently noticing white flesh above her stockings. Elvira handed me a serviette. "For your drool." I took it.

After the meal, which, thanks to Monica's entirely hands-off approach, was delicious, the guests loaded the dishwasher and Felix, who was Israeli, took a quick call from his parents. They were Christmasing in Nazareth. When he was done, he passed on their seasonal greetings.

"I didn't think Jews celebrated Christmas," I said.

"That's a bit anti-Semitic," said Henk.

"Tish." I pooh-poohed him. "If I wanted to be anti-Semitic, I'd bring up the whole Christ-murdering thing. But you know, not today, eh?"

"They don't exactly celebrate," said Felix. "They just love all the…"

He paused long enough for Henk to jump in with: "All the bullshit."

"Exactly. So they go to Nazareth, look at the giant tree and buy Santa hats. They did a 'Follow the Star' Wise Man Tour in Bethlehem yesterday."

Nix did an elaborate shrug. "Harry Potter has tours. Why not Jesus?"

"I've just realised, we are pretty much a Republican's Christmas nightmare," said Henk. "We have gays, lesbians, a black man, a Jew, and a Muslim."

Nix laughed. "All we're missing is a wheelchair and a trans and we'd have Diversity Bingo."

"Who's Muslim?" I wondered aloud, adding, "If it is to be known."

Cristina raised her hand. "I was raised Muslim. But for the record, I believe in nothing." Everyone laughed, except Doug, who, I was beginning to realise, had no sense of humour.

For the next couple of hours, we drank, played games, sang Christmas songs and laughed. We laughed a lot. At one point, in a minor lull, I said, to no one in particular, "We were supposed to be in Sofia now."

So we talked about Kras, forcing ourselves not to dwell on the injustice of his death and instead wilfully celebrating all the love he'd brought into our lives. And just as we'd finished toasting him, a high-pitched scream cut through our grief and ruined Christmas forever.

5.12

The scream came in two short, sharp bursts. Monica was halfway up the stairs before the second scream sounded. Nix and I were right behind her.

Before I'd even reached the top of the stairs, Nix had stripped to his jeans and socks and dived over the side of the boat, while Monica tossed the nearest lifebuoy in after him.

This is Amsterdam's East Dock, in front of the Science Museum, and while it's not perhaps as dangerous as open sea, the water is deep and in December, ice cold. It was also dark and slightly misty by now, making this a distinctly life-threatening situation.

Nix came back to the surface of the water. He had one arm around the waist of a predominantly naked woman. She didn't appear to be alive.

"Bring her to the steps," shouted Monica.

Using the lifebuoy, Nix managed to get the woman's body back to the side of the boat, and there at the foot of the ladder, thank God, she began to exhibit signs of life, coughing and flapping about in a panic.

Once we knew she was alive, Monica ran off to fetch warm things, and Lizzie and Sylvia helped get the woman back on board. The bankers, at this point, were nowhere to be seen.

Monica returned with a pile of towels, blankets and duvets, and just as the wet woman stepped back onto the boat, shivering outrageously, Monica set about wrapping her up in as many layers as possible.

It was then I noticed that the woman — who was wearing stockings and suspenders and nothing else — was the lady with the lemons from earlier. As Monica and Sylvia helped her onto one of the sofas in the middle of the room, she replied to their questions through chattering teeth. Her name was Zuzana. She was from the Czech Republic.

Meanwhile, Nix had made it back onboard, where he was regaled with congratulations and towels. Also shivering impressively, he took a couple of the towels back to Monica's quarters to recover himself.

All the while this was happening, loud drum and bass was belting out from one of the cabins. Only one of the bankers had emerged and was hanging around, keenly observing what was going on. He wore only boxer shorts and a t-shirt. He had red hair. This one, I'd later learn, was Rupert.

On the table between the sofas, aside from bottles, glasses, credit cards and two silver straws, was a glass ashtray almost filled with cocaine.

Monica turned up the heating and dispatched Henk to go fetch an electric radiator, which was then plugged in and set down near Zuzana.

When Monica asked her what had happened, Zuzana paused, and Rupert answered for her.

"No big deal — just a little mishap." I felt myself bristle. "We were just clowning around and… buff! In she went!"

Monica turned to Zuzana and said: "Is that what happened?"

"Hey, hey, hey," Rupert interrupted. "If I say that's what happened, then that's what happened, OK?"

At which point Nix returned wearing only a towel. He set about picking up his discarded clothes.

Monica said: "Do you mind if I just talk to Zuzana?"

"She'll tell you the same thing," said Rupert.

I'm sure I wasn't alone in sensing something of a threat in Rupert's tone. My fists were clenched. Monica addressed Zuzana directly. "Do you want to come to my cabin so we can talk for one moment?"

Sylvia said: "I'll go get her clothes." She stood up and said to Rupert, "Can you give me her clothes, please?" Then Lizzie reappeared with a cup of hot herbal tea and handed it to Zuzana.

Zuzana took the tea and said to Monica, "I'm fine, thank you."

"You see, she's fine," said Rupert. "So maybe you can all go back to your little party now and leave us in peace, what do you say?"

"I say you're a fucking… dick, my friend."

"*Wesley*," admonished Monica.

I don't know where "my friend" came from. It sounded very wrong coming out of my mouth. *Dick* too, felt forced and weird. I wasn't surprised that Rupert laughed.

"Well, that may be true," he said. "But I'm a dick who's paying a fortune to stay on this boat and not be insulted by… whatever the fuck this is." He gestured vaguely in my direction. "OK? Ye olde English cunt."

Though his tone was mock-friendly, I flinched. What the fuck did my age have to do with anything?

"*Wesley*," Monica repeated, keen to head off any unpleasantness.

"Really I'm OK," Zuzana said. "Thank you for your help."

"Yeah, thank you," added Rupert. "We're so grateful. Please, let me offer you a demonstration of our gratitude."

As Rupert went to fetch bribe money, I heard Zuzana pleading with Monica not to call the police. Presumably there were questions concerning her legal status. Monica reluctantly agreed.

As Rupert entered and exited the cabin containing his cohorts — Trevor had joined them mid-morning — he released two brief hectic blasts of drum and bass bedlam. On his exit, he was followed by the sound of male laughter. Then he grinned his way towards Monica and said, "Please, Monica, take this money." He looked incredibly pleased with himself. "A token of our appreciation on this special day."

Monica shook her head. "I don't want your money."

"No? Suit yourself. What about our Nubian prince over here?" He turned to Nix and held out the cash.

Nix glared at him. "Are you fucking serious?"

Part of me so wanted Nix to lamp him. I envisaged a proper brawl — guides versus bankers — a no-holds-barred, eye-gouging fistfight. Like the old days.

"Oh don't be coy," Rupert continued. "You're a hero, dude. You deserve it. Take the money, please, come on. I want you to have it." He shook the notes at Nix, as if taunting him. Nix continued to glare, seemingly unable to believe Rupert's crassness. After a short silent pause, he turned away and headed back to Monica's.

"I'll see you back in there," he said over his shoulder.

"And there he goes," said Rupert. "The Noble African Warrior."

Nix stopped and turned to face him. "What is with you, man? Are you trying to upset me? Do you want me to fight you? We can fight if you like. I'm pretty sure I'll fuck you up."

Rupert laughed. "What is it with you people? Lighten up, for God's sake! It's Christmas Day! Zuzana's fine. She had a smidgeon too much to drink, she took a tumble. No harm done. Let's move on!" Only when his voice cracked did I realise just how intoxicated he was.

"Are you sure you are OK?" Monica asked Zuzana.

Zuzana nodded and Rupert moved towards her. "Come on, Zuzu. Let's get you back to the party and get you warmed up. You'll take a little more of my money, won't you?"

Zuzana stood up and gathered her blankets while trying to hang on to her tea and the towel wrapped around her head. Rupert took her tea from her and carelessly led her away by an elbow.

Monica stood up. Sylvia laid a hand across her back.

We that remained watched Rupert lead Zuzana back into the room with the drum and bass. A few raucous cheers went up and the door slammed shut.

Back in Monica's kitchen, the atmosphere had changed entirely. *Ruined* is a word that's far too readily bandied around at Christmas but in this case, it was entirely appropriate. Christmas was ruined. None of us was in any doubt that Rupert the banker was in some way responsible for Zuzana ending up in the water.

Monica opened her laptop.

"So," she said. "Who wants to see what really happened?"

5.13

At 4.30pm, Rupert was in the communal area with Zuzana. They were taking cocaine. Rupert's brother, Russell, was there too, and another mostly naked woman. Then Zuzana was on her knees between Rupert's legs and Russell and the other woman disappeared into one of the cabins. As Zuzana went down on Rupert, Rupert held his hand against the back of her head. She appeared to gag. Low gender esteem cringed through me and I looked away.

Monica fast-forwarded.

At a certain point, Rupert lifted Zuzana's head to his face and leant forward to kiss her on the mouth. She moved her head to one side to avoid him. He pulled her face back and tried to force a kiss. In order to stop him, Zuzana brought up a hand and pushed his face away. At which point, Rupert grabbed Zuzana's face in one of his hands and although it was not easy to make out on the film, he appeared to squeeze her cheeks together, bunching up her lips. He held her in this position for a while as he talked. With no sound on the film, it was impossible to know what he was saying.

"Nothing good for sure," said Sylvia.

Standing up abruptly, Rupert then took hold of Zuzana's left hand and dragged her unceremoniously across the floor. With his other hand, he reached out to the door that led to the narrow strip of deck that snaked around the entire boat, and they both disappeared out of frame.

"It's pretty obvious what happened, I think," said Sylvia. "She wouldn't kiss him so he threw her overboard."

I imagined her screaming as he lifted her up, then screaming again as he threw her into the water.

"He's a fucking animal," said Felix.

"What are we gonna do?" I asked.

"We can't call the police," said Monica, explaining that Zuzana had specifically asked her not to.

As we debated what to do, there was movement on the live feed. The door of the cabin with the music had opened and Zuzana and two other women had stepped out into the communal area. One of the bankers accompanied them. The English one. We watched as Trevor led the women out onto the deck and presumably, off the boat. While he was gone, Rupert resurfaced, approached the table in the centre of the room and racked up more lines. Minutes later, they were all sat together at the table, snorting coke and drinking cognac.

In Monica's kitchen, we watched in silence.

"I wish I could hear what they were saying," I said.

"You can probably imagine what they're saying," said Lizzie.

"Yeah, I just want to know the full extent of their hideousness."

"Why?" asked Lizzie.

"I dunno," I said. "Because it's there. I want to understand it. Or at least be fully aware of it."

"I don't think they're necessarily any different to most people," said Doug, apparently now a paragon of forgiveness and acceptance. "I mean, we're sitting here watching them like they're a completely different species. They're just people."

"Nah, they're not," said Henk.

"People have souls," I said. "These are rich, self-centred white men. They're the end of the world."

Doug rolled his eyes. He didn't see it that way.

"I want coffee," said Monica. "Somebody else want coffee?"

She set about making it. Henk poured Baileys.

Some half-hearted conversation ensued but the fun had gone out of it and none of us could really tear our attention from Monica's laptop.

"Anyone read *American Psycho*?" asked Cristina.

Nix laughed. "Yeah, right. It's like a live feed."

Just as Monica finished pouring coffee, the bankers rose from the table. Rupert cleared up the cocaine and they each returned to their cabins, emerging a short while later, looking ready for a night on the town.

"It's a shame they're so hot," said Cristina.

Henk agreed. "If they weren't so obnoxious, I totally would."

At which point, sounding really quite exasperated, Doug interjected. "What do you mean, *if they weren't so obnoxious*? I mean, I know that one we spoke to was a bit of a twat, but how much do we really know about the others? Didn't you say they were quite charming, Monica?"

There then followed some discussion about exactly how obnoxious they were and how much actual proof of their obnoxiousness had thus far been established. Doug clearly felt, under the circumstances, they should be given the benefit of the doubt. He argued — persuasively — that condemning a person for their wealth was just as bad as condemning a person for their poverty. As he spoke, the rich men in question reconvened at the sunken table and racked up yet more lines of cocaine.

This was my moment.

I jumped up, grabbed my coat and scarf from Monica's hat-rack and said: "Right. I'm gonna find out."

"What are you doing?" asked Henk.

"I'm gonna surveil them." I zipped up, fully scarfed. "I'm gonna find out just how obnoxious they actually are. And I'll let you know. No charge."

"Do you want me to come with you?" asked Nix.

"Nah," I said. "I'll be less obvious alone. I'm like a ninja." I tripped over a chair leg, deliberately.

"I think this might be a very bad idea," said Lizzie.

I shook my head. "You may be right."

5.14

As I passed along the deck next to the main room, I glanced inside. My targets were back on their feet, making their final preparations to leave.

I unlocked my bike, revitalised by my sudden sense of purpose. Then I cycled along the jetty to the main road, stopped under a tree, and waited. The bankers emerged. They headed west, towards the centre, crossed the street and turned onto Peperstraat. I cycled slowly after them, from a very safe distance, closely observing.

Like pack animals linked by culture and genetic code, they each stopped walking simultaneously and bowed their heads, consulting in unison the shining little superbrain they each held in their hands.

Then they turned round and walked back in my direction. When they reached the Peperbrug, they stopped again. An Uber pulled up. I cursed. An Uber might well scupper my surveillance. Generally speaking, in the centre of Amsterdam, bikes are faster than cars, but the streets were Christmas Day dead, so it was possible they'd get away from me. And if they were heading out of town, they'd lose me for sure.

They weren't heading out of town. From Peperstraat, the Uber followed the one-way system all the way round to Nieuwmarkt, where their journey came to an end. It was a four-minute journey.

In Nieuwmarkt, I parked up and continued my surveillance on foot. I wore my old parka with the deep-sea diver zip-up hood, the old furry face-frame. I wore it up, with my scarf covering the lower half of my face, just in case. I didn't want Rupert to recognise the *olde English cunt* from the boat. That would be embarrassing, and might reflect poorly on Monica.

Nieuwmarkt was busy for a Christmas Day. It was 6.20pm. The Albert Heijn supermarket was still open. People were sat at restaurant tables under heated awnings. Some had gathered around a giant hot waffle stall.

The bankers drifted around the main square next to the old weighing house and former public execution site, like ordinary tourists. They were a little bit rowdy, but not what you could genuinely label obnoxious.

Then one of them tripped over a tree root and stumbled into a small Japanese woman, headbutting her about the shoulder. He didn't knock her to the ground but she was an elderly lady and you could see she was physically disgruntled. By way of apology, the banker performed an elaborate bow. I knew it wasn't a hate crime, but did the bow itself constitute a racial slur? If not, the obnoxious laughter that sprang up around it definitely did. More importantly, not one of the bankers showed even the slightest concern for the old lady, and for that reason, I spoke the incident into my phone and declared it: Strike One.

Three young women wearing flashing Santa hats passed them in the street and one of the bankers — I think Trevor — made some remark. I would bet good money that the remark was a salacious one, but of course... objection sustained.

Next they went into the Jolly Joker coffeeshop on the corner of Monnikenstraat. I sat on the window ledge outside with my phone, smart-feigning, occasionally glancing inside till they re-emerged.

No more than two metres from where I perched, staring into my hand-screen, they lit a couple of joints and set out back along Nieuwmarkt, taking a right down Bloedstraat.

I watched. I waited. I followed.

Twenty metres into Bloedstraat, the bankers stopped and turned to face the first of the women behind glass. When one window opened and one banker pushed another banker towards it, they all laughed, one of them doubled over. It was disrespectful and adolescent. But I let it slide.

A short distance further on, a white-haired woman with a bucket of hot bleachy water and a stiff-haired broom was cleaning up some street atrocity or other. After an exchange of words, the woman shouted an obscenity and swung her broom at the bankers, tracing an arc of steaming water through the air. For whatever they said to upset her: Strike Two.

On the Oudezijds Achterburgwal, they passed the Moulin Rouge sex theatre, with the beefy bouncers out front, hands stuffed in pockets, calling out to groups of women as they walked by. "You wanna see some big penises tonight, ladies? Live sex on stage. Come and see the Christmas cock."

Further along the same street, one banker took a photo of another banker making an obscene gesture next to a woman in a window. The woman banged on the glass and pulled her curtain across. The bankers laughed outrageously. Strike Three. When a passer-by admonished them, they laughed some more. Strike Four. How many strikes, I wondered, was I going to allow them? I guessed I'd know when it happened. Not many more.

At the next junction they stopped off at the Old Sailor, a rough and ready boozer where I'd been just once before, with my dad. I leaned against the railings of the bridge outside, staring in through the front door. I wondered what to do. I was getting bored, and my feet were numb. I wanted to go home but I felt I hadn't quite achieved what I'd set out to do.

It felt like I was looking for a reason to hate them, which if I'm honest, didn't feel massively Buddhist. I knew in my heart that my duty was to extend loving kindness to them, and to everyone. I wanted to too, if only they'd let me. I still wanted to make the

333

world a better place, but to do that, I had to fully understand it. And to fully understand it, I had to observe it. Ultimately then, that's why I was there, freezing to death in the Red Light District on Christmas Day: to make the world a better place.

That's why I followed Rupert and Russell and Trevor back down the Oudezijds Achterburgwal, where they produced and smoked another joint, upset yet more sex workers by taking yet more photographs, and then disappeared for five minutes into a sex shop.

That's why I then followed them stumbling their way further down the street and watched as they made their way into the Theatre Casa Rosso.

That's why I hung around for almost an hour and a half in front of the building works in front of the theatre, waiting for them to re-emerge, drunk as fuck and coked to the gills.

That's why I continued to follow them, on a freezing cold Christmas Day night, with teeth chattering and fingers and toes frostbite-numb, back into the dark and foggy backstreets.

And that's why I watched Rupert, standing in front of a window on Stoofsteeg, peeling a fifty-euro note from his wallet, taking out a lighter and setting fire to it.

To make the world a better place.

I was maybe five metres away at the end of the lane when Rupert burned the money. I moved closer, watching in horror as one of Rupert's friends creased up in laughter, while the other filmed with his phone. The curtain had long been yanked back across the window.

My voice when it came was calm but strident. "Why are you doing that?" Like I really wanted to know.

The bankers turned to face me as the half-burned note pirouetted to the wet ground. A thin drizzle was now falling in the mostly deserted lane. The banker that was filming — Russell — continued to film, pointing his phone at me. They all walked towards me.

"Who the fuck are you?" This was Rupert.

"I'm just trying to understand," I whispered.

As Rupert moved towards me, I unclenched my fists and took a deep calming breath.

5.15

I could have parried Rupert's hands as they reached for the fur around my face. I could have ducked and directed his forehead at the wall directly behind me. But I chose not to. I chose to take the blows. I chose to crumple in a foetal heap after the headbutt, and absorb the kicks and stomps that Rupert and Trevor administered to my body and head. Russell, I observed, continued to film. It didn't last long. The moment someone shouted and came running down the alley to my aid, the bankers scarpered.

As I lay there, head throbbing, footsteps all around me — some receding, some approaching — I felt for a few brief seconds peculiarly at peace. I'd wanted to see what they were made of, these bankers, and they'd shown me.

The sex worker who'd closed her curtain on the burning of the note came out from behind her window just as the guy who'd given chase arrived on the scene. They both crouched over me and asked if I was OK. I said nothing for a moment, enjoying the peculiar sensation of achievement. My face was pounding, my eyes were watering, but I think I may have been smiling.

"You should call the police," said the guy, a middle-aged Dutchman with white hair and a long, lined face.

"There are cameras," said the woman, a middle-aged Eastern European with long blonde hair and a provocative cleavage. She gestured down the alley. "They will find them."

I climbed to my feet. The drizzle was turning to rain.

"I don't want to," I said. "I'm OK. Thank you both."

"You are bleeding," said the woman. "Come in for wash."

I thanked the man again and shook his hand and wished him zalige feestdagen. When I followed the woman into her tiny room, she closed the curtain and said, "Sit. Take off hat."

I loosened my hood and pulled off my scarf, which had quite a lot of blood on it. I sat on a single bed, on a thick black plastic cover, as the kind woman took a large wad of kitchen roll and wet it under the tap in the corner of the room.

I smiled. "Thank you for helping me."

She tutted and wiped at my nose, mouth and chin. Her eyes were tired and bloodshot. She was mid-50s at a guess. I flinched from the pain of her touch.

"Is not broke I think." She tossed the bloody wad into a bin. Then she tilted my head back and pressed fresh paper towel against my nose. "Hold here till blood stops."

I did as I was told. "What's your name?"

She tutted again and didn't answer.

"I'm Wesley. I really appreciate your help." No response. I brought my head back into a normal position and checked the paper towel. There was a little fresh blood but not much. "Where are you from?"

She lit a cigarette. "Bucharest. You know where is?"

"Romania, right?"

She nodded. "Clever boy." She smiled, and my heart blistered. Tears welled behind my eyes.

"I saw what they did to you."

She shook her head sharply and flicked her cigarette hard against a plastic ashtray.

"I'm so sorry they did that."

Again she scowled and shook her head. "Is not first time."

I stood up and checked my pockets for cash. I had seventy euros in tens and twenties. I handed it to her and she recoiled.

"For what?" She seemed angry.

"For you. For helping me."

She pushed it away. "*Nu!* No fuck, no money."

337

"Please." My voice cracked as I spoke and I realised I was crying again. "Please take it. For helping me. For Christmas! It'll make me feel better. Please. Take it for Christmas."

She looked into my eyes, with the tears streaming down my cheeks and blood still trickling out of my nose and she said, "OK." She took the money from my hand. "Thank you."

At which point, I brought the paper towel back up to my face and started sobbing. As I sobbed, I felt the woman's hand patting me on the head. I don't know what she made of me.

Eventually, I composed myself, dried my face and stood up, ready to leave. "Happy Christmas. And I hope everything is great, you know, in the future. I hope you get what you want."

As I reached for the door, she said, "Renata", and held out her hand.

As I shook her hand, I started sobbing again and Renata laughed and said something in Romanian that sounded, tonally, like kindly disparagement. "Go!" She smiled. "Go home! Happy Christmas you too."

When I stepped out back into the alley and waved goodbye to Renata, two women passed and giggled at what they imagined they'd just seen, exactly as they had with my father, back when everyone was alive. I glanced down and saw the burnt remains of the banknote on the wet ground. I picked it up. Then I walked back to my bike feeling warmed by my encounter with Renata and distinctly chilled by what had preceded it.

I cycled home and had a shower. In bed, I sent a text to Monica: "Obnoxiousness confirmed. I'll fill you in soon. Thanks for today. Buon Natale!"

The next day I worked, but my heart wasn't in it. I couldn't stop thinking about money. I couldn't get the image of Rupert and his money out of my head. How he'd tried to paper over the boat incident, then burning a fifty in front of Renata. I thought about the Bullingdon Club, which required future Prime Ministers of England to burn banknotes in front of homeless people. Boris had done it. Cameron too. Patrick Bateman does it. All the psychos do it. But I'd never seen it before. I'd never seen — in reality and with my own eyes — anyone stoop so low.

After my tour, having okayed it with Monica, I returned to the Miss Adventure. Monica was shocked. "My God, Wesley. What happened to your face?"

My right eye was swollen and vibrant with red and purple bruising.

I told Monica exactly what had happened. I showed her the charred remains of the fifty-euro note. She was livid. And disgusted. She wanted them off the boat. Obviously this was not possible. Just a couple more days though, and they'd be gone. They had their conference on the 29th, and they were flying back to London the very next day.

Currently they were elsewhere, having left the boat not long before I arrived.

"What will you do?" Monica asked.

I shook my head. "Nothing." Even as I said it though, I knew it wasn't true.

Back home, I wrestled with the question. What would I do? Because surely, I had to do something. It was my moral duty to oppose such inhumanity, such evil. The Reverend Malthus saw it that way too, and he had God on his side.

Although I knew that Rupert and his friends were just three out of millions of ghastly creatures roaming the earth (forty or fifty million, to be imprecise), for me they had become a symbol of everything that was wrong with the world. Especially that repugnant twerp Rupert. The moment he burned that money, he became the physical embodiment of every despicable human male. He was that arsehole on Warmoesstraat tossing bricks in the air; he was the celebrity footballer who tried to rape Monica; he was the murdering pimps who destroyed Krastyo and Donka's dreams; he was every banker, every last despicable vampire locust one of them; and he was The Sociopath Jack Hammer. He was all sociopaths. And I had made a decision: it simply would not stand.

5.16

At just after midday on the 27th of December, 2019, I packed an old pair of sandals, a thick pair of woollen winter socks, a thick woollen winter beanie hat, an A4-sized mirror, a black garbage bag, some beard adhesive and my Bulgarian mystic outfit (beard, wig, robe) into my rucksack, and I rode into the Vondelpark, where I parked up, and wandered off to find a place to change.

Even in the winter, when most of the trees were naked, there was still a lot of dense perennial foliage and plenty of places to hide in the Vondelpark. I found an isolated spot in a small clearing between a ragged collection of trees and bushes, somewhere near its heart.

Once completely hidden from view, I took off my coat, trainers and socks, and placed them in the garbage bag. Then I took the clothes and accessories from my rucksack and transformed myself into Spas Daskalov, complete with winter hat. The mirror was to ensure I got it right. If I couldn't get it right, if I felt I looked in any way like I was wearing a bad disguise, then I would take the whole thing off, call the whole thing off and go home. But I looked pretty convincing. I looked good.

I took my normal clothes from the garbage bag and placed them in the rucksack. The rucksack I placed inside the garbage bag, which I stuffed into the middle of some dense evergreen bush. Then I strode out of the undergrowth, back through the park and to a hardware store on Kinkerstraat. There I purchased a sturdy steel lino knife. The knife had a hook-shaped point, like the upper mandible of a bald eagle's beak. It was perfect for all kinds of things.

Then I walked back to the park, changed back into my everyday clothes and went home. The experiment had been a success. I'd road-tested my outfit, and felt pretty comfortable with it. I'd also purchased something with which to exercise my moral duty.

At home, Nix was in his bedroom with a woman. Beyond the music, I heard laughter and later, moans of pleasure.

After a while, I retired to my bedroom and lay on my back imagining everything that might go wrong. I felt incredibly tense and irredeemably lonely. The year filled with love that I'd yearned for in January had not come to pass. There'd been a couple of women I probably could have loved, but they'd been tourists, and tourists never hang around.

Bloody tourists.

Time passed.

I lay still in the dark for more than an hour. Then I made a decision. I'd do it after the conference. I'd creep up behind Rupert the banker, dressed as a Bulgarian mystic, and I'd slice open the banker's throat with my eagle-beak knife. And damn the consequences.

5.17

In the build-up to New Year's Eve, the sound of fireworks became more or less constant. They exploded throughout the city at all hours of the day. I had absolutely no idea why. This is yet another aspect of human behaviour that baffles me entirely. It also puts me terribly on edge. So I was already feeling agitated when I turned up at the square for my last tour of the year. Or, of course, ever. It was December 28, the day before the bankers' conference.

At the square, Henk asked me how I was feeling. The bruising was less fierce now, but with the reds and purples already fading into oranges, blues and yellows, I looked like a kingfisher. I said I was OK, but it lacked conviction.

Ultimately, today's tour turned out to be one of my favourites of all time, thanks entirely to a curious, excitable 8-year-old Australian girl called Amy. Now, excitable kids can make a tour, for sure, but they can also make you want to accidentally nudge them into the nearest canal. At first I wasn't sure which way it was going to go with Amy, but within ten minutes, I think it's fair to say I had fallen deeply in love with her.

Pretty much as soon as I began, Amy started in with the questions.

"What's a dam?"

"A dam is pretty much the same as a dyke."

"What's a dyke?"

"A dyke is basically a wall, or mound of land, created to control the flow of water. They had to control the water, Amy. Do you see? Or they'd drown! There was water everywhere." I left a pause. "A dyke is also a lady who likes to kiss other ladies. Is that too much?" I directed the question at Amy's parents, both of whom threw up their hands as if to say, "She's your problem now, mate."

Amy's slightly older, much quieter sister Megan was also present, but it was Amy who stole the show, always standing at the front of the group, always staring intently as I spoke, always with the questions.

"What's a heron?" "What's a hippy?" "What's a Prosetant?" [sic]

After a few minutes, I had to limit her to one question every ten minutes, which she agreed, begrudgingly, was fair.

"What's a pimp?"

Apparently she knew what a prostitute was so the hard part was done. After checking again with her parents that I wasn't doing irreparable damage to her childhood, I said, "A pimp is a man who makes a woman work as a prostitute. So she... kisses other men? For money? And the pimp takes some, if not all, of the money for himself. It's a beautiful world, Amy, but it's full of sad, sad, sad, sad things. Let's move on."

Amy laughed. "You're funny."

I caught my breath. I mean, I know I'm a pushover, but there was just something about the purity of Amy's acceptance and sincere appreciation of me, and of her voicing it so instinctively, so innocently, that made me want to grab hold of her and jump headfirst into the water. Not... I just mean that her words broke me, and I wanted that feeling and those words and the perfect child that had uttered them, to last forever. But I managed to hold it together. "Thank you," I chirruped. "So are you."

At the penultimate stop, the water stop, I hopped onto a bridge railing on the Keizersgracht. And while I was there, talking about the people who fell foul of the water, mostly drunken men with their zips open, Amy moved one step closer and slowly and softly rested her head on my right knee. Then Megan did the same with my left knee, her head a little lower, her hands rested on my calf.

344

They both just rested there. I didn't know why it had happened. I didn't know what had prompted this spontaneous show of seeming affection, but it immediately cut right into my heart.

I stopped what I was saying and said, "Awww." Then I felt tears gathering in my eyes. It was too obvious for me to hide it entirely, so I wiped my eyes and laughed through it. "Wow. This is a first."

A few of the group also gave out involuntary *awwww*s and a few more of them smiled indulgently. I felt we were seconds away from one giant group hug, but I soldiered on and we finished the tour ten minutes later at the Homomonument.

I was happy that Amy's family hung around at the end to ask for food recommendations, as it gave me the opportunity to let them know how much I'd loved meeting them. I didn't say "especially Amy" but I think it was clear.

They thanked me for my patience and for what was basically "cheap as chips childcare" for the afternoon and then the mum said, "Do you have kids yourself?" When I said I didn't, she was surprised, "Oh, I'd have put money on it. You should definitely be a dad. Not everyone should. Lots of people who do have kids definitely shouldn't, but you should."

I thanked her. I thanked them all. Then we said goodbye and I made my way home, still feeling moved by the whole experience. I loved what the mum had said to me, but I didn't agree. Even though they might be able to click with kids and have fun with them, I thought that some people were just not genetically fit to procreate. I felt sure that my own genes, for example, were wildly unfit. Plus I was always rattling on about over-population and needing a new plague. It would've been a tad hypocritical, therefore, to turn around and start procreating, even though, theoretically, and ironically, a family might have sorted me right out. I shrugged. It was too late now. Not because I was nearly fifty, but because tomorrow, I would kill a man.

Another one, I mean.

Home alone that night, I called Monica. A very large part of me wanted dearly for Monica to tell me that everything had changed, that she'd made friends with Rupert, Russell and Trevor; that they'd shown her a tender, caring and selfless side of themselves that had completely taken her aback. Sadly, no. On the contrary.

They'd had more women back the previous night. The music had gone on till around 5am and this morning, there were plants, books, pillows and a duvet floating in the dock. And God knows what else beneath the surface of the water. Monica called Remi. He came to the boat, fished the items out of the water and went to have a word with his guests.

Monica watched on the stream as the scene played out in all its venal predictability. Rupert appeared at the door, Remi reprimanded him, Rupert paid him off. Then Remi returned to Monica's cabin and gave her another hundred from the sheaf in his right hand. "Just two more days," he said. And that was that. Monica felt rotten about the whole thing.

After a lengthy, ineluctably sad silence, she perked up. "Va bene, Wesley. What are you doing for Capodanno?" She invited me to the New Year's fireworks. "On the Prinsengracht. Near to Sylvia."

I told her maybe, but I knew that realistically there was a very good chance I'd see the new year in behind bars. "Ti voglio bene, Monica."

Ti voglio bene is Italian for non-romantic *I love you*. It's reserved for family and close friends.

"Anch'io, Wesley, ma che c'è?" *What's wrong*, she wanted to know. My voice must have betrayed me.

"No, I'm fine. Just feeling… grateful. Ecco. I wish you an amazing new year, just in case I don't see you before."

"You too, Wesley. But I hope we see each other."

"OK." I took a deep breath. "Goodnight, Monica."

It was just gone 8pm.

Gazing down at Amstel Bay, I drank a glass of red wine and watched the last of the day's boat tours wrapping up. Tomorrow it would be busy again. Tourists would come and go, New Year's Eve would come and go, spring, summer, babies and burials, same as it ever was, but one thing would be different: I, Wesley Bell, would have done my bit.

5.18

The next day I spent pondering, as you can imagine. The words *if not me, who?* swirled round and around my head like a particularly ominous earworm. Preparing myself for a life behind bars was the hardest part to ponder. I'd be sad not to make it back to South-East Asia, amongst other things, but as long as I got to explain myself, I'd be satisfied. I imagined writing the story of why I killed Damo and Rupert from prison. It would be a coruscating condemnation of man's inhumanity to woman, primarily, as well as a provocative yet compelling argument as to why removing sociopaths from the realm of existence — aka psycho-cleansing — was an *Objectively Good Thing*.

I imagined my words touching the hearts of good humans everywhere. I imagined them organising into groups of moral mercenaries, a kind of international league of sociopath hunters, devoted to carrying out Malthus's edict and eradicating evil wherever it was found. I imagined somehow creating real and lasting change and ultimately, saving the entire human race. Then I had a pizza, and waited.

I checked the website of the Stock Exchange for the umpteenth time. Nothing had changed. The conference finished at 7pm. I would be waiting, and if I saw them, it was fate. I'd stroll up to Rupert and slice his throat from behind. As he fell to the ground, I'd walk away like butter wouldn't melt, like Michael Corleone. I'd then cycle back to the park, change my clothes, ditch my bike and knife, and make my way home on foot.

Much more likely of course: I'd be in prison by 8pm. So be it. I was ready for that. Whenever I wavered, I thought of Zuzana and Renata and the countless other women who Rupert — I had no doubt — abused on a daily basis.

348

I went to the Vondelpark just before 6 and changed and hid my clothes in the bushes as before, perfecting my costume as best I could. It was harder in the dark, by the light of my phone, but I managed. I left my phone in my rucksack but took my wallet with me. I didn't want a fine for not carrying ID added to the murder charge. That would just be annoying. Then I cycled slowly to Beursplein, Stock Exchange HQ and arguably, along with a couple of other spots in Amsterdam, the birthplace of modern capitalism. There I dismounted and walked my bike through the crowds.

It was much busier than I'd anticipated, with gangs of tourists and shoppers gawping at giant Christmas boxes composed entirely of tens of thousands of fairy lights. I made my way to a lamppost about five metres in front of the main doors of the building. It was a very ornate lamppost atop a cubed metre of prettified concrete. I leaned my bike against one side of the concrete and locked it. I leaned myself against the other side, and waited.

I expected to get a lot of attention in my ridiculous get-up but the opposite was true. There were a few double-takes but most people looked straight through me. Consequently, I felt like a ghost.

It was 6.30. I had half an hour. I was ready. Finally, I was about to do something positive. Or if not *altogether* positive, at least proactive. At least I wasn't just sitting around complaining anymore. I thought about the Death Wish Lady. She was still wrong. I wasn't destroying Amsterdam. On the contrary, I was actively improving it.

Not long after 7, identical men in suits began to appear, streaming out of the Stock Exchange in loose, oily mergers, shaking hands and swapping cards. Which was when it occurred to me that if I didn't spot *my* banker, maybe I should just kill another one at random. Chances were, they'd be equally odious. But of course, I wasn't serious.

Then I saw Rupert and his unmistakable ginger barnet. He loitered for a few minutes in conversation, before setting off with two other men. Rather than kill him there and then, as I'd planned, I told myself there were too many people and I followed on foot, left down Papenbrugsteeg, then left onto Warmoesstraat. Once again, it started to rain.

At the end of Warmoesstraat, they were joined by three other bankers, two of whom were Russell and Trevor, and all six went into Het Elfde Gebod, a lovely little boozer on Zeedijk. There they stayed for half an hour or so while I loitered across the street, hanging around the doorway of St Olaf's like some throwback to the 80s.

Sometime after 8, they left the pub and Rupert, Russell and Trevor said goodbye to their friends and wandered off up Zeedijk. I was growing impatient. I grasped the handle of my lino knife in my right robe pocket and willed myself to act. And I swear, I was just about to do it when they dipped into a fast food snackbar. I hung back, turned around, walked slowly back down to St Olaf's, turned again and walked slowly back up Zeedijk. When I passed the restaurant, they were all sat at the window bar eating noodles. I kept walking and stopped at the next corner. Then I thought about Amy.

Sweet Amy. The daughter I never had. The daughter I used to dream of. I pictured us together, sometime in the future in one of the other universes. "Why did you kill that man?" That's what she'd ask. "Daddy," she'd insist. "Daddy. Why did you kill that man?"

"He was a bad man," I would reply.

"Is there really such a thing as *a bad man* though?" she would wonder, patiently. "Are not *all* humans equally capable of being both good *and* bad? Although, frankly, the terms themselves are naïve and... reductively asinine. One might even say *jejune*."

Forced to concur with my imaginary, peculiarly precocious and persuasive child, I loosened the grip on my lino knife. *Shit*. Of course she was right. We were all monsters now and then. I'd never burned a banknote in front of someone in need, or thrown a woman over the side of a boat and left her to drown, but I was no angel.

And that was it. I changed my mind. I decided there and then that even if culling lowlifes like Rupert really *was* the way forward, it wasn't for me to decide who was for the chop. Maybe I was a coward at the end of the day. Maybe I just didn't have enough self-belief. And maybe that lack of gumption was the only thing separating me from genuine madness; and *maybe, at exactly the same time*, it was the one thing holding me back from greatness, from existential harmony, from true purpose fulfilled. Ultimately, it didn't matter.

My opinion of myself would continue to fluctuate like Rupert's money numbers, but I had made my decision. I was killing no one. The Universe could go fuck itself.

Frankly, it was a crushing anti-climax. But also, an enormous relief.

I was just about to make my way home when I saw my merger of bankers making their way out of the snackbar and back into the drizzly night. I watched Rupert guffawing at something or other and I thought to myself, *You have absolutely no idea how close you came, you terrible, terrible gobshite*. And then, just as I turned to leave, everything went black.

5.19

When I regained consciousness, I was sitting in a chair behind a cash register in a tiny Chinese supermarket next door to the snackbar. Rupert was bending over me, clicking his fingers.

"Hey, Lebowski! You alright, buddy?"

I blinked open my eyes.

"Yeah, he's good. Chalk it up to experience, man." Then he walked briskly out of the store, rejoined his friends on the street and headed north.

I blinked and tried to figure out where I was. I brought my hands to my face, less to explore the pain that was throbbing at the top of my nose, more to make sure that my beard and wig were still in place. I suddenly felt very vulnerable, but my woollen hat and robe hood combination still seemed to be holding everything together. I felt for my knife through the fabric of my robe, noticing fresh blood down my front. It was still there. My left hand returned to my face. My beard was also wet with blood and I was in a tremendous amount of pain. I felt like I'd been hit with a brick.

A middle-aged Chinese man, the shopkeeper on whose chair I was seated, addressed me: "You walk?" It was part question, part command.

"What happened?"

"Crazy man, kopstoot." He did a little mime. *Kopstoot* meant *headbutt*. It seems I was head-butted into unconsciousness by a passing crazy. "Tumeh isuh cayinsah owarey."

"Sorry?"

It took me a few more very slow repetitions, but eventually I was able to figure out that two men... in suits... had carried me inside... out of the rain.

"One man with red hair?"

"Ja, re-air."

I thanked my new, almost entirely incomprehensible Chinese friend, and walked slowly back out onto Zeedijk. As I stood in the street trying to figure out what I needed to do next, I experienced a wave of what felt almost like drug-induced euphoria. I was overjoyed that I hadn't killed anyone and that empathy had won the day. Glancing back at the Chinese supermarket, I noticed a row of four laughing Buddha statues in the window. I laughed out loud and squeezed the handle of my lino knife. I didn't need a diagnosis to know I was insane. But fuck it. Who wasn't? We're all walking a tightrope, sanity-wise.

My entire head was throbbing with blinding pain. I'd been head-butted again! Why did people keep head-butting me? First Rupert, then some passing stranger, dispensing karma. I laughed again. It was payback, I knew, for all the violence I'd inflicted over the years. I deserved it. I took it on the chin. Or thereabouts.

I headed in the rough direction of my bike. Before turning left onto the Oudezijds Voorburgwal, however, I decided to stop off in the Mata Hari pub, if they'd let me in. They might not, considering it was the nicest pub on the street and I looked like a Charles Manson impersonator who'd just lost a fight with the real Charles Manson. I recoiled from my blurred reflection in a wet window. Blood had wept from a crack in the bridge of my nose and congealed in clumps all over my facial hair. I looked dangerously insane.

Thankfully, the staff in the Mata Hari not only let me stay, they even encouraged me to wash up my face in the bathroom. I silently nodded my agreement. But first I ordered a double Jack Daniels in my Bulgarian mystic voice and knocked it back. Then I headed to the bathroom.

In the light of the bathroom mirror, I was actually quite shocked. Not only was I a mess, I was also an *unconvincing* mess. Some of the gum behind my moustache had been washed away with the blood and the rain. Half of my moustache was folded over on itself. I was clearly wearing a disguise. Rupert must surely have noticed. I wondered if maybe he'd recognised me and said nothing. No. Much more likely he'd noticed nothing and couldn't care less. The bar staff must have noticed though. My cheeks buzzed with shame. I was a fucking joke.

I used paper towels to get rid of most of the obvious blood and I tried my best to regum the loose facial hair but it was a lost cause. I decided to butch it out. Trump it. Pretend it's not happening. Pretend it looks perfect.

So I returned to the bar and ordered two more double whiskeys. One for the pain, one for the road. I left a couple of twenties, waved away the change and took my drinks to a corner table for a long, leisurely sip.

As I sipped, I replayed the drama of the preceding hours. I shook my head. A man I'd been on the verge of good-murdering in cold blood had just helped me in off the street when another man had struck me down. I shook my head some more. Life was nothing if not endlessly unpredictable.

By the time I stepped back out into the world, it was just gone 10pm and the rain was falling heavily. With my head down, I marched along the Oudezijds Voorburgwal like a man with a purpose, which, thank God, I was not. Not anymore. Thunder rumbled somewhere in the distance. Fireworks fizzed and popped in the background. I picked up my pace. The rain followed suit. Then I stopped. I'd noticed something, a disturbance, an altercation to my right and down a narrow alleyway. I took a couple of steps back and looked more closely.

354

Assessing the situation in a second, I saw a large bald man kicking someone on the ground and instantaneously, for better or for worse, I decided to act. I figured, if I managed to stop at least one person being hurt, then the evening hadn't been a total washout. So I tightened my grip around the handle of the lino knife and I approached the altercation, the sound of my fast footsteps lost in the pandemonium of what was now torrential rain.

I was six metres away when the man on the ground managed to scramble to his feet, and the man that had been kicking him backed away for a second. Then, as they faced off in the glare of the red light from the window, I noticed two more things: first, I noticed that the bald man — the aggressor — had just pulled a knife from inside his jacket; second, I noticed that the man who'd just got up from the ground, the man without a knife, was Nix.

I started to run.

5.20

If I'd missed the bald man's spinal column, perhaps he'd have survived. But my aim was true. I hammered the point of the lino knife hard, down into the base of the man's fat neck, just to the left of the vertebrae, and I pulled the blade backwards in as violent a yank as I could manage, like I was trying to remove a tablecloth from beneath a coffin, without moving the coffin. A woman screamed. I stepped out of the way of the man's falling body, and he slumped onto the alley floor, face down. Blood pumped out of his neck and disappeared into the violent rain.

Eyes peered through a crack in closed curtains. To the left of the window, an open door. Charging through that open door, another man. This one shorter and darker and pointing what appeared to be—

Before I'd even consciously registered that I was being shot at, I threw myself against the wall to the right of the door. The noise of the shot made my ears ring and whistle but the bullet hit the brickwork opposite. The gunman then made the mistake of extending his weapon past the threshold of the door and I took my opportunity. I sliced my lino knife through the air and into his hand. There was a shout of pain as his gun, and his right thumb, both fell to the floor of the alleyway. I moved quickly.

With my left hand I grabbed hold of the gunman's hair and pulled back his head. With my right hand, I sliced open his throat. It was exactly the same trick I'd pulled with the other man's spine, but this time with the oesophagus. When I let go of the gunman's hair, he too slumped to the ground, his top half landing on the legs of his dead cohort. He spluttered and gurgled and grabbed at his throat, his whole body bucking as the life leaked out, begrudgingly, out through the hole that I'd made in his neck.

As he lay dying, I noticed three more things: first, I noticed that Nix had completely disappeared; second, I noticed that the guy with the gun was the same guy who'd called Donka a bitch back in October; and third, I noticed that the woman in the window, was Donka.

I looked at her. We made very fleeting eye contact. I wanted to tell her who I was. Now that I'd recognised her, I wanted to do more to help her, but I realised I had to get out of there. So I nodded at her in what I hoped was a meaningful manner and I went right back to marching.

Stuffing the lino knife back into the pocket of my sodden heavy robe, I marched through to the other side of the alley. Thunder rumbled and lightning flashed almost simultaneously overhead. The rain continued to rattle to the ground. Only a shower of toads would have made it more dramatic.

I pretended that nothing had happened. Like that time I stole an autograph book from Jopling's department store and just walked out onto the street like Michael Corleone. Only that time I was apprehended and publicly humiliated. This time, I was hoping to get away with it.

I turned left onto Warmoesstraat, then right onto Papenbrugsteeg and right again onto the Beursplein. My bike was still there where I'd left it. The square was deserted. Murdering in heavy rain was clearly the way to go.

I rode to the Vondelpark, located my rucksack and changed into my real-world clothes. I cleaned the knife as best I could and tossed it into the middle of a nearby pond. It was safe there. No one magnet-fished ponds.

Just in case anyone had spotted a man meeting Daskalov's description riding a bright yellow Batavus with blue tyres, I left the bike unlocked under a bridge in the park. Someone would take it. And it'd be gone, like the whole thing never happened.

Then I walked briskly home.

I made it home by 11.30 and went straight to Nix's room to tell him what I'd done. When there was no answer at his bedroom door, I went in, but he wasn't home. Part of me was relieved. I was so tired.

I climbed the stairs to my room. I really needed a shower but also really needed to lie down just for a moment. I stripped off my clothes and lay on my bed. I guess I was asleep within minutes. I dreamt I'd written a book called *The Good Murderer*. On the back cover were the following words: "Sometimes murder is an act of purest empathy." It was a good dream.

I slept till noon the next day and when I woke up, I was in quite a bit of pain, but I wasn't in prison.

I also had a voice message from Nix.

"Hey. Wesley," it began, and immediately I knew that something was wrong. There was a lack of levity in Nix's voice I had heard only once before. "I don't know if you've made plans yet for tomorrow night. Either way, please come to Sylvia's flat between 8 and 9 in the evening. Your presence is politely requested. Please let me know you've heard this and that you'll be there. I'm out of town till then. We need you there, Wesley. Hope you're OK."

I messaged that I'd be there. I had no plans.

I did nothing for the rest of the day except sit around thinking about what it was like to end human life with your own hands. On the one hand, it felt awful and I wasn't even sure I'd be able to live with it. On the other hand, under the circumstances, knowing what I knew about these men, it felt like exactly the right thing to do and I reckoned I'd probably be OK.

5.21

On the morning of the last day of the year, I got a haircut. Then I bought a couple of bottles of nice Prosecco for the evening and I went home for a shower. In the afternoon, I drank one of the bottles of Prosecco. I hadn't intended to, I swear, but I had a nice bit of cheese and… well, one thing led to another.

I turned up at Sylvia's apartment just after nine. Amsterdam was already insane. It was like a war zone. Bangs and booms, crackles and cracks, whistles and the occasional scream peppered the night air, liberally. The sky was also alive with colourful sparkles and trails of light.

Nix was there already. He was wearing a shirt, which was unusual. He was sitting on a small sofa in the living room. He rose to greet me with a hug before returning to his rather formal seated position. Monica sat in one armchair, with Sylvia perched next to her on one of the arms. The second armchair was waiting for me, so I accepted a glass of wine and sat. There was a weird atmosphere in the room. It felt like an intervention.

"So um…" I began. "What's going on?"

Nix picked up a piece of paper from the coffee table between us. He turned it over to reveal a black and white printed photo of a man with wild hair and a large unkempt beard. The man had a sign around his neck saying: FREE HUGS. Nix held it up with the image facing me.

"Do you know this man?"

I began to feel terribly cold. "Where did you get it? Do the police have it?"

"We print it here," said Monica. "From YouTube." I smiled. I would never not love the way she always put the emphasis on *Tube*.

"Do you know this man?" Nix repeated.

"No," I chanced.

Nix sighed. "I put it to you that you *do* know this man. I put it to you…" He paused. "…that you know this man *very well indeed*."

"OK, OK," I snapped. "You've worn me down. It's me. I confess."

"If I were you, I'd ask your friend to take that film down from the internet, because if the police happen to come across it, you will go to jail. They're not putting a lot of effort into finding you — or rather *him* — but if it gets handed to them on a plate, they will come for you."

I said nothing to Nix, but I didn't much like the idea of talking to Bryson. I couldn't ask him to take down the film without telling him what I'd done, and I didn't want him to know what I'd done because in truth, I was afraid of his censure. But then if anyone was going to understand why I'd done what I'd done, it might very well be a physical interventionist like Bryson. I was in two minds. I'd figure it out later.

Nix had gone to the police the morning after the incident. He'd told them exactly what had happened. He'd gone looking for Donka, as he apparently had repeatedly since he'd got back from his stand-up tour. He figured it was less dangerous to go out alone.

I had no idea. I felt deeply guilty. I should have been with him. But then, if I had been….

On this particular occasion, another Bulgarian woman had told him exactly where Donka was working. So he went to see her and waited for her to be free. Once behind the curtain, he asked her straight out what had happened to Kras.

She immediately became hysterical. She said it wasn't safe for him to be there. They were always watching, she said, or listening. They would kill him too, she said. When Nix implored her to go to the police, she said she couldn't do that. They would kill her. She had no doubt at all that they would kill her.

Then they showed up. Fisnik and another Albanian — the same guys we'd run away from the first time we went looking for Donka. The police confirmed that they were sex traffickers, both well known in Amsterdam.

"So the big one came in first and punched me in the face," said Nix. "I made a run for it and was just getting through the front door when he hit me with a baseball bat, so I fell out into the alleyway, which was when he started kicking me and the next thing I know, fucking Moses here is ripping his head off."

Sylvia covered her mouth.

"He didn't rip his head, Nix," said Monica. "Don't exaggerate."

"Sorry, can I just clarify something here, so we know exactly what's going on." This was Sylvia. "Wesley." She looked me in the eye. "Did you really… kill two sex traffickers and save Nix's life?"

I held her gaze. "Much as I might enjoy the idea, we don't know for sure I saved anyone's life. But yeah, I did… um… I mean, I guess I did… kill those guys. Yes."

Sylvia gasped. Monica just looked at me, nodding slowly.

I asked Nix what the police had said. Apparently, they had CCTV footage of what had happened in the alleyway. They also had footage of Spas Daskalov hanging around the Red Light District earlier that night, where he appeared to have been involved in another altercation, in which he was randomly attacked and carried into a Chinese supermarket. They'd later tracked his progress on the city's network of cameras. They knew that after the first altercation, he'd gone to the Mata Hari. They knew that after the murders, he'd collected his bike and then, as he cycled south through the city's back streets, they lost him. They'd also circulated grainy photos of the killer, but they suspected he'd be halfway back to Albania by now. They told Nix they were fairly sure he was avenging some personal grievance he had with the two victims. They were convinced it was a premeditated execution, even though all signs pointed in entirely the opposite direction.

One of the policemen interviewing Nix said outright that there was very little chance they would ever find him, and that they wouldn't try particularly hard, adding, "Saves us a bit of work when they kill each other."

I shook my head, momentarily stupefied.

"How did you know it was me?"

"I didn't at first. I ran when you arrived. I came home, tried to find you to tell you what had happened. You weren't there, so I went to see Monica and told her. Then at some point it just hit me. I remembered the film. Checked it online and I was like…" He made a shocked face. "I knew it was you." He broke off and laughed for a moment outrageously. "What the fuck did you do, Wesley? Who even *are* you?" Then he bounded across the room and hugged me excitedly.

"So when I got back last night," he continued, "I came into your room and you were passed out. But your rucksack was there and I looked inside and saw your Moses robe, so… well, then I knew for sure. Which is when I decided to go to the police just to see if I could find out what they knew. And yeah, it looks like they couldn't give a shit. So it looks like you might just have got away with it, man." He looked thrilled. "Not only did you stop me getting stabbed, potentially killed, but you also avenged Krastyo's murder." He hit the flat of his fist twice on his chest as a sign of respect.

I didn't know what to say.

I felt weirdly calm about the whole thing. As at every other distinct step along this dark, remarkable journey, I just kept waiting for the dreadful kickback. All of my life experience so far told me that taking a human life — especially with your own goddamn hands — was not conducive to serenity. But I had no regrets about Damo, and so far, I had no regrets about the Albanians. On the contrary, I actually shared some of Nix's apparent excitement. I was keeping it under wraps because I didn't want to appear like a maniac, but if I was totally honest, at that point in time... I felt pretty good about what I'd done.

Monica asked me what I'd been doing in the Red Light District and I told them everything. I talked them through my thoughts and my actions over the preceding few days. Everything. I was totally honest about the whole thing, holding nothing back. It felt pretty good. They seemed to understand me. They were with me. There were tears and gasps and hugs and when we were all quite recovered, Sylvia asked me if I was hungry. I said I could eat, but it wasn't a priority.

"What about mushrooms?" Nix suggested, with a non-culinary twinkle.

"Magic mushrooms?" asked Monica. "No. Is it a good idea?"

I shook my head firmly. "It's *always* a good idea, Monica."

5.22

Nix took from his backpack a large paper bag of dried spindly psilocybin mushrooms. "If we take 'em now, we should come up smiling by 11.30, then we can head straight out for the fireworks."

Monica really wasn't sure, but everyone else was, so we peer group pressured her. Then we spent the rest of 2019 drinking wine and discussing the morality of murder. By the time we headed out to the Kees de Jongenbrug, just around the corner from Sylvia's place, opposite the Anne Frank House, at fifteen minutes to 2020, my mental state was remarkably altered.

The fact that this was the same bridge where Spas Daskalov had first incarnated to give out free hugs to the righteous, was lost on no one. It was perfect, and eerily appropriate. I thought about Bryson. I wanted to talk to him about coincidence. Then, as if by magic, there he was, shuffling alongside. I called out his name with a laugh and when he turned to face me, I saw that it wasn't him at all. It was a bearded stranger, a full metre shorter. I was tripping balls.

We made our way to within ten metres of where the fireworks were set out, which meant we'd be standing directly below the display. Dutch regulations regarding such events were routinely ignored, which is precisely what made New Year's Eve in Amsterdam such an exciting, undeniably dangerous experience. Every year people got badly burned and one or two lost a finger, or an eye. And of course, people died. And then people who knew the people who died complained and campaigned to make all personal firework use illegal. So it goes.

The bridge was packed. The moment we stood still, I began to feel physically disconcerted. As my ego unravelled in the mushroom meltdown, the feeling of the crowds pressing in on me began to stress me out. I began to feel like I'd made a terrible mistake. I felt something like panic creeping into my bones and then Monica, sensing it, took hold of my hand. Immediately, it passed; I became soothed.

Midnight came. Midnight went. People hugged and kissed and the firework display kicked off in earnest.

I had never been directly below a huge fireworks display before. It was quite an experience. First of all, there was the noise, which was very close to overwhelming. Second, there was the falling debris, of which there was a hell of a lot. I'd never considered it before but of course it made sense that the often substantial post-coital firework casing had to come back down to earth. Third, and most overwhelming of all, especially if you happened to be flapping about in the midst of a ferocious mushroom trip, were the visuals. The visuals were… insane.

Looking up under such circumstances felt dangerous. Like things could go wrong. As it transpired, things did go wrong, but not immediately.

At first, the anxiety, all of the anxiety I was feeling, all of the anxiety I'd ever felt, entirely drifted away. As, for a moment, did the *oooh*s and *aaah*s and the cheers and screams of the hundreds of people standing all around me. All I could see for a while was the outrageous display of pyrotechnics directly above our heads. There were magnificent feather boas of phosphorus, cascades of sparkling ephemeral jewels fleetingly unfurling before exploding into the past. All of it spectacular, all of it ending, constantly ending.

Then, things sped up. I didn't know how much was genuine pyro-talent on the part of the witches and wizards who dreamt up these magical firesticks, and I didn't know how much was whatever the mushrooms were doing to my senses. All knowledge, in fact, was a thing of the past.

I was in motion; suddenly, I had moved up inside the kaleidoscope and I was being fired up into the sky, through the sky, through the solar system at the speed of light. Shifting into hyperspace like the Malthusian Falcon, light dropping past me, dripping past me, as I was shot forward into the future, into the end of time and beyond.

I don't know how much time passed, between the last thing I remembered and the silence that would come all at once, but in that transient, microscopic, timeless eternity, everything was perfect. I was back on the forest floor in Pucallpa in South America, dissolved in the arms of mother ayahuasca and understanding true faith for the first time, feeling true faith, feeling god, feeling every living atom of the universe as clearly and as lucidly as I could feel my own fingertips; seeing things, once and for all, as they truly were.

I remembered the whispered conversations as the sun came up way beyond the forest. I was there because I believed I had blinded a man. I was there to renounce violence. Under the close guidance of two veteran shamanic healers, I renounced a major part of who I was.

The conversation came later.

In a revelatory medley of Spanish, Italian, English and bestial grunts, this must have been the first time I was made aware of the Malthus edict. Not from some fusty old overprivileged English reverend, but from some jungle-dwelling Peruvian shaman, both in their own ways self-professed mediators between different realms of existence, but coming from very, very different cultures and standpoints.

366

As the rising sun started to burn its way through the dense canopy of trees, I became aware that violence was not only occasionally acceptable, but also, that it was an absolutely necessary part of the human ecosystem. I was enlightened by the notion that humans need violence — good violence; loving violence — and it's just something that happens. It's not much spoken of, because it's not much understood, and it's a dangerous concept — it's not knowledge you want falling into the wrong hands. Still, it abides. Killing with love. Turns out it's a thing. It's a beautiful thing.

And then — all at once — silence.

5.23

When I opened my eyes, Monica's mouth was pressing hard against mine, her crow-black, blue-black hair falling softly across my face. She smelled wonderful. *"Yes!"* she gasped.

And I did, I confess it all, I did for the smallest of moments, the most infinitesimal of time particles, I did genuinely believe that I'd been proven wrong, and that sometimes, in the weirdest of circumstances, pale, chinless gingers like me did get to kiss women like Monica Gandolfo.

"He's alive!" she cried.

There was a crowd of people gathered round. An ambulance was on its way, although it would have its work cut out reaching me. I was pretty sure I was having some kind of cardiac incident. The last thing I remember feeling, before the noise cut out, was heat; dark, painful heat that quickly became completely overwhelming.

I still felt the pain, in dirty great waves, throughout my chest, my neck, my left arm. I was breathing again but it was not coming easily. It felt like a conscious effort to force breath through my throat. I realised, in that moment, I was dying.

Monica was kneeling next to me. Sylvia was crouched next to her. Nix was crouched on my other side. They all looked terribly concerned and I felt guilty that I was keeping them from the fireworks, which were still exploding all around. I felt guiltier still that I'd ruined their trip.

"You stopped breathing," Monica said. I took a deep, staggered, painful breath. "I gave you mouth and mouth."

"Thank you," I wheezed. Then I said something that Monica didn't catch, so she brought her ear close to my face. "I killed Damo," I whispered. "I spiked him… with acid."

Monica shook her head, her hair still falling across my face, her magnificent smell still filling me up. "No, you didn't," she said, but she must have known I was telling the truth.

"I'm not sorry," I said. "He was the Devil."

The burning sensation in my chest began to spread through my body like a really dark orgasm. It was happening. "I'm dying, Monica."

"No, no, no. Stai qui, Wesley. Stai con noi."

I must've lost consciousness for a second, because when I came to, Monica was physically opening my eyes with one hand and slapping my face with the other. I drank her in. She had never looked more beautiful.

"Stai, Wesley. Stai con me."

She tied up her hair. With the fireworks still exploding behind her, and the psilocybin still muddying up my bloodstream, Monica's face had never been so alive to me. It flashed and flared and flickered and twinkled. It rippled and billowed and surged. And when tears fell from her nose and landed on my bruised and scabby forehead, right between my eyes, it stung and it felt like a blessing.

If Monica's face was the last I saw, I figured then mine was a full, rich death; a good death. I smiled, or tried to, because I knew how ridiculous it was to be lying there dying, drifting like doomed plankton into the very jaws of death, and still be consumed by Monica Gandolfo, and how much I adored her. Also, I knew I'd never get the chance for a more cinematic death.

I closed my eyes. I let it come. I knew it was right. I knew that unless you were incredibly wealthy, you couldn't really go around killing people — even horrible misogynistic devil-men — and expect to get away with it.

"It's OK," I whispered to Monica, my breath weak, like I'd swallowed a wasp. "It's good… it's time… I want to die."

My eyes blinked open for a second, but I saw nothing. My senses were closing down. My hearing, the last to go, registered explosions, and sirens, and Monica, screaming out my name and the last words I ever heard: "I want you to live!"

Epilogue

Wesley Bell's notebook was found in his apartment on the Amstel six weeks after his death. At his funeral, Nix did an hour and a half of stand-up and totally owes his subsequent comedy career — as well as his life, let's not forget — to Wesley Bell.

No. Not really.

How could that even work? I'm fucking with you. One last time.

I'm alive!

Apparently — and I don't know if I necessarily believe it, but *apparently*, I died twice that night. And on both occasions, Monica thumped on my chest and blew air into my lungs, and *ping!* Back I came.

I had indeed had a heart attack. Doctors confirmed this. As it was my first, however, and as I was under 65 and there were no complications — alleged double-dip-death aside — the doctors agreed to let me fly to Da Nang on January 4th as planned. They figured spending three months relaxing on sun-drenched beaches was probably the best thing for me.

The day before I left, I received a message from Elvira telling me to stop by the Beachams office. There was something I needed to pick up. When I got there, Elvira handed me an envelope. Inside the envelope was a very short letter. It said: "Thank you for the honourable thing that you did. Krastyo would be very proud. I go back to Sofia today. I'm going to stay with Krastyo's aunt. I will never forget you. Lots of love, Donka."

"And she brought those," said Elvira. "God knows why, but… please take them away." She gave me a tight-lipped smile and gestured behind the office door to three green-tinted glass demijohns on the floor. I had no idea how Donka had got hold of

371

them, but there they were, like a gift from Kras from beyond the grave. I was very moved.

I said goodbye to Elvira, took the demijohns home and flew to Vietnam the next morning. Most of my first month was spent riding around on motorbikes, lying around on beaches, and swimming in, and eating from, the South China Sea.

Two weeks in, I heard the word coronavirus for the first time. As my trip progressed, I heard it more and more. Ten weeks in, which is where I am now, and they're starting to close the airports.

It's time to go home.

On the last day of February, I received a long catchup email from Fitch. In the three months since we'd seen one another, lots had happened.

"You remember you said that you hoped his kids would find the empathetic father they deserve? Well, it looks like they already have. The really weird thing is... it's me!"

Fitch had gone to see Kim as soon as he got home. Obviously she was devastated, so he comforted her as best he could. As it transpired, she needed a lot of comfort, and one thing, maybe inevitably, led to another.

"We're keeping it quiet for the moment because we don't want to seem ghoulish. I'm not sure ghoulish is the right word but you know what I mean. It's all a bit quick. But when you know... you know. I'm crazy about her, Wesley. The kids too. I feel terrible about Damo, obviously. His death is one of the worst things that's ever happened to me, but also... No, I can't even bring myself to say it. I just feel like my life is turned upside down in the best possible way. I can still hardly believe it. How's that for a silver lining?"

I was ecstatic. I couldn't stop smiling. *Each man's death touches so many other lives.* I wrote back immediately. "It couldn't happen to a nicer man, Fitch. I'm absolutely made up for you. This is glorious news."

I can't deny too, that part of me felt entirely exonerated.

I'd been convinced that the world would be a better place without Damo, and the Universe had wholeheartedly agreed. It had even rewarded me for my courage and determination. Indeed, there could be no clearer sign, no more definitive indication that if I were to meet other men in the future, men who convinced me that the world would be a sweeter, less painful place without them in it, then making the world a sweeter, less painful place should definitely be my priority. Or even my duty.

I don't think it will happen though, because — extraordinary circumstances aside — I'm done with killing.

Still.

It is good to know.

Fuck DJ Khaled.

One more thing…

If you enjoyed this book, please tell people.

Word of mouth is everything when you're doing it alone.

Leave a review if you can. Send one to me if you can't.

Maybe buy copies for any readers you know, for their
upcoming birthdays.

And what about Christmas?

And so on.

Aww, go on.

Tell the world.

Spread the word.

Thanks.

Thanks also for sticking right to the end and even
reading these words. I mean, nobody reads these words.

Just you.

You know what?

I kind of love you.

Special thanks

Angelique Aguerri, Charles Batho,
Axel Blaauw, SG Collins, Karen Crombie,
Carole Jordan, Melloney O'Connor,
Blue Jim Oliver, Mariana Rodriguez, Roxane Roussac,
Amy Shrack, Shaun Trevisick,
Shex Bomb, Fay Weat, Morana Žunec
and last but probably most,
Liz Monument

~keep breathing~

Printed in Great Britain
by Amazon

23204525R10219